HEAD FULL OF DARK

THE THIRD STORY OF HIS MAJESTY'S OFFICE OF THE WITCHFINDER GENERAL

PROTECTING THE PUBLIC FROM THE UNNATURAL SINCE 1645

D1742745

Also by Simon Kewin

Stories of
Her Majesty's Office of the Witchfinder General

The Eye Collectors

The Seven Succubi

HEAD FULL OF DARK

THE THIRD STORY OF HIS MAJESTY'S
OFFICE OF THE WITCHFINDER GENERAL

PROTECTING THE PUBLIC FROM THE UNNATURAL SINCE 1645

SIMON KEWIN

Elsewhen Press

Head Full of Dark
First published in Great Britain by Elsewhen Press, 2023
An imprint of Alnpete Limited

Quotes are included from: *Daemonologie*, James VI of Scotland, 1597,
Edinburgh: Robert Waldegrave; *Dracula*, Bram Stoker, 1897, London:
Archibald Constable and Company; *Folklore of the Isle of Man*, A. W. Moore,
1891, Isle of Man: Brown & Son; *The Hound of the Baskervilles*, Sir Arthur
Conan Doyle, 1902, London: George Newnes Ltd; *The Lady of Shalott*, Alfred
Lord Tennyson, 1832, London: Edward Moxon; *The Mabinogion*, from the
translation by Lady Charlotte Guest, London: Longman, Brown, Green and
Longmans, 1848; *Macbeth*, William Shakespeare, 1623, London: Edward
Blount and William Jaggard; *The Merry Wives of Windsor*, William
Shakespeare, 1602, London: Arthur Johnson; *Le Morte d'Arthur*, Sir Thomas
Malory, 1485, London: William Caxton; *The Raven*, Edgar Allan Poe, 1845,
New York: Wiley and Putnam. Quotes from documents in the internal
archives of His Majesty's Office of the Witchfinder General that are no longer,
or have never been, in the public domain, are used with permission.

Elsewhen Press, PO Box 757, Dartford, Kent DA2 7TQ
www.elsewhen.press

British Library Cataloguing in Publication Data.
A catalogue record for this book is available from the British Library.

ISBN 978-1-915304-28-5 Print edition
ISBN 978-1-915304-38-4 eBook edition

MALEFICOS VIVERE NON PATIERIS

Nihil obstat: Dorothy Aphrodite Coldwater
Imprimatur: Thomas Quirk, Lord High Witchfinder of
the Isles

CONTENTS

For Andy Yates

1 – Hagridden

The Night Hag belongs to that group of indistinct spectral entities – the nightmares, the shadow people – that haunt humanity when they are asleep (or half asleep) and therefore vulnerable. Night Hags, specifically, are often explained away by modern science as "sleep paralysis", the distressing experience of waking but being unable to move, or alternatively by "somnambulism" or "dream-enactment disorder" when the opposite happens: the sufferer can move, even walk around, but is not aware of the fact. While these scientific explanations are doubtlessly accurate in some cases, it is certainly not in all. Hagridden individuals again and again report the presence of a hideous, perhaps demonic figure squatting upon their chest or abdomen, pinning them down, preventing them from moving or even breathing. In other cases, these entities cling to their victim's back like some grim horse rider. Why these demons perform their actions remains a mystery to cryptozoologists. They may be cruel by nature – or it may be that they are the instruments, the weapons, of a malign sorcery, filling their victims with helpless horror and darkness.

– Dr Miriam Seacastle, *White Dragon, a Second Bestiary of Modern Britain*, 2003

Anders Kropotkin opened his eyes, but found that it didn't make any difference.

Had he gone blind in the night? There should be *some* light: the radiance of the alarm clock digits from the table beside his bed; the familiar sodium-orange glow of the

Edinburgh street lights through his curtains. *Something.* Not this heavy black darkness, smothering him like a thick felt blanket. It was a physical weight pinning him to his bed, squashing the air from his lungs.

He was dreaming, that was it. Dreaming he was awake. Damn, he hated it when that happened. He'd suffered a few bouts over recent months, his nightmares becoming more and more vivid. Confused, panicky episodes when he was caught between illusion and wakefulness, as if his dreams were bleeding into his daytime reality.

The nightmares he'd suffered as a child, when he was bound in strips of some dark material, bound tight so that he couldn't see or hear or breathe, had come back to haunt him thirty years later. It probably didn't help that he was so exhausted from not sleeping properly. A vicious circle. He hadn't been sleeping well at all since the weird incident with the dogs. A pack of them, huge, their eyes red and their fangs dripping and their panting, panting breath on his neck, chasing him through the backstreets of Edinburgh, up flights of steep stone steps and through the vennels of the Old Town. How were they even allowed to roam free like that? Why hadn't the Council *done* something? Why wouldn't the police believe him? Were they even dogs, or was that merely the impression his panicky mind had conjured up? In truth, their forms had been … hazier than that. They'd been like patches and scraps of shadows coalescing to form shapes. Darkness yearning to take on form and pursue him.

Whatever had chased him, it hadn't been a dream; it had been damn-well real. The experience had shaken him; he hadn't been able to do *anything* well since. It was like he'd been cursed, the Evil Eye put on him. He didn't believe such nonsense, but an experience like that, well, it made you think. Such creatures had no place in the rational world. The memories replayed in his mind when he was falling asleep, when he didn't have the strength to push them aside, and then the nightmares came. He would wake up floating in his own sweat, heart pounding, or else he'd emerge into consciousness paralyzed, like now, synapses firing but utterly disconnected from his body, his limbs distant, remote things that he couldn't move, couldn't reach.

And the troubling thought that always came to him at such moments was, how was he still breathing? How did his heart know to keep pumping if his other muscles were disconnected from his nervous system? If he stopped concentrating, stopped willing his heart's laboured *lub-dup*, would it simply stop?

Confused, lost in his nightmares, he imagined the weight as a demon squatting atop him and leering its evil grin, exuding darkness into his thoughts. A *Night Hag*, Jenny had called it when he'd admitted what he'd been suffering. A goblin sent to torment you. This had been just after he'd woken up in panic the first time, a couple of weeks before she'd left. She'd been amused at first, shown him some old painting on the internet, Fuseli's *The Nightmare. Yes!* he'd said, *Like that! That's how it feels!* When she'd seen that he wasn't joking, her smile had faded.

The Night Hag had been the final straw for her. Damn, how he missed her, irritating as she could be. He didn't blame her for leaving; he hadn't been much fun to be around since the nightmares began. Weird, though, the fantasies the brain conjured up to explain the anxieties it was attempting to process. Somewhere there was a rational explanation. Had to be. A *Night Hag*. Dear god. No wonder their primitive ancestors had believed all manner of fantastical tosh when they didn't have science to provide simple, factual explanations.

He needed to persuade his brain that the weight wasn't real. He needed to force himself to make a movement, any movement, the slightest twitch, in order to break the spell and send the damned demon back to Hell, bring the world crashing back in. That was all he had to do. Any tiny twitch of a muscle.

The effort of it was like trying to lift up the edges of a mountain to see what lay beneath. He was so drained by the blood tests the doctors had given him, testing him for anaemia and infection and who-knew what else. The tests had triggered several fresh nightmares in which unnamed, misshapen horrors had come for him in the night to drain yet more blood. Nightmares that had felt sharply real.

He tried to flex his fingers, forcing his brain to connect to his limbs. After long moments of concentrated effort, he managed it. His fingers moved a few millimetres. He was back in the world. He wasn't paralyzed. At some point in the night, he'd apparently thrown his arms wide; his left hand was trailing across the bedside table. He walked his fingers across the surface, exploring the familiar clutter: phone, glasses, the fantasy book he'd been reading, his alarm clock, a glass of water, then onto the bed. If he could slide his hand over the quilt to the imaginary weight – still pinning him to the bed – the lack of any actual mass there would persuade his subconscious to pull itself together and wake up properly.

With an effort, he worked his hand upon onto his chest – and found, not empty air, but the soft, squishy touch of something like … flesh. He withdrew his hand in shock at the contact. What the hell was that? There was no one else in the tenement, not since Jenny. He began to breathe more heavily but it was hard, so very hard, to inflate his lungs with that weight pressing down on him.

The Night Hag was there, sitting on top of him. He wanted to cry out in horror but could not. Or, no, they weren't real, were they? He was getting confused. He was still asleep, dreaming he was awake. Asleep, dreaming he was awake and deciding he was still asleep. Was that possible? He was spiralling into ever-deeper circles of confusion. Night Hags *were* real, but they were just metaphors. Representations of very real, perfectly natural physiological conditions, that was all.

The odd thing was that his thoughts felt clearer and harder with each passing moment. In his dreams, everything was impressionistic, misty. He could never hold onto ideas, like trying to grab hold of a feather floating on the summer breeze. But now his thoughts were arranging themselves into hard lines. This was no dream, no hypnogogic delusion.

It was the black dogs all over again. This was real. Something cutting him in the night and now this. Craziness. He was awake, he was *sure* of it, but it remained utterly dark and the dead weight upon him hadn't budged. There was a slurping, gurgling noise, like someone breathing through liquid. The sound was so hideous that, finally, he was able to move his body. With a superhuman jerk of strength, he kicked off his duvet, swung his legs around to sit on the edge of his bed. The weight slithered away. Or, no, it had obviously never been there. Dear god. He needed to get help, go see the doctor again. His dreams, his troubled sleep: they were getting out of control.

He breathed. It was good just to breathe. He'd survived another night. It was still dark, though. That didn't make any sense. He cast around with his gaze in the hope of detecting stray photons. There was nothing. No sound from outside, either. That realisation sent alarm bells clanging through him. His eyes *and* ears couldn't both have stopped working at the same moment, could they? Had something gone wrong with his brain? Was he suffering some sort of – the word was ugly to contemplate, despite sounding so superficially pleasant – a stroke? There *had* to be sound. Maybe a power cut could explain the lack of lights, but there was always noise in the city: the rush of cars, the calls and laughter of people in the street, the trundling trams, the rumble of jets overhead.

Something touched him then, stroking the side of his face, like the tendril of an underwater beast feeling for him. He spun round, but of course that made no difference. He was standing up, although he didn't recall climbing to his feet.

Something leapt onto his back. A weight. Bony, sinewy limbs gripped him around his waist, his neck. He flailed around trying to dislodge his attacker. The appendage around his neck cut off his breathing, making panic rise within him once more. He still could see nothing and hear nothing, but his pain-receptors were fully functioning. He bashed his shins against the hard edge of something – the bed most likely – then his nose thudded into a wall as he flailed desperately.

He was very definitely awake. He'd had nightmares where he'd been pursued, attacked by nameless horrors, and the shock of it had always been enough to jar him out of sleep. That was not happening. He roared his frustration and horror – or tried to. His strangled throat worked, but no sounds emerged.

The bony grip about his windpipe tightened further. Desperately, he tried to loosen the hold, tear it away. In his frantic efforts, he crashed head-first into another cold surface – but this time it was glass, not stone.

The glass shattered.

Cold air engulfed him, rushing past his face as he spun and whirled. He fell, plummeting from the tall window of his third-floor tenement flat, down to the hard cobbles of his street. He screamed. Finally, he screamed. The burden on his back was gone. The ligament around his neck was gone. He was free.

Free and falling.

He seemed to drop for long, long moments, so long that he began to think he was in a dream after all, that he would land upon his bed, finally awake, panting and drenched in sweat.

The hard stone of the Edinburgh pavement rose up to meet him, proving that idea wrong too.

2 – Welsh Gothic

No mourners attended the interment and the entire ceremony, according to the spoken recollections of the chapel's preacher, one Jebediah ap Rhys, was concluded but briefly. A heavy rain conspired to soak those few individuals standing at the sepulchre as Owain Williams was consigned to his final resting place. Mr Williams, it is believed, was a recluse, his family all having already passed on or left the area some time ago. And, indeed, so inclement was the weather on that final day that it may be considered a blessing that others were not exposed to such violent and chilling storms, for fear of their also being consigned to the graveyard where Mr Williams was duly lodged, with respectful but brief ceremony.

– Black Mountain Reporter, *In Memoriam* column,
1814

The graveyard of an abandoned Welsh chapel at the dead of night.

The place was everything that I, Danesh Shahzan, newly-promoted Adept in His Majesty's Office of the Witchfinder General (we'd just been renamed, as a result of recent events), had imagined it was going to be. Ivy crept across the lichen-encrusted, crumbling headstones that canted from the ground like broken teeth. A few leaned at alarming angles, as if a writhing presence were beneath the soil, thrusting for the air. People long-dead had paid for their names to be carved onto slabs of granite, but weather and the years had slowly scribbled the words out, reducing them to illegible marks, back to blankness. The names and dates of the forgotten. Angels, their expressions of lamentation worn away to emptiness, watched from atop their sepulchres as I and the man I'd paid to accompany me to the graveyard entered the scene.

Every surface was silvered with frost. Even the cobwebs that festooned the creaking lich gate were pearled with ice. My breath billowed from my mouth. The glow from my phone sent shifting pools of light dancing around my feet, picking out little mists of gossamer spun between the blades of grass, like the frozen exhalations of unseen night time creatures.

Overhead, a crescent moon scythed through the ragged clouds that fled across the sky. Despite everything, the dangers out there in the darkness, the creepy eeriness, the scene was … satisfying. It was what I'd imagined it was going to be. It was all in a day's work for an operative of the Office of the Witchfinder General.

Or, in this case, all in a night's work.

I flashed my light up the stone wall of the old chapel. Glassless windows gaped darkly. A parade of gargoyles and their cousin grotesques ran along the roofline, a succession of fabulous beasts carved in stone. A dragon; a two-headed lion-like creature; a fierce bird with pronounced fangs. Hardknott-Lewis, had he been there, would not have approved. One of the carvings I picked out was badly broken; at some point over the centuries the weather had got into it and snapped its head in half. Now it was the most hideous of them all, locked forever in a gaping, quiet scream.

Were they all merely stone carvings, I wondered, or were any of them *gargoyle* gargoyles? Living, demonic entities or possessed statuary, watching us from their perches? Now wasn't the time to find out. They weren't doing me any harm. I'd leave them in peace if they'd do the same for me.

The early spring day had already been fading when we set off on our trudge through the wilds, and it had taken us over an hour to reach the old chapel, abandoned and disused as it now was. The map on my phone marked it as a rough cross within a round clearing. The path was a simple dotted line leading to it, but in reality we'd had to hack through dense undergrowth. My companion, the gravedigger, had assured me that the path was passable – *well-used* was the term he'd used – but even he struggled at times. I'd wished I'd brought a machete. We'd climbed a winding, narrow path, its floor a patchwork of flat stones worn smooth by the countless Sunday feet that had, in ancient times, walked up from Pontannwn, the nearby hamlet hiding away in a valley of the Black Mountains.

We'd passed silently between high banks that reached above our heads, as if those feet had worn the path away, sinking it so deep into the ground that the surrounding countryside was lost to view. Tree roots had writhed from the earth around us, their excavations exposed by time and weather. Between them, and the spiky skeletons of the previous year's brambles, and the fresh-growing ranks of chest-height ferns, it had been hard to escape the feeling that the local vegetation was doing its best to stop us, grab hold of us, bar our way.

Finally, we'd emerged at the old chapel, its graveyard choked with more rambling greenery, to discover that night had settled upon the world. I'd planned to get there in the light, late afternoon at the worst. But being there in the darkness: like I say, there was something satisfying about it, too. It was hard to imagine bright sunshine ever lighting up this place.

The building's roof was completely gone, ripped away by some storm or simply the passage of time – although the local legend, I knew, was that a local giant had torn it off in a fit of anger at the worshippers' loud singing. Maybe that was true. Whatever the cause, the chapel's stone interior now gaped open to the sky. The place hadn't seen a burial or even a congregation for nearly a century.

My companion with the shovel and crowbar slung across his shoulder – Gwethenoc the gravedigger – stopped and glanced up into the night, as if taking his bearings from the hard, jewel stars sparkling away up there. He left the path abruptly, plunging into the forest of gravestones. His black leather boots were the colour of Welsh bibles. In his free hand, he carried an actual oil-and-wick lantern for illumination, a brass and glass contraption that wouldn't have looked out of place in a museum. It was as if the previous two or three centuries hadn't yet worked their way up through the valleys to find this remote spot. Although, when I'd tracked him down in the snug of Pontannwn's *Yr Hen Lew Goch* – The Old Red Lion – I'd noticed him swiping through a late-model iPhone, laughing at some video like any normal person.

Perhaps he simply liked to stick to the gravedigging traditions passed down to him by his father and his grandfather. Or perhaps he relished the role of mysterious and cantankerous local so he could amuse his mates later with tales of the look of horror on the city boy's face. I needed him either way. You can't just go around digging up graves; there are formalities to these things. The chapel might no longer be in use, but it was still consecrated ground, and the title of official gravedigger, I'd learned, was one jealously guarded by Gwethenoc.

Once I'd told him what I needed, and funded three rounds of double whiskies from my meagre Office expenses account to *fortify us against the cold*, he'd become amenable enough. The delay while we drank partly explained the late hour of our eventual arrival at the chapel. The slow journey up to the heads of the valleys had been the other. Interminable road works, the gradients and the weather had conspired to slow the Mini's progress. I'd had *all* the weather: it was one of those strange April days when the elements are having a spring-clean, throwing out each scrap and remnant left over from the other seasons. A vicious, gusting wind had given way to blinding sun, to be followed minutes later by squalls of hail. The tops of the Black Mountains were white, in contravention of all the rules about accurate geographical naming.

Grateful to be inside while the elements calmed down a

little, I'd taken the opportunity to get to know Gwethenoc – trying all the while to set aside the notion that he was deliberately prevaricating, steeling himself for an approaching ordeal. He was just tapping me for free drinks. That was definitely it. Couldn't blame him for that.

"Will you pass the job on to your own son?" I'd asked. That seemed to be how it worked: digging the graves was apparently something of a tradition in Gwethenoc's clan.

"Daughter," he'd replied, his eyes sparkling in the lights from the quiz machine as he sipped at his whisky. Actually, it was whiskey; he preferred an expensive Irish malt with the added *e*. "And that's a very good question. More concerned with enjoying herself in the fleshpots of Cardiff, that one. Can't say I blame her, did plenty of that myself in my younger days, like. But she may come back to it. It's not the money, that's a pittance, but it's the tradition, isn't it? Good to keep them alive. There's the upkeep of the graves, and there are the occasional cold case disinterments for the police that still need doing, too. You did say you were the police, didn't you?"

"Yes," I'd said. "We're definitely something like them." I'd shown him the forms that I'd brought with me – all completely official and countersigned – but the small wad of banknotes I'd also offered as the *required payment* had been what had really caught his attention.

He'd nodded, then thrown back his drink and set it down on the table, studying it intently as if trying to grasp the concept of *empty glass*. And I'd gone to the bar for yet another round.

Finally, hours later than I'd planned, we'd made our ascent to the churchyard. I could see little evidence of the upkeep that Gwethenoc had mentioned. Inch by inch, clearly, the forest was winning the war against civilisation, reclaiming the site.

Now, we picked our way between plots and unmarked mounds in the turf, trying not to walk across the dead but, I suspected, not always succeeding. Gwethenoc knew the path to take through the labyrinth, and in a moment, stumbling forward warily, I lost him. I stopped, trying to get my bearings, work out the route to take. A bird screeched from the darkness, an owl maybe, doing its best to add to the general gothic ambience. I could *feel* eyes watching me from the darkness, my primitive hindbrain summoning up all manner of monsters and horrors lurking beyond the reach of my meagre light – a response that wasn't helped by the fact that I could catalogue and describe quite a few of the monsters and horrors that really might be watching.

Standing there, cold and alone, my worries about Gwethenoc resurfaced. I'd sought him out, but he'd only been a name; I didn't really know much about him. Was it possible he was a member of some local cult antagonistic to outsiders? Worse, was he secretly an English Wizardry foot-soldier? I'd come up to Pontannwn because I was slowly, quietly, tying up the loose ends from the Succubi case, their attempt to weaken and destroy the Office by attacking its seven Keyholders. Had he been waiting for me here all along, planning to get me alone in the wilds? Several locals had seen us together in the pub, watched us set off – but for all I knew, they were in on it, too. That was how it worked in all the films, wasn't it? Setting up some overcomplicated execution ritual?

The grouping of nationalistic wizards had gone quiet since the destruction of Evangelina Mormont. Too quiet. I wasn't fooled for a moment. They were still out there, probably more pissed off than ever at the state of the world, at modernity, at the Office, at me. Word beneath the street was that they were regrouping, rearming, preparing to come back even harder. I was 99% sure that Hywel Williams, *El* so-called *Encantador*, wasn't one of them, and that he was concerned only with defeating his malign ancestor Owain – but I needed to be sure. And if Hywel *were* one of them, maybe this Gwethenoc was, too. Back in the pub, I'd caught a glimpse of him messaging someone on his phone, thumbs a blur, when he'd thought I was at the bar and not watching.

I caught a glimpse of him, shadows playing about his face in the glow from his lantern through the branches of a low-hanging tree. Keeping my eyes on the light, I stumbled across the broken ground to find him.

As I approached, he gave me a nod then looked down to the ground. Apparently, he wasn't springing an ambush in this lonely spot after all. He'd stopped at an imposing tomb, a raised oblong of stone surrounded by a high iron fence. I wondered who bothered to fence off a grave – and whether they were trying to keep something out or something in. More ivy knotted the ironwork, obscuring the tomb within.

"Are you sure this is it?" I asked. My breathing was still laboured from the long ascent, but he wasn't remotely out of breath.

"This is it. Final resting place of Owain Williams, 1732-1814. Bit notorious this one, lots of stories about it."

"What stories?"

Gwethenoc's accent was musical, as if he were incanting the words of a poem he'd learned by heart.

"Daft stories people come out with; hear them all the time in my line of work. The dead climbing out of their graves to trouble the living and ghosts drifting through the moonlight on cold winter evenings. Skeletal hands reaching up through the soil, as if we don't know how to do a proper deep burial. You know the sort of thing."

"Have you ever noticed anything like that happening?" I asked.

Gwethenoc looked like he was going to respond facetiously, but then thought better of it when he saw I was being serious. "No, no. Never seen nothing like that. 'Course, you hear things when you're alone up here, but that's just your imagination galloping away with you, isn't it? The dead stay dead, in my experience. It's the living you have to look out for; they're the troublemakers. Up here, it's peaceful. I like it. A man can think."

"What do people say about Owain, specifically?"

"These days? Nothing at all. All ancient history, that is, long-forgotten. But my father passed the old tales on to me along with this shovel, tales he'd been given by his father. Owain was an expeller, see, a cunning man, a wizard right enough, and a good man in his early days so they say, always happy to help, cure a disease here, sweeten a spring there."

"But things changed."

"As things do, right enough. There was a woman that he loved, and they had a child, but it all turned to worms. Owain listened to the whispers in the night, daft bugger, and off he went to the dark side. Consorted with the devil and walked with the Tylwyth Teg, the fairy folk. Became something less than human. More, too."

"You surely don't believe any of that?" I asked.

"'Course not," Gwethenoc replied gruffly, as if I'd insulted his masculinity by suggesting such a thing. There was also, I thought, a note of defensiveness in his voice, a pride, as if he would fight anyone daring to question him or his heritage. He needn't have worried. I was fairly sure that all of the stories he'd just summarised were completely true. They were more or less exactly what Owain's descendant, Hywel, had told me. Owain, hundreds of years old, quite possibly a wraith or a lich or some other member of the revenant community, had unleashed the cyhyraeth that had nearly killed me. But I didn't know how widespread belief in the stories were in the area. It sounded like folk memories of the evil and hideous Owain were fading.

I thought of a newspaper clipping I'd unearthed from my researches, an image-matching hit from a MORIARTY scan. A grainy, pointillist newspaper picture of a man standing in a Cardiff street in 1922, his features crisp even though the traffic – horse-drawn carts and trams, a few cars – and the pedestrians around him were a muddy blur. He must have stood still for a moment, watching the long-dead photographer as he worked. There was no name assigned to the figure, but, despite the old clothes, ragged and yet oddly formal, the man could have been a doppelganger for Owain – or, at least, for the sketch I had of him from his journals. That thin, cadaverous face was unmistakable. At the same time, it might have been Hywel staring out at me, hand raised to his forehead, some similarity around the eyes undeniable, although the shot had been taken sixty years before Hywel's birth. Perhaps it was simply some forebear who bore a striking resemblance – and perhaps it really was Owain, caught by the camera.

I knew what I thought.

Away in the south-east, glimpsed through the branches of the trees, Orion was picking itself off the horizon. I'd devoted quite a bit of time to pursuing Owain in the couple of months since Evangelina Mormont's demise. I'd traced down leads in the archives, staked out abandoned houses that might have had a connection to him. I'd never come close. Once, I think, I'd glimpsed him, a hurrying figure in the distance on a deserted Monmouth backstreet. If it was him, he'd moved unnaturally quickly. I'd raced after him, turned a corner, and he was gone, vanishing into the Welsh drizzle, stepping between the raindrops into some other dimension.

Once or twice, I confess, as I hit another dead end, I'd begun to doubt Hywel's tale of a malign ancestor pursuing a long vendetta to wipe out his own bloodline. Was it possible Hywel had played me, spun me a fantastical yarn to escape arrest? I'd uncovered enough incidental evidence in my research to suggest that the tales of Hywel's family ghost, the literal skeleton in his proverbial closet, *might* be true. Owain *might* be out there, working to ensure that none of his bloodline survived, thus preventing them from sealing the breach in reality he'd opened by sacrificing his own son. There was certainly a pattern of unfortunate, often gruesome, deaths in the family, particularly among the young – but I needed to know for sure. Hence my visit to the grave.

Gwethenoc delved into his backpack and fished out a bracelet-sized iron ring upon which ten or more large, rusting keys were strung. He was certainly doing his bit to play his part. He selected one of the keys by the light of his lantern, seeing marks upon it that I couldn't pick out. He squatted down and proceeded to thread the chosen key into the lock while I hovered over him, providing illumination with my phone. The mechanism resisted, then succumbed with a harsh squeal. Gwethenoc hinged open one whole side of the tomb's railings and stepped inside the little fenced-off area.

"How long will it take to open the tomb?" I asked. My voice sounded fragile in the icy air.

Gwethenoc bent down to consider the bulk of the stone oblong from all angles.

"You don't want to actually lift the remains, yes? Just see if they're there?"

That was the plan. Hywel had insisted that Owain hadn't died early in the nineteenth century; that he'd faked his own burial so he could continue his unnaturally long existence in peace. If there *were* remains in there, I wanted to know. I also wanted to be able to identify them. There had to be a very good chance that they weren't Owain's at all. If I could get Hywel to consent, I could compare against his DNA and maybe get some answers.

"I'm authorised to remove the skull so we can use the teeth for analysis," I said. "The rest of the bones can stay where they are."

Gwethenoc nodded. He pulled a set of short, sharp wooden spikes from his backpack. They looked like the stakes vampire hunters use in the books and the films. They weren't going to be much use here. Even if Owain were a vampire – which *was* a remote possibility – and even if for some reason he'd chosen to slumber in this lonely, remote grave, a few pointy sticks weren't going to make much difference. Vampires are fearsomely powerful entities, almost impossible to kill. Kill, unkill, whatever. I'd done a bit of research into the subject, picked up a few clues – my family on my father's side, so it appeared, once had a reputation for the craft. Ensorcelled wooden stakes do work, when cut from the right trees and carved with the right incantations, but they're vanishingly rare despite what popular culture would have you believe. They need just the right undeath spells woven about them in lines of black smoke, by someone very much in touch with their darker side. They can take years to craft. It seemed very unlikely that Gwethenoc had a whole set of usable stakes in his backpack.

"I hardly think they're necessary," I said.

He looked up, the light from his lantern giving his features a haunted, hollow-cheeked expression. In the distance, its timing impeccable, another night-time creature chose that moment to fill the air with an alarming screech, like someone in the throes of the cruellest agony. City boy as I was, I at least recognized that call. A fox. Their calls could be weirdly human-sounding. We had them in London, too, although ours obviously had cockney accents.

"These?" said Gwethenoc. He sounded confused. "How else are we going to wedge the lid of the tomb open?"

Right. Not what I'd thought at all. "They're … wedges."

"What else would they be? Stone lid like this will weigh a ton. Like, literally, a ton. We'll lever it open a crack with the crowbar and drive the wedges in. Need a crane to do the thing properly, but this will give us a glimpse of what's inside. Take it gentle so we don't break the stone. If we can get the gap wide enough, we can reach in and lift the skull."

I stepped back, considering the situation. It had seemed so straightforward sitting at my desk in Cardiff. Open the grave, check there were remains buried inside, try and get an ID. Things looked a little less straightforward in the darkness of the abandoned graveyard. Reality was dirtier.

"I don't get it," I said. "Why go to the expense and difficulty of building this memorial? From what I can tell, Williams had no immediate relatives to pay for anything. Hard to believe anyone would have wanted to go to all this trouble."

"People are weird about death." said Gwethenoc as he felt around the lid of the tomb for a crack to begin his work. "Perhaps Williams insisted on having a grand grave when he was gone, and he spent all his money on it. Can't see what good it would have done him, but there we are, that's folk for you. Or perhaps the locals went for a really heavy lid to make sure he couldn't get out again."

He was joking. I was pretty sure he was joking.

"I assume there'll be a wooden coffin inside the stone tomb."

"Normally they rot away, but this one was lead-lined, from the accounts I've seen."

"Why would they do that?"

Gwethenoc shrugged, stroking the weathered top of the tomb, sizing it up with his eye as if it were some great beast he'd darted and brought to ground. "To help preserve the body in case they wanted to check something afterwards. Or because his will demanded it. Who knows? Like I say, people get funny about death."

Had there been some other reason? Was the lead a component in some warding incantation, there to keep whatever was in, in? Perhaps it wasn't actually lead but iron and the story about the lead was put about to hide the truth, explain the weight. Many conjured and otherworldly entities hate iron for reasons I'm hazy on, the Tylwyth Teg among them. It disrupts them, or repels them, or they're allergic, and I was pretty sure the people of that time would have been well-aware of the fact. A coffin made of iron might keep something sealed away for a long time. Despite myself, a little shudder of cold horror ran through me. Was it possible that he was still alive? Still … moving, anyway? Had he been down there all this time, locked in his tiny iron cell, screaming screams no one could hear, awake and alive but unable to do anything to escape? That he wasn't working the streets of Wales, hunting down his progeny?

It didn't bear thinking about. I tried and failed not to do so. And, if he were in there, did I really want to let him out?

Working together, we inched the stone lid aside. An earthy, wormy smell breathed out of the darkness, the sickly tang of old decay in it. We carried on, our grunts of effort loud in the quiet night. We drove the wooden wedges into the gap as we worked so we didn't trap our fingers. The weight of the lid had to be enough to crush bones. It hadn't occurred to me how dangerous gravedigging could be for simple, mundane reasons as opposed to, well, other reasons.

A skeletal hand grasped suddenly at us from inside the tomb. In my imagination. In reality, no such thing happened. So that was good. I had my thaumometer running, and I peeped at its display surreptitiously when I had a spare hand. It was registering nothing, no spikes in the general background level of magical activity, no incursions of the transmundane beyond normal Welsh background levels.

It took us the best part of an hour to reveal enough of a gap to be able to reach inside the tomb and pull out a skull. We were careful not to push the lid too far back: if it toppled over and crashed to the floor, it might crush our toes, and there'd be no way for the two of us to lift it back into place.

Despite the icy conditions, I was sweating from my efforts. Under my waterproof, my tee shirt was plastered to my back, and a bead of perspiration had trickled into my left eye, making it sting. I blinked through it at my phone, switching the light back on that I'd deactivated to preserve battery. The light picked out the carved edgings of the tomb, the tableaux of weird beasts, their features also eroded away almost to nothing. Around us, the vast darkness sat and waited to see what would happen.

I shone the light into the corner of the tomb that we'd opened up. Instead of the inner coffin, or bare stone, I glimpsed, unmistakably, the white glint of bone.

"What do you see?" Gwethenoc asked from behind me, his voice softer from his exertions.

My voice echoed hollowly as I replied. "A skeleton. He's in there."

19

Dismay sank through me. I was wrong, then. Hywel *had* spun me a yarn and I'd fallen for it gratefully, believed every word. Which meant, most likely, that *he'd* summoned the cyhyraeth and *he'd* worked the runes that had so nearly spiralled out of control, threatening both me and, indeed, everyone else.

And I'd believed his nonsense and let him go, believed his cunning hiding-in-plain-sight crap magician act. Then there was the other unfortunate truth: since events at the warehouse, he'd vanished. Completely vanished. El Encantador had stopped performing, dropped off the net, refused to take calls. The pre-schoolers of Newport and Cardiff had been deprived of his shows; he'd dematerialized as completely as one of the doves in his tricks. I hadn't been able to decide if that was because Hywel was protecting himself from his malign forebear – or if there was some still darker reason.

And the possibility that swam through my mind at three in the morning was this: maybe Hywel, the man I'd met, didn't exist. That *that* had been Owain, right there in front of me, still walking the Earth after all these years. He'd told me his *own* story to put me off the trail, weaving more layers of the deception. The family resemblance I'd convinced myself about: the truth was simpler. Owain simply looked like himself. I'd checked, and there was certainly documentary evidence of the existence of Hywel. Birth certificates and National Insurance numbers and social media accounts and the like. Bureaucratically speaking, he existed. But actually? I'd wondered.

At least the presence of the bones told me that little waking nightmare wasn't true. Owain was here, where he'd always been. And Hywel? The good news for him was that he existed. He was a dabbler with some power, clearly – but he was deluded. A fantasist. I needed to track him down and ensure he didn't endanger anyone else, but, most likely, the biggest threat he posed was to himself. A user in the grip of paranoid delusions could cause themselves considerable harm.

"Let me see," said Gwethenoc. He kneeled to take my place, peered inside the tomb, and then reached down inside, as if that were the most normal thing in the world to do. I could see the look of concentration on his face as his fingers explored the inner landscape of the sarcophagus and its occupant.

"I've found the skull. It moves; it feels … disconnected. Want me to bring it out?"

"Will it come up in one piece?"

"I think so. It feels weird, though. It's like…"

"What?"

"Let's get it into the light."

He felt around for a few moments, frowning as, I imagined, he tried to hook his fingers into some convenient orifice. Forensic investigation this was not. Finally, he had it and fished it from the depths.

What he pulled from the grave most definitely wasn't human. The skull was elongated, bestial. There were two wide, round eye sockets in it, one on each side of a pronounced central ridge. There were also two short horns coiling off it, horns making the skull awkward to manoeuvre out of the tomb. Black cracks marred it where some rot had got in, and the nose section appeared to be completely missing. As Gwethenoc held it up to show me, it was hard not to read a sneer of malevolence on those white features.

"Do you know what this is?" I asked.

"This? You don't live round here and not see these. It's a goat, I'd say, maybe a sheep. A ram most likely."

"It's a *goat's* skull?"

"An entire goat, I'd say, judging by what I could feel in there. What's gone on here and where the remains of Owain Williams are, I don't know, but he clearly wasn't in the coffin they lugged up here and buried all that time ago."

"But someone wanted the world to believe that he was in there," I said. "Used the goat to make the weight feel right." Or as a component of some malign act of sorcery, I didn't add.

Gwethenoc looked puzzled at my words. "Why would anyone do that?"

I chose not to answer. "Any sign of the lead-lined coffin the archives mention?"

"None at all. The whole story must have been invented. What did they do that for?"

"Let me take a few pictures of the interior of the tomb, then I'll help you get the lid back on," I said. "I don't think we'll be needing any DNA samples after all."

Gwethenoc looked like he wanted to say more, then thought better of it. To another cry of anguish from the unseen fox lurking in the Welsh darkness, we set about our work.

An hour later, as we threaded our way back through the frost, thoughts whirled through my brain as I tried to slot together the pieces of the jigsaw puzzle. Hywel's story about Owain appeared to be true. At least, I hadn't proved it wasn't. Problem was, I didn't know for sure how many puzzles I even had. How many pictures I was trying to build up. I could still see no connection between Owain Williams and English Wizardry, other than the fact that they'd both worked magics at the Mermaid Warehouse in Cardiff Docks – a coincidence that could be explained by the presence of a magical node, the *crucible*, at that location.

Gwethenoc walked ahead of me down the narrow path. I couldn't see how he could have any connection to my enemies, but I couldn't resist asking him.

"Tell me, Gwethenoc, what do you think of the English?"

The reply came out of the darkness. "Some of them are complete dicks. Most of them are fine. Same as everyone."

3 – Bridges to the Otherworld

> Black dogs and dire hounds are to be found in
> stories and reports throughout the British Isles –
> notable examples including *Black Shuck* (Norfolk,
> Suffolk, Lincolnshire), *Padfoot* (Yorkshire), *Cŵn
> Annwn* (Wales) and *Moddey Dhoo* (Isle of Man) –
> but there are many others. It is not known if these
> are all the same creature, or simply members of the
> same species. The creatures are generally reported
> as large, black beasts, often with glowing red eyes.
> They are quite frequently spectral in form and are
> able to change their shape, pass through solid walls
> and so forth. They can be dangerous and malicious
> creatures. Several accounts report less ghostly
> versions of the dogs attacking people in the dead of
> night, ripping out their throats and baying with
> blood-curdling howls.
>
> – Dr Miriam Seacastle, *Red Dragon, a Bestiary of
> Modern Britain*, 1999

Back at *Yr Hen Lew Goch*, the pub closed now, its
windows dark, a familiar black car was parked at the side
of the road. The Jaguar's electric motors were silent, but
the vehicle's metal body ticked as it cooled from its
recent run. A fan whirred from within, keeping its
occupant warm. By the interior light, I could see he was
in there. He watched me walking nearer, expressionless,
then stirred into life. He stepped out into the freezing
Welsh night to meet me, his movements the familiar
sequence of rapid actions, as if he were walking
constantly though the choreography of a fight.
Gwethenoc, perhaps sensing this might be a fraught
situation, or simply because he was tired from his

labours, nodded his head to me and turned up the street to leave without a further word.

"Danesh," said Campbell Hardknott-Lewis, Lord High Witchfinder of All Wales, "did you find the goat's skeleton in the grave?"

He was my superior in the Office and a man I considered both a friend and a foe at the same time – which was awkward. In many senses I trusted him utterly, but his opposition to the use of magic – to *unnatural* powers – was absolute, and that meant he was opposed to me, too. I had accepted what I was, but I knew he never could. Yet, despite everything, his suspicions about me, he had remained my steadfast defender. It was a strange situation.

Without admitting it, we were both aware of the unbridgeable divide between us, but, for now, we functioned. Facing common enemies could do that. I had to destroy the Office, I understood. Its strictures were ridiculous, hugely damaging to users like myself and Sally who surely posed no great threat to polite society. You could not go around denying people their nature just because you didn't like it and thought you knew better. I told myself that I remained in my job because we also did good work fighting malign magic use – and also because I had a better chance of weakening the Office, bringing it down, by operating on the inside.

My situation was awkward. You might even say, *unquiet*. But that was also a situation I was comfortable with. My background had primed me well for living with such contradictions; a conflicted sense of belonging was my day-to-day experience. Not just my semi-Asianness, also the fact that I was an Englishman living in Wales. Borders on the map are so clear and hard. Those in our heads, not so much. Ask anyone from my background whether they feel fully at home in the UK – ask anyone English living in Wales or anyone from the Celtic nations living in England come to that – and the answer most will give will include the word *complicated*.

The Crow, apparently, had also accepted the situation

– hoping, perhaps, that I would eventually see the light and return to the one true path. Or, maybe, preferring to keep me close so he could keep his unblinking eye on me.

And, unexpectedly, here he was. I had kept this expedition up the valleys out of official Office logs. Amongst my various crimes and misdemeanours, I had chosen to let Hywel Williams go in that warehouse in Cardiff docks, and that meant that both he and I were at risk if the truth came out. We were both magus law renegades. The Crow might ignore my contraventions of the rules if they were ambiguous, but I doubted even he could tolerate an operative letting a powerful and dangerous sorcerer walk free.

"I found it," I said, talking about the skeleton. "Are you saying you already knew it was there?"

An amused little smile passed across the Crow's features. "I came up here thirty years ago to tread the very same path, open the same grave."

That was troubling. So far as I knew, he had no clue about Hywel's family ghost.

"What were you investigating?" I asked. "What brought you up here?"

He considered me for a moment. "First, let me ask you a question. Your visit here, there is no record of it on our systems, and you clearly aren't being accompanied by another operative. Can you explain this to me?"

What did he think – that I was consorting with unnatural powers? That I was slipping further from him? If that were the case, he'd be wrong – in this, at least, we were on the same side. Owain, summoner of cyhyraeth and writer of malign runes and whatever the hell else he was, was a threat we could both fight.

I tried to sound as innocent and unconcerned as I could. "The name of Owain Williams came up in the succubi case. I was tying up loose ends."

I could see his steel-trap brain working as he made the connections I'd made several months previously.

"You suspected *Hywel* Williams before identifying

Evangelina Mormont as the perpetrator of those crimes. Are you saying Owain and Hywel are related?"

"I can't be sure," I lied, grateful for maybe the millionth time that he didn't and couldn't have any sort of magical means of knowing that I wasn't telling the truth. "The connection of the name seemed worth investigating, but it's obviously very common, in Wales especially."

"I don't understand. How did your investigations bring you up here to Owain's supposed grave? How did his name *come up*?"

Lying is like exercise. The more you do it, the easier it gets. "I ran a MORIARTY search on cold cases and this particular Williams appeared."

The Crow thought about that. All I could see were the holes in my alibi, but, somehow, he managed to see the tissue holding the holes together. My explanation appeared to appease him.

"You should know that I have had some dealings with Owain Williams," he said. He was frowning, in a way that told me the case seriously troubled him. "I thought I had marked all of that work as classified, but you must have found a mention that I missed. My, as I believe you might say, bad. Without delving into the details, I will also say that the presence of a surviving descendant of Owain Williams would be highly significant. That family has suffered a very great deal of misfortune over the years, a fact that I certainly do not put down to chance. My working assumption is that Owain has no relatives left. That he has rather … burned his way through them. Perhaps I should have searched harder."

The Crow's use of the present tense wasn't lost on me. I tried to sound surprised. "Are you saying Owain is still alive?"

The Crow waved that away as if it were of no importance. "Oh, yes, that is completely clear. Whether he is technically *alive* is open to debate, of course, but he is certainly still with us, walking the world. I have pursued him off and on for years. If your Hywel is related, then this changes the complexion of the succubus case considerably. I doubt the presence of Owain Williams' offspring would be coincidental. Whatever he has become, he or it is extremely dangerous. The word I might choose is *malevolent*."

"Hywel almost certainly isn't related," I said, trying to stick to the story I'd put into my reports. "Kerrigan and I checked out his stage magician act, and it was pretty unconvincing."

"Did Hywel claim he was related to Owain?"

"No. He didn't mention an Owain Williams at all."

The Crow thought about that some more, but, with a nod, clearly decided to let it go.

I hoped.

I tried to change the subject. "Can you give me any details of your dealings with Owain? Why is there a goat in his grave?"

"I think we can dismiss the goat. The poor beast may have been slaughtered in some historical ritual, but my assumption is that it was placed there to make the supposed burial of Owain more believable. As to the ongoing investigation, well, you will be familiar with the Office joke."

It took me a moment to work out what he meant. "You mean the *continuing situation at Caerlech*? I didn't think that was real." The phrase was shorthand for any long-running difficulty that has no real solution. Something we just have to live with. Something we can ignore away; kick into the proverbial long graveyard grass.

The Crow nodded. "I am afraid that particular situation is very real. It is, in fact, perhaps the most troubling situation we face, although the danger is held in abeyance for now. At some point we will have to tackle it."

"What is the nature of the situation?"

"As I say, better we leave it in the dark. It is contained. You probably know something of what I would say in any case: a terrible supernatural danger; an existential threat to our very survival. To some extent, the usual. Although if Caerlech does ever get out of hand it would be very bad, very bad indeed."

"And you believe Owain is connected?"

"I have good reason to connect the two. There is some evidence that the Caerlech situation has been ongoing for many decades, perhaps many centuries, and Owain is, if my calculations are correct, currently nearly three hundred years old. He may be responsible, or he may have simply been attracted to it, drawn like a death's-head moth to a lantern flame. If there is a connection between Owain and Hywel, even a distant one, even one that Hywel is not aware of, then he needs to be very careful. He faces a very great threat to his survival. We, on the other hand, should do all that we can to protect him. We should track him down, bring him under our protection. Not only for his own safety, but because he might well prove useful."

"He's disappeared," I said. "I assume that events in the warehouse freaked him out."

"Well, quite. You should redouble your efforts to find him, bring him under our protection. But tread carefully; doing so will inevitably place you at significant risk. Once again. And be vigilant, always, for Owain. Or whatever it is that Owain has become."

I was cooling down after my hack through the Welsh wilderness now. Icy tendrils of night were beginning to find their way through to my skin. I assured him, not for the first time in our relationship, that I would be careful.

"Sir," I said, "can I ask why you're here? How did you even know I was in Pontannwn given that I failed to log my actions?"

"As to the latter, I left strict instructions with the gravedigger to contact me if anyone ever came calling."

"You said that was thirty years ago. Gwethenoc would have been a child at the time."

Hardknott-Lewis stared into the distance as if he could still see the gravedigger's back. "I remember him. A most rambunctious child. It was his father who accompanied me on my visit, and I am gratified to learn that he passed my instructions onto his son. Gwethenoc contacted me while you were in the pub. He, ah, said he would keep you talking to give me chance to drive up here and address the situation."

"He did?"

"Yes. And he sent me a surreptitious photo of you so that I could identify you. At that point I told him he was safe to continue with you to the graveyard."

"Right. I had no idea."

"Well, no, that was rather the intention. I saw no reason for you not to know about Owain, although I was intrigued to find out why you were interested."

"You didn't need to drive all this way to do that. We could have talked about it in work tomorrow."

He nodded his head from side-to-side, in a way that suggested things weren't quite so simple. "I wanted to talk to you in complete confidence, with no possibility of us being overheard, technologically or magically. Much as I disapprove of your not properly logging your activities, you might like to know that I was inspired to do something similar myself. The truth is that no one else knows I am here. Flouting the rules like this, it is disconcerting, but also, I admit, rather exhilarating."

He smiled a little smile to himself as if amused at the words coming out of his own mouth. The thought of him coming to find me without anyone knowing was troubling enough, but his frank admission of rule-breaking was almost worse.

"Talk to me about what?"

"Let's go inside and get warm, shall we? I love Wales in the winter, but it can get chilly after a time."

He strode towards the locked door of the pub and knocked three times. Twenty seconds later, lights came on upstairs and the muffled voice of someone calling out came to my ears, followed by the thump of footsteps on stairs. The barmaid who'd served me earlier in the evening threw the door open, a woollen shawl clutched around her shoulders, a curse half-formed in her throat until she saw who was standing there.

"Who the bastard hell … oh, it's you, Campbell. Don't just stand there freezing, man, come in, come in."

29

"Thank you, Mafanwy. We will not impose on you, but a table to sit at out of the cold would be welcome."

The barmaid – Mafanwy, apparently – cast a glance over me, then smiled back at the Crow.

"Take as long as you like, plenty of room with all the bloody punters gone." She stepped back to grant us admission. "I'll pop a few more logs on the fire, no point you freezing in here."

"There is really no need."

"Nonsense. Can I get you a drink? Still on the tea, is it? Can't offer you something stronger?"

"A cup of tea would be most welcome. From a teabag if at all possible."

She nodded, glanced at me again. "For you too?"

"Is there any chance of a coffee?"

She sniffed as if I'd asked for the rarest brandy. "How do you like it?"

"Black and strong, please."

"Well, I can probably manage that."

She swept away to sort out the drinks, and I sat down at the very table I'd shared with Gwethenoc earlier that evening.

"They know you here?" I asked.

"In *Yr Hen Lew Goch*? Yes, indeed. I offered them some help with a problem they were having a few years back. A nasty incursion in the beer cellar."

"What was it?"

The Crow took his coat off, and, rather than hanging it over the back of his chair like any normal person, scanned around the room for a peg to hang it off. Once he'd returned, he sat and set about answering my question.

"What do you make of the name of this village?"

He'd been encouraging me to pick up whatever smatterings of Welsh I could. I'd failed badly so far. "Pontannwn," I said, trying to dissect the syllables. "Pont is bridge, so bridge over the *Annwn* river maybe?"

"Excellent logic, and normally you would be quite correct – but I am afraid the river here is not the Annwn.

You have the wrong preposition. The translation should be something like bridge *to* Annwn."

"Right, Annwn."

"You are obviously familiar with the name."

I obviously was not, but it rang distant bells from the Crow's various lectures and explanations over the years. "Annwn is … the Welsh otherworld, yes?"

"Just so. Annwn, Tír na nÓg, Hy-Brasil, Avalon, there are many names for it. It lies alongside our own, woven in and around our reality like brambles through a hedgerow, intertwined like Celtic knotwork. Our reality is but a thin façade: pierce the veil, lift up the curtain, peer through the mirror, and you'll glimpse Annwn. So people used to believe, anyway. I am strongly inclined to believe that there is a core of truth to the tales."

I nodded. That made sense, at least. "There are otherworlds in every culture I know about. Realms just out of sight, hidden beneath the ground or in the clouds. Hindu cosmology describes so many you need a SatNav. Do you think they're all the same? Or all near each other?"

"They may be. Assuming they exist."

I couldn't help peering down at the floor, thinking about the fell gateway to this otherworld beneath my feet in the cellar.

"There's something like one of the Oblivion portals in the beer cellar?"

Oblivion. I needed to find a way to sneak inside that grim dimension, and to do so without being spotted or having my life-force sucked from my lifeless, frozen husk. Evangelina Mormont's words at our showdown had stayed with me. *Go to Oblivion and see. See who else has been lying there all this time.* Had she been trying to spook me or was there truly someone there I needed to know about? The problem was, the only reliable gateway I had access to was the part-time broom cupboard in the Cardiff office, and that was very well monitored – and usually nothing more exciting than an *actual* broom cupboard.

"Yes and no," the Crow was saying. "Annwn is not

closely connected to Oblivion if I understand the topography of the alternative dimensions with any accuracy."

He'd given me a reading list of classic Welsh literary works to absorb, in particular the Four Branches of the Mabinogi – some of the names in which had been used as pseudonyms by Sally Spender and the other members of her supposed reading group. My reading hadn't got much beyond the pictures on the books' covers.

"Annwn ... remind me. Are we talking heaven or hell?"

"That is not a meaningful question, I would say. Annwn is neither. Or maybe it could be considered both. I really do recommend you re-read the tales, immerse yourself in Welsh myth. There are often nuggets of truth to be found in such flights of fancy."

He'd said something similar at the time of the eye case. I nodded, as if this was sound advice that I would immediately heed.

"But you found the bridge?" I asked. "It's possible to walk across?"

"There is no literal bridge, or at least not one that I was able to identify. No. There *are* certain places where the walls between the worlds are thin, as you know. Some planes are simply nearer, easier to reach from certain places, that is all. There is the chamber where Evangelina Mormont summoned her succubi, for instance. This village is another. From here it is relatively easy to at least glimpse the otherworld although, under normal circumstances, it is not possible for a mortal such as you or I to enter Annwn. Unfortunately, that does not mean that it is not relatively easy for something from the otherworld to step hither. I assume you spotted the ravens thronging the trees on your way up? The creatures are attracted to places like this."

I hadn't, but chose not to acknowledge the fact. "And something did step, um, hither?"

"They had a bad case of the *Cŵn Annwn*. And no one wants that, do they?"

He knew damn well that he'd have to translate.

Sometimes I felt he enjoyed his wise old sage act just a little too much.

"*Cŵn Annwn* – okay, the *something* of Annwn?"

"Hounds. Spectral hounds with night-black, burning red eyes and dripping fangs. Vicious creatures like big wolves with bad toothache. They are traditionally considered to be harbingers of death, although I suspect that is simply because they have a nasty habit of slaughtering any mortal they come across. They are, in that regard, something of a self-fulfilling prophecy. My guess is that there used to be a cave in the ground here, a tunnel or a river course, and the pub was built on top of it, perhaps to use the waters to brew beer. Somehow, the hounds found their way through. As with the ravens, they appear to be attracted to portals. It made changing the barrels distinctly precarious as you can imagine, and their blood-chilling yowls were not good for business. People in these parts have got used to putting up with much, and they are remarkably relaxed about contact with the ineffable, but there are limits."

"You managed to put a stop to these hounds."

"I did what I could. I restored the universe to its proper order and sealed the breach to the best of my ability. Mafanwy was extremely grateful, as you can imagine."

He glanced over to the bar, and there was a moment when I saw a haunted look pass across his features. Perhaps Mafanwy had been a little *too* grateful, come on a bit strong. I had no idea if there was a Mr Mafanwy, and I still had very little insight into the Crow's love life. From a backroom behind the bar, I could hear the steamy rush of a coffee machine making fresh espresso, a happy and glorious sound. Mafanwy peeked around the doorway as if to satisfy herself we were still present, smiling at us in an approving way.

The Crow continued, as if he felt I needed an explanation. "I sometimes come up here if I need to, well, find a little perspective on events, sit and think for a time. And to check that the *Cŵn Annwn* are not breaking through again."

"Have they ever?"

"Not so far. If I had time, I would complete my work on the movements of the spheres. I believe there are patterns to their motions and that, if one only knew enough, one could predict the moments when such dangers might present themselves, like being able to predict the reappearance of a comet or the tides in Cardiff Bay. There we are. A pleasant task for me to turn to in retirement, perhaps. For now, we have more pressing matters. We have to identify who, exactly, our adversary is."

Mafanwy arrived with a tray holding our drinks. She'd also summoned up a plate of biscuits and found a jug for the milk. She set them down with a satisfied smile.

"Earl Grey," she said. It took me a moment to work out that she meant the tea. She set my coffee down next to it. It looked good: bubble galaxies swirled in the crema.

"Thank you," said the Crow. He took a sip, making that little eyes-closed expression of delight tea drinkers often make. "Excellent. Most kind. We will let ourselves out once we are done if you wish to go back to bed."

Mafanwy adjusted the belt of her shimmery dressing-gown very slightly. "Oh, I can wait."

"There is really no need; we may be some time. Several hours, I imagine."

"Will you ensure everything is satisfactory downstairs before you go?" she asked.

"Naturally," said the Crow, his expression absolutely fixed. "You have my word."

"Right, well, make yourselves at home. Have more drinks if you need them."

"Thank you."

"If you need anything, you know where I am." There was the faintest pause partway through her sentence. The merest suggestion of suggestiveness.

"Yes," said the Crow, his voice level. "Thank you again."

When she was gone, he rose and fetched his black leather notebook from the inside pocket of his coat.

As he sat back down, I said, "You don't really think this will take several hours, do you?"

"Perhaps that was a slight exaggeration."

I couldn't stop myself grinning. "You lied to get rid of her. I'm actually slightly shocked."

"Well, it is theoretically possible the discussion might take that long. As with the veils between the worlds, sometimes the walls between lies and truth can be vanishingly thin. Shall we get down to business?"

"Fire away," I said. "Which particular enemy do you wish to discuss?"

The Crow took out a folded square of paper from the notebook and flattened it out on the table between us, the surface sticky with decades of spilled beer. The paper contained a list of names, hand-written in the Crow's distinctive, flowery style. Several had been crossed out.

"English Wizardry," he said. "The Office traitor. These are the names of everyone who was in and around Downing Street on the day of the Westminster Bridge attack."

He'd explained at the time that the meeting had been altered to 13 Downing Street, the private offices of the Witchfinder General, at the very last moment. His assumption was that, since the attack had then taken place nearby, at that precise moment, someone attending the meeting must have given orders to Thomson Fulger, the English Wizardry foot-soldier who'd carried out the atrocity.

It didn't quite add up for me, though. "The whole thing could have been coincidence. Maybe English Wizardry staged their attack in central London simply because it's the obvious place to use. I mean, it's literally central, isn't it?"

"As a matter of fact, we now know for sure that that was not the case," said the Crow. "Another matter I have been looking into. You will recall that the Assay of Thomson Fulger returned nothing useful; that his brain was fogged, his thought-patterns hexed?"

A fact I was extremely pleased about, given that I'd shown my hand and killed Fulger with a very illegal magical attack.

"Yes," I said, keeping my features straight.

"You will recall, also, that there were a whole series of encrypted messages between Fulger and someone in Cardiff, someone we now assume was Mormont. What we did not initially spot was that there was also a text message, unencrypted, sent a minute or so after we decided to switch venues. I presume Mormont panicked and resorted to a text to be sure of getting through to Fulger. The message very clearly said, *Urgent. Change of plan. Switch Westminster Bridge.*"

I thought about that. "Right, so Mormont told Fulger. The question is, who in London told Mormont?"

"Unfortunately, we have not been able to locate Mormont's phone in order to examine it for incoming messages."

"But it must be someone in the Office."

"No one else knew about the change of venue."

"Right, which is why you came up here without telling anyone," I said. "Without even logging your movements."

"I have learned not to commit my suspicions about these particular matters into MORIARTY, even in encrypted form. In this, I do not know who I can trust."

"You're trusting me," I said.

There was the little smile around his mouth again. "Well, yes, when it comes to English Wizardry, there can be no doubt about your loyalties. They probably hate you even more than they hate me."

I studied him for a moment, then looked to the list. "So, one of these is secretly working for English Wizardry, betraying everyone in the Office as well as everything they stand for."

"An individual with a foot in both camps, the Office and English Wizardry. Yes. I am convinced that one of these people was behind the trail of eye-extraction murders that you investigated and then the release of Evangelina Mormont from Oblivion, resulting in the summoning of the seven succubi. Shall we proceed, Danesh?"

I nodded. "Yes. I think we should."

4 – Infected by Shadows

Ate a hearty breakfast and took a good, long walk along the cliffs to steel myself. Nothing like a strong westerly to blow away the cobwebs, clear the mind. This really is a most beautiful island. Then, destroyed the ancient and malign wight haunting these parts, with the capable assistance of Hardknott-Lewis, my somewhat joyless but infinitely reliable colleague. Whole process took four hours: long, gruelling hours. Both of us nearly died, but we prevailed. Some fights you survive more than win. Lesson here: obvious clues can be hiding in plain sight. The name of this island was right there, and I didn't see it. We put out some nonsense about it coming from ancient Celtic words and Latin mistranslations and the like. Hopefully people believe it.

– Thomas Quirk, Lord High Witchfinder of the
Isles, *private journal*, 2002

The Crow's list started with the seven Keyholders of the Office of the Witchfinder General, followed by their lowly minions. People like me. The list was oddly formal, with titles and roles provided even though the Crow clearly knew the individuals well. Who did that when they were making scribbled notes for their own usage? Hardknott-Lewis did.

The list went like this:

Keyholders of the Office of the Witchfinder General
Talvin Epenesa (Overseas Domains)
Mac Ferrier (Ireland)
~~Mason Greentree (England)~~
Earl Grey (All Britain and the British Isles)
~~Campbell Hardknott-Lewis (Wales)~~
Ian Majkowski (Scotland)
Thomas Quirk (Isles)

Acolytes and Advisors
Gwenn Altandubh (Isles)
Dan Box-Templeton (Ireland)
Per Lyndstrom (Overseas Domains)
~~Danesh Shahzan (Wales)~~
~~Lincoln Umenyora (England)~~
Herbert Wigwe (Scotland)

He had, of course, written the names in alphabetical order. Only six acolytes, though. I tried to think back, replay my memories of the day. I'd been distracted by events elsewhere, the things I'd witnessed in the ghost station and, later, by the horrors on Westminster Bridge.

"Doesn't Earl Grey have an advisor?"

"Not one that was present. Lincoln Umenyora would have been the closest, although obviously his focus is England. As so often, there is a certain amount of elision between England and the wider territory, a fact that causes tension at times."

"Mason Greentree is crossed off because he's dead," I said. "I see you've crossed your own name off, too."

The Crow grimaced in a way that he did when facing some distasteful task. "I checked into poor Mason; in case his unfortunate demise was some macabre ruse to put us off the trail. Being dead is such a good alibi, is it not? There can be no doubt about him; he is gone. We can discount him."

"And you?"

"Well, by all means cast your net over me as well. You know that I have always encouraged that. This is simply the list as I have written it, and I know myself to be innocent."

"But you would say that if you weren't."

"I would say it if I were, too. You will see that I have crossed you off by the same token, as well as Lincoln."

"Why discount Lincoln?"

"On reflection, my assumption is that it would take a Keyholder to engineer the events we witnessed, to free Mormont from Oblivion and so forth. And, if Mason is innocent, then I believe that means Mr Umenyora is in the clear as well."

"You can't be sure of that."

"No. I am weighing up probabilities."

"If what you say is true, we could cross off all the acolytes."

"I think I agree. Shall we? I wanted to hear your views before I did so."

I took a sip of coffee. It was hot, it was black. It was good. "They may be involved, as Peter Warder was, but they aren't going to be giving out the orders. Let's do it."

The Crow unscrewed the silver fountain pen (the one that he naturally carried with him at all times) and crossed off more names. I considered the list, recalling what details I could of that day in Downing Street. And also, another day: one of flickering candles and horror; of my showdown with Evangelina Mormont in the nexus chamber. Her intent gaze boring into me and the words she spoke. *He has resisted so far. It won't last.*

He. Who was he? If I knew who Mormont's enemies were, I might know who her friends were, too. Mormont had been English Wizardry's most feared protagonist – save, perhaps, for the individual controlling it.

"Surely you can cross a few other names off?" I said. "The attacks on Ian Majkowski, Talvin Epenesa and Mac Farrier all stopped before the death of Mason Greentree. Our assumption was that those assaults had been successful. Their semen had been harvested; they're victims, not perpetrators. Thomas Quirk, too – he succumbed towards the end."

The Crow sat back in his stained, plush seat, his gaze still on the list. Something was troubling him.

"Possibly so. I have ... mentally crossed some of those names off. Again, we need to be sure. Our enemies are clever, and what better way of diverting suspicion than to frame yourself as a victim? This is the area I have been looking into."

"What have you found out?"

I imagined all manner of forbidden mystical powers being brought to bear: spirits consulted, runes read, tea leaves examined, the spirits of the deceased called forth through the veils. But that wasn't it.

"The five cauldrons that Mormont was making use of to develop her cambions: before we destroyed them, we took samples for DNA analysis."

"You can get a genetic trace from a witch's brew?"

"You can if they contain gametes; spermatozoa or ova. And if you are lucky. The results took a while to come through, partly because I had to resort to a certain amount of bureaucratic sleight-of-hand to acquire samples from my fellow Keyholders."

Well, you would. "I'm surprised at you, sir."

"I was a little surprised at myself, to be brutally honest. Still, needs must."

"What did you find?"

"More or less what we suspected, I think. We retrieved viable samples from four of the five cauldrons. As well as Mason, we were able to match against Ian, Talvin and Mac. I believe, yes, that we can most probably discount them, too."

"Unless one deliberately consorted with Mormont as an alibi."

He did his little head jiggle, weighing-up-of-possibilities thing. "I judge that unlikely; anyone doing so would be putting themselves at significant risk. The blood magic of the chalices would make the cambions, the children, potent entities, with the power to control and harm their kin. Specifically, their parents. I doubt any Keyholder would put themselves at such a risk, especially if they were the one in control of the whole operation."

I dipped my head in assent. The Crow crossed more names off the list. Now it said:

Keyholders of the Office of the Witchfinder General
~~Talvin Epensa (Overseas Domains)~~
~~Mac Ferrier (Ireland)~~
~~Mason Greentree (England)~~
Earl Grey (All Britain and the British Isles)
~~Campbell Hardknott-Lewis (Wales)~~
~~Ian Majkowski (Scotland)~~
Thomas Quirk (Isles)

Acolytes and Advisors
~~Gwenn Altandubh (Isles)~~
~~Dan Box-Templeton (Ireland)~~
~~Per Lyndstrom (Overseas Domains)~~
~~Danesh Shahzan (Wales)~~
~~Lincoln Umenyora (England)~~
~~Herbert Wigwe (Scotland)~~

"You got DNA from five of the cauldrons," I said. "The mother: I assume it was Mormont?"

"Of all of them, yes. If the foetuses had been allowed to come into existence, they would have been half-brothers and half-sisters. Mormont had clearly acceded to ovum-extraction at some point, possibly before she was even committed to Oblivion. One obviously accepts that modern families are often singular in nature, non-standard, but this was perhaps going too far."

"If the Cambions are so much of a threat to their parents, why would Mormont have consented to the whole arrangement?"

"Because she was instructed to, I suppose. Our enemies are not strong on issues of consent. She followed her orders."

I studied the list again. "And no hint of a match on Thomas Quirk?"

"One of the cauldrons did not give us viable DNA;

regrettably, we could not connect its contents to anyone. There was something there, but not enough."

"Assuming it was Quirk's, that only leaves Earl Grey himself. Two of the cauldrons were empty; presumably they were for you and Earl Grey once the attacks on you were successful. But, for all we know, maybe Earl Grey's was never going to be filled."

"And that is a most troubling thought, is it not?" said the Crow. "I would go so far as to say that it is impossible for the Witchfinder General to be our nemesis. I trust Earl Grey utterly; it is because of his guidance and inspiration that I am here today. The attacks upon him were particularly vicious and I have seen the physical evidence, the scars, that demonstrate this."

Was Hardknott-Lewis right, or was he struggling to come to terms with an unwelcome truth? I knew what *that* was like.

"Then, who?" I said. "That doesn't leave anyone else."

"My hope was that you might come up with a fresh perspective."

I tried to give the whole situation a helicopter view. I leaned back in my chair, then regretted it as the wooden bar dug into me.

"There *were* others there that day in Downing Street," I said. "People not part of the Office, I mean. Staff in Number 13 for one thing. Others, too: I mean, for all we know, the Prime Minister himself was there and was aware of our gathering. I sat in the garden at one point, and we know that it's shared between several properties. It's well-known that they have parties there, right?"

"If the PM were present, I'm sure the Doctrine of Unseeing would apply," said the Crow.

"And that is…?"

"Ah, a long-standing arrangement in force when members of the Office come into close contact with colleagues in the more mundane branches of government. We agree to hold our gatherings in secret as much as possible, while they agree to simply not see us should we happen to meet."

"They can legally claim to have not seen anything that they have, in fact, witnessed?"

"In my experience, some of our politicians become extremely adept in the art. If you showed them video evidence to prove that they had been present with us in a room, they would be genuinely amazed and would probably claim it was faked. There we are. The wonders and frustrations of our unwritten constitution. Perhaps we in the Office are somewhat to blame for fostering generations of politicians skilled in the art of dissembling. But it is true that staff or politicians in the other buildings in Downing Street might have seen something. This is an area I shall continue to pursue. I have one or two contacts in the relevant departments of the Civil Service."

"There was one other person inside the offices that day."

The Crow looked puzzled. "Who?"

"Talking to Earl Grey. The two of them seemed to be arguing about something."

The Crow looked puzzled. This was news to him. "You didn't mention this before. When was it, exactly?"

"Immediately before you all went into the chamber. I'd forgotten all about it; I assumed you all saw him."

"I did not. Can you recall what he looked like?"

"The light wasn't good. He was taller and older than the Witchfinder General. I didn't get a look at his face. Oh, and he wore, like, ecclesiastical robes."

"Was it, perhaps, the Archbishop of Canterbury?" The Crow asked. "You will recall that we conversed with him outside Number 10 as he was leaving. Perhaps he doubled back to press some liturgical point home."

"No, I don't think this was him. The man I saw inside Number 13 was hairless."

"Interesting. Another mystery to pursue. Most likely, another functionary of the church discussing a point of doctrine."

"The Archbishop of Canterbury, though," I said. "As you say, *he* knew we were there, and he's also fully aware of who and what we are. You told me that yourself. Doesn't that make him a suspect?"

The Crow looked amused. "I did briefly consider that possibility. The modern church is liberal, broad-minded, but I doubt even they would resort to summoning demons to defeat their enemies. I applaud your creative thinking; it is, as I believe the saying goes, outside of the box. But, perhaps too much so. No, I very much doubt that the Archbishop of Canterbury is the controlling mind behind the evils of English Wizardry."

"Then what do you want me to do? You must have a plan for me to have come all this way."

The Crow sighed as he screwed the cap back onto his fountain pen and returned it to his inside pocket. "Question marks remain over Earl Grey and Thomas Quirk. And, arguably, over myself. Are we agreed?"

"I think so."

"Then there is anyone else who was at Downing Street that day, including this mysterious figure you glimpsed. I suggest a two-pronged approach."

"Go on."

"It is more natural for me to be in Downing Street and Whitehall, at the heart of the Office's operations in London. I shall return there on some pretext, learn what I can about anyone who was present that day. As I say, I find it hard to believe Earl Grey is capable of such treachery, but I may learn something. He is a strong-minded man, but it is conceivable that some baleful magic was brought to bear on him, some glamour."

"And my prong is Thomas Quirk?"

"There is no clear proof that his semen was harvested. It is possible that he is our shadowy figure and that his cauldron was a fake, set there for show."

I remembered my impression of him: tall, slightly stooped, in his sixties. His hair was wild, as if he were constantly battling against some violent gale. An austere but friendly man, full of wiry enthusiasm.

"What do you know about him?"

"I have fought alongside him several times, tackling

ghasts and wraiths and vampires, even a bridge troll or two. I would say he is also a good man, utterly dependable. The two of us once discovered why, exactly, the *Isle of Wight* is called that."

"Oh. Why is it?"

"A most fearsome revenant haunted the place. Thomas was always formidable when we went on operations together. Although, these days, we converse rarely. Given his patch he does tend to be a somewhat peripheral figure. I suppose it is conceivable that he has strayed without me noticing."

"Which *Isles* does he cover?" I asked. "Britain is all islands."

"Various smaller territories that either are now or once were separate from the larger countries. The Hebrides, the Orkney Islands, Shetland, the Isle of Man, the Channel Islands, Anglesey, the Scillies and various other rocks and outcrops around the coast, including one or two with lonely and deserted lighthouses. Rockall. One or two islets in the middle of inland lakes and lochs, Seaforth and so on. Also, a number of landmasses that used to be on the maps but which aren't there anymore – in Cardigan Bay, for example. Then there are the temporary islands."

"How can an island be temporary?"

"Places like Lindisfarne, which is only an island when the tide is in. Office jurisdiction there is a little hazy."

"Anglesey is Wales. Some of those others are Scotland or England."

"The delineations of the various Keyholders' responsibilities are somewhat archaic. As you know, we do cling to our traditions rather."

The Crow wasn't wrong there.

The irony wasn't lost on me, either. We spent all our time battling the arcane, while doing our absolute damnedest to stick with our own arcane practices.

"Why would Thomas Quirk be a member of English Wizardry? That makes no sense."

"For what it is worth, he is, in fact, English, although

he comes from Manx stock on his father's side, which explains the name."

"Is there any indication at all that he might be on their side politically? Or that he might be a user, come to that?"

"None whatsoever, but my feeling is that you might be able to sniff him out, as it were, if he has gone to the other side. Identify any hidden magical powers he may be wielding, or that are controlling him."

So that was it. The Crow didn't spell it out any further. He knew I was a user and he was calculating that I might be useful in spotting the activities of another user. Set a thief to catch a thief. I wondered how he squared this with his personal abhorrence of magic. It was acceptable to get me to do things he wouldn't and couldn't do himself?

"Where is he at the moment?" I asked.

"Well, now, that is, in fact, a very good question. Since the Star Chamber meeting in Downing Street, he has rather, well, disappeared."

"Like, *magically* disappeared?"

"I assume not. He has simply dropped of the maps. Most likely he is on manoeuvres somewhere, working undercover."

"Hasn't he logged anything in MORIARTY either?"

"There is nothing relevant in his diary, a fact that is odd. He has always been rigorous in following the rules. A stickler even by my standards."

"He's definitely worth looking into then," I said. "The question is, where should I start?"

"His base is on the Isle of Man, conveniently located in the middle of the British Isles. Douglas, the capital, would be my first port of call. Do you know it?"

"Never been there. I don't see how I can just turn up there and start asking questions. If Quirk is our adversary, he's going to be extremely suspicious."

"Well, we *are* attempting to foster inter-department links, as you know, break down the old barriers, *work smarter* as I believe the saying goes. But I agree, it might seem odd for you to turn up, especially given your prominence in events on Westminster Bridge. I thought about saying you were on our new Adept Training Program, being sent around the different offices to gain experience. It still might seem suspicious."

"So, what's the thinking?"

The Crow pulled a second notebook from his breast pocket.

"There is this."

"What is it?"

"What do you know about Night Hags?"

"Just what everyone knows."

"Well. It occurred to me that we might attempt to kill two birds with a single stone. This is a case that urgently needs looking into. One more supernatural threat to our way of life, I am afraid, fraught with risks and uncertainties. It is also, I believe, utterly unrelated to our English Wizardry problem, a fact that might help to keep things simple."

"Are you sure there's no connection?"

"Reasonably so, I think. It is a mistake to see the Warlock's hand in every infernal horror we face. I suspect that is how he wants us to react, to perceive his baleful influence in every bad thing that happens."

"Or *she*. We don't know that the Warlock is one of the Keyholders. The Office's traitor may simply be taking orders from a higher power."

"Just so. Although, Mormont referred to *him*, of course. But then, perhaps she was simply throwing us off the scent. Pronouns can be slippery, can they not?"

He handed me the notebook. "I have jotted down everything that I thought might be useful, but you should obviously retrieve what we have on MORIARTY as well. The Librarian might also be helpful."

"Why her?"

"Read the notes; it should become clear. It is a nasty case. The three victims that we know about, I should mention, were all operatives of the Office of the Witchfinder General."

"Is this where you tell me to be careful? That I'll face terrible dangers?"

He smiled at that. "It might be, yes."

"Three officers killed. That sounds very much like something English Wizardry would be behind."

The Crow nodded in a way that suggested he saw my point. "By its very nature, our work involves battling hideous and unseen dangers, though. It is inevitable that our death rate by, well, *unnatural* causes is significantly higher than that of the general population. I am convinced that this case is unrelated to our Warlock problem, but of course I may be wrong. By all means find a connection if there is one."

"What's it about?"

"One victim refers to being *infected by shadows*, a striking phrase. Night Hags may well be involved, or some similar species of demon. Two of the cases also make passing reference to sightings of hellhounds or some local variation of them. All three victims lost blood as part of their attacks."

I thought about that. "The *Cŵn Annwn* you said had been sighted in this pub: do you think this place is connected somehow?"

The Crow leaned back in his chair and looked around, as if expecting to see giant spectral dogs stepping from the shadows. None did.

"I don't believe there's a direct connection, no. Perhaps you will see links that I do not, but I simply felt that the location might be instructive, especially if any of the creatures happened to manifest this evening. As I have explained, I have noticed before that entities such as the *Cŵn Annwn* are attracted to doorways opened between the worlds. I suspect this pub is simply one such place. My suspicion is that the creatures are attracted to the scents they pick up coming through such portals."

"As in, the smell of possible prey?"

"Yes."

"Any other connections between the cases?" I asked. "Did the victims know each other?"

"As far as I can tell, they were not connected in any way, other than being Office operatives. I do not believe they even all met."

"What about vampires?" I asked.

He frowned at that word, as if it were distasteful to him. "Why do you mention those creatures?"

Perhaps it was simply my imagination running away with me after my visit to the tomb. "You said blood-letting was involved in each case. Then there are the hellhounds; vampires can transform into wolves as well as other creatures, right? Perhaps that's what people saw."

"Again, I applaud your open-mindedness, although modern cryptozoology asserts that vampires cannot, in fact, transform into bats or wolves or anything else. Their grim powers lie elsewhere. But who knows? The worlds are wide and wonderful, and there are no laws about such things."

"What do you believe is going on with these cases?"

"They may be nothing other than coincidence, although my suspicion is that something malign is going on. It is almost as if Night Hags are being wielded as a weapon, a means of execution. Or, it may be a case of possession by some unknown entity. Or it may be some other, barely-understood magical effect. I can tell you that the three Officers – the three people – died in the most upsetting ways imaginable. We must not forget that. But the case also has the advantage, if that is the correct word, of involving victims from across the British Isles. One here in South Wales, a colleague of our own, Jamie Tavish who you may have heard of. Then one in Scotland some years ago and, conveniently, a more recent case on the Isle of Man."

"Your thinking is that it won't appear suspicious if I turn up in these places asking questions."

"That is my hope."

I thought about that. "Still, it will look odd if I ignore the local case and immediately head off to investigate the others. I'll spend a little time here finding out what I can first. I have a few loose ends to tidy up before I leave."

"As you see fit," said the Crow. "My advice is not to leave it too long, though. We must suck out this poison before it kills us. Be sure to assiduously log your activity in MORIARTY, so that your pursuers do not think it odd when you do head off for the islands."

"I'll leave a good trail. What about the Owain Williams situation?"

The Crow looked out of the window, although it was obviously utterly dark out there. "I imagine that conundrum will still be here when you return. I believe it is also unconnected to the new case, but if it turns out that everything is interrelated, that we face a complex spider web of evil, then you may surprise Owain by coming at him from an unexpected angle."

I nodded and took the second notebook from him. Anything to help in the fight against the Warlock and his righteous army of magical bastards. Plus, the thought of getting away from Cardiff was appealing. I had certain other leads I wanted to pursue, other people I wanted to speak to, and I'd be more comfortable not having the Crow perched on my shoulder as I did so.

I opened the notebook. The first page was given over to the name of the case, penned in Hardknott-Lewis's purple ink. The words didn't make a great deal of sense.

They said, simply, *Head Full of Dark.*

5 – Charnel House

> One need only undertake the briefest investigations
> into certain powerful, indigenous beings to
> understand that these islands are hallowed, special,
> set apart. As with our native magical arts, so with
> what me might term our mystical aristocracy. We
> are fortunate, indeed, to benefit from their diligent
> shepherding, as we are their most welcome
> protection. The natural fear that we may, from time
> to time, feel should be understood for what it is: the
> deep, ingrained understanding of our inferiority and
> their superiority.
>
> – Samuel Bedfellowes, *The Old Ways*, 1847

Sir Jacob Charnel, first and so-far only Viscount
Grimsby, lifted the silver goblet to his lips and sipped at
the warm blood that his silent servant had poured.

The bouquet was salty and earthy at the same time, rich
with the stone and soil of Old England. He could taste the
history in it, the deep roots, the memories. Yes, the
provenance was very fine, pureblood, no doubt about it.
There was no hint at all of the foreign in it – of what his
three visitors might dismiss as taint or tang. His cellar –
dungeon might be a better word – was undoubtedly
extremely well-stocked, surely the finest in the land.
There was a whole community down there, cut-off, self-
sustaining, unknown to the outside world. It had served
him well over the centuries.

Nor did It only contain his herd of two-legged cattle
kept for bleeding. Housed separately, unknown to each
other, were the coterie of clairvoyants that he employed
to monitor the world's financial markets. The *Financial
Wizards* as he liked to think of them. It was their

predictions, the killings on the markets they made, that funded his lifestyle and his activities, and that had done so for a very long time. The recent buzz from them was all about cryptocurrencies – a fact that amused Charnel, given their physical location literally in a crypt.

To keep his financiers keen, he held out the promise of immortality to each of them, and every now and then, he would escort one away to be granted ascendance to the vampiric ranks – or so they thought.

Blood and money and power. They were all he needed, and he had ready supplies of all of them.

Then there was the vampire Magor, his oldest friend, his bitterest foe. Magor was entombed down there, too, isolated in his own private sepulchre, pinned into place by the power of the *Norskrang* artefact, seething with helpless fury. Four hundred years previously, he, Charnel, had walked into the fortress they had once shared upon the nearby tidal island. *Holy Island.* He'd descended into the crypt that Magor and Valian still dwelt in to strike the decisive blows, killing one, skewering the other with the fearsome ensorcelled spike of yew. They'd had no idea the artefact had come to light, let alone that Charnel had retrieved it. Even if they had known, they'd surely have doubted that any vampire could use the foul weapon. Could even bring themselves to be near it.

To maintain your position of power, you had to be prepared to carry out the distasteful.

Magor and Valian, though: one that he hated and one that he had loved, in his own way. Both that he had feared, for that was how it always was for his kind. They were animals. He didn't flinch from the truth. He was under no illusions. The three of them had accompanied the rats and the lice and the dogs that had tagged along behind the nomadic humans as they crossed Europe: nomads that they fed off and begged off. His kind were parasites wearing the clothes of lords.

Magor was an issue he would need to address at some point. Why had he, Charnel, even allowed his compatriot to live for so long? Was it – the thought sent a shudder of distaste through him – some relative of human sentimentality that had stayed his hand? The fact remained that Magor was too great a threat. Valian had been too dangerous to keep around, and the same was true of Magor. One day soon, Charnel would go down and destroy him.

Charnel ran the glutinous liquid around in his mouth, across his palette, letting the subtle notes in the symphony sound. The metallic tangs, seaweedy iodine, the floral undertones; yes, it could not be faulted. He swallowed, then nodded his approval with the slightest movement of his ancient head.

Not that he cared about *purity* for a single moment. He was well aware of the irony of that little word, given his own origins in the hills and woodlands of eastern Europe – but there were certain pretences that had to be kept up even for him, certain roles that had to be played. He, after so many centuries, was a master at it. A word-perfect performer. This little sect, his *coven*, the Order of the British Vampire as they now styled themselves (the name a ridiculous private joke that had somehow taken on a life of its own) – it was his alone, and he set the tone for it. It had gone by many other names over the years – the General Sinod, the 1622 Committee – but whatever the title, it was always little more than a front for him. He knew well that his three guests, sitting around him in the shadowy room, preparing to share in the meal he was offering them *did* care about purity of the bloodline. They cared very much indeed, so much so that it defined them. Including them in his affairs, it was a necessary evil. Which was fine; he liked a necessary evil. In his terms, though, they were little more than parvenus, the nouveau riche – if one could allow the passage of two or three centuries to still constitute *nouveau*.

Which, he most certainly could. It was the slow blink of an eye. These three were his allies, his foot-soldiers, but they were narrow-minded fools. Each drank in his stories about ancient bloodlines, fantasies that he had invented and that he actively fostered. Ultimately, ancestrally, everyone was an African, were they not? One only had to go back far enough through the generations to see that. His kind had started there too, diverging from the common herd under the influence of some ancient act of chance or witchcraft. These three, though – they would never accept such assertions. The very notion was repulsive to them, facts be damned. They believed absolutely that Britain was both his and their origin. That it was a special place, a land they had arrived within by some mystical, elevated means. That they had emerged from its very soil, sprouting between the roots of its ancient oaks. That they were set apart from the lowly cattle, the humans that they preyed off even while they prized *purebloods* above others.

Well. Let them drink. Their blindness to inconvenient truths was useful. His fellow vampires did not need to know, for example, that he, Jacob Charnel, had walked to this land from his dimly-recalled home, crossing the now-submerged and lost domain of Doggerland some seven thousand years previously, at a time when there simply was no North Sea, when this island hadn't been an island at all. He, Valian and Magor had come to take up dominion over the primitive and distinctly unpromising tribes of that time, setting themselves up as tyrants or kings, whichever suited their purpose at the time. A plan that had, indeed, worked well enough.

It was all a matter of perspective, of the story told. The myths were useful, just as the myths of these islands were useful. The power of fantasy. His trick had been to convince his prey of his superiority. His right to rule. He knew well that such notions, repeated enough, gilded with sufficient jewellery and pageantry, became truths. Or something even better than truths; they became things people *believed* in.

Things that they were prepared to live by, and so to die for.

The candle flames flickered, sending glints of light across the table, reflected in the polished silver and gold of the cutlery and the goblets and platters. Such baubles, too, were a part of the play. The patina of age and wealth and privilege; the accumulation of expensive *things*. The carved stones of his grand home, the oak panelling, the portraits on the walls and the fine stained glass: it was all an act. Behind the four of them, adorning the walls, were oil paintings of his supposed forebears. They were, of course, all him. The costumes changed but the face remained the same. He would go quiet for a few years and then re-emerge as the *next* Viscount Grimsby of the line, and people accepted it. Who really knew what went on in remote ancestral piles such as his? The world was obviously kept at a long arm's length.

As the servants stepped forwards from the shadows to fill the goblets with the blood that he'd approved, the conversation began.

"My Lord, I believe events in London did not go quite to plan?" Gereint Summers, the Duke of Gravesend, sitting on his immediate right, was the first to break the silence. Of course. Summers was young – by the standards of the group – and impatient. He felt the need to act, but it was an urgency born of weakness. He required constant reassurance of their dominance. His words were critical, almost a challenge, but Summers was no threat.

Charnel smiled to himself at the other vampire's words, being always careful to reveal nothing on the outside. Once, long ago, such notions of insecurity might have run through his mind, too. Back then, days when people *saw* his kind and knew what they were, his life and his position had been precarious. Now it was different; now he ruled over millions and millions of them, carefully husbanding them so that there was never any serious danger to the supply. Humans didn't even know that this was all they were. A resource. A crop. So successful had he been – he and others in other lands – that from time to time he had to instigate culls of one sort or another to maintain the viability of the herd. Once, as the human population teetered on the brink of collapse, this would have been unthinkable. These days, one could very easily absorb such losses. Sometimes, in order to win the war, it was acceptable to lose a battle. Necessary, even. But Summers would not see that; he lacked the perspective that came from thousands of years of existence.

Charnel considered Summers for long moments before replying. "It is true that our friends in English Wizardry have received something of a blow to their designs. We need not concern ourselves. Useful as they are, our position remains secure. Indeed, in many ways, I believe the new situation is preferable. And, they will recover. They are strong."

Heston Godwin, on his left, snorted his amusement at the mention of English Wizardry. Godwin was less ambitious than Summers. He was another of the newer recruits, having been inducted into the Order in the late nineteenth century. Charnel suspected that Godwin still had trouble believing that he had been chosen for ascension to the ranks. There were times when Charnel had doubts about that decision, too. He valued obedience, loyalty, yes – but independence of thought was essential as well. This was *why* fresh blood was occasionally brought into the inner circle. They survived by maintaining a close understanding of the modern world, by adapting to it even as they shaped it to their own ends.

"English Wizardry are fools," said Godwin, his voice dismissive as he picked up the theme. "We should never have allowed them to flourish."

"Fools, but useful fools," Charnel replied, letting the tones of a kindly schoolmaster enter his voice. "Their readiness to intervene in events when we would prefer to, well, remain in the shadows provides us with a useful lever in the control of public opinion. They commit their atrocities and the terrified people respond by flocking to the familiar, to easy explanations, to the reassuringly powerful. In short, to us. To tradition."

He did not add that the myths concerning the supposed *old ways* propagated by English Wizardry were useful fabrications, too. He, after all, had essentially written them himself, magically beguiling writers to set down his ideas as if they were their own.

"What do we care about public opinion?" The voice from opposite him was little more than a growl. Lord Tremaine, the oldest of his trio of visitors, a vampire for three hundred years now, finally spoke. "Does the farmer care about the opinions of his cattle? Does he worry that his sheep might be sad?"

Charnel sipped at the blood from his chalice, letting the taste wash around his mouth. Tremaine was the only one in the little group who was any sort of threat. He wasn't anywhere near the power of Magor, naturally, but he was a vampire to be taken account of.

Charnel averted his head to one side and raised an eyebrow, instructing his servant to provide a refill, before replying.

"Yes, I believe that he should. Not because he is concerned for the wellbeing of the animals in his care, nor from any misguided sense of altruism or, worse, *morality*, but simply because he wishes to make the task of containing them and controlling them easier. Do you not see that? Contented cattle grow happily fat, ready for the slaughter. Oblivious to the slaughter. Denying, even, that there is any such thing as a slaughter. Celebrating, even, the very fact that they are part of it."

"And I see a sect of wizards and spellcasters running out of control," said Tremaine. "They endanger us all, summoning entities into our world they have no understanding of, throwing their magic around. We should not allow them the freedom to act."

"If you are referring to Evangelina Mormont, then there, at least, you have no reason to fear," Charnel replied.

"She is gone then?" Godwin asked. The note of hope in his voice was pathetic. "Truly this time?"

Mormont – the so-called Sorceress – was dead, of that there could be no doubt. Charnel had checked very carefully. It was a satisfactory outcome in many ways: the one, indeed, that he had privately hoped for, the one he had manipulated events to achieve. He had calculated that she might survive, weakened, but that had not been the case. So be it. Mormont had been a powerful ally, a useful attack dog, but powerful allies couldn't be allowed to become too powerful. It had been his instruction to pull her out of Oblivion, place the powerful playing-piece back on the board. In time, her towering magical abilities would have become a threat to his own. She wouldn't have been the first. They operated in different spheres, perhaps, his blood and death glamours very different to the summoning sorcery she had wielded so capably, but she would have seen him as an obstacle to her own designs in the end.

Now, she had been removed from the game, and it was their opponents in the Office who were seen to be responsible. Both facts could only strengthen his hand. The conflict between the Office of the Witchfinder General and English Wizardry was manufactured of course, a war that he had created to consume the passions and energies of people and entities who wielded magic. Keep them divided, tearing – metaphorically or actually – at each other's throats. That was the idea. It was also a thing of beauty. Let the puppets fight; it distracted the audience from seeing the strings.

These titles, though. How ridiculous they were, how laughable. *The Sorceress.* By the dark gods of the underworlds, sometimes he had to laugh at the infantile stories people concocted without any bidding. Still, he had to concede that such affectations could be effective. They caught the public imagination. He'd had titles of his own over the years, of course. The Lord of Dragons, that had been one of his favourites. The Shadow Who Walks in the Night. The Lamentation. The Sword of Death. All good, solid names.

The point was, he had not been Sir Jacob Charnel when he walked into this land. He hadn't been able to resist *that* little joke when the title was offered to him. Over a long, long existence, you had to take your pleasures where you could. He had accumulated other labels more recently, as well, including one in particular that seemed to have stuck. None of the epithets were *him*, but they could all be useful. People feared an impressive or shadowy figure, and fear, ultimately, was the best way to keep people in check. Stop them having – the horror – ideas of their own.

"Truly," he said out loud, finally deigning to answer Godwin. "The Office of the Witchfinder General, ridiculous as they are, managed to scrape together just enough wit and skill to achieve this miraculous feat."

A little ripple of amusement washed around the table at his mention of the Office. It was satisfying to hear. In earlier days, troubling times during the late eighteenth century in particular, there'd been moments when he'd been seriously diverted by the Office and the threat it posed to his dominion. They wished to impose their drab, mundane little view of the world upon everyone, and that could obviously not be allowed. In the end, he had allowed them to survive mainly because their sister organization, the Mystical Council, had been even worse. The Office shunned more or less all forms of magical activity, a puzzling fact that weakened them considerably. The Council had had no such qualms, and the presence of powerful wizards cooperating on achieving the aims of the British state had turned out to be too dangerous. After all, those aims might not coincide with the needs of a controlling cabal of ancient vampires – although it was surprising how often they did.

Now, the Council was long-gone and the Office was weakened, ineffectual, deprived of resource and credibility. He allowed it to survive, to appear to be operating successfully, but it was another illusion. To any dweller of the British demi-monde, to anyone or anything sorcerous or magical in nature, they were an inconvenience at most – something to be feared, perhaps, but certainly not as much as *he* was feared. They were weak, useful enough when they kept certain magical powers in check. So long as they didn't become too successful, they could be allowed to continue.

Probably.

"Do you really claim your influence over the Office remains undimmed?" Tremaine asked. His voice was low, a snarl in it.

"Naturally," said Charnel. "I have my puppets among them, as you know. I play my detuned violin and they dance my tarantella. I was in Downing Street recently, handing down my orders to one side and another, making suitable arrangements. All is in hand."

"Westminster Bridge?" asked Godwin.

"Just so. A little demonstration carried out by our, if you will, paramilitary wing. English Wizardry were only too happy to do my bidding, even if the main effect was to weaken themselves further."

He didn't mention the unexpected resistance he had encountered when giving his orders. The dissent. You made monsters and sometimes they took on a life of their own, started thinking for themselves. It was troublesome, another situation he needed to keep a watchful eye on. The British government had its official shadow cabinet, made up of opposition politicians, but the truth was that his cabal of vampires was the true shadow cabinet. The *shadow* shadow cabinet. It worked, too: the damned Prime Minister of the United Kingdom of Great Britain and Northern Ireland had taken his orders readily enough, as he or she generally did. But both the Office of the Witchfinder General and now English Wizardry were a different matter. The irony really was amusing. The time might come when both had outlived their usefulness. Then, it would be time to destroy them.

Tremaine's gaze was still intent, as if he were attempting to bore into Charnel's mind, see his innermost thoughts. As if Tremaine's glamours would ever be powerful enough for that little trick to succeed on *him*. Charnel, by the same token, could easily see the colours of Tremaine's mind. His fury, his fear, the violent distaste he bore towards any and all members of the herd. He was driven by hunger and very little else. Which was by no means unusual or unreasonable for their kind, but it did mean he was a danger.

"Not all your puppets dance to your tune," said Tremaine.

So, he had heard some whisper of the situation. There was, also, a clear note of challenge in Tremaine's words. Charnel approved – up to a point. He and his fellow vampires were untamed creatures. The hierarchy was strict, like any pack of wolves, but from time-to-time vicious violence broke out as individuals vied for position, attempting to rip the top dog to shreds in order to take his position. The hunger for this was in Tremaine's mind now. The time was coming when he would have to slaughter Tremaine; turn him to dust, scatter his burned and broken bones to the winds so that he could never come back. Again, he wouldn't be the first. The ashes of many an ancient vampire drifted upon the winds of Britain. Those that had thought to challenge him.

"They do as I tell them," Charnel said. "Are you doubting my word?"

Tremaine stood suddenly, sending his heavy gilded chair careering backwards, a wordless growl in his throat. He loomed over the table with his thin height, casting his shadow across them. It was well done, Charnel had to concede. Tremaine threw a glance around the group, calculating who was with him, who might support him if he attempted to seize control of the Order. Neither Summers not Godwin, Charnel noted, met Tremaine's gaze. They were not with him, not yet at least. Still, his little show of defiance was clear. Charnel had pushed him a little, flushing him out to see what he would do, and Tremaine had dutifully responded.

"Sit down," said Charnel after another sip, another pause. He kept his voice low and quiet, as if he were bored. Which, in truth, he was. "No one is impressed with your little games. Perhaps, in another thousand years, when you have drained enough life from your victims, we might be quaking in our chairs. As it is … no."

To his credit, Tremaine pressed on, refused to sit. "You are losing your grip, Charnel. Where is your sting? Do you really deny you are no longer in complete control? I have heard the whispers, as we all have. The Office is kept busy fighting its little fires, but not everywhere and not completely. They take their toll upon us. They encroach. The ancient fortress that you yourself once dwelt in, not thirty miles from this spot, has been uncovered and ransacked – *cleansed* by the operatives of the accursed Office – yet it seems you do nothing. Cardiff, too, are becoming a thorn in our side; they refuse to dance your dance. You tried to break Campbell Hardknott-Lewis and you failed. His strings have slipped through your fingers. And not just his; it was Cardiff that destroyed Mormont. It may even be that they know where Arthur Stonewall has been hiding all this time. We know they have been consorting with those who are protecting him."

Stonewall. *The Destroyer.* Yes, there was another problem that needed to be resolved. To think that he had once considered Arthur Stonewall a possible ally. That he, Charnel, had attempted to bring the man into the fold of English Wizardry to be considered for ascension to the vampiric cabal. Stonewall had proved himself to be extremely capable, his powers enormous, the lengths he would go to truly impressive. But he had turned his back on everything that had been offered him. Stonewall *was* tainted – with the disease of morality, with his misguided and childish concern for right and wrong, as if such notions were *real* and not just ideas that people made up in their heads. Well, it was Stonewall's weakness; it would be his demise in the end. The powerful controlled the weak; that was the natural order, but Stonewall had refused to see it. He preferred to spend his days among the cattle, pretending to be like them. Pretending to like them.

"The Office will hardly be on the same side as Stonewall," said Charnel. "Do you need me to explain the delicate balance we maintain?"

Tremaine, still standing, leaned forwards, his hands on the table. His gaze upon Charnel was intent, sharp enough to skewer any mere mortal into abject terror. It had precisely no effect on Charnel.

"I know what they are, how they oppose the *unnatural*, whenever they encounter it," said Tremaine. "That is their mission, their very reason for existing. They play individuals like Stonewall off against English Wizardry and ourselves, intending to weaken both sides. I say the Office are a threat that you have allowed to survive for far too long."

What Tremaine said was true, up to a point. The playing piece became a player if it was allowed to. He recognized the fact because he played such games himself, sliding his chess pieces around the board, manoeuvring them to maintain the happy stalemate where he, the king, remained inviolate. The Office's desecration of his ancient home was, indeed, an outrage, but Charnel hadn't simply let the act go unpunished. That little spider's web had been left alone, to see who wandered into it. It had already proved useful.

Tremaine also had a point when he mentioned Cardiff. The Welsh Witchfinder, Hardknott-Lewis, was one thing, a notable-enough foe, but another name had come to Charnel's ears recently. A new piece on the board. A mere pawn, perhaps, but one bearing a name that he was very familiar with. There was a new Shahzan in the Office, and that was a cause for concern in ways that Tremaine would not understand. Jacob Charnel had had dealings with the Shahzan clan before. He had assumed that little nest of cobras had been neutralized, but not so, apparently. You stamped on cockroaches and sometimes, when you lifted your foot, the insects came back to life and scuttled away. Really, it was galling. The boy, Danesh: he would be ignorant, unaware of wider matters, oblivious to his true heritage, but he would be learning quickly. He would be coming into his powers. He would outgrow the Office. English Wizardry with their parochial little prejudices would be of use in controlling him, naturally, but he doubted they would be enough. Cardiff was becoming a situation that he needed to address with some urgency.

He could take the direct approach, confront the

Shahzan boy in person, destroy him where he stood. Once, that was precisely what he would have done. These days, he preferred to stay in the darkness, pull the strings quietly. Partly it was to protect himself, and partly, he admitted, it was because he enjoyed the game, the subtle political play. Ripping the human cattle to tattered shreds of flesh and blood, hearing their sobs and screams as they died – it was all very well, but something of the satisfaction in that had left him over the centuries. It now felt a little … adolescent.

At the same time, he'd found a growing satisfaction in wielding the subtle power of rumour. Whispers of unseen hands, of figures secretly controlling events, were invaluable. They added to the myth. The Office was always meddling, picking out enemies to confront. There were many individuals and entities in thrall to him, powers that lurked in the shadows who feared him for one reason or another, particularly among those who had one foot in unlife. And it was true that he had his marionettes inside the Office. He would simply take one or other of those tools and use them, put them on the trail of Shahzan, use them as the glove to conceal his own hand. People wouldn't know who was responsible, but they would suspect. They would whisper. And, of course, he had planned for this eventuality, or some version of it. There were other Shahzans and one, at least, was under his control.

Charnel shrugged, deliberately not meeting Tremaine's stare, dismissing it as unimportant with a wave of his hand. He didn't stand to meet the challenge of his underling. To do so would be to imply that he took the threat seriously. He let the silence grow in the room, waiting to see if any more dissent would be voiced, letting Tremaine maintain an awkward stance that he wouldn't dare push any further.

Charnel sipped at his goblet. No one uttered another word. Outside, the wind off the North Sea rattled at his doors and windows, moaning and seething through the gaps, but the walls of his ancient home were solid. The flames of the candles guttered again, sending more glints of light across the polished silverwork.

"Very well," said Jacob Charnel. "Unless there is any other business, we will leave it there. The Office and Cardiff; Stonewall and English Wizardry: I will ensure that none pose any serious threat to us. We will continue to play to my tune. Are we agreed?"

A look passed between the gathered vampires, but there was only silence in the room, and no one voiced a further word of dissent. Charnel suppressed the laugh that rose up within him. The other vampires he controlled were little better than cattle themselves. Weak, misguided, pliable. They amused him and repulsed him.

He let none of that show as he sipped at his goblet.

6 – Who Watches the Watchers

Even your superiors must be treated with the same scepticism, the same suspicion. Too many evils have been allowed to take place because no one dared to raise their concerns about someone supposedly older, wiser, more powerful. I repeat, *semper vigilans*. Always vigilant. Always.
– Earl Grey, Witchfinder General, *Office of the Witchfinder General Handbook*, 1999

Back in Cardiff the following morning, I dutifully logged my thoughts about the *head full of dark* case – better to start laying the trail of deception as soon as possible – then spent a fun-filled hour navigating the very real horrors of airline and hotel booking websites to sort out my trip around the British Isles a few days hence. Once that was done, I rang Lincoln Umenyora.

We hadn't spoken for a while. He'd been suspicious of me at first, as I'd been of him – not least because he'd claimed Peter Warder as a friend. I figured we'd learned to trust each other. At least, *I* thought we had, and if I had a few doubts about him, well, what I was about to suggest cut both ways. He had given me useful intelligence on the communications involving Thomson Fulger – which it was his job to do, but he could have taken his time about it, left out details. The fact that we'd faced death together, walked into the mists on Westminster Bridge to face demonic horrors summoned up from the cold waters by a twisted and racist sorcerer had something to do with how I felt towards him. Experiences like that bring you closer together. Don't you find?

"Hey. It's Danesh."

"Danesh. How's it going?"

He sounded a little surprised to hear from me. Understandably so: he didn't know the number I was using, because, feeling slightly ridiculous, like I was in some clichéd spy thriller, I'd bought a throwaway SIM at my local newsagents that morning, slipped it into one of the impressive collection of rusting, discarded handsets in my bedside table drawer.

We did a few moments of playful banter while I left my desk and walked outside. I didn't want Kerrigan or Digbeth or Olwen or anyone else hearing what I was about to say. Once there, standing in the balmy Welsh drizzle, I got to the heart of the matter.

"Do you have, like, a private number you could call me back on?" I asked.

"For real?"

"Please."

"You do know the rules for operative phone calls. Office-approved devices only."

If I was being recorded, I figured I'd be covered by the fact that the Crow had also gone off-piste.

"Please. I have good reasons."

He sighed. "OK, bro. Bear with."

I hung up. Two minutes later, the lamephone buzzed, a number I didn't recognize. I imagined Lincoln doing what I was doing: standing in the street outside his office in London. I hoped it wasn't raining with him.

"Hey," I said again.

"What's this about?"

"I need to talk to you."

He laughed at that. "Well, here you are, talking to me."

"Off the record. Is this okay with you?"

"It's cool. What is it?"

"It's about Mason Greentree and Hardknott-Lewis."

"Go on." It was hard to miss the sombre note that had entered his voice. He'd liked Mason, no doubt about it.

"What's been happening since Mason was killed?" I asked.

"What's been happening? Lots been happening, bro. Lots always happening around these parts, you know that."

"Do we know who Mason's replacement is going to be?"

There was a pause before he replied. "Names have been put forward. The Star Chamber is deliberating, and we await their decision. Why are you interested?"

"Always interested in Office politics, obviously. Plus, I'm keen to find out what's going on in our upper echelons. Something I'm looking into."

"Right, right. Quis custodiet ipsos custodes."

Why did everyone in the Office keep quoting Latin at me? I expected it from the Crow, Lincoln not so much. Shows you what I know.

"Huh?" I said, displaying all of my own dazzling intellect.

"Quis custodiet ipsos custodes. Who watches the watchers?"

"Aha, yeah. Something like that. You know about the late switch of venue just before the Westminster Bridge attack I assume?"

"You figure someone there that day gave English Wizardry their orders," he said.

"It's a fair assumption."

"If I had a mortgage, which obviously I don't because I live in London and I ain't a billionaire, I'd bet my house on it not being Mason. The guy was a straight old white dude but he was also as decent as they come. He would do anything for you."

"The candidates to replace him – is your name in the hat?" I asked.

"Sure. Gotta put yourself forward, right? No one else gonna do it for you."

Now he sounded like my mother. My mother before the thing happened to her.

"I really hope you get it," I said.

"You do?"

"It's about time the Office dragged itself into the twentieth century."

"This is the twenty-first; you do know that right?"

Now it was my turn to laugh. "Twentieth would be a start, though. What's the delay, any idea?"

"Oh, man, who knows how these things work. Wheels within wheels."

"I could talk to Hardknott-Lewis, put in a good word for you."

"Can't do any harm."

"Actually, it was mainly him I wanted to talk to you about."

"Now we get to it. Go on."

"What you said about Mason – I believe you. Hardknott-Lewis though: I think the same as you do about Mason, I really do. Still, there's a question there."

Lincoln made no attempt to hide his shock. "You're doubting the Crow? I do not believe it."

I'd forgotten he knew my secret name for Hardknott-Lewis. I let it go.

"*Doubting* is a strong word, but something underhand was going on with the succubi. Hardknott-Lewis: it's possible he was the one giving English Wizardry their orders, yes. It's not impossible, let's say. He's somewhere inside the big Venn Diagram of suspicion."

"Why would he be commanding a bunch of English nationalist fascist dickheads?"

"Good question. Because fascist dickheads aren't rational by definition?"

"Sure, sure, but Hardknott-Lewis? I don't believe it. He's as Welsh as, I don't know, the Welsh hills. You do have hills, right?"

"You've never been here?"

"To the mythical lands beyond Reading? Gotta be kidding."

"We do have hills, plenty of them," I said, "and I don't believe it about Hardknott-Lewis either, not really, but I need to be sure. Thing is, he's going to be spending more time in London, looking into the whole Downing Street, succubi, Westminster Bridge thing, and I figured..."

"You figured you'd get me to keep an eye on him?"

"I figured I'd let you know my suspicions. You need to be aware, especially if you're going to be a Keyholder, right? If it helps, he encourages us to think like this, challenge each other. If he knew we were having this conversation, I'm pretty sure he'd approve."

"Yet we're having it off the record."

"There's *someone* in the loop we can't trust. I just don't know who it is."

"What are you asking me to do?"

"I'm just saying he's there looking into this thing, and while he's doing so, someone could look into him."

"See how good a job he does?"

"That sort of thing. And also, see who watches him while he's doing it."

"Apart from me."

"Apart from you."

"And what about you, bro?" Lincoln asked.

I wondered how much I should tell him. Feeling bad, I stuck to the party line. "I'm on a different case, completely unrelated. You know how it is."

"Sure do. Still take care, though, right? Sometimes things are more related than they seem. At some root level, everything is interconnected, right?"

"Sounds dangerously mystical. I'll be careful. You take care, too, Lincoln, yeah?"

"Always do, bro."

I had a list of people to see, places to go before I left Cardiff. I thought about ringing DI Zubrasky, because we'd left things hanging and the guilt kept panging at me. We'd agreed to go out for a drink, but whether that was as friends or it would be a date, I wasn't sure. And I wasn't sure she was sure, either. She'd said the timing was bad for her, but that it would be good to meet up somewhere, sometime. In the end, I sent her a text, suggesting a drink and asking how she was. I made it clear I wasn't tapping her up for information or requesting unofficial *Heddlu* help. I was just saying *hi*. I watched my phone for a while, hoping to see a reply pop up, but none did. Maybe I'd burned my bridges there.

Next, I did as the Crow had suggested and dropped by the Librarian's lair to seek her advice. Not that one really did *drop by* the library. Going down there wasn't like nipping out to the coffee shop; it was more of an … expedition. I always had to resist the urge to pack a knapsack, maybe even take a torch and supplies for the road before delving below ground.

I hadn't seen Lady Coldwater since our fight against Mormont at Mermaid Warehouse. The good news was that my pass still admitted me. I took my time to approach her hexagonal desk at the centre of Level -1, deliberately making noise, humming a tune and stepping firmly on the attuned floorboards, in precisely the way you're supposed to walk through the woods when there are bears about, just to let them know you're there.

She sat in a pool of light at her desk, one hand held up towards me, telling me not to interrupt, while she transcribed a passage of text from an old, illustrated tome into her private notebook. I could see her lips moving as she wrote, and the frown on her features was enough to tell me she was making notes on something she thoroughly disapproved off.

Finally, with a decisive nod of her head, she set her pen down, closed both books, and looked up at me.

"Danesh. Why are you here? You don't have any books out on loan. You're not planning to borrow one, I hope?"

Perhaps it simply didn't occur to her that people might come and see her for other reasons – such as, for example, to see if she was okay or if she happened to be the one person in the Office they actually felt they could trust.

"I've come for some advice."

"Ah. I suppose that does fall under the remit of *Librarian*," she said, although she sounded distinctly resentful. "I trust your mother continues to improve?"

"Better and better with each passing day. We've talked about her maybe moving to Wales so I can see her more."

"That's good; it sounds like she's emerging from her

shell, her safe place, getting ready to face the world again. And you? Are you looking after yourself? I assume you're practising all your skills and abilities diligently, keeping up your training."

I was pretty sure she meant magical skills as much as physical. I chose to ignore the suggestion. "As much as I can."

She snorted, as if she knew I was doing nothing of the sort. I changed the subject.

"And you – you've destroyed Evangelina Mormont's soul maze amulet I take it?"

Her eyes visibly narrowed. "Why do you wish to know?"

"Just … wanted to be absolutely sure she isn't coming back."

Lady Coldwater considered me for a moment. Then she opened one of the drawers in her desk and pulled out a small black leather sack. From this, she tipped shards of colourful glass onto the desk and stirred through them with the tip of her pen.

"This is all that remains of Evangelina Mormont. For your information, I wove the relevant wards and incantations very carefully around the gem to seal her in place, embedding her soul within the gem's crystalline structure by the light of the waxing and then the waning moon. And then I smashed the stone into a thousand pieces with a very large hammer, shattering the Sorceress into pieces, too. Yes, I can assure you, she is not coming back. She's profoundly dead. She does not exist anymore."

"Not even some other aspect of her hidden away on some other plane of existence? An avatar or a fragment?"

"Not even that. She was all here, her essence tied to this gem, and now she is gone. Death comes for us all. At least, it should, if events are allowed to follow their natural course."

"I don't really approve of the death penalty, but … good."

"It seems as though many people are interested to know whether she is genuinely gone."

"Someone else has been asking?"

"There have been … incursions I have become aware of. Magical presences in the aether from those trying to ascertain the truth."

"Which people?"

"I have no idea. Someone as powerful as Mormont would have had many friends and many enemies. Quite possibly, the same individuals might have been both."

"Did they get the same answer?"

"I believe so. A presence like Mormont is hard to miss. Was there anything else, or were you simply satisfying your idle curiosity?"

I explained what little I knew about the Crow's *head hull of dark* case. "Hardknott-Lewis suggested you might have useful background information."

"Oh, he did, did he?"

"He did."

Lady Coldwater studied me through her glasses. There may or may not have been magic brought to bear in that stare, but it damned-well felt like I was on the receiving end of something … withering.

"I know of the case," she said eventually. "The Pale Sisters have a certain connection to the affair."

"They do?"

"There's a history there. Also, a certain book which may well be connected to the events you describe."

"Does the book have a title?"

"It's generally referred to as *The Book of Shadows* and sometimes the *Book of Seventeen Darknesses*, although, in truth, it's a handwritten tome and bears no title."

"May I ask where it is?"

"It is here, in my care." She was clearly reluctant to admit the fact.

"May I see it?"

She frowned for a moment, as if my words confirmed all her fears about me. "What do you wish to learn?"

"I don't know. That's why I need to look."

"I would have to remove the tome from … containment. It is heavily warded."

"But if you did that, I could see it?"

She come to a reluctant decision. "If anyone else came asking, even Campbell himself, I rather suspect you know what answer I would give. But I suppose that after our adventures together and what we know about each other – well, perhaps I can trust you a little. You certainly may not have the book; as you know, I strongly discourage people from considering this" – a shudder seemed to go through her at the words she was uttering – "*a lending library*. But in my presence, you might be allowed a glimpse of its pages. If it would help you to tackle this evil."

"Now?"

"Come back in a couple of days. Unweaving the wards around the deeper books is not a simple matter of opening a few locks. The incantations are complex. There are the phases of the moon to consider, for one thing. The tides."

It was the best I was going to get. I thanked her and returned upstairs. Back up in the land of signal, my phone buzzed to tell me I had a text. DI Zubrasky had responded.

It said, *meet for a drink?* That was a win. I replied saying I was heading out of Cardiff in a few days' time and to let me know if the timing of that worked for her.

Back upstairs, while I was checking to see how my travel bookings were progressing (answer: badly), a lumbering bulk appeared to my side, blotting out the light of the fluorescent tubes.

"Well, well," said Kerrigan. "The face is vaguely familiar but I'm struggling to put a name to it."

I gave up on the travel arrangements and turned to my colleague. "I should have logged my actions," I said. "Guilty as charged."

"Seems to me you've been going off book a lot of late," he said, sitting down beside me so his head was on my level. "I'm a bit worried about you, laddo, I'm not going to lie."

This was Kerrigan all over. His shaggy, man-of-the-wilds look belied the fact he was basically our mother hen, fretting about us all. I loved him very much. I obviously couldn't tell him about my nature as a user though, something I regretted.

"If it's any help, I was with Hardknott-Lewis," I said. "Check with him if you like."

That was a bit of a dangerous line to give out. Kerrigan was unswervingly loyal to the Lord High Witchfinder of All Wales, but even he might wonder why the Crow hadn't logged anything in MORIARTY either.

"Curiouser and curiouser."

"There are good reasons, trust me."

Kerrigan considered me with narrowed eyes for a moment, then obviously decided to let it drop. Maybe he did trust me and maybe he didn't, but his faith in the Crow was unshakeable.

"Just don't take any stupid risks, laddo. Any *more* stupid risks, I mean." He indicated my screen with a nod of his head. "Planning a little holiday, I see."

"The case Hardknott-Lewis gave me. Actually, I did want to ask you about it."

"Oh?"

"You must have known Jamie Tavish."

Kerrigan sat in a chair to consider me. "You're opening up that cold case, are you? Plenty of hot cases to pursue, if you ask me."

"I do as I'm told. Obviously."

Kerrigan looked amused at that. "I don't get it, though. Why the secrecy?"

I shrugged, like it didn't make a ton of sense to me, either. "A lot of the victims were Office staff. Perhaps Hardknott-Lewis didn't want to set off too many troubling memories."

"So why the travel? Has something happened elsewhere?"

"There's a chance that events we hadn't connected follow a pattern. You know how it is; we're getting better at correlating data across the territories. Someone once told me Jamie went out to investigate a haunting and *got lost in the mirrors*. What does that even mean?"

"I presume you looked the case up on MORIARTY?"

"The bare facts are all there but nothing about mirrors. He failed to turn up for work one day and was never seen again. He'd filed a possible Code 11 for his own home, but this was nearly a year before he disappeared."

Code 11: a haunting or other spectral presence. It had been investigated and nothing had been found. The implication from the notes was that Jamie wasn't well, seeing things that weren't there. Was he connected to the other case? The details in the Crow's notes had been unhelpfully vague. A few individuals had died in a variety of troubling and disturbing ways, but there wasn't much else to connect them. The deaths had all taken place after dark, true, and there was a recurring mention of the victims suffering nightmares. But most deaths occur at night, and bad dreams are common enough. It was surely just as likely that the deaths weren't related at all.

"Mirrors, yeah," said Kerrigan, his voice taking on a hushed tone. "He had a bit of a thing with mirrors did Jamie."

"What sort of a thing? Were you one of the people who investigated his place?"

"Jamie was old school, came from a long line of witchfinders. I sometimes think that's a bad idea; that all the magic gets into the genes, scrambles them up a bit. Like, I don't know, prolonged exposure to radiation. That's why they bring in virile studs like you and me to keep things fresh."

"But, the mirrors," I said. "Mirrors are just mirrors, right? They reflect light."

"Depends who made them, what spells have been worked upon them, where they came from. You know this: mirrors can be portals to the otherworld. People once thought the same about mountain tarns and the like. Jamie became convinced he was being watched from the mirrors around him. That they weren't mirrors so much as windows onto some other plane of reality. Apparently, he'd harboured these fears all his life, some childhood trauma clinging to him, but his anxieties grew and grew as he got older. He claimed someone or something was trying to come through, get at him."

"I mean, that could happen."

"We found no evidence of any such incursion taking place. He assured us that some demonic entity was creeping into his room at night, but we found no evidence for it. Jamie … I think maybe the stress got to him. He went a bit off-planet towards the end. At least, that's what we assumed. It wasn't just mirrors towards the end; it was any reflective or shiny surface."

"I assume his house was investigated?"

"Both to protect him and then to look for any suggestion of the unnatural after he'd gone. We found nothing."

"Who carried out the investigation?"

"Why?"

"I might talk to them if they're still around, see if they can recall anything out of the ordinary."

"I don't recall. Not me, anyway. Look on MORIARTY."

I did so – probably something I should have done already. The notes, when I found them, were brief and uninformative.

"Digbeth," I said. "Other than the madness with the mirrors, nothing was found, as you say. Was the house left untouched?"

"It was declared *in camera*. Dark. Demapped. Officially speaking, the house does not exist, just in case there is something malign going on there that we haven't worked out yet. If there's a presence in the ground there, we can't just let people live in the place. These cycles have a nasty way of repeating."

Haunted or cursed ground checks: one of the less well-known aspects of the property searches your solicitor dutifully carries out for you when you buy a house. In fact, the solicitors don't know they're doing it, either. Land Registry searches cover a lot more than you'd think.

"The body was never found," I said. "It has to be

possible that Jamie will come back some day from … wherever he's been."

"Maybe. We generally follow the year-and-a-day rule for disappearances, and it's been ten now. We left everything in his house untouched on the off chance he returned or in case we'd missed some vital lead among his stuff. In hindsight, maybe we just couldn't admit to ourselves that we'd lost him. But, sure, you never know. I hope so. He was a nice guy. Very keen walker in his spare time, loved to do a bit of bird-spotting, too, as I recall."

"I'd like to go check out his house," I said.

"Want me to come with?"

"No need. Like you say, this isn't an active trouble-spot; it's just a house that doesn't exist. I can go alone, once I've tied up a few other loose ends."

Kerrigan didn't like it, but eventually he conceded with a grunt through his beard. "Just be sure to log everything you find, yes? And also, record *when* you're going, so we know you haven't got lost in the mirrors, too, okay laddo?"

"Of course," I once again lied.

7 – Lost in the Mirrors

She left the web, she left the loom,
She made three paces through the room,
She saw the water-lily bloom,
She saw the helmet and the plume,
She look'd down to Camelot.
Out flew the web and floated wide;
The mirror crack'd from side to side;
"The curse is come upon me," cried
The Lady of Shalott.
– Alfred Lord Tennyson, *The Lady of Shalott*, 1833

First thing the following morning, I jumped into the Mini and set the controls for the heart of *Dyffryn Gwy*, the Wye valley. I was soon out of the Cardiff sprawl and tanking down the M4, through the Brynglas tunnels without even slowing for once, as if they were nothing more than a normal part of the British motorway network. From there, I cruised past the giant metal red dragon (a statue that the Crow surely couldn't approve of) overlooking the Newport roundabout, then sped up the lovely Usk valley to Monmouth. I crossed the old stone bridge into the Forest of Dean. The road down the Wye valley to Tintern was like driving through a green tunnel, the tall trees overhanging the road, dappled sunlight shining through the budding canopy and the silvery ribbon of the river running nearby on my right. For a few minutes, the world was impossibly beautiful. Crows played chicken on the road ahead of me. In Tintern, I crept past the soaring gothic ruins of the abbey squatting beside the road, awestruck as always at how large and impressive they are, then took a turning up a narrow, twisty track snaking up the side of the valley.

Jamie Tavish's officially non-existent house nestled in a dip in the ground some way back from the main road and out of sight of any other dwelling. As well as being officially dark, it was also actually dark, no lights on, curtains across the windows. The little garden rampaged away around it, creeping ivy slowly reclaiming the stones. As with the chapel Gwethenoc and I had reached, it looked like no one had been near the place in years. The rotting wooden gate resisted me as I pushed at it, then relented to grant me access. A few of the stalks of the overgrown grass near my feet, I noticed, had been crushed. That was odd. I crouched down and was able, faintly, to make out a line leading from the gate to the front door. Someone had walked that way recently. A seriously misguided postal worker, perhaps, or some woodland creature, a fox or a badger. Or the local kids? I wasn't a good enough tracker to work out who or what was responsible.

I ran a quick thaumometer check on the area in case there was some unnamed horror, something we'd missed, lurking within. It might have been slowly mounting in strength and fury all this time. Fortunately, there was nothing.

Kerrigan had given me the keys to the house. There was no power, but light trickled in past the curtains and the torch on my phone showed me the interior once my eyes had adjusted. There wasn't even the traditional pile of unpaid bills and pizza flyers behind the door. Even the Post Office thought the house didn't exist; whoever had walked through the garden, it hadn't been someone from *Post Brenhinol*. The interior smelled damp and dusty at the same time, as if the same air had been trapped within all this time. It smelled neglected; clearly nobody had lived there for years.

As Kerrigan had explained, though, the place *looked* inhabited at first glance – perhaps by someone who'd shunned every trend in interior design for the last decade. There was furniture and clutter. An old-fashioned, steam-powered TV stood in the corner. A copy of the Black

Mountain Reporter from ten years previously lay on the coffee table, with headlines about catastrophic floods that I had no memory of. In the kitchen, tins of food were quietly rusting away, and plates and cutlery waited patiently in the drying-rack. The fridge had been emptied and left open, but everything else had been simply left. It was like one of those ghost ships that the crew mysteriously abandons for no known reason, leaping overboard or being abducted by aliens or whatever it is.

Then there were the lights. His house had a *lot* of lights. Ceiling lights, table lamps, standard lamps, lines of bulbs strung across curtain rails and doorways. But not only those: battery-powered hand-held lanterns were all over the place. One looked very like the brass lantern Gwethenoc had carried. There were candles all over the place, burned down to frozen puddles of wax in their saucers. Jamie had really liked light. The whole house must have blazed with illumination.

But then, oddly, there was the black paint. It was hard to miss the black paint. Jamie had gone to a lot of trouble to cover every glass and metal surface with it. It wasn't only the mirrors: the windows had been covered, too, although the pigment was flaking off now. Interior glass doors had been sloshed with paint, spattering the carpets and walls with specks of black, no attempt made to save the decor. Even pictures on the wall had been painted out. Wouldn't it have been easier to take them down, turn them round? It spoke of someone losing his grip on reality, seeing faces and hearing voices and thinking he could paint them out of reality.

Even the TV screen had been coated in thick black paint. In the corner of the hallway stood a grandfather clock, its pendulum stilled. That also had been daubed over, its face covered. Tavish had been really, really convinced something was watching him or coming for him.

I made a mental note to myself to take all my allotted holidays while I remained an operative of the Office of the Witchfinder General. Poor Jamie must have been sane, once, but whatever he'd experienced had taken its toll. There'd been mention in the MORIARTY notes of his insistence that he was being stalked by packs of large, black canines – perhaps even wolves – prowling in the woods around his house after nightfall, baying at the moon and the like. Maybe there was another Pontannwn-style portal nearby – or maybe he'd simply not been in a good mental state.

Upstairs, I found the room he'd used as a studio for his painting. Like Sally, Tavish had also daubed landscapes, drawing on the beauty of the valley and the woods around him. But even these hadn't escaped his delusions. Or maybe they catalogued them. Some of the paintings – the earlier ones judging by the dates in their corners – looked normal enough. Tintern Abbey nestling in the green, green valley. Sunsets, sunrises. The blue silver Wye winding its way down the valley to Chepstow and the delicate, spindly lines of the bridges across the Severn.

But then, in later paintings, I saw that there was more and more black. It started as a few brushstrokes in the corners of the sky, like storm clouds were sweeping in to mar a sunlit scene – a sight that is not altogether unbelievable in Wales. In subsequent paintings, however, the condition progressed. More and more of the landscapes were blacked out, daubed over with thick lines of heavy black paint. All around the edges and then across the centre. Splashed across hillsides, overlaid over forests and villages. Had he created the scenes beneath and then painted over them? Or had he just sloshed more and more black pigment onto his canvases, trying to capture the darkness clouding his mind? I studied one picture closely. Clearly, the crude black lines were on top of fine brushwork underneath. Apparently, he had painted his scenes with intricate, subtle care – then obliterated them.

By the end, the canvas still standing on the easel, there was barely a glimpse of light peeking through the heavy blackness. An oval of green here and there like an eye peeping through the shadows was all you got. His last works were a long, long way from the beautiful landscapes he'd started with.

"Jamie, Jamie," I said out loud, "what the hell happened to you?"

There was still no flicker of a reading from the thaumometer. If I'd had to guess, I'd have said Tavish had suffered a breakdown. This wasn't malign magic, it was psychiatric illness. By the look of the paintings, it had been growing inside him for a long time.

I stepped up the creaking staircase to his bedroom. The bed had been stripped by someone, but the sheets had been left in a heap on the floor. Again, the room looked like it had simply been abandoned one day. There were two mirrors in the room: one bolted to the wall opposite the bed, and then a free-standing one in the corner. The one on the wall had been painted over, but the other hadn't – because there was no glass in it at all. I could see only the wooden backing where the mirror had once been. Except, there were a few fragments of glass still stuck in the frame. There had been a looking-glass there, until someone had smashed it. Puzzled, I reached out to touch the wood – and fell to the floor as another of my fun episodes of confusion and delusion struck me like a blow from a hammer.

I was suddenly writhing in darkness on the ground. The confused visions threw themselves at me: a doorway receding into the distance, another rushing towards me. Or perhaps it was a square frame that I was falling into through an infinite void. I saw a face, oddly frozen in a smile as if it were painted onto wood, then black clouds, or black liquid, washing over everything, obliterating everything. I tasted it in my mouth, smelled it in my nose. Cloying, bitter blackness corrupting my senses.

I hadn't suffered such turns for a while, not since I'd admitted to myself that I was a user. I knew what they were: my magical powers refusing to be bottled up, forcing themselves to the surface. It had never occurred to me they might be useful though. Now, as I writhed in sickening rigours of pain, I also felt myself rising above them, like I was learning to swim within their seething, turbulent waters. They were an ability I could, perhaps, channel.

Because, there was something here, in this house, in this room, I knew it. I could feel it. A presence. Something here we'd missed, something the thaumometers didn't pick up. If I could attune my senses, practise practise practise, as the Lady kept telling me to, maybe I could hear the voices whispering just beyond hearing.

I stood, my legs weak and wobbly. The sickness still washed through me, but it was like I could perceive two realities at the same time, intersecting, overlaying each other. The real world and the confused realm of nightmare horrors, both of them there in front of me. It was like seeing a reflection in a mirror *and* glimpsing what lay through the looking-glass, there on the other side of reality.

Through the frame of the mirror, I saw a formless black landscape, stretching away to meet a uniform grey sky at some huge distance. The horizon between them was a pencil line of hills, as if that entire dimension of reality was still being sketched out. The landscape resembled Oblivion. Perhaps it was another corner of that plane, and perhaps it was utterly separate. I could see no grave markers.

Near to hand, inches away (if that term made any sense in this dimension) a faint line of runes glowed in the gloom. They'd been drawn across the ground, directly in front of the portal on the other side. Perhaps they were the magic that had opened this doorway between the worlds. The ground through there was also littered with jagged shards of glass. That was where the mirror had gone. Something had smashed through or been thrown through, from the bedroom across into this other plane. I peered closer. There was something else there, a black shape huddling on the black ground, not moving.

I tried to step through the mirror but could not. I met only the wood of the frame as I tried to climb in. I held up my phone and shone the light in. Somehow – don't ask me how the physics of this works – the light was able to pass through the frame. The illumination it gave was scant, but it was enough to let me pick out the outline of the shape more clearly.

A body. A body lay there. Jamie Tavish, it had to be. Had he died here, in this dusty bedroom in Tintern, or had the force of being thrown through the mirror done the damage? Or had he smashed his way through, driven on by some madness or delusion, only to find that he couldn't live in that other dimension? That whatever had lured him there had tricked him?

I called to him, shouting out his name. Nothing happened. Jamie was beyond my voice, beyond my help.

The reports had said Tavish had been *lost in the mirrors*. They'd been talking about his obsessions, but the grim irony was that the phrase was literally true. I made another mental note to speak to Kerrigan or the Crow when I got back, see if we could at least retrieve his body from this no man's land. They might question how it was I was able to see into the other plane, how I was able to work such magic. But that was their problem, not mine. It was the least we could do for Jamie.

I turned to consider the room again. Waves of sickness still washed through me, but they were receding now. They'd done their bit, alerted me to the mirror that was actually a portal.

I breathed. But they weren't done with me. They flared up again, and I was assaulted by a clamour of disembodied shouts, more visions of square frames and oddly wooden faces leering at me, shouting at me. I staggered but this time stayed on my feet. I cast around, trying to work out the meaning of the visions. Some of the cries came from behind me, the free-standing mirror, but not all of them. There was something else in the room.

It could only be the other mirror. I crept towards it, and it was suddenly like battling up a steep hill against a powerful wind. Whoever or whatever was there did not want me to get near. I pushed forwards, leaning into it, gritting my teeth. Using my magic, the abilities I barely understood, to swim through the onslaught rather than be thrown back by it.

I reached out to touch the other mirror. It was cold. Weirdly cold. An unheated house in Wales can be on the chilly side of bloody freezing, but it was rare for ice to form. The glass was intact by the look of it, although heavy layers of paint had been plastered over it again and again, thicker than anywhere else in the house. There was a little square in the corner where the paint was heavier, as if something had been stuck there. I couldn't see what it might have been. The mirror was from the fifties or sixties maybe: a steel rectangular frame with curls in each corner, a basic attempt to make the thing look a little decorated. It was firmly attached to the wall, the heads of the four screws also painted over. I slipped out my pocket knife to try and budge them, but they were solid. I scraped away a little of the paint with a blade and found glass underneath, just as you'd expect from any self-respecting mirror. I could see my own eye there, peering back at me.

A brief search of the house turned up a fine selection of screwdrivers scattered in kitchen drawers and the like. Using my knife to excavate the lines in the heads of the screws, I eventually managed to get enough purchase to make them turn. It was surprisingly hard work, and I may have grunted out loud more than once. Eventually I had them: four screws, each maybe five centimetres long. The mirror wasn't going to be *that* heavy. Whoever had secured it had wanted to be really, really sure it stayed in place.

Even with the screws removed, the mirror remained attached to the wall – held there by the many layers of paint that had been applied over both. I slid one of the longer screwdrivers behind it and carefully levered it away. It resisted manfully for a while, then finally came away. I lifted it off the wall. The voices swirling around in the room reached a crescendo, howling at me, whispering words into my ears that I couldn't understand. I had the sensation of birds flying at me, feathers fluttering at my face, smothering me.

Then they faded. The mirror that I held was just a

mirror – but behind it, in a little brick-sized recess hollowed out of the wall, wedged inside, there was something else. I reached in to pull it out. As I touched it, I felt a sharp jag of pain as if something had bitten me or as if I'd been hit with an electric shock. I heard something between a scream and a snarl, a noise that was maybe only in my head. It was angry, no doubt about it. The sound rose in pitch, then either faded or passed beyond my hearing. I pulled back my fingers to examine, but there was no sign of a wound or a puncture. Some kind of magical trap. It didn't appear to have done me any harm. Either it had faded in power over a period of time, or else the innate resistance that I'd discovered within myself in Mermaid Warehouse had also protected me against … whatever this was.

More warily, I reached in again. This time, there was no prick of pain. My fingers gripped something soft. It seemed to writhe and skip in my hand, but when I pulled it into the light it was just a doll: crude, lashed together from twine and corn stalks and rags, a bit of wood for a head. Scraps of random objects – twigs and shells – were tied up in the knots of wool or twine around its body.

It was old, judging by the black blotches upon it, the greyness of the corn, the scribble of cobwebs wrapping around it. My guess was that it had been there a long time. There was something malicious about it, cruel. With my inner ear – is that a thing? – I swore I could hear it laughing at me, taunting me. I ran my thaumometer over it and got nothing, but I didn't need the device to tell me the doll was sorcerous in nature. Our technology doesn't pick up every hex and curse employed by users. As I studied the object, turning it over and over, a sharp edge caught me, embedding a tiny splinter into the tip of my finger.

"Bastard thing!" I swore out loud. Was the doll attacking me?

I resisted the temptation to throw it to the floor. Maybe I was overreacting and the thing was just roughly made. I tried to tweezer the splinter out with my teeth, but it was too small.

With my thumb, I brushed away the cobwebs that formed a thick fuzz around the doll's head. A head with a faded, painted face smiling out from it. There was the gleeful, malicious leer that I recognized from my visions. Turning the doll over, I saw a finger-sized hole in the back of its head. Something had been stuffed in there. With the light from my phone, I tried to peer inside. I could see nothing; it was hard to get the angle right. I should have bagged the doll up, taken it back to the office, but I needed answers; there was something malevolent about the doll, and I wanted to be free to bring my magical powers to bear if need be. Slipping my phone into a pocket, I tried feeling around inside the head with my little finger.

Once again, something sharp pricked me, like a needle being jabbed into my finger. This time I did drop the doll, my muscles recoiling in horror of their own accord. I watched as hundreds of tiny, tiny spiders – a black cloud of them – swarmed out of the hole. They had to have filled the little nut-sized head of the effigy. A tiny red dot on the tip of my finger showed where one had broken my skin.

"Bastard thing," I said again. Someone had clearly woven defensive hexes into the object. I let the creatures creep away, then placed a holdfast next to the doll and activated it. Whatever this thing was, I didn't want to drive around with it working its voodoo on me. Once the thing was frozen into temporary stasis, I slipped it into a plastic evidence bag, being very sure not touch it with my fingers again, like I was a proper policeman and all.

With the doll immobilised by the holdfast, the nausea and disembodied shouting stopped immediately. Cut out, gone. No doubt about it, the doll was the source. And Jamie? How much had he been aware of this thing hidden away in his bedroom? He must have slept in there with it, for years maybe, while it howled away magically at him.

He hadn't simply succumbed to stress or depression. This was an attack. This had been done to him.

I scoured the rest of the house but found nothing

untoward. I'd include in my report the recommendation that the site could be opened up again, now. I had no idea whether Jamie had family, but maybe someone somewhere would appreciate the inheritance. Or maybe they'd come live here. The place needed to be looked after, lived in again. The light let in.

It was getting late, the world outside the house sinking into a drab, teatime gloom. The sky had clouded over, roofing the world in grey Welsh slate. I needed to return to the office to log everything that had happened and to secure the doll within a proper, heavy-duty holdfast locker in accordance with supernatural evidence gathering protocol. Before that, though, I had one more journey to make, and this one, I wasn't going to enter into MORIARTY.

I pulled up outside the remarkably unremarkable bungalow on the outskirts of Cardiff that Bella Mine – the pseudonym Sally Spender had used, not that this would be her real name either – had hidden away in while she recovered from the dire magical effects of her battle with Evangelina Mormont. The last time I'd seen her, the *pilipalas* fluttering away in my stomach, she'd stopped being the vital and decidedly lovely young woman who I'd accompanied to Faebrook Folly and had basically turned into her own grandmother. Possibly, great-grandmother. She'd assured me the effects would unwind eventually and that she'd be back to herself.

Which perhaps was true. A week previously I'd driven idly by – yeah, right – to see the *For Sale* sign hammered into the gravel of the driveway. Sally had clearly moved out, moved on. In a good way, I hoped. I'd tried the number she'd magically hacked into my phone under *Goddess* and got no response. Number unavailable. Had she recovered? Gone into deeper hiding? Whatever the truth of it, I both wanted and needed to see her. Wanted because, well, damn she was lovely. Needed because I had to get help with my whole coming out, *admitting I'm a user* thing. I needed a guide, a mentor, some basic instruction before I magically blew my own head off. For many reasons, Sally was the best person I could think of to help me.

I liked to think she'd have left a subtle trail of clues for me to find, like the thing with the copy of *Dorian Gray* and the message on the canvas that the Grafton Projector had revealed. I could have borrowed (borrowed, stolen; language is a slippery beast) the device again to spin back through time and see if she'd left any other messages. It would have felt intrusive. Creepy. She also knew I had access to the device and would probably have made sure that the same trick didn't work again, just to be contrary.

I could have broken in using the *sesame* trick I'd employed on the house on Cathedral Road and scoured the house for clues in some other way. I could have used my powers – the Office ones, not the magical ones – to smash my way in without any need for search warrants. Instead, I'd killed two birds with one stone and – somewhat brilliantly – made an appointment with the estate agent advertised on the board to have a look around. My cover story was that I was looking at possible properties for my mother to come live in – which was sort of true, although it would have been news to my mother. But it did mean Kerrigan wasn't going to get twitchy about me heading off alone to face the ineffable. Neither he nor the Crow nor anyone else needed to know about Sally.

The estate agent let me in, and after showing me around and pointing out the many fine features of the property, left me to have a little look around on my own. She waited outside the front door, long red fingernails blurring across the keyboard on her phone, while I quietly looked for magical clues. And, sure, checked out the many fine features the property had to offer. If Sally had bought the place, the chances were it was sound and not constructed on top of a disused coal mine or a forgotten burial pit.

The place was much as I remembered it – the same bland, magnolia walls and pastel carpets. It was an estate agent's dream. All the furniture was gone, though, the kitchen cupboards stripped. In the back room where she'd lain, there were only four indentations in the carpet from the bed's wheels. They looked oddly like the footprints of a deer. But I figured they probably weren't.

The estate agent showing me round – Belinda – hadn't been able to tell me much.

"Do you know why the place has become available?" I'd asked.

"Ooh, I don't know, sorry, love. I just came to show you around."

"But you must have had dealings with someone? Received instructions?"

One of Belinda's artfully sculpted eyebrows had raised. "Sorry, I can't talk about that. Private, that. Why do you wanna know anyway?"

I let it lie. "No reason. Just wondered."

I spent five minutes waving my thaumometer around and closing my eyes trying to *feel* for magical auras – and feeling pretty stupid as I did so. There was nothing. Belinda would be getting suspicious; she probably already thought I had some very dodgy motivation for being there.

My experiences in Jamie Tavish's house gave me the idea. The mirrors. There was one by the empty coat racks near the door, and one in the *tastefully redecorated bathroom and WC with shower over*. The former revealed nothing, but when I studied the latter, I found it.

More magic worked on mirrors. It seemed a hell of a coincidence. Was Sally somehow involved in Jamie's case? In what had been done to him? But maybe Sally had left clues and hints in a variety of places, and that had happened to be the one I noticed.

In any case, her message was there. I breathed on the mirror and watched as words were written in the mist I made. Letters that faded rapidly as the moisture on the glass evaporated. It was a neat trick. I breathed on the mirror again, fascinated as to how it worked, but this time nothing happened. It was strictly a one-time deal.

I could read what she'd written though. I'd imagined the name of some obscure castle or beast in a Welsh literary classic – which perhaps it was, because the long stream of letters I read there made no sense to me.

It said – and I wrote this down very carefully – *Gadeklawklawklawiriol.*

What the hell did that mean? Couldn't she have simply left an email address? Were they the syllables of some dire spell, or was it perhaps a word in Welsh that I didn't know? Or was it just some unnecessarily cryptic clue, one that I was supposed to understand when others didn't. On reflection – heh – I suspected the latter.

As I turned to leave, the image in the glass changed very briefly. Instead of your dashing young investigator, Sally was there, very briefly. Faebrook Folly and a collection of eyes Sally; young, delightful, infuriating Sally. She grinned at me as if it was all a joke – and then physics got fed up with the intrusion and reasserted itself. My own reflection returned.

Outside, Belinda was waiting for me with a wide smile. "Did you see everything you needed to see?"

"I did, thanks."

As she locked up, she said, "Oh, I found out about the vendor. Got in touch with the office."

"That's very good of you."

"She's emigrated, apparently. Left it up to us to sell the place."

"Aha. Did she give you a name?"

"I shouldn't tell you it. That's against the code."

"The code of the estate agents."

"That's it."

"If I buy the place, I'll find out anyway."

Belinda shrugged like she really didn't care either way and glanced at her phone to check she had it right. "Strange name for round by here, it is. She's called Mormont. Evangelina Mormont."

8 – The Book of Shadows

It was the following morning. I'd slept fitfully, half-remembered nightmares chasing me out of the land of sleep to send my heart pounding. Now, Lady Coldwater eyed the doll I'd brought down to show her with clear distaste.

"This is ugly. Very nasty. Where did you find it?"

"It's magical then?"

"Do you really need me to answer that?"

The holdfast had worn off now, and the tattered scrap of straw and twine lay on her desk, peering innocently up at us. I could definitely feel the malevolence coiling off it like a bad smell. The librarian poked at it with the tip of her pencil.

"It was in Jamie Tavish's house," I said.

"It was? Any indication how long this poppet had been there?"

"Poppet?"

"Doll."

"A long time I would say," I said. "Years, maybe."

She thought about that. "So, it was probably there when we searched the place a decade ago, and we missed it. I missed it."

"I didn't know you were involved in the operation."

"I took a look. I should have found this."

"Could it explain the problems Jamie had? What happened to him?"

"This is malicious magic, a powerful curse. Jamie was susceptible, I believe, but this could well have tipped him over the edge."

She flipped the doll over and studied the little hole in the back of its head. "Was there anything inside?"

"A swarm of tiny black spiders."

"Ah."

"I think one bit me."

"Show me."

She studied my fingers. "Here? This tiny speck?"

"That's a splinter I picked up from handling the object. This is the bite that cut my skin."

She studied both pinpricks on my fingers for a moment, peering through her reading glasses.

"Hmm, well, I expect you'll live."

"Good to know. Why were there spiders in there?"

"Do you ever do any research or do you just swan around in fast cars chasing zombies?"

"I've literally never chased a zombie. I'm fairly sure you don't need to chase them; you can just amble up to them."

She sighed. "This is sympathetic magic, obviously. It explains a lot. Jamie said he sometimes had trouble differentiating nightmare and reality. He once told me his bad dreams seemed to bleed into the waking world, and that he couldn't always be sure which was which. I assumed his condition was something medical, but I was wrong. Damn, damn, *damn*. I could have helped him, and I failed."

"This doll was bound to Jamie, and the black spiders in its head affected his mind?"

The librarian nodded. "Foul sorcery. If this was near him when he was growing up, it's no wonder he suffered so much. A doll like this can be used to heal or to harm. Or to act as the focus for some summoning incantation. Clearly, this one was malign. It would have been like having spectral spiders eating away at your mind. The question is, how did it get there? And who put it there?"

"Jamie came from a family of witchfinders," I said. "Is

96

it possible this thing was put there to attack a forebear? For all we know, it might have been cursing his family for generations."

The librarian thought about that. "Do we know that his family had lived in the same house for so long?"

"I checked."

She exhaled. "It's possible. Still, I doubt it. Dolls like this can have a general effect, but the fact that it was Jamie who was driven mad by it suggests that he was targeted. There is probably something of him in its construction. A lock of hair, a drop of blood. Semen, bile, tears – anything uniquely of him."

Like the good witchfinder that I wasn't, I'd carefully logged all my findings into MORIARTY. Kerrigan had read them and had assured me he'd do what he could to retrieve Jamie's remains. Her words, though, reminded me of something else I'd read in the case notes.

"He did report that blood had been taken from him against his will."

"When was this?"

"A few months before he disappeared. He reported waking to find a puncture wound in his arm that hadn't been there the night before."

"Probably bitten by an insect."

"This was a big puncture," I said. "Enough to make him bleed over the sheets. I wondered about vampirism."

Lady Coldwater frowned, trying to make sense of this information. "Vampires? Perhaps. Nasty bastards they are. Why do you mention them?"

"Just a thought."

She considered the doll again. "This doesn't smell of vampires, though. I can also tell you that you wouldn't need much blood for this little horror. By the sound of it, it must have been working its magic for much longer than a few months. But, if what you say is true, it's possible someone took his blood to renew the hexes woven into this little horror, to finish him off. Such curses don't last forever; they need to be reworked from time to time."

"Why would anyone do any of that?"

"I've no idea. You're the investigator; I just look after the books."

"Kerrigan said we should destroy it."

"Kerrigan is correct. Burning it is best."

"Before we do that, can you work anything out from it? Like, who made it and when? Perhaps, I don't know, there's something like the cartouches you get in runes. A fingerprint of the maker."

The Lady flipped the doll onto its back and peered closely at it. She sniffed at it, then licked it. Sometimes I thought she did stuff like that for show.

"It's possible. With folk magic like this, there are regional styles, local traditions. The materials and the knots vary from place to place, the incantations woven into it, too. I'll look into it before I destroy it. I can't promise I'll find anything."

"Thanks."

I tried a different tack. "While I'm here, can I ask if this word means anything to you?" I showed here my phone with a picture of Sally's message.

"*Gadeklawklawklawiriol*," she read. "What on Earth is that?"

"That's what I'm asking."

"Have you tried searching the web?"

"I got nothing. I wondered if it meant anything to you. Does it sound Welsh? Or a component of a spell perhaps?"

She wrote the word down on her pad, because she trusted paper. "I'll look into this, as well, if I can spare the time. These books don't look after themselves, you know. This is related to Jamie?"

"It's an unrelated matter. It may be nothing. The doll is the main thing."

I thought about asking her again whether Evangelina Mormont was truly gone, given the name that Belinda had given me. I decided against it – not only because I was terrified of Lady Coldwater's withering gaze, but mainly because I'd decided this was nothing more than Sally's idea of humour. If the Sorceress had purchased a nice little bungalow in the Cardiff suburbs – *decorated to a high standard through out, easy to maintain* – I doubted she would have used her real name. Just as Sally hadn't.

Instead, I said, "The tome you talked about? Can I see it now?"

"Tome?"

"The *Book of Shadows*. You said you had to remove all the wards upon it."

"Of course. Yes, you can look at it. This *is* a library, or hadn't you noticed?"

She crossed the room to lock the outer door so that no one could sneak in and try and read a book while she wasn't watching, then returned. Together, we took the stairs down. I'd passed through the portal to Level -2 once before, when she'd given my rune-infected phone to the bookwyrm entity to interpret. Everything looked the same on that level as we emerged from the bottom of the spiral stairs: the smooth, concrete walls and the dry, regulated air. The ancient-looking wooden racks of chained tomes.

We went past the isolated display case where the bookwyrm dwelled. I stopped momentarily to watch as the little illustrated dragon, as brightly coloured and as beautiful as the stained-glass windows of a mosque or a cathedral with the early morning sun streaming through them, crept across the top of a page of cramped, handwritten text. It paused for a moment, then spread its wings and flew, across the gutter of the book to land on the opposite page. It sniffed, exhaled a few stylized curls of flame, then settled down for a good read.

"What book have you given it now?" I asked.

"Best you don't ask."

"Have you ever thought about setting the creature free?"

"It is free. It has everything it wants. You're thinking spatially, but it inhabits concepts. It can go anywhere."

"You'll run out of books eventually."

She snorted, as if that was a ridiculous concept, but she didn't reply.

We crossed the floor to the door down to the next level. This was a modern steel vault door, the sort to be found in banks in all good heist movies. It had codes and locks and several layers of biometric protection that required the Lady to place her fingertips on a screen, have her retinas scanned and her breath sniffed.

"Do you really need three different sorts of biometric protection?"

"They can all be stolen."

"Eyes and fingers I get, but how do you steal someone's breath?"

"Why do you want to know?"

I didn't reply. The Lady finally satisfied the locks and heaved the door open. It was heavy and massive, twenty-centimetres or more of blast-proof steel. I wondered if it was to protect the books down on Level -3, or if it was to protect *us* from whatever was down there.

"The books on the next level down," she said, before we passed through the gateway to descend, "they're much more dangerous than those up here. You remember I said that the books on Level -2 aren't dangerous as such? That the danger lies in what people do with the knowledge they contain?"

"Yep."

"That's not true on the next level. The books down there are intrinsically hazardous."

"You make it sound like they're alive."

"You've seen enough possessed objects in your time, I'm sure. It may be that they are. Before we venture down, let me repeat: don't touch any of the books. Don't open any of them and especially don't read any of them. Reading these books is bad for you."

"So, standard library advice then."

She ignored my hilarious jest and opened a little cupboard set into the wall next to the door.

"We'll also need this."

She pulled out a brass contraption that looked something like a miner's safety lamp, except that it had far too many dials and switches set into its base. Instead of a light, I could see a complex set of tubes and reservoirs containing a blue liquid.

"What is it?"

"Don't they teach you anything? It's a Feynman's Thaumic Exposure Tube. Obviously. It's essential equipment for anyone venturing deeper into the library."

I did know what the device was – although we called them FTETs and the ones we carried were the size of a pen and battery powered. Like a cross between a Geiger Counter and a thaumometer, they gave you an indication of your long-term exposure to magical fields. Essentially, they gave you an approximate indication of the moment to run like hell and not look back.

"This must be an original," I said. "How old is it?"

"It functions perfectly," the Lady said. "I wouldn't trust my life to anything else."

She twisted little knurled brass wheels on the contraption, then pumped little pistons that sent the blue liquid from one tube into another.

"As we're exposed, the level in this tube will fall," she said. "When it reaches this red mark on the glass tube, we leave immediately, no questions asked. Is that understood?"

"I may ask questions once we've left," I said.

She picked up the FTET by its wire handle and, holding it out like a lamp to reveal the way, opened the door.

We clanged down a spiralling iron staircase to arrive upon the floor of Level -3. Unlike the floors above, the lighting was very subdued down there, and there was something electric in the air, a crackle of barely-suppressed and restless life. I could hear rustles of paper, low growls, snorts, as if the level were a zoo for malevolent magical creatures. Or maybe my imagination was hearing voices in the ventilation system. There weren't many books down there, and each was kept isolated in its own locked display case, picked out in a little pool of light. What was the Librarian afraid of – that they started communing and cooperating if they were placed next to each other on shelves? That they could reproduce or fight?

I didn't ask. Moving quietly so as not to wake the sleeping monsters, we padded along the shadowy aisles between the books. Lady Coldwater stopped me at one in the middle of the room. As well as locks and chains, the other tomes had lines of something more magical in nature binding them, lines of smoky black criss-crossing over them. I swear I saw several of the books struggling against their constraints.

The book the Lady wished to show me had no such magical wards containing it. It was small, bound in red leather, something you could slip into a pocket. It didn't look particularly impressive, but for some reason I thought about the notebooks soldiers might have used to tally the names of prisoners herded onto trains for execution. The place was having an effect on me. The Lady cast a warning glance at me, then she set down her Feynman's Tube and set about unlocking the case.

"How do we know this book contains the magic used in the case I'm exploring?" I whispered. "What's the connection?"

"There may not be one, but the sorcery you describe, this filling people's heads with their own nightmares, making them think it's deepest night even when it's day … that's what this book is all about. We know Night Hags have those effects, and the book mentions several rites for summoning such demons."

"Is this book the source of the spells, though?"

"Users copy what they've learned or glimpsed into their own books. Sometimes they get it wrong and what they copy is inert. Other times, they inadvertently create something wildly destructive and out of control. This one is old, but there may be older tomes with originals of the same spells. If there are, I don't have them."

She slipped on a pair of white cotton gloves to protect the ancient paper from her touch – and maybe to protect herself from its touch, too, then opened the book and turned the pages. I saw … shadows. Clouds. Patches and blotches of blackness drifting over a background that contained scribbles of text, odd little diagrams of trees and the alignments of the spheres and symbols I barely recognized. The similarity to Jamie's later paintings was striking.

"Where did you acquire this?" I asked.

"We retrieved it from the library of an Oxford college. Someone was researching ancient folk practices."

Oxford. I thought about Peter Warder. "When was this?"

"Victorian times. They weren't in the know, just dabbling in quaint folk practices that they should have left well alone. Some students were murdered in horrible ways, nailed upside-down to an oak tree and allowed to bleed dry."

"Those student pranks really can get out of hand."

She ignored me. "We were called into the college and we retrieved a number of tomes and objects."

"*We* as in the Office?"

"*We* as in the Pale Sisters."

In her head, this library she guarded wasn't the property of the Office of the Witchfinder General at all. It was hers, and occasionally she let us visit.

"Why is it filled with these black clouds? Is that why you think it's connected to the case I'm looking into?"

She was grimacing as she turned more pages, holding each by its corner as if it were hot to touch. "It's badly decayed. The spells in it; they run out of control, like weeds overgrowing a garden or a plague spreading through a village. The book is fairly far-gone – it was when we retrieved it – but it is still potent. I believe it touches on the magic that Campbell says might be involved. He is usually right."

"The book has become infected by its own magic?"

"The sorcery this tome contains is like a cancer. It runs amok, out of control, causing harm rather than growing and repairing. Yes, it is slowly destroying itself. It wasn't originally called the Book of Shadows; that was simply the name the Oxford academics gave it."

"What was it called originally?"

"I told you, it didn't have a name, suggesting it was for someone's private use only. A scribbled note slipped inside it suggested they referred to it as, simply, *The Book*."

"Why don't you let the bookwyrm loose on it?"

"This is one of very few volumes that I wouldn't let it go near. It could be sucked into the shadows and never emerge."

"Can the magic infect us, too, here in the physical world?"

"Have you not been listening to anything I've been saying?"

I took that to mean *yes*. "There isn't a lot of the text left, by the look of it," I said, helpfully. "Can you clear away the black clouds so we can see the spells?"

She turned more pages, but it was all the same. She shook her head. "It's too far gone. I was afraid it was so. Containment has stopped the rot from spreading, but there's not a lot left. Perhaps it would be better to commit the book to the flames and have done with it."

"Where did Oxford get it from? What do we know about it?"

"It's sixteenth or seventeenth century, although obviously there may be older source books. It was retrieved from a private collection in Suffolk. The Oxford academics weren't very good at keeping records in those days, unfortunately."

"Then, I don't see how it helps me much."

She'd stopped turning the pages. She withdrew her hands as if she'd come across something distasteful.

"Well, there's this."

I peered over her shoulder. One page was relatively clear of the fogging blackness. There was a rough pencil sketch filling the page, surrounded by a variety of symbols and runes. The picture, unmistakably, very closely resembled the doll I'd retrieved from Jamie Tavish's house the day before.

I peered closer. "It could be the same one. Whoever

made the doll I found might have used this book as their instructions."

"I told you, there are regional variations, local traditions. This may not be very close at all to the totem you found. Except, these knots…"

She had a picture of the doll on her phone. She placed it next to the book for comparison.

"See? The way the twines are twisted and woven to form its body. I told you, they're diagnostic. This one … yes, it's close. These tiny bat bones tied in here. This oak gall and seashell … your doll could have been worked from this depiction, or at least a close copy of it."

"The symbols around the edge – do they tell you who created the spell? Like a signature? If I can get something I might be able to follow the lead."

She pulled out a little brass magnifying glass from a cardigan pocket and peered in closer at the page.

"Alignments, syllables of the incantation, how to arrange the entrails of slaughtered rabbits and crows … no, there is nothing identifying an individual. Except…"

She was studying a particular symbol in the corner. To my untrained eye it looked like a squashed beetle, but the Lady appeared to find it fascinating.

She let out a sighing breath. "Well, well, well. There's a mark I haven't come across in some time. What are you doing there?"

"Are you speaking to it in the hope of getting a response?"

"Of course not. Don't be ridiculous."

"The symbol is a name?"

"Of sorts. It's the mark of the Sisterhood."

"The Pale Sisters? It's *your* mark?"

"No, no, not the Pale Sisters, the Blood Sisters. Obviously."

"Who are…"

I was about to extract more information from her, but the Feynman's chose that moment to release a stream of bubbles within one of its tubes. The Lady's attention jerked from the book to the brass device.

"We have to leave. Now."

"But…"

"*Now*. Unless you want to spend the rest of your days locked in your own nightmares."

I really did not. We closed the book, closed and resealed its case and then ran for the door. As we pounded up the stairs, black dots swam in my vision. I hoped they were from the sudden exertion.

Back upstairs in the reassuring surroundings of Level -1, I sat while the Lady poured us both tea from her flask. Her hand was shaking as she worked.

"I, uh, don't really like tea," I said.

"Drink. It's hot and sweet, and it's what you need."

The liquid tasted as vile and sickly as I recalled, but I swallowed it down anyway.

"Another?" she asked.

"I'd honestly rather not. How much were we exposed?"

"Hopefully not too much. I set the sensitivity of the Tube to low. You are carrying your Stebsen's Ward, I assume?"

I wasn't. But I assured her I was.

"Good, good. Are you experiencing any side effects?"

The black blotches were still there, swimming around in my peripheral vision like amoebae glimpsed through a microscope. I decided not to mention them. They'd go away soon enough. Probably. On the way back across Level -2, I'd surreptitiously scanned myself with my thaumometer and found nothing. Okay, maybe that didn't prove anything, but it made me feel a little better.

The Librarian sank into her wooden chair and looked, for a moment, old and tired. Then all her normal wiry enthusiasm returned. She poked the scrappy little doll on her desk with her pencil again, teasing aside a few strands of the tangled knots making up its body.

"Definite similarities, wouldn't you say?"

She clearly had a keener eye for the subtleties than I did. "These Blood Sisters you mentioned. I don't know who they are."

She threw me another of her *Why don't you know anything?* glances. "You will at least be familiar with the witch trials of the seventeenth century? Matthew Hopkins and his ilk? I mean, you are literally a modern-day witchfinder."

I obviously didn't feel particularly proud of the Office's origins. I wasn't responsible for the sins of my forebears – but I did get that I needed to acknowledge them, even try and atone for them if I could.

"Terrible mistakes were made. They basically hated women, or were afraid of them. Seems to me the original witchfinders were sexually repressed, too, afraid of their own desires. I mean, come on, they loved to go around looking for women with a third nipple. Not to mention the *witch prickers*, going around shaving women of their hair and studying them for special marks."

The Lady regarded me for a moment. Her tone softened a little. "There's something in what you say. Or they were suffering some mental disorder, a moral panic. Or, perhaps it was … some other sort of disorder."

"Are you suggesting the early witchfinders were being magically controlled in some way?"

"It's an idle theory, something I haven't put much work into. There obviously *were* witches in Britain, as there always have been and still are. Cunning men, too. Sorcerers, alchemists, summoners, oneiromancers, enchanters, necromancers, the whole spectrum of magical practitioners. They were and still are among us, despite the best efforts of the Office. They weren't doing anyone much harm four hundred years ago, give or take the odd curse, but someone may have decided they were a growing threat and acted to control them."

"Who?"

"Who do you think?"

"You're talking about the Warlock."

"That's what we call him – it – right now, but I believe there have been other names over the centuries. It's possible this entity inspired the entire witchfinder craze by working glamours on profoundly religious men. By

SIMON KEWIN

doing so, ultimately, the Office as we now know it was born."

"That's quite a theory."

"One I have little proof for, although I see evidence for this Warlock's hand in a number of key events in British history. The Armada, the Gunpowder Plot, perhaps others. No matter, those are stories for another time. The point is, one reaction to the persecution of the witches was the founding of the Sisterhood. You will be familiar with the case of Alis Treacle."

"Assume I'm not."

The librarian regarded me for a moment, as if wondering why she was bothering to even talk to me. "She was a wise woman, a witch if you like, quietly going about her work. Hopkins heard about her and subjected her to the blunt knife trial. You will be familiar with that, at least?"

"Remind me."

The Lady sighed. "Treacle was held down and her left arm was cut off at the shoulder. They used a blunt knife to make the process as slow and as agonizing as possible. This was obviously long before anaesthetics or antiseptics – not that Hopkins would have used them even if he'd had them."

"Bloody hell."

"Quite literally, yes. I'm sure you're familiar with the twisted logic. The idea was to see if the woman bled. If she didn't, she was a witch and was executed. If she did, well, she was going to die anyway, from the trauma or the blood loss or from infection. Poor Alis bled profusely as you might imagine, so she wasn't executed. She also managed not to die from her terrible injuries. What she did – eventually, once she'd recovered – was vow to get her revenge."

"I mean, good for her," I said. "Hard to argue with that. She started this Sisterhood?"

"They were a secretive group of witches who set aside their work at healing and curing and soothing, and put their skills to other uses. They devoted their lives to using their magical arts to attacking Hopkins and his little army. It was a quiet, desperate war. A brutal one, too, at times. They were sometimes called the Blood Sisters, and not without reason. They felt that they had to go out of their way to be as cruel as possible to their oppressors in order to right the balance."

"What happened to Alis?"

"Oh, the witch finders caught her in the end. What they did to her – these supposedly civilised, religious men – it is hard to believe. The brutality of it, the barbarism. I couldn't bring myself to read to the end. Almost the worst of it was the way they recorded what they were doing so carefully, setting the bare facts down as if they were simply tallying up their household accounts. Implements brought to bear and body parts removed. I can tell you that she was blinded with hot pokers early on. Her sufferings were long and terrible, tipping her into raging madness."

"Fucking hell."

"Yes."

"How do you fit into this? The Pale Sisters?"

The Lady sat back in her chair. "The Blood Sisters gave us the name. It was intended as term of abuse."

"They did?"

"After a century or so of bloodshed and horror, a few of us turned our backs on the Sisterhood and the bloodshed and tried, instead, to devote ourselves once again to healing. To setting a better example, rising above, making a positive change in the world. The Blood Sisters, as you can imagine, were scornful. We were turning against everything they stood for. It was a bad time, sister against sister."

"Why did they call you *Pale*? I'm willing to guess most of the women on both sides were fair-skinned right?"

"*Pale*, in this sense, means bloodless, ineffectual. The Blood Sisters thought we were betraying them, letting the enemy walk all over us. They thought we were too afraid to fight. We, on the other hand, thought they were just as bad as those who were trying to kill us. We took on their insult as a badge of honour and started calling ourselves the Pale Sisters, proud of what we were."

"I've never heard of these Blood Sisters."

"No, well, they haven't existed for a long time. Their approach went out of fashion."

"Then it seems unlikely they're behind the attacks on Jamie Tavish and the others."

The Lady nodded her head at that. "I'm sure they don't exist anymore, but that doesn't mean someone hasn't unearthed one of their old spellbooks, a copy we don't hold."

"Who?"

"If I knew that I would obviously tell you."

"When did these Blood Sisters cease to exist?"

The librarian frowned, gazed into the distance. "It's hard to be completely sure. Before this, I'd have said that remnants clung on no later than the start of the twentieth century. Now, who knows?"

"Will you look into them? The Pale Sisters must have some idea who belonged to the other group. Sister against sister, you said. If you could find out who had a copy of this spell, it might allow me to narrow down who has access to the magic in the modern day."

"They didn't write down much. They were hunted and persecuted and they preferred to pass on their wisdom by word of mouth. So far as we know, the book downstairs is the only surviving work containing those particular hexes. But I'll see if I can dig out anything useful. It's unlikely, but the connection to Blood Sister curses … it might be a thread for you to pull on."

I nodded my head, trying to work out how to make use of the connection. I couldn't quite see how it would help – but then, I was finding it a little hard to think with all the black clouds floating around in the corners of the room.

9 – Cryptic

There is an old tale goes that Herne the Hunter,
Sometime a keeper here in Windsor Forest,
Doth all the winter-time, at still midnight,
Walk round about an oak, with great ragg'd horns;
And there he blasts the tree, and takes the cattle,
And makes milch-kine yield blood, and shakes a chain
In a most hideous and dreadful manner
– Shakespeare, *The Merry Wives of Windsor*, Act 4,
Scene 4, 1602

I sat at my desk trying to clear my head with our closest approximation to strong, black coffee. It wasn't working. The machine referred to it as *instant coffee*; but in my view it was neither of those things. It took the damned thing about thirty seconds to produce, basically, black-tinted water. After I'd suffered through two cups, the leaden clouds were still there, lurking in the corners of my vision. When I tried to focus on them, they skidded away to hide in another corner of my sight.

I'd already seen what had happened to Jamie; I did not want to succumb to something like that. I'd go see the Lady again if they got worse, but they also reminded me that I needed to pursue my own magical development, my own abilities. I was essentially in the dark about how this stuff worked, and for all I knew, the symptoms I was experiencing were nothing to do with recent events but were another side-effect of my suppression of my nature as a user. Maybe they'd stop once I fully embraced what I was.

I checked through the notes on Jamie's death in MORIARTY again, to see if there was anything I'd missed. There was very definitely no mention of a cursed witch's doll. The house had been searched and nothing malign had been identified. Hardknott-Lewis had recommended the place be placed off-limits, just in case there was something going on we hadn't discovered. While I was in the system, I also checked into the other cases that the Crow's case notes mentioned. One was Morris Crossley, the cover for my visit to the Isle of Man. The other was one Charles Raneleigh. He'd died thirty years previously in the Outer Hebrides, a fact that made his case particularly cold and the one least likely to turn up anything useful. The digitized notes I had access to on Charles were brief, nothing more than a title and a few sentences of summary. There was no mention of anything like a cursed doll. There was some talk of bleeding wounds and, weeks previously, the possible sighting of a spectral hound, and there was the suggestion that Charles had been suffering with some troubling personal issues, but the hard details were scant. If I wanted to read the full account, I'd have to visit Edinburgh.

The usual background hum of the office went on around me: the rattle of an air-vent and the shuddering clank of our ancient heating system underpinning the murmur of conversations being held. The place was busy for once, not much going on in the field. The spooks were having a day off, so the spooks were having a day off. Kerrigan was engaged in an animated argument with someone on the phone, but it appeared to be about car insurance rather than the incursions of primal evil. McLeland was typing up some report into MORIARTY, while Digbeth, sitting opposite me, was staring idly into space, doing very little. Which, to be fair, was normal for him. He was maybe only ten years older than me. Baby-faced, he'd also perfected the grizzled, unkempt look. A week's stubble was giving way to what might be called a beard, and his straggly hair hadn't been cut for a while. He looked like a choir boy whose life had gone seriously off the rails after discovering a taste for communion wine. No doubt it all helped when he went undercover to investigate some supernatural incursion. Not that he seemed to do that very much.

He caught me looking at him, his eyes coming into focus. He grinned at something going on in his head, then returned to pressing keys on his computer, one after the other.

Olwen slumped into the chair beside me, complete with her new pixie-cut hair style. It suited her, I had to say.

She folded up her legs as she considered me. "You look rough. Hangover, is it?"

Friend as she was, she didn't need to know the truth. "No need to look so delighted about it."

"Kerrigan tells me you're heading off under mysterious orders from our glorious leader."

"I mean, that *is* our job."

"I could do with a break. A tour of Britain sounds ideal."

"Love to have you along, really, but this place would fall apart without you."

She smiled ruefully at that. She was much more active in the field these days, but she also multitasked to keep everything in the office ticking over. She was basically the mirror image of Digbeth. It was fair to say that the Office was still struggling to get its head around the tricky concept of equal gender roles.

"I assume you've just been down to visit Gilroy?" she said. "You could probably get drunk on his fumes if you stood near enough."

That threw me. "Why would I go see the tame necromancer? No one's died as far as I know."

"People die all the time in my experience. He said he wanted to speak to you."

"First I've heard about it."

"Apparently he has a message to pass on."

Gilroy was kept in a very comfortable but very isolated prison in the sub-basement – which sounds bad when you put it like that. Which, in my view, it was.

"How is that possible?"

She shrugged. "You'll have to ask him."

A thought staggered blinking into the light of my consciousness. "Oh, hey, Olwen, you're Welsh, right?"

"Our ace investigator. Not much gets past you, does it?"

"I mean, you know the language."

"Speak it like a native, I do."

I showed her the word I'd read in Sally's mirror. "Does this mean anything to you? Is it maybe a place name? Like that town on Anglesey with the 18 syllables."

She frowned, turned her head on one side as she considered the odd jumble of letters on my phone. Finally, a smile of satisfaction passed across her face.

"Cryptic. I thought you were the smart guy who did all the crosswords and puzzles."

"Is it Welsh?"

"Partly it is, and partly it isn't. It's multicultural, like."

"What does that mean?"

"Take a stroll down Charles Street. I'm sure you'll work it out."

"Or you could just tell me."

"I could, couldn't I?" With a smile to herself, she unfolded her legs and slipped off to do all the many things required to keep the Office ticking over.

Downstairs, I rang Gilroy's bell and waited. And waited. There wasn't much to look at except for the blank, painted concrete walls and the camera in the corner monitoring him to make sure he didn't escape.

Eventually, his head appeared, sagging jowls and florid, puffy face and all. He had work-out machinery, but his incarceration clearly wasn't doing his health much good. Perhaps it wasn't better than Oblivion after all – at least there, he wouldn't be aware of how miserable his existence was.

He greeted me with all his usual warmth. "The fuck do you want?"

"Olwen said you had a message for me."

He stepped out of his inner sanctum to look at me through the glass of his outer door. His locked outer door. "If you visited more often, I could have told you myself."

His words threw me. I'd once seen him as this unpleasant racist necromancer that we kept around because he was useful. I'd been completely wrong about him. Apart from the *unpleasant* thing. He could definitely still be that.

"I should have come down here more. I'm sorry."

"Yeah, well. I'm sure you have a life to lead. Not sure I need you coming down here to taunt me with how much fun you're having out there, the women you're sleeping with, the wild parties you're enjoying."

He really did not know me very well. "No taunting, I promise."

"Glad to fucking hear it."

"Can I come inside so we can sit down?"

"No, you fucking cannot."

"This message that Olwen mentioned – does it exist?"

"'Course it exists! Why else would I have said it?"

"I mean, you're isolated from the outside world; no electronic communications can get through to you. No one can write to you or talk to you in any way unless they come down here and knock on your door."

"Shows you what you know. What part of *necromancer* don't you understand?"

"Are you saying you've received a message for me from someone who's dead?"

"The brightest and the best, fucking hell. Are you always this slow? You sound like that's an insane idea, but you literally come down here and make me talk to the dead all the time. Which, by the way, since we're on the subject, I bastard-well despise. The dead are pissed off, angry and confused, and they do not welcome me dropping by for a fucking chat, believe me. Their language can be fucking awful."

"Right. Who is this message from? I thought assays only worked on the recently deceased."

"What, now you want me to teach you how necromancy works, do you?"

In truth, I wouldn't have minded. But now wasn't the time. "Is it someone I know?"

"I don't know; I don't keep up to date with your social calendar. Did you ever meet Jamie Tavish?"

"Wait, what? That can't be right; he died years ago."

"What does years mean when you're talking about different planes of reality? Don't you know any damn thing? *Years ago* from our perspective might be right now or in the future in other dimensions. Or maybe his fading spirit has been locked away in some closed bubble universe and was recently released."

"That … is a possibility."

"There you fucking go, then."

"What was the message?"

"He said, Stay awake, stay in the light. Darkness is when it comes for you. It lives in the darkness. It is the darkness."

"What does that mean?"

"How the fucking buggery fuck should I know? Who do you think I am, the bastard Oracle of Delphi? The dead are often confused and traumatised; maybe it's utter bullshit."

"Anything else? Is he definitely dead?"

"Oh, he's dead. He sounded terrified, but then people in his position often are."

Another possibility occurred to me, something that had been nagging away in my subconscious. "When you touched his mind, even though he was dead, was Jamie definitely … human?"

"What the fuck does that mean?"

"He'd gone to a lot of trouble to black out all the mirrors in his house, like he was terrified of reflections. Then there was the blood taken from him. Is there any possibility that he was undead?"

"He was as human as you or I. That doesn't mean he hadn't been attacked, or wasn't expecting to be attacked. Maybe he was just a delusional fuckwit, seeing phantoms where none existed."

"Maybe."

I noted down the words Gilroy had given me on my phone for later consideration. "Well, thanks. And I'm … I'm sorry you're still stuck down here. It isn't right. If any more hauntings in expensive hotels crop up, I'll try and get you posted there again."

"Oh, well, that makes me feel a whole lot better, doesn't it? Tell you what, once you're Witchfinder General, just make sure you set me free."

"I would, I really would, but somehow I don't think that's very likely."

I nodded in what I hoped was a sympathetic way. I turned to leave, but something else occurred to me.

"Can I ask you a question?"

"If you're quick. I have a packed schedule of meetings to go to."

"My grandfather. You said you fought alongside him. What was he like?"

"You've got relatives, haven't you?" he barked. "Ask them."

"Actually, there isn't much left of my immediate family. There's only my mother, but her memory is patchy these days. Hardknott-Lewis has told me a little. I know that my grandfather fought against English Wizardry and I know that they killed him, perhaps by trapping him in a runic circle with some shadow realm nightmare. I was told by one English Wizardry agent, Peter Warder, that there was no mention of Amoor at all in the records. Maybe that was a lie, and maybe my grandfather was simply written out of history. It happens."

Gilroy hesitated uncharacteristically. He glanced up at the security camera winking away in the high corner of the lobby. The camera I'd deliberately turned away from before speaking so that my lips couldn't be read.

"Come inside," he said finally. "I'll tell you what I know."

"Really?"

"What, you think it's a fucking trap or something?"

He turned and disappeared into his lair, leaving his inner door open. After only a moment's hesitation, I typed in the code to open his outer entrance, then followed him.

I'd imagined he lived in a bachelor's *pit* (I could talk), pictures of naked women all over his walls, empty gin bottles lying everywhere, splashed pizza topping up the walls. I was very, very wrong. The rooms he lived in were immaculate: smart, modern, scrupulously tidy. He did have pictures on his walls, but they were Picasso and Miro prints. Whole walls were taken up with bookcases, their shelves full, tomes ancient and modern carefully arranged by subject matter. Lady Coldwater would have been proud of him. He stood there, this shabby wreck of a man, four or five days of stubble on his sagging chin, looking utterly out of place in his own world. And I saw why: the Gilroy we knew wasn't the real Gilroy. *This* was the real Gilroy. He played the role of the unhealthy, foul-mouthed man as an act of defiance. A small way of keeping the real *him* safe and hidden.

He looked hesitant for a moment, oddly unsure of himself, guilty at revealing himself to me, then indicated a chair. "Please, sit. I'll tell you what I know about Bi Bi."

My grandfather's name had been Amoor, but his friends had all called him Bi Bi. It seemed an oddly down-to-Earth epithet for the serious, stern figure I'd seen in family photographs. According to my mother, I'd met him, although I had no memories of him. I wished I had.

"Did you know him well?" I asked.

"No, no. I was young at the time and he was high-up, but we were involved in a few operations together. I spoke to him a couple of times, too. He was always friendly. He was ... impressive."

"As a person?"

"That, yes, but I mean magically, too. He was a big man, tall, and he loved life, had a very infectious laugh. He had a way of ... filling a room when he came in, if you know what I mean. He was powerful, too, and he despised anything evil that threatened life. Anything demonic, dark, vampiric, soul-eating: he hated it. Did you know that you come from a long line of such people? Revenant dispellers and vampire hunters?"

Gilroy's language was markedly different, too. Here in

his own domain, he hadn't sworn at me once. It felt weird.

"I need to find out more about it all," I said.

"Well, you should. He told me something about it, the demons and ghosts his forebears fought to dispel and destroy in India. The *vetala*, for example; I recall him talking about how he almost lost his own grandfather battling them in a charnel ground in the south of India somewhere. This would be late in the nineteenth century. Bi Bi was an expert in the incantations required to defeat such horrors, wherever they arose. I guess darkness is the same the world over. We all fight the same evil even if we give it different names."

I thought about commenting on the whole troubled matter of identifying *evil* with *dark*. It was obviously a common enough trope, in fantasy literature and elsewhere, but take that too far and you ended up with English Wizardry in their pristine white robes and their xenophobia. I said nothing. Because, also, setting race aside, this case was seemingly about darkness in its literal sense. The seeping of nightmares across into the waking mind was a real thing. I needed to separate out the two senses of *dark*.

Gilroy was shaking his head as these thoughts ran through my mind. "You, though. I definitely see something of you in him. His thoughts used to wander off like that, as well. You want my advice? Don't deny what you are, boy. Embrace it."

"I'm trying. It's complicated."

"Ah, *complicated*, right. The modern world. It seems simple to me. It seems to me you need to try harder at being *you* or you'll get yourself killed. Or you'll tear yourself apart trying to run in two opposite directions at the same time."

"Was my grandfather in the Mystical Council?"

"You've found out about that, at least."

"I've picked up a few mentions."

"That was long-gone before I knew your grandfather, but I suspect he was involved once, yes. He would have been very junior, eighteen or so, when it was disbanded.

It must have been immensely frustrating for him; the Council would have been just his thing. He was a team-player, you know. He wasn't particularly interested in leading or commanding, but people naturally followed his suggestions anyway."

"And Arthur Stonewall – was he involved in any of this? The man English Wizardry call the Destroyer?"

Gilroy scratched at his stubble with a clawed hand. "That's an interesting question. I saw even less of Stonewall, but he was most certainly around, there in the background. I think, perhaps, I saw him and your grandfather working together once, but I'd need to check on that. Wait here."

He rose and hurried into another room. I glimpsed more book-lined walls through there, a desk with papers strewn upon it. Whiteboards with pictures stuck to them and boxes drawn in red, lines connecting them like any movie cop trying to figure a case.

Gilroy returned carrying an armful of dossiers. Before he opened them, he said, "I'm showing you all this on the understanding that it goes no further, yes? I'm showing it to you because you're Bi Bi's grandson, and because you've treated me fairly. My stay in that hotel looking for poor Maude Woebegone was welcome."

"I'll tell no one anything about what I've seen in here," I said.

"Good. Make sure you don't."

He plonked the pile of manilla folders onto his coffee table. "This is what I spend my time doing. Remembering the old days, yes, like any old fool, but also putting the records into order. So much has been lost that might still be useful. They let me have anything I want so long as it stays here with me."

"You should talk to the librarian. She'd approve, I'm sure."

"Dorothy Coldwater? I doubt it. We don't communicate much. Haven't spoken to her in a while."

That statement struck me as sad. The librarian was his near neighbour; they both lived out their lives in the

120

basements, she in her library, he in his upholstered cell. They were only separated by a few metres of rock and stone. And it seemed more and more like they had a lot in common.

He began to leaf through the papers one of the binders contained. I saw scribbled handwritten notes, some typed reports, the occasional photograph. He mumbled to himself as he searched. Then, finally, he fished out the picture he'd been looking for.

"Here. This is it."

He held out a black and white photograph of a group of men and women standing proudly in a semicircle. Some held wands, others blades with runes engraved on them. A couple held delicate glass bottles containing colourful liquids while one or two held only old books. A man with impressive muttonchop sideburns, almost meeting under his chin, stood erect while holding a curved Japanese sword. One or two of the group wore smart, sensible suits, but others were dressed more unconventionally, with long flowing gowns or garb that might not have looked too out of place in a middle eastern suq. Or at Glastonbury festival. One man appeared to be wearing an elaborate silk dressing gown adorned with moon and star symbols. On his head was a matching cap complete with an impressive tassel. Most bore expressions of pride, although standing at the front there was a short pugnacious man who looked like he intended to leap out of the photograph and tear you limb from limb.

One of the group, unmistakably, was Amoor Shahzan, my grandfather, although much younger than in any of the family photographs I'd seen. He was tall, but his face was that of a boy. He wore what appeared to be a three-piece tweed suit, and his hair and moustache were carefully lacquered into place. I traced my fingers across his likeness.

"Stonewall is in this picture?" I asked.

"Here, at the back. This tall man with the trimmed beard. There aren't many images of him in the record. He always liked to stay in the shadows."

The man that Gilroy pointed to was laughing at something with an open, warm guffaw. He stood at the back of the group and had his arms held wide, as if trying to embrace everyone there.

"I assume this is the Mystical Council?"

"Most of it, as far as I know. A gathering at Chequers to celebrate a victory over some malign foe. Perhaps their efforts to thwart Soviet attempts to open portals to hell around London."

"They tried to do that?"

"Crazy, uncontrolled magic. You're just as likely to get sucked into the other realm yourself."

"When was this taken?" I asked.

Gilroy flipped the photograph over. Written on the back in purple ink was the inscription, *MC, 1949.*

"My grandfather would have been 17 or 18," I said.

"The Council didn't survive for long after this. A year later, it was gone."

"Why exactly? Who was behind that? It seems mad given how important their work was."

"You lot are mostly to blame, of course. The Office. But … perhaps others too. It's something I'm looking into, picking through the archives for clues."

"You know something?"

"Hints, suggestions, nothing more. The Council members were discredited, one by one. It was as if someone was quietly bringing them down, coercing them to act against their will. Seems to me they were too good at their jobs. Some would have seen them as a threat."

I thought about the succubi; the attempt to control the Keyholders of the Office. Had something similar happened here?

"English Wizardry," I said.

"I suppose so."

"Was my grandfather coerced in any way? Controlled?"

"From what I can tell and from what I recall, no. He wasn't good at doing what he was supposed to do, what others wanted him to. If you wanted him to perform an action, the best approach was to order him to do the precise opposite. I'll bet he resisted any attempts to control him if they were made. When the Council folded, he would have been ordered to stand down, stop using magic, but he simply carried on the fight. He died in, what 1995?"

"1996."

"All that time, then, he was quietly waging the war against evil magic use in Britain. He wasn't alone, naturally, but he was resolute. He was a damned good man. If you weren't his grandson, I wouldn't have let you in here."

"Who are the others in the picture?"

"Don't know. They were powerful sorcerers and illusionists and conjurors, but they were useless at writing minutes. Or perhaps it was deliberate; they were obviously secretive. A snatch of handwriting can be used against you if you know what you're doing."

I was sure there were details and connections here I was missing. Something in those smiling faces. My brain was mush, though, refusing to focus. It was like trying to see through fog.

"When was this taken?" I asked.

Gilroy looked at me with a frown on his face, his eyes narrowed. "I just told you that."

"You did? Yes, of course, you did. Sorry, I was distracted."

He frowned, then came closer, kneeling in front of me to study my face. His closeness was disconcerting. I could feel his breath tickling my nose.

"Damn," he whispered to himself.

"What is it?"

"You've been hexed," he said, sitting back. "You're definitely under the influence of malign magic. I can see the shadows of it in your eyes."

"I ... came into contact with something."

Gilroy began to pack away the papers. "You need to leave. You ought to get that looked at before it consumes you. I've seen it happen."

"I'll fight it off. I seem to be good at resisting these things."

"That's what your grandfather used to say."

"And was he?"

Gilroy hesitated for a moment, before picking up the binders. "Actually, yes, he was. He seemed to be naturally resistant to evil magic. Handy when you've devoted your life to banishing demons and turning the unliving. Partly it was because he practised the mantras his family had handed down to him, all the training he'd done."

"Mantras, yeah."

"You know them, I assume? You use them to train your mind and body?"

Like I say, he was really very like the Librarian, right down to the patronising advice on doing my exercises.

"I, um, no. I actually have no idea about them. My family is a bit broken."

"Then you need to unbreak it. And you need to find out about your grandfather and your father and how their magic worked. I think you're going to need it. Let's not beat about the bush; you're a Shahzan, with Shahzan powers if I'm not mistaken. Quite what you're doing in the Office, I don't know, but you need to look after yourself. But before you do any of that, you need to get out of here. You may have good resistance to these things, but I do not, not after all my years living in isolation. Leave now. Please. Leave and get some sleep. You look like you can barely keep your eyes open. And if it doesn't go away, go see Dorothy, or Hardknott-Lewis. See *someone*."

I rose. The room lurched around me for a few moments, more shadowy pondlife blobs swimming through my vision. Then the hard lines settled down. I worked my way back to the door.

Sleep. Yeah. I needed to sleep.

Gilroy stopped me in the vestibule between his inner and outer doors.

"Everything you've seen here … you tell no one, understand?"

"I understand."

"Make sure you fucking well do."

There he was, the familiar Gilroy back again. Weirdly, I'd missed him. I knew where I was with that Gilroy.

"Will you carry on your research?" I asked. "I need to know about the Mystical Council. Who was in that picture, who their enemies were. Anything about Stonewall, especially. And my grandfather."

"How exactly am I supposed to contact you if I unearth anything?"

"Who brings you supplies most days?"

We were standing outside now. This appeared to be the trigger for the return of the full-on reactionary Gilroy that we all knew and didn't love.

"That pretty young piece with the nice arse."

"Are you perhaps referring to Acolyte Olwen Morgan?"

"Didn't catch her name; I was too busy admiring her a..."

I held up my hand to stop him. "I get the idea. If you find anything, pass it to Olwen, and she can relay it to me."

"Trust her, do you?"

"With my life? Absolutely."

"That's not what I asked, is it, twat features? I'm talking about you, your dark secrets, your true nature as a practitioner of the unnatural arts."

He had a good point. I wasn't sure Olwen was ready for that little confession yet. "If you need to communicate with me, tell her to tell me to visit. Or put a message in a sealed envelope so only I read it."

"A paper envelope," he said, his florid face lighting up. "Fuck me, yeah, that'll keep the bastards out."

I thanked him for his time for the benefit of the CCTV camera, then walked away.

125

10 – In Camera

Oh, the terrible struggle that I have had against
sleep so often of late; the pain of the sleeplessness,
or the pain of the fear of sleep, and with such
unknown horror as it has for me! How blessed are
some people, whose lives have no fears, no dreads;
to whom sleep is a blessing that comes nightly, and
brings nothing but sweet dreams.

– Bram Stoker, *Dracula*, 1897

I considered investigating Charles Street, as Olwen had
suggested, but I really was not thinking straight. The little
black clouds in my peripheral vision joining up into one
big brain fog. My mind was experiencing power-cuts and
outages across all suburbs. I clearly wasn't going to be at
my best until I got over it, and I certainly wasn't up to
fighting anything malicious that came for me.

Plus, I needed to do some washing ahead of my jaunt in
pursuit of Thomas Quirk. He was still AWOL, no sign of
him on MORIARTY. I, on the other hand, had recorded
my adventures with the Jamie Tavish investigation
extensively – obviously making no mention of my
debilitation, in case English Wizardry seized upon an
opportunity to send their ghouls after me. I figured I'd
spent long enough in Cardiff, laid enough of a false trail.
Focussing hard through the mists, I came up with some
possible connections to look for in the case of Morris
Crossley, the Isle of Man victim. I logged my intention to
pursue them, too. It was Thursday now, and I had a flight
booked from Bristol on Saturday morning. Cardiff
Airport would have been much more convenient, but it
turned out that no one had yet worked out how to fly
from Wales to the little island in the middle of the Irish

Sea. It was good to know that there were still some feats of human endurance and enterprise waiting to be achieved, some impossible expeditions there to be pioneered by brave explorers.

Back home, I stared at myself in my bathroom mirror. I tried sweeping the fringe of my black hair into place, but it wasn't helping. I looked rough. I felt like I was hungover without having had any of the fun of drinking too much the night before. Which just wasn't fair.

Now it seemed to me that the black clouds were in the room with me, lurking in the high corners and behind the furniture. More than once, I'd found myself glancing to one side in the hope of catching them. Each time, they scudded out of the way. Was that what it had been like with Jamie? Perhaps that explained all the lights and lamps and candles: Jamie had attempted to illuminate every nook and cranny of his domain, give the shadows no corner to lurk in. It obviously hadn't worked, because the darkness was in his eyes, in his head.

My guess was he'd been driven mad by the attacks upon him, and that had triggered him to daub every reflective surface in black paint. He'd decided that the mirrors were where the darkness was coming from. Maybe he'd been right; after all, someone *had* opened a portal to another dimension through that mirror in his house. Was that why he'd jumped into the other domain? Had he been driven delusional by the torment or was he in hot pursuit, determined to put a stop to the user attacking him? Whichever, it hadn't ended well. Poor guy.

Well. I wasn't going to fall into madness like that. Yet I also found myself peering into my bathroom mirror, trying to stare *through* my reflection to see if anything was lurking there. It's an odd thing to study yourself so intently; it feels uncomfortable to stare into the eyes of someone so close by, even though it was myself and I was alone. I saw nothing out of the ordinary. The mirror was nothing more than a flat sheet of silvered glass, slightly tarnished at the edges where the humidity had got into it. Still, I found myself covering it with a towel before I left, wedging the material behind the mirror to hold it in place.

I wasn't crazy, oh no. I could stop this behaviour any time I wanted.

I had a few other little mirrors about the place, one near the door, a tall one in the bedroom. There were also the windows that acted like mirrors when it was dark outside as well as a couple of pictures on the walls with reflective glass. Once you started looking you saw mirrors everywhere. Easy to see how the paranoia could spread. I pondered how I might cover all these up, too – then decided I was being ridiculous. That way lay black paint splashed everywhere. I undressed, dropped my clothes onto my floordrobe and collapsed into bed. A good night's sleep, and everything would be fine.

It seemed like only a few moments passed before the dreams started. I was dimly aware of being restless for a time, caught between sleeping and wakefulness, unclear about what experience lay within which domain. And then the tired old footage of my familiar, recurring nightmares began to flicker in my mind.

Have I mentioned them? Probably too predictable to bore you with. I was a boy again. I was also me, older Danesh, the Office operative who'd fallen asleep in his Cardiff bed, but, in the way of dreams, it didn't seem remotely odd that I was both of those at once. I was back on that day with Az, my brother, the day we lost him. These are the events that haunt me. We were playing some game of hide-and-seek, full of breathless excitement. I knew our mother was somewhere about, a reassuring presence, but we'd rampaged off into the woods, lost in our fun. The floor was awash with a thick layer of fallen leaves; running was like splashing through water. I found a place to hide inside the hollow of the wide trunk of a tree and peeped out, hoping to catch a glimpse of Az.

As always, this was the moment when I became aware

of the looming, indistinct threat, lurking within the folds of my dream. It knew where I was, and it was coming for me, coming for the both of us. I felt it as a weight settling upon me, a fizz of alarm in my gut. I was both frantically aware of the imminent danger and also completely oblivious to it, lost in our game. On some other level, I was also aware of what this was: a recurring nightmare that couldn't harm me, something I suffered through at times of stress. Each time I experienced the dream, the pursuing horror crept a little closer. I could run and I could hide, but it knew where I was and nothing could stop its relentless progress towards me.

In some versions of the nightmare, I found myself looking out through the eyes of the pursuer. The monster. And when I caught up with my victim it wasn't me after all, but it was Peter Warder and it was Thomson Fulger combined. Sometimes, worst of all, the shifting, screaming features of my victim were those of Az.

Now, though, I'd lost sight of my brother. I needed to warn him urgently, flee with him. My twin brother; we were inseparable. This was the crux of my dream: it was my guilt at surviving when he didn't, replayed over and over. I shouted his name, but whether I produced any sound, I couldn't tell. I could hear his voice, though. This was the worst part of the dream. His thin, frightened, boy's voice calling to me from afar but also nearby, whispering in my ear. *Don't leave me, Danesh. Help me, help me.* But I hadn't, had I? I'd escaped and left him behind. I knew I couldn't be blamed; I was only a child. Still, I did blame myself. Of course, I did.

Danesh? Danesh? Where are you? Don't leave me, Danesh.

I set off into a desperate run through the trees, but my legs seemed incapable of making contact with the ground. I barely moved. I put more effort into it. Was I running towards Az or away from the danger? I didn't know. I had to do something, that was all. I saw the shadowy figure, directly ahead of me. The grey boughs of the trees rose around us, regularly spaced like the columns in some cathedral. The knots in their bark were eyes, peering at me. The dark shape drifted down a colonnade of the trees, drifting directly towards me. Had it already taken Az? I no longer cared. Desperate panic took over; I had to get away. Fear thundered through me. The urgency of escaping that unspeakable horror blotted out everything else. I forced myself to move, willing my feet to touch the ground and give me forward motion.

I progressed, but not quickly enough. The shadowy presence was a smudge of deeper darkness within the gloom. It was growing larger, larger as it neared, sweeping down the aisle of tree trunks. It was nearly upon me, reaching out for me. I felt it as a sickness in my stomach, the pounding of pain in my brain. It loomed over me, and now I saw its face. This time, it was the indistinct scribble that my mother had described. Was this my own memory, or her account seeping into my subconscious? Then, for a moment, the face changed, and it was Az there, his frightened child's face crying through the features of the entity that had consumed him.

Don't leave me, Danesh. Help me, help me.

Desperate, I ran harder. A strangled sob rose in my throat. I had to get away. Then I felt a rough hand grab my shoulder, a sharp point of pain in my neck, a talon cutting into me.

Boy and man in unison, I screamed…

…and awoke, panting, my bed liquid with sweat, that gasped cry dying in my throat.

It was dark: a solid darkness that was like being swaddled in thick felt, tightly enough to restrict my breathing. I could see nothing and hear nothing yet, somehow, I knew I was in my room in Cardiff, the familiar mattress beneath my back. I tried to sit but could not. What was going on? There was always light in the city, always the rush of traffic or the siren calls of distant alarms. Now, there was nothing. I blinked, but it made no difference.

I was still asleep, that was it. I was lost in the labyrinth of the landscapes in my head. I'd dreamed I'd woken up.

It was a new phase to the nightmare, a thing that had never happened before.

I heard a sound then: a rustling, whispering sound like the faint flutter of feathery wings, the swish of silk. My gaze snapped to the side to see what was there. There was a patch of deeper darkness the size of a standing figure, right next to me. I knew such impressions made no sense – black is black – but there it was, in the room with me, any stray photons falling into it. The figure from the earlier phase of my nightmare had pursued me to this layer of my consciousness, stepping down through the years to the present day. How could that be? It couldn't, of course. Except, it could; this was a dream, nothing more. Understanding came and went. I was no longer clear what was real and what wasn't.

I heard a voice. For some reason I expected it to be a man, but it was a woman's voice I heard, little more than a whisper of air in the darkness. It might have been young and it might have been old, but it was no one I recognized. Someone my brain had invented.

It said, So the witch hunt begins. Witch finder.

It made no sense; if I was hunting a witch, the chase hadn't just started. The twisted logic of the nightmare. Again, I felt the visceral need to flee. Whoever this was, I knew they were malign, wished to do me harm. I struggled harder, desperate to throw off the crushing weight pinning me down. It was as if my muscles were no longer connected to my central nervous system. I put all my strength into it. Also, my magical power, coiling away inside me like a wyrm, a serpent rousing from its subterranean slumbers. The unfocussed power of it was dangerous; it could burn me, but right then I needed it.

I let the storm build in my mind, lightning to put a crack in the dark clouds, then hurled it outwards at the thing attacking me…

…to be met with a solid wall of darkness, absorbing, reflecting the magic I'd hurled at it.

The voice came again, a whisper with an edge of pure hatred in it.

No you don't, witch finder. No more. Never again.

I writhed under the weight of the assault. Never again what? Was my brain trying to tell me something, send a cryptic message? Sometimes my dreams gave me clues, ideas, as my subconscious worked on untangling the problems I was facing. The sting of pain came again. This time something sharp was driven into the crook of my elbow. The darkness was holding me down, pinning me to the bed like a butterfly in a collection. The pain intensified. With a mounting fury, I lashed out, kicking with my legs as well as unleashing another unfocussed blast of magical fury.

This time, I hurled the smothering weight aside. My muscles were finally connected to my brain. I threw myself from the bed to stand in that utter darkness. The carpet was soft beneath my feet and the air was cold on my body. I could still see the shadow that had attacked me, the monster of my dreams, there in my room with me, lurking a short way away.

I lunged for it, tired of fleeing, tired of the recurring nightmare playing over and over. I'd dispel it, destroy it. Show it I wasn't afraid anymore. Perhaps that would finally exorcise it. As I lunged, the shadow swam backwards, and I succeeded only in throwing myself off balance. The universe whirled, and I caught against something with my knee. The chest of drawers came up to strike me on the side of the head.

The darkness, seeing its chance, flew at me to consume me, and this time there was nothing I could do.

When I awoke, there was light, and the rush of traffic outside, and the mocking cries of the gulls. I was in comfortable, familiar Cardiff. The relief of being back in the real world was glorious. I was also lying on the floor. At some point in the night, racked by my nightmares, I'd fallen out of bed. One of my legs was knotted up in my twisted bedsheets. My shoulder was numb from the uncomfortable position, and my back ached. The side of my head throbbed; I must have hit it on something for real. I was also bloody cold. Still, as I looked round, there were no black blobs clouding my vision, no lowering banks of grey obscuring my thoughts. Whatever nasty little hex the *Book of Shadows* had infected me with, I'd sweated it out, shrugged it off.

Perhaps the nightmares were me battling it, forcing it out of my mind. Who knows how this stuff works? It seemed I did indeed have natural immunity to such curses, but I also knew I'd been lucky. A stronger spell might have taken root, felled me on the spot. Sometime soon, I'd visit London to see if my mother had any useful notes handed down through my father and grandfather, something on these mantras Gilroy had mentioned – but before that, I needed to track down the one person who was alive now and who was very definitely capable of giving me what I needed when it came to harnessing my powers.

I had to find Arthur Stonewall.

I sat up, rubbing my head and my numb shoulder and my arm, and it was then that I saw the blood staining the white sheets of my bed. There looked to be a lot of it. Someone had bled profusely – presumably me, since I was, alas, sleeping alone. That wasn't good. At the same time, my hand touched something slippery and wet on my arm. I lifted my fingers to study. More blood. Fresh-looking blood.

What the fuck?

I stood in a whirl, breathing hard. There was a puncture wound in the crook of my elbow. It must have bled freely for a time. What the hell had done that? Had I been bitten by something? An insect? But this was Cardiff, not some rain forest full of deadly bugs. My own words to the Lady came back to me; our conversation as we discussed Jamie Tavish. He'd had blood taken from him in the night, too, enough to stain his sheets red.

What the actual fuck?

I bent my arm to stem the flow, my gaze darting around in alarm in case my attacker was still there. I looked into every room, behind every door, trying not to drip blood anywhere, but nothing was out of place. No unspeakable horror leapt to attack me. I crept back into the bathroom to clean myself up. The towel was still in place on my mirror; I pulled it down so I could watch warily behind myself as I worked. I ran my arm under the tap to clean it up. The blood had more or less stopped flowing by now. The puncture was, in fact, tiny; it had found my vein precisely. The quantity of blood had made it look worse. It had surely bled more than it should have. Didn't some insects do that, inject anticoagulants to keep the stolen blood flowing? There were sharp pains all up my arm and across my shoulders from where I'd struggled and writhed in my sleep. Or had some toxin also been injected? I used the towel to dry my arm.

When I was done, I checked on my reinforced steel door, complete with its m/tech wards. Nothing had come in or gone out. The windows, too, were intact. Could I have inflicted the wounds upon myself? I couldn't see how. I stripped the bed, pulling off the soiled sheets. No needles or spikes had somehow gotten in there to cut me as I turned over. I didn't need to be an ace investigator to know that something magical had attacked me. The *Book of Shadows* curse? The Lady had said nothing about the black clouds coming at me armed with a blade.

The whispers I'd heard, the words dripping with malice: had they been real or some echo of my nightmare? Probably the latter; they didn't make a lot of sense. Something had come for me, though, and the question was why? Was it the same antagonist who'd attacked Jamie? There were obvious parallels with his case: he'd seemingly suffered attacks from mysterious shadows, too, and he'd reported having blood taken from him. Okay, blood is an active ingredient in many spells and incantations, but, still, it seemed more than a coincidence. But why only *some* blood? Why not take all of it? And why had I been left alive? Maybe my struggles had saved me, or maybe the intent was not to kill me, not there and then. To prolong my suffering? To give me a warning? But, if so, I had no idea what it was a warning about.

Grappling with these thoughts, I showered and threw my sheets into the washing machine. The bleeding had stopped. I folded some more clothes into my suitcase in readiness for my journeys around the British Isles.

I needed to get away, yes. More than that, I needed to fight back, pursue those that were – seemingly – pursuing me. Was this English Wizardry or had I stirred up another hornet's nest to further complicate matters?

I needed to know. I needed to find out what the hell was going on.

I strode up and down Charles Street a couple of times, past buildings erected in a hotchpotch of architectural styles: Georgian townhouses converted into offices and clinics; the cubes of more recent buildings given over to shops, the ornate red and grey gothic arches of the Roman Catholic cathedral. It was here, walking by for the second time, that I finally twigged what Olwen had worked out the day before.

Eglwys Gadeiriol Caerdydd, the sign outside the building said. *Cardiff Cathedral*. The word I'd grappled with was *Gadeklawklawklawiriol*, but it wasn't nonsense and it wasn't a Welsh place name. It was the word *Gadeiriol* with klawklawklaw in the middle of it. And that wasn't anything to do with claws or the names of ancient dark gods as I'd vaguely assumed. Olwen had referred to the little puzzle as multicultural. She was right: it was the English word *walk* spelled backwards within part of the Welsh for *cathedral*.

Decoded, it simply said walk backwards three times inside the cathedral. Easy.

I paused for only a moment, then stepped inside the building. It was beautiful in there, airy and hushed. I stood in a large, vaulted space with beams of sunlight shining through the stained-glass windows to my left. Many flowers had been set in pots and upon stands, white lilies along with red and purple blooms that I couldn't identify. The air was heady with their sweet aroma. Most of the interior was taken up with lines of wooden seats. I stepped down the nave between them, each step a crisp *clack* on the stone floor. The only person in sight was a woman wielding a yellow duster. She paid me no attention.

Feeling faintly ridiculous, I walked up to the steps that led to the altar, then began to walk backwards, feigning an interest in the fine wooden ceiling above me. I repeated this dance two more times, pretending to study the windows instead, in what I hoped was something like rapt attention. The polisher glanced my way once but still didn't say anything.

I completed my manoeuvres, then sat in one of the pews waiting for the thing to happen. It didn't. What did I expect? The manifestation of some mystical entity next to me? Sally to appear in a theatrical puff of smoke? A worshipper came in, a man in a flat cap, but he sat on the other side, far away from me, lost in his own thoughts or prayers. He didn't look like a messenger from beyond the veils. Had I missed something? The sun faded for a moment then blazed back into life. I was on the point of trying again when I worked out where I'd gone wrong.

I'd been too literal. I'd worked out the answer to the puzzle, but I wasn't supposed to walk around inside one of Cardiff's cathedrals. Sally hadn't said anything about Charles Street, Olwen had. Sally's house and the flat where I'd had various adventures were on Cathedral Road. She must have meant one of those. Maybe she'd even meant the road itself.

Twenty minutes later I was walking up that familiar tree-lined streets with its grand houses and up-market offices. I tried ambling forwards and backwards, this time feigning interest in something on the other side of the street to cover up my odd actions. No one paid me any attention. Again, nothing happened. It looked like I did need to go inside Sally's flat or her house opposite.

Just as I was approaching the flat – the place I'd first conversed with Sally – DI Zubrasky texted to suggest a place in town as a place to meet up that evening after work. It sounded good to me. I emojied a reply then returned to my crimes of trespass.

This time – after ringing and receiving no answer, and then making sure no one was watching – I did use a *sesame* to despatch the flat's inconvenient locks into another dimension for a few moments, as well as deploying a holdfast to hush its alarm.

The flat was deserted, with no sign of recent habitation. I tried walking backwards three times, figuring now to move around in a circle, because that felt more magicky. I attempted the manoeuvre in every room large enough to swing a dead cat in, but everything remained relentlessly mundane, no messages from the beyond passing through the mists, no words splashed in blood upon the flock wallpaper. Nothing.

It took a little longer to attempt the same trick in the larger house across the road. The first room I tried was the cellar where I'd encountered the Pestilential Presence – now, happily, despatched to its own fell dimension thanks to my blow with the clothcutter blade. There was no sign of any other demonic presence, no stench of rot or brimstone. It was a cluttered, slightly damp basement like any other. The first time I tried circling backwards three times, I stumbled over a paint pot and had to start again, because doing that probably broke the enchantment. Once I'd finished the process successfully, precisely nothing happened once again. I climbed through the house, attempting the manoeuvre in each room, feeling more and more ridiculous all the time.

The last room I tried was the loft where she'd painted. It was maybe my best shot, although I was beginning to think the whole thing was a red herring, another of Sally's jests. Maybe she was watching me from afar via some magical seeing stone, her and her coterie of users laughing uproariously each time I backed into a wall or stumbled over.

The attic, though, was the closest she'd had to an inner sanctum, a private space where she could be herself. This was the room in which I'd deployed the Grafton Projector to reveal her earlier message daubed beneath a watercolour of the Sugar Loaf above Abergavenny in sun-washed blues and greens. That particular picture was still there, leaning innocently against a wall. The other landscapes were just as I remembered them.

Something was different, though. I studied the photographs I'd taken last time on my phone to confirm it. Yes. Sally, it seemed, had recently taken to painting people. Set upon an easel in the middle of the room, beneath a skylight, was a semi-complete self-portrait, the unmistakable features of young Sally Spender, artfully suggested by a few simple lines of charcoal. The likeness was good, I had to admit. Maybe portraiture was her thing.

I set about circling the easel that held the sketch, stepping backwards carefully in case I knocked something and broke the spell. If there even was one.

I completed my circumnavigations and stood in front of the portrait, trying to decide where I should go next, how else I could get in touch with her.

Then, no doubt about it, I felt the rush of magic swirling through the room, sweeping through me like a cold wind from a window that didn't exist. I stepped backwards, one hand going to my clothcutter, just in case. Then Sally's depiction on the canvas blinked once, twice, and the suggestion of her features became animated, the lips curling into an amused grin, her eyes narrowing in disapproval, and she was talking to me.

"You took your time," she said.

"Where are you?"

"I am, obviously, elsewhere."

"But we're talking; this isn't some sort of recording?"

"I'm elsewhere but not elsewhen; think of this as a magical FaceTime call. I've been waiting for bloody ages for you to put the clues together and get in touch. Are you really the finest that the Office has to offer?"

"I mean, you could have left an email address or a phone number. That might have been quicker."

The lines of charcoal moved across the canvas to suggest a laugh. "But where's the fun in that?"

I had to admit, this was cool. We in the Office spent so

long worrying about the dire effects of malicious magic, we forgot about the positive uses. Not just healing people and making the world a better place, but also the fun stuff, the exciting stuff. Sure, why use email when you could talk via an animated sketch?

"Last time I saw you, you weren't doing too well," I said.

"I recovered. It took a little time to unravel that bitch's curses and the effects of the dimension I dragged her to. But I got there."

"Are you fully recovered? It's a little hard to tell through the charcoal."

"Rude. You're seeing a strikingly accurate and beautiful depiction. Yes, I'm my old self again. By which I mean my young self. You, though: the word on the street is that you destroyed the amulet, obliterated what remained of the Sorceress."

"We did. Which, now that I think about it, you should have done when you trapped her in there in the first place. It would have saved some trouble."

I swore I picked out a shrug in those indistinct features. "Perhaps I wanted to see what you did with it. Besides, you know what they say: beware of geeks bearing gifts."

"How do you know, though?" I asked. "The word on what street?"

"It's a metaphorical street, obviously. An event like that – the aether buzzes with it. The grapevine. So, what next? Why do you want to talk to me?"

"Do I need a reason? I thought we were friends."

The features on the painting froze for a moment, like the real Sally was deep in thought on the other end. Like the screen of an app freezing as heavy processing is going on in the background.

"Yes. Sorry. Sometimes I forget how to be … normal. You know, hang out, do stuff. It is good to see you again, even if you are a hated representative of our oppressors. This isn't just a social call, is it, though? You need something."

I gave her an outline of recent events on Planet Danesh.

"The truth is, I still need help," I finished. "There's the Warlock and the rest of English Wizardry. There are weird patches of darkness within the shadows coming for me and books that curse you just by looking at them. There's the foul thing that just attacked me in my sleep and bled me. There's every damned other weird and demonic presence out there. Mainly, though, I need to protect myself from myself, before I blow my own head off in some magical explosion. Last time you refused to help me. I've come to ask again. I don't know where else to go."

Her features softened, and that beautiful face was there. Sally as I saw her in my daydreams. One or two *dream* dreams, too. You don't need to know about those.

"I'd like to, I really would," she said. "I'd like a lot of things to be different, but they're not. I can't help you. I explained last time: the risk to us is too great. Maybe I believe you when you say you're not trying to infiltrate us, but for all I know someone in the Office *is* using you to get to us. We have to be careful; there aren't many of us left, now."

"If you can't help me, then tell me how to find Myrddin. Arthur Stonewall. I know you know how to contact him. The trail of stolen eyes would have led English Wizardry through you to him."

"Danesh, you've literally just destroyed one powerful magical user. You have to see that this sounds a little like you're now gunning for another. What this sounds like is standard Office procedure."

"No."

"What are you trying to do here, Danesh? Who are you really trying to bring down, English Wizardry or the Office? Which side are you on?"

"Does it have to be one or the other? Both need to go sooner or later. I know that. Right now, my position within the Office is useful in the fight against English Wizardry. Once that's done, and if I'm still around, the Office is next."

"Until Hardknott-Lewis sits you down and explains

about the next supernatural threat and asks for your cooperation and compliance. And then the next and the next."

Anger flared within me. "If someone would give me the guidance I need, help me understand my own powers, maybe I wouldn't be so damn dependent on the Office! But no one will, will they? You tried to bloody recruit me into your *Unnatural*, and now you're turning your back! I protected Oliver Auchter and I've protected you. I've magically slain two English Wizardry operatives in clear contravention of all Office rules and at significant risk to myself. I'm pretty sure Hardknott-Lewis knows very well what I am, and for all I know I'll be carried kicking and screaming into Oblivion next time I go into work. I helped destroy the Sorceress and I stopped English Wizardry using the eyes of their victims to find you. What the hell else do you want me to do?"

The sketch of black lines on the canvas suggested a complex set of emotions. Regret. Annoyance. Mostly, amusement. Whether this was because the painting was great art or great magic, I had no idea.

"You're cute when you're angry, you know," the charcoal lips said.

"You can see me through those charcoal eyes, can you?"

"Naturally." She considered me for a moment, the picture pausing again save for the occasional blink. "Look, I get how you must feel, I do. But you're still an Office agent and, not only did you not leave them, you actually accepted a promotion."

"I could hardly refuse."

"Couldn't you?"

"I thought you wanted me to stay on the inside to infiltrate them?"

"I'd prefer it if you left."

"Look, will you help me or not?"

The eyes closed for a moment. I imagined her sighing. Then she said, "Everything you've done ... you're right. In truth, I have relayed it to Myrddin, but I'll speak to him again, pass along your request. And I'll also tell him that I trust you."

"Does he know my name? Does he know I'm Bi Bi Shahzan's grandson?"

"I don't know who Bi Bi Shahzan is, I'm sorry."

"*Was.* It doesn't matter. The point is, Stonewall does. They worked together, fought together. Tell him that. He probably knows, but tell him anyway. Tell him I'm my grandfather's grandson. If the name means anything, Stonewall has to help me."

She nodded. "I will tell him all of that, I promise."

"And then? What obscure and unnecessarily complicated way will you choose to get in touch with me?"

"We'll be in touch. Enough games. Either I'll text you, or, if you're very lucky, no promises, Stonewall may even contact you himself."

11 – The Cloak of Manannan

> Manannan became jealous of Cuchulainn, with whom his wife Fand had fallen in love. He shook a cloak of invisibility of forgetfulness between the two and carried off Fand with himself to fairy-land.
> – A. W. Moore, *Folklore of the Isle of Man*, 1891

That evening, my packing and travel arrangements more or less complete, I slipped inside the wine bar that Zubrasky had suggested. It was a modern, brightly-lit, casual sort of place. It definitely said *friends meeting up for a chat* rather than *intimate date*. The happy babble of relaxing shoppers and workers released from wage-slavery enfolded me as I stepped inside, whispering to me that all was well with the world.

The DI herself was already there, sitting alone in a quiet corner. It was the sort of table where you had a good view of the rest of the room but no one would notice you. Maybe it was her police training kicking in and she was checking the sight lines, and maybe it had been the only table available.

Once we both had our cocktails, we skipped rapidly through the obligatory small talk. She fixed her green eyes on me as she sipped at her brightly-coloured drink. "So, we had a report of someone acting very suspiciously at a couple of addresses on Cathedral Road. Naturally, I thought of you."

"You're normally the one complaining about me talking shop."

"Ah, so you admit it. See how easily I drew a confession out of you?"

"I was checking up on something. I guess I should have informed you what I was up to."

She smiled. "Trust me, we have far better things to

worry about. For the record, yes, it is worth logging your activities, to avoid complications."

She sat back in her chair before continuing. "So, did you find what you were looking for?"

"I did."

"This would have something to do with the mysterious Sally Spender?"

"Do you really want to know?" I asked.

"I'm just checking what this is." She indicated the table, the two of us sitting together, the evening, with a wave of her hand.

There was something about her tone that troubled me. She looked sad, a little beaten down. She was normally effortlessly impressive and professional; now her hard edges had softened a little. Perhaps she'd simply had a bad day bringing the criminals of Cardiff to justice. I wondered, though. One of the things I knew about her from my Office investigations into her past – and which she hopefully didn't know that I knew – was that she'd suffered abuse as a young teenager. Perhaps it explained some things about her, and perhaps it didn't, but as we sat there, I thought I glimpsed a well of sadness in her eyes that I hadn't noticed before. I guess the Zubrasky I normally got to see was the Detective Inspector version, not the off-the-clock human one.

I nodded and looked down to my own ridiculously fluorescent drink. Stirred it unnecessarily for a moment then looked back at her.

"Honestly?" I asked.

"Please. Lying to a police officer is an offence, you know."

"Honestly, if you'd asked me that question a few months ago I'd have said that what I wanted more than anything was for this, us, to be a date. That I regretted using you as a police contact and that I really wanted to get to know you better. Now…"

"Now there's Sally."

"Yeah. I mean, I *still* regret using you and I still would like to get to know you better, but Sally … well, I obviously experience things that I can't tell you about, and that's not a very good basis for a relationship."

"Also, you fancy her."

"I … yeah, I think I do. I'm not completely sure who the real Sally is, to be honest. I'm sure you're mainly amused and relieved, but for what it's worth, I'm sorry."

She smiled a watery little smile that vanished rapidly. "It's okay. I'd pretty much worked all that out. And I was telling the truth when I said things were a little complicated with me right now. I recently broke up with someone, and I'm not ready for another lap around that circuit right now. Honestly, it feels like I never will be. That's partly why I was reluctant when you asked me out. If that was what you were doing."

"Whoever he is, he's an idiot for losing you."

"*She*, but the principle applies."

"We can still get far too many drinks and you can tell me all about it," I said. "Or not, if you'd prefer. We can just do the drinks bit."

Now there was a hint of genuine warmth back in her smile. "I'd like that. Be good to just do fun stuff for a change, no bullshit."

"No bullshit," I promised.

"Won't the lovely Sally be jealous?"

"I seriously doubt it," I said. "She and I …. it would be a bit like a police officer dating a member of the criminal underworld. I don't know how she feels about me. I suspect I'm somewhere on her vague acquaintance-annoyance spectrum, nothing more."

Zubrasky thought about that, her head slightly on one side as she considered me. "My guess is that's completely untrue. If the timing had been different, I'd have said yes, you know that don't you? Don't undersell yourself. A decent haircut, some sharper clothes, one or two jokes that are actually funny, and anyone would be thrilled to have you."

"Now you tell me."

"Don't worry, I'll still be prickly and offhand when we meet up at a crime scene."

"Wouldn't have it any other way. I will also try really hard to reciprocate on the professional help front. As much as I can. Although, since we're being open, I'm actually not sure how long I'm going to be an Office operative."

"Are you in danger?"

"Yes, obviously, but this is more of a matter of … professional advancement. I've decided the Office might not be quite the right place for me."

"Ah. Because the use of unnatural powers is absolutely forbidden by your people and you can no longer live with your internal contradictions."

There was very definitely a sparkle in her green eyes as she looked at me. She'd already worked out what I was saying. Did everyone know my secret? Had they known it before me?

"Something like that," I admitted. "Walking a tightrope gets exhausting after a while. You have to concentrate so damned hard."

"For what it's worth, it sounds like the right thing to do. You have to look after yourself. Although, I don't really understand why you have those restrictions. The police are allowed to use a certain amount of force to prevent greater crimes from happening. Why isn't it the same for you? Why can't you use your powers for good?"

I shrugged. It was a good question.

She took another sip of her drink. "You said you were heading out of town for a while?"

"Yeah, jetting off tomorrow. Well, propellering anyway."

"Is this a holiday? You sound like you need a holiday. Forgive me, but you look like you need it, too. There are great shadows under your eyes."

An unfortunate turn of phrase.

"It's a work thing, unfortunately," I said. "I could do with a break, I really could, but there's some stuff I need to sort out. There are never enough of us to go round, which I'm sure is familiar. But there are some specific people and … things … that pose significant threats."

"To you or to all of us?"

"Both."

"Aha. Well, let's forget about it all for an hour or two."

"Sounds good. Sounds very good."

"And when you're back, let me know so we can catch up, okay? I'd like that. Just as friends. Law-enforcement colleagues letting their hair down after a day's work."

"I will."

"And, wherever you're going, be careful, yes? Don't go getting eaten or possessed or whatever it is."

Why did everyone keep telling me to be careful?

I promised I'd avoid all those things and went to the bar to order another round of cocktails.

The passengers on the flight to the Isle of Man were a mixed bunch. They looked to be mostly business people in their suits, frowning at laptops or reports on actual paper. There were also one or two families making the hop across the Irish Sea for a holiday. A few people maybe visiting family too. I thought I caught a woman travelling on her own, her hair dyed purple, her ears and nose elaborately pierced, glancing at me out of the corner of her eye, but I put it down to paranoia and decided to ignore it.

Landing at the airport on the island was an alarming experience. The plane itself was tiny; it was essentially a van with wings, small enough to be thrown around by every passing gust of wind. Possibly my post-cocktails hangover wasn't helping. The approach involved skimming low over the choppy green waters of the Irish Sea with no land in sight from the passengers' windows. Then, at the final moment, just as we were about to plunge into those inhospitable depths, a line of jagged rocks appeared out of the window and *they* were what we were going to crash into. And then, miraculously, at the last second, we were over green fields, skimming a road and a fence to touch down on the tarmac of the runway. A grim-looking building like an Evil One's fortress stood right next to the boundary of the airfield as we taxied in.

Outside the airport, I was met by an Office operative called Simon. He was tall and thin, with a mop of thick hair despite him being (I'd guess) in his late fifties. He was going a little grey at the temples. He greeted me with a friendly shake of the hand and showed me to his Merc. I'd never met him before, but his name was familiar from emails and MORIARTY case notes and the occasional Office shindig.

His surname sounded local. I asked him about his background as we drove from the airport towards Douglas, the island's largest town.

"Kewin, yeah, it's a Manx name. The equivalent of Johnson. I was born here, went to university on the mainland, Great Britain I mean, stayed there several years, then came back on a posting after the Office recruited me. This was a long time ago. I'm, ah, actually leaving the service soon."

Getting out seemed to be in fashion at the moment.

"Wait, you can leave?" I asked.

He grinned. "Oh, sure, once you've signed all the solemn pledges in blood not to reveal anything."

"What do you plan to do?"

He glanced at me, and I got the clear impression that he'd been planning this conversation, wanted to ask me something.

"Actually, I'm thinking of writing."

"As in ... books?"

"Seen a lot of odd and weird things in my time, as I know you have. I figured they might make for, you know, fun supernatural thrillers. It's something I've always wanted to do."

"Quirk would let you get away with that? Even with the pledges? You may be outside UK criminal law, but you're very definitely within magus law jurisdiction."

He moved his head in a way that suggested it was a good point. "They'd have to find me first. I've found a quiet place in the middle of nowhere I can sit and write. I guess we're a little more relaxed about our folkloric roots on the island; we're not so, you know, *us and them*. And our Keyholder is somewhat … absent. I'm actually not sure what his response would be. I mean, he wouldn't approve, obviously, but if I change a few names and a few details, maybe I can get away with it, especially if I pretend I'm just writing fantasy. I've, ah, actually found a publisher willing to take the risk of putting the books out."

I could only imagine Hardknott-Lewis's response – and Lady Coldwater's come to that – if I suggested such a thing. I also wondered why Kewin felt he was safe to admit this to me.

"Brave of this publisher. Probably foolish, especially if your books are published in the UK. Even if the Manx Office is relaxed, the other regions won't be. They'll stop you, believe me."

"I'm sure they'll try."

"What subjects are you going to tackle?"

A line of motorbikes roared past, five, six, seven of them.

"There's lots of material here on the island; it has its own menagerie of supernatural threats. As well as *themselves*, the *Mooinjer veggey*, the fairies I mean, there's the *buggane*, the *fyonderee*, the black dog *Moddey Dhoo*. Then there are the magical mists that shroud the island sometimes, to keep enemies away. The Cloak of Manannan."

"Manannan being…"

"Celtic god, otherworld king. Manannan mac Lir, son of the sea. It's a long story. In fact, it's several long and contradictory stories. Don't you have Manawydan in the Mabinogi? They're the same figure, if I understand it properly."

My knowledge of the Welsh classics might be patchy, but that name I knew, at least. Manawydan had been the codename adopted by Evan Cornwallis, the first victim I'd come across in the eye collector case. Funny how it went.

"The weather was good and clear for me today when I flew in," I said. "No mists at all."

"Excellent. The island has obviously decided you're welcome." He looked pleased for some reason. "I, ah, actually requested this assignment so I could speak to you about my plans."

"You did?"

"I'm obviously aware of your recent exploits from reading your MORIARTY logs. I thought they might be of more general interest than events on this little place, given the wider changes to British magical culture in play, I mean."

I didn't know what to say to that. "You … want to put me into your books? That's weird."

"Only with your permission, of course. And with anything too incriminating changed."

"*Is* there anything incriminating?"

"No, no. You know what I mean. Personal. I might have to alter a few facts here and there, leave out a few details, the *really* weird and dangerous stuff so people don't get too alarmed."

"People won't believe it's real."

"Most probably won't. That's fine. I plan to put in just enough detail to make people wonder."

Once I'd have said no, absolutely not. The very idea was unthinkable to the secretive and officially insignificant Office. Now, though? Now that I wanted to get out, now that I saw all the damage the organization did, I was pretty comfortable with the idea. In fact, I think I approved of it. Maybe somewhere, somehow, it would do some good. This hidden world needed to be brought out into the open.

"Also," he said, "I am a little worried about, you know, cultural appropriation."

I wondered which culture he was talking about. "I guess only you can decide what's acceptable. Culture isn't an archipelago of isolated islands, is it? Everything's blurred, connected."

He nodded his agreement. "Still, it's a tricky area."

"This is fiction, though, right? Change the details until you're comfortable with them."

"I guess that makes sense."

"You will need to change my name."

"Of course."

"And make me out to be an intelligent, resourceful and deeply sexy individual."

He laughed at that. "Well, I'm still learning the craft, but I'll do my best."

Quirk, though. I'd come to the island to investigate him, although so far as the Office knew, I was investigating the *head full of dark* plot. Here was a chance to combine them both.

I breathed out. "Then, sure, go for it. If you really figure anyone will want to read them. Tell me, though: if you've seen my log entries, you'll know why I'm here. The death of Morris Crossley, the Office operative supposedly consumed by his own nightmares. *Eaten by them*, as one note put it. Tell me about it. Was It your Lord High Witchfinder who carried out the investigation?"

"Yeah, although we all pitched in. I remember it well; I obviously knew Crossley. It seemed like a case of early-onset dementia at first. Terribly, terribly sad, of course, but not unknown. He began to lose more and more of his memories, like there were holes appearing in his mind. He actually said that to me, once. *There are these holes in my memory and the darkness is shining through. I try to plug them, but the more I do, the more that appear*. It's a terrible thing to happen to anyone, but this was different. He had long stretches of lucidity, and at those times he would tell us, insist very forcefully, that he was under attack."

"Did you take his claims seriously?"

"Absolutely we did. We're well aware of the dangers we face."

"The case notes don't mention any investigations into possible attackers."

"We didn't find anything. We did everything we could, we really did. He was one of us, you know how it is. Maybe it shouldn't matter, but it does. We scanned his house and his possessions, picked over everything in minute detail. We traced people he'd come into contact with, followed the threads of all the cases he'd ever worked. We used every means at our disposal. Nothing. If he hadn't known what he was talking about, you'd have assumed he was suffering serious delusions."

"Did you work closely with him?"

"It's a pretty small department. When he was lucid, he was completely normal, talking like we are now, the way anyone would. Politics and football and the weather and last night's TV. But then he'd explain to us in great detail about the malign magic being worked on him. The way something was breaking into his mind, clouding his memories, locking parts away so he could no longer reach them, filling his waking hours with his own nightmares. He was losing himself, and he knew it."

"Do you have recordings?"

"There are transcripts. We were still getting to grips with modern technology at the time. Still are, to be honest."

"Can I see them?"

"I don't see why not. We have boxes and boxes of handwritten case notes that we need to digitize."

"What happened to his house? The notes on MORIARTY don't mention it."

"It ... ah, wait."

We were driving beneath a canopy of overhanging trees, something like the Tintern Abbey road I'd recently blasted down. There was a little white stone bridge ahead, the road passing over a stream maybe. The trees and the bridge were festooned with streamers and colourful scraps of paper. The sign, as we approached, read *Fairy Bridge*.

As we passed, my companion declared out loud, "Good morning, fairies!"

I looked at him. He seemed to think his behaviour was perfectly normal.

"You, ah, just attempted to communicate with a race of dangerous supernatural entities," I said.

He shrugged as he drove. "Everyone does that here. It's a quaint old custom for most people, a bit of fun. Obviously, you and I know better. It does not pay to antagonize *themselves*, trust me. Better to maintain the détente."

Again, I wondered what Hardknott-Lewis would say. I let it pass.

"So, his home."

"Yes. It was demolished."

"Because you wanted to exorcise the site, make sure no one ever lived there again?"

"Actually, as I recall, it was to make way for a housing estate."

"What happened to all his possessions? I presume they passed to his descendants or other family members?"

"Morris was the last of the family line. His family had been witchfinders for generations, but it stopped with him."

"Any idea why that was?"

"I guess he just never found the right person. Being in the Office makes it hard to start a family, right? Especially if you can never tell them what it is you do all day. How you got those wounds or curses or whatever it is."

"Yeah, can be tricky," I admitted.

"There were some cultural artefacts, as I recall. Morris was a bit of a collector. Nothing very valuable, folk art and that. There were quite a few pieces that had been passed down to him by his forebears."

That was interesting. *Folk art* is one of the euphemisms people employ when they should be saying *dangerous magical objects* but they've been brainwashed by the Office into thinking such things are childish nonsense.

"What happened to those? Was any of it dangerous?"

"It was all low-level stuff. They went to the museum in Douglas. It has a collection of such things. The rest, I guess it was sold off. The Witchfinder might know."

"Quirk?"

"Witchfinder Quirk, yes."

"Quirk who seems to have disappeared off the maps. There has to be a way to find him, get in touch with him."

"He'll turn up. He covers a lot of ground, scattered islands all around the coast. We don't see him for months on end sometimes. He can be a bit ... scattered himself, to be honest."

I wondered about that. It sounded to me like a useful cover story if you were, say, secretly the head of English Wizardry.

"Do you suspect his mind is going as well?"

"Not at all. He's as sharp as a sharp thing. It's just ... he's one of these people who gets so occupied with higher matters that he forgets to eat or get dressed."

"I'd really like to talk to him, get his insight into the Crossley case. He may have ideas or see connections that didn't reach MORIARTY. We must have some idea where he is."

"There's his house. It sounds a bit daft, I know, but I suppose you could go there, try knocking on the door. He often doesn't answer his phone, or even remember where he's put it. Or that he has one. So far as I know he's not on the island, but I've seen him get so absorbed in arcane research that he fails to notice the days and the weeks slipping by. It's possible he might be holed up in his library surrounded by his books. I've been meaning to go check myself."

I wondered if Lady Coldwater knew about that. If she had any idea what tomes were to be found in his private library.

"Is Gwenn Altandubh around?"

"Do you know Gwenn?"

"A little. She was in Downing Street with Quirk on the day I was there with Hardknott-Lewis. The day of the attack."

"She's not on the island. I think she's somewhere in the Channel Islands, dealing with a Nixie sighting. They're quite a common problem in coastal areas. Interestingly, they're cropping up more and more farther south. Climate change maybe."

"Is it possible Quirk is with her?"

"I doubt it. She'd have mentioned it even if he hasn't."

I tried a different tack. We were nearly in Douglas now, driving down a steep hill with the town laid out in front of us. "Do you know if blood was ever taken from Morris?"

My companion threw a puzzled glance at me at that. "I don't recall it being mentioned. When the bad thing happened, he was taken to hospital; I suppose they might have taken some for matching. Why?"

"Just looking for patterns."

"Do you see any?"

I let out a breath. "Honestly? Only if I squint and turn my head sideways."

12 – Artefacts

I shall curse you with book and bell and candle.
– Sir Thomas Malory, *Le Morte d'Arthur*, c. 1469

I checked into the safe house the local Office had provided – actually a rather nice converted crofter's cottage, with white-painted stone walls and a thatched roof held on with weighted ropes. It sat alone amid the purple heather, nestling within rolling hills. The views across to the shining waters of the Irish Sea were incredible as the sun spotlit them. Distantly, a line on the horizon, I could make out the hills and mountains of what I presumed was the Lake District.

Inside, the place had all mod cons. The large stone fireplace was now merely decorative as under-floor heating and heat-pumped radiators kept the interior toasty. There was a good coffee machine and a well-stocked fridge. It would do nicely. I dropped off my bags, then drove the hire car into Douglas, the capital.

Weather happened quickly on the island. By the time I'd parked in town, the wind had picked up. Waves were leaping over the iron railings of the promenade as I strode by, like they were attempting to grab hold and pull me in. I made a mental note to be polite to the fairies; they probably had aquatic cousins. The gale streaming in off the Irish Sea, blasting into my face, smelt of salt and seaweed. It was invigorating, the cold spray enough to wake me up, clear away the cobwebs clogging up my mind. Not as much as a decent cup of coffee, obviously, but it was something.

The museum lay a little way back from the seafront, at the top of a short, near-vertical road. I showed my Office card at the reception desk and was met with a nod of recognition, as if this was an everyday occurrence.

"Will you be wanting the, ah, folk collection?" The lady behind the desk asked. Her eyes were blue behind her gold spectacles. She smiled in the friendly, helpful way that, say, librarians are supposed to have. She wore a black knitted shawl wrapped around her shoulders, held together by a fine piece of Celtic knotwork.

"That's it," I said. "I presume you don't have it all on display?"

"Oh no, there's far too much of it, I'm afraid, and some of it … well, you know. Best it's kept under lock and key, isn't it dear? But obviously you'll be safe."

She seemed to know all about the Office and what we did. Small islands for you, I guessed. You didn't get that in Cardiff or London. I followed her through the halls of the museum, past the towering skeleton of an Irish Elk, its splayed antlers wider than I am tall and its skull eyes empty, past displays of rusting swords and stones marked with Ogham and Viking runes, then through a secured door marked *Staff Only*. A flight of narrow stairs led to a storage basement. Once the fluorescent lights had flickered on, I was greeted with rows and rows of steel shelving, lined with plastic crates marked with serial numbers.

"The hidden collection is this way," my guide said, striding around a couple of corners to another locked door. I very definitely caught a flicker of something magical coming off it, a whisper in my mind. Someone had woven strong wards into the entrance. Was it her, this friendly lady who'd brought me down here? Was she a member of some Manx chapter of the Pale Sisters or whatever witches they had here? I should have quizzed Lady Coldwater more closely.

There were fewer objects held in the inner sanctum; the crates were marked with individual names rather than the numbers of an indexing system. She led me to an orange box marked *Morris Crossley*.

"It's all here, everything we had from him."

"Do you remember the case?"

"Not really. Your colleagues handled everything. Very polite, they are."

"You didn't know Crossley?"

"Terribly sad what happened. A thing like that upsets everyone. To take your own life; it's a hard thing to understand, especially when you have so much to live for. So very sad."

"The artefacts in your hidden collection ... have they ever given you any trouble?" I asked.

"Oh, all safe and sound in here, dear. If you need to take anything out, well, you obviously know best, but I'd be careful."

"So, you have had problems."

"It's all sorted now, isn't it? Take your time, I'll make sure no one else comes down while you're working. The doors all open from the inside so you can't get locked in, but make sure they're shut fast behind you when you're finished, won't you? Don't want anything ... unfortunate to escape. Not after the last time."

With another sweet smile, she left to return upstairs to greet the museum's visitors.

I set my thaumometer down and then, wary of long-term exposure after the events in Cardiff, placed my electronic equivalent of the Lady's Feynman's Thaumic Exposure Tube next to it. The box containing Crossley's special artefacts revealed several items of interest, each carefully wrapped in brown paper. There were long, hollow bones with holes drilled into them – musical instruments, I presumed, the sort you probably played while dancing round the fires at Beltane. There were highly-polished stones with smooth holes in them, something like the weights holding down the thatch on my cottage. There were carved figurines of little, ugly humanoids. There were fishbone combs and silver rings.

Then I unwrapped something that I very definitely *did* recognize. It had the same twists of straw and twig and rag lashed together with twine and with the same hollowed-out nubbin of wood for a head. A doll like the one I'd retrieved from Jamie Tavish's house. As before, the thaumometer picked up nothing, which no doubt explained why the local operatives had dismissed it. If the doll was sorcerous, it was of a sort the device couldn't pick up or wasn't attuned to. Either that, or the doll had run out of potency. Wary of both more splinters and, indeed, more magical curses, I didn't touch it directly. I sniffed at it – I couldn't bring myself to lick as the librarian might – and my inner thaumometer did pick up the brief flicker of an enchantment.

I took photographs from every angle, using a pencil to flip the doll over. There was a hole in the back of this one's head, too, but no nest of tiny black spiders came boiling out. I peered inside using the light from my phone, but I couldn't see anything. It sounded hollow as I tapped it with my pencil. To my untrained eye, the doll looked like the work of the same hand as Jamie's, but I'd send the pictures to the Lady and see what she could make of it.

A few minutes of this and the first of the little line of LEDs on the FTET device glowed. This device, at least, *could* detect something coiling off the doll. I did *not* want to have the black clouds back in my eyes; I wrapped the doll back up in its paper and returned it to its box so I could put some distance between it and myself.

Back upstairs, the doors locked safely behind me, I stopped off at the reception desk. The same lady was on duty.

"All sorted, dearie?" she asked. "Did you find what you needed?"

I replied quietly so that no one else would overhear. "The objects down there; I realise this is a museum and you're trying to preserve historical artefacts, but there's one item in the Crossley collection that I'd recommend destroying. The crude doll. At the very least it should be moved to somewhere more secure. Away from people."

Once again, she studied me through her spectacles, her magnified eyes wide. "Oh, don't worry about us. We're quite used to handling ... delicate objects. Some of our objects, well, let's just say they're never going to go on public display and leave it at that. Come back if you need to see anything else, won't you?"

I drove out of Douglas heading for my secluded safe house in the hills. The weather had changed dramatically once again: the wind had dropped completely, and the island's uplands – *the mountain* as my contact in the Office had called it – was now shrouded in either a thick fog or maybe a low cloud that had gotten itself snagged on the peak of Snaefell, the highest point. Within a couple of kilometres of the town centre, my car was completely wrapped in it. I felt like I was driving across the sea bed at the bottom of a murky ocean. The twisting mountain road had steep drops down one side, which made for an exciting journey when you could only see a few metres ahead of you. I took it slowly, ignoring the idea that Manannan had decided I wasn't to be trusted after all and had thrown his cloak over the island to lure me to my death.

Whether he had or not, I reached my cottage safely. There were some tyre tracks in the gravelly patch of mud next to the house that I didn't recall seeing before. Probably nothing; someone turning round on the narrow mountain road. The doors and windows were as intact and locked as I'd left them. Inside, coffee brewing, I sat to log all that I'd learned. It turned out the old stone cottage had an excellent internet connection. I couldn't tell if Thomas Quirk was reading my notes, but if he did, he'd hopefully be reassured that I hadn't come looking for him.

I also sent the pictures I'd taken of the poppet directly to the Lady, in case she didn't bother to look at my MORIARTY logs. She hadn't responded with any further information about the first doll; perhaps the second would allow her to work something out. For all I knew, it was typical of Manx folk magic.

I was more and more intrigued by the matter. Distraction as it was supposed to be, I was becoming convinced there was something to it. It looked more and more like a coordinated attack, a campaign of revenge. Both Jamie Tavish and Morris Crossley had suffered significant mental afflictions, consistent with the workings of a destructive curse. They'd also both been operatives in the Office from long-standing witchfinder families. Jamie had reported blood being taken from him; I needed to know if that was true of Crossley, too. I made a MORIARTY note to pursue that next. The case was troubling, especially given my own recent experiences, but it at least made my cover story more convincing.

I had the notes that the Crow had given me, and I could access everything pertaining to the case in MORIARTY. There were, in fact, three Office operatives named in the Crow's notes as possible connections to the case: as well as Jamie Tavish and Morris Crossley, there was a Scottish agent called Belinda Carraway. Her connection with the case was far less clear; she'd reported some ill effects consistent with a curse, but she was very much alive and kicking. I vaguely knew her; she was an Adept working out of the Edinburgh office. We'd talked briefly about a possible kelpie attack on some children in mid-Wales. I read through the Crow's notes on her again. The parallels were not conclusive, the connections forced. My guess was that she wasn't connected after all. She'd had a few troubles, the sort anyone could have, and had managed to work through them. That was all.

Scanning through recent entries from Edinburgh brought something else to my attention, though. Another Scottish operative had investigated the apparent suicide of a man called Anders Kropotkin. He'd thrown himself out of his third-floor tenement window in the middle of the night – which, okay, was tragic, but wasn't necessarily of interest to the Office. It was the statements Kropotkin had given to the police that had caught the Office's attention and now caught mine. Kropotkin had talked about shadowy presences in his room at night, demons coming for him, attacking him. Lurid, traumatic episodes when he'd awoken to find himself pinned to his bed by *some vicious bastard creature* that was delighting in torturing him. Nightmares becoming real and coming for you in the night.

Yeah. I knew what that was like.

Then there were the hellhounds. Some weeks before the fateful night, he'd reported being pursued through the alleys and streets of Edinburgh by a pack of huge black dogs. *Red eyes and dripping fangs and growls that made my bones shiver inside me.* I thought back to the *Cŵn Annwn* that the Crow had described, the hounds that came loping through the otherworld portal in the pub's beer cellar. I found myself glancing out of my own window into the gloom of the fog, half-expecting the island's own version of the black dog to be there, red eyes peering in at me. There was nothing.

Had Anders Kropotkin been the victim of something genuinely malicious, or was he as delusional as the local police reports assumed? They'd referred him to the local medical services, but it appeared he'd refused to cooperate, claiming it was *no use, the wrong sort of help*. The police reports said he'd been suffering night traumas and possibly psychotic episodes for several weeks, but also that he'd had a record of such problems stretching back to his childhood. I could only sympathise with that. According to one report, he also had a history of inflicting abuse upon his partners, although no charges had ever been brought.

Unlike Jamie Tavish and Morris Crossley, Kropotkin had never been connected with the Office in any way. There was no mention of any other Kropotkin anywhere in the archives. These differences suggested Kropotkin wasn't connected to the matter I was looking into – but then there was a police note from a month before he died when he'd claimed that someone or something had drawn blood from him in the night. Held him down to do it.

That little detail was enough to make me stop and stare at the screen. For a moment, ice ran through my veins. I'd thought fleeing Cardiff for a time might give me some safety, but then here was Anders Kropotkin, hundreds of miles away in Edinburgh reporting the same experience. How were we connected? So far as I knew, I'd never met the man.

I added another MORIARTY entry, tagging the Crow to draw his attention to the matter. Perhaps he'd see connections to Kropotkin that I didn't. Scotland, though. That might be useful. Wherever Quirk had vanished to, Alba had to be one of his likelier destinations. The country was extremely well-furnished with islands. Its coast was thick with them. If I needed an excuse to track Quirk into the Highlands, then Belinda Carraway and Anders Kropotkin between them provided it – not to mention Charles Raneleigh, the supposed victim from thirty years ago, also mentioned in the Crow's notes.

For now, I set all that aside. I needed to pursue Thomas Quirk, and his possible role as the Office traitor and the shadowy head of English Wizardry. I'd sent him a few inconsequential questions about the Crossley case but had received no reply. There was his house on the island I could go and look at – doing that might draw Quirk out, elicit some response from my enemies.

I hadn't unpacked, but I was too exhausted to do so. I could live out of my suitcase for a time. The bed looked fluffily comfortable, and I was soon able to confirm that this was, in fact, the case.

I drifted off to sleep. It seemed like only a few moments passed before the baying, alarming spectres that haunted my dreams were back with me.

13 – Witches in the Dream House

The remit of magus law is wider than that of any one criminal legal code, as the Office of the Witchfinder General covers several mundane jurisdictions. Jersey, Guernsey and the Isle of Man, for instance, while passing all their own parliamentary acts, are still subject to magus law when it comes to more supernatural matters. This constitutional curiosity might well become the spark for political dissent and unrest – if it weren't for the fact that the truth is deliberately hidden from the public gaze.

– Mirabelle Glee, *Magus Law*, 1982

This time, as I ran headlong in breathless panic through the dark forests of my nightmares, my brain conjured up something new.

I emerged into a clearing. The nameless horror pursuing me was behind me somewhere, lumbering between the boughs, whispering my name, but I was suddenly in the open air. The grey sky overhead was thronged with heavy clouds, flecked with the stationary squiggles of black birds. The leafless branches of the trees were silhouetted against that gloom, leaning over me as if trying to grasp me. I was aware of the chortling of water. The light from it reflected brightly on the boughs in shimmering patterns, as if I stood upon a little wooded island in a lake.

A woman dressed head-to-toe in black knelt on the ground in front of me. There was a small graveyard there, I saw – or, at least, two mounds of earth, side-by-side.

The soil of the broken ground was reddy-brown. The heads of animals and birds had been set upon poles in a circle around us. Their eyes were open, watching, and despite the lack of a body they grunted and cheeped and screeched in a grim cacophony. Small stones marked the two graves, no words carved upon them. They were decorated not with the usual flowers but with the twig and twine dolls, four of them in a little line. Once again, although the scene was vivid, I knew on some level that I was dreaming, and I marvelled at the way my brain picked random events from my real-world experiences and jumbled them up to form these dreamscapes.

There was another example of this: the kneeling woman looked up, and it was the purple-haired passenger from the aeroplane. When she opened her lips, she had far too many teeth. A mouth full of cruel, pointed teeth. For no particular reason, I was aware of a hammering pain in my finger, the one in which I'd picked up the splinter. That was odd in itself: I didn't usually feel physical sensations in my dreams, but this was impossible to ignore.

I expected some bestial growl to come from the crouched woman's throat when she spoke, but instead I heard the voice that had come to me before, in my dreams in Cardiff.

Oh, you've come too early. The grave isn't ready for you yet. Our little witch hunt has barely begun.

Disquiet wormed its way through me. There was something unusually solid about this dream: there was a realness to it, a muddiness. The air was icy cold; I could feel it in my bones. The black birds – some sort of crow – croaked and cronked away in the sky, although they weren't moving. They might have been sketched up there in ink.

Who are you? I asked. I knew the question was pointless. This figure was the confused conjuration of my troubled imagination, nothing more. Wasn't she?

My name? Perhaps you will find out before the end. Perhaps you won't. It doesn't matter.

She looked amused at her words. She turned back to the little grave, straightening the four dolls as if they were sad, drab playthings. One, in particular, looked tatty and faded.

Why are there four dolls? I asked. Perhaps there was a logic to my dream-self's questions. Perhaps this was how my mind was making connections, working out what was going on. I only knew of two poppets: the one that had affected Jamie Tavish and the one from the Museum, Morris Crossley's.

Four of the six, the shadowy woman said, not looking up at me. One missing, one removed, but there's room for you, too. Always room for you, witch finder.

I could make no sense of the numbers. What did I expect? Advanced mathematics wasn't going to be one of my subconscious brain's strong points. My conscious brain's, come to that. From somewhere nearby, like it was directly behind me, a quiet little voice giggled, but when I snapped my head around there was nothing there.

Why six? I asked.

Because there were six.

Am I one of the six?

Of course not! But you could join them. I'd make an exception for you.

I was about to quiz this invented phantom further, try to pull some order from the tangle of clues buzzing around in my mind, but the other formless, nameless horror – the one that had pursued me through the woods of my nightmares for years – chose that moment to appear at the edge of the clearing. I felt it rather than saw it: a baleful dread washing through me, obliterating all my other thoughts.

I stepped backwards away from it. I soon reached the water. This was an island, but not in a lake. A stream split in its course, leaving this isolated patch of earth cut off from the wider woods. Was I safe? No. The looming entity drifted easily across the water. I ran in blind panic. In the illogical way of dreams, the water was no longer there, and hard ground was beneath my feet.

I ran and ran, headlong into the dark of the woods. However much effort I put into escaping, the patch of deeper darkness within the shadows grew inexorably nearer. I could never outrun it. In a moment, I felt it right behind me, a grim presence. Its slow, patient breathing. I threw a glance behind me, and it was right there, its face the scribble of lines, its arms reaching for me. I tripped on some tree root or stone and the ground flew up at me hard. The taste of dirt filled my mouth.

I flipped myself over, panicky, terrified. I tried to backstroke myself away, but it was no use; the shadow leaned over me, blotting out the trees and the sky. It would have me now. It reached down, its hands tendrils worming their way into my mouth, my ears, my eyes. I felt it inside me like frost spreading across the surface of my brain. My last conscious thought was to ask myself what happened to you if you died inside your own dream.

Then, unexpectedly, gloriously, there was light. A green-white glow shining out through the nearby trees. The shadow over me fell backwards from that effulgence, shrinking from it. I found myself back on my feet. Shading my eyes against the radiance, I tried to pick out who or what was making it – and what it signified in the symbolic language of my dream.

I caught sight of a figure there. Details were hard to make out; it was like staring into a low sun on a winter's day, the last blaze of light above the horizon. The figure shifted, and there were horns there. No, antlers, deer antlers. A human figure with horns sprouting from their head. Or were they the branches of the trees? The light grew brighter still, and I could no longer look at it. The shadow that had pursued me, lumbered after me down the years, was tiny now – shrinking to a dot or receding into some distance.

The light blazed brighter still and brighter, consuming me, and I could only close my eyes from its brilliance.

This time, when I woke up, at least I wasn't drowning in my own sweat. Dread and relief, darkness and light, fought within me as my chest laboured. I felt like I'd run a marathon. Or at least, how I imagined I might feel if I ever attempted such a thing.

I lay on my bed. A grey light was filtering through the curtains. Morning was coming. My head pounded with solid thumps of pain, making it hard to think straight. Think anything.

I sat up, holding my head in my hands as I tried to form ideas. Despite the natural immunity I'd fondly imagined for myself, I hadn't recovered from my contact with the two ensorcelled dolls and the *Book of Shadows* after all. At least there was no blood this time. But, if anything, I was worse. The visions I'd just experienced were so much more vivid, all my senses engaged, whereas my dreams were usually more distant. Silent black and white films. And then there was that quiet giggling. The memory of it sent a shiver up my spine; I seemed to still hear it, but it wasn't coming from anywhere in particular. It wasn't a *sound* as such; it was in my head rather than in the air around me.

I'd been fine the night before, though. Slept peacefully and long. What had happened? Travelling had knocked me out of my routine, maybe. Then the chuckle came again, and this time it very clearly came from outside my head, from the room. As in Jamie's house, the sounds brought a sickness with them, an alarming vertigo. Visions of leering, laughing wooden faces assailed me. I knew what was going on: if anyone else had been in the room they would have heard nothing, seen nothing. This was my magical ability flaring.

The whispering giggle had come at me from several directions, bouncing off the hard stone walls, but as I turned my head it seemed definitely loudest over by the fireplace. The hearth was unused: a decorative pile of fir cones lay in the open grate along with a spray of desiccated thistles in a little vase. That was where the sound was coming from. A sound and something else, too. A sense of wrongness, like the taint of decay in the air. I'd tasted that little tang before.

Despite the hammering in my head, I rose and approached the fireplace. The whispering susurrus grew louder, more insistent. I moved the vase of thistles and crouched down to peer up the chimney using the light from my phone. The stone of the hearth was cold on my cheek. The flue above me contained only darkness, a breath of icy air. I reached a hand up the chimney, feeling the rough old stones of the walls.

After a moment, my hand brushed against something soft. There was an item wedged up there. Maybe it was something old, a bird's nest that had fallen down. I certainly hadn't checked the previous day. I scrabbled for it with my fingertips, lying in the grate to reach up far enough.

A sprinkle of old soot cascaded onto my face as I snagged the item. It came loose in a shower of dust and grime. Crouching there, brushing the black carbon off it, I recognized it immediately. There could be no mistake.

Jamie Tavish had had one and Morris Crossley had had one, and now, it seemed, I had a doll all of my own, too.

I let it lie there in the hearth, peering innocently up at me. I thought about my nightmare, the three dolls in a line on the shoddy little grave. Had I known? Had my subconscious already worked it out? Taking a tissue – being very careful not to touch the doll – I brushed away some of the grime on its twigs and straws. The cuts of the ends were sharp. They looked fresh to me.

I spoke to the poppet as if it were alive. "How on Earth did you get there?"

It had affected me, I was sure of it. Was I the intended victim or was this an older magical crime? I took pictures, flipping the doll over using the iron poker set in the fireplace for show to take more. There was another little hole drilled in the back of the doll's head, but this time I didn't delve around in there. Once I had good photographic evidence, I slapped a holdfast onto the poppet to neutralize it, then sent the images I'd captured to Lady Coldwater to see if she could identify any similarities to the other dolls. We were getting quite a collection.

Wrapped in my dressing-gown, I stepped outside for some fresh air. The misty chill felt good on my brain, dissolving the fug. I rang the local operative who'd fetched me from the airport the day before. I got through after only a few rings. Despite the remoteness, I had a good signal.

He sounded bright and cheery on the phone. "Danesh! Good morning. I trust the bugganes didn't come for you in the night."

I was in little mood for banter. "Tell me," I said, "who knew I was staying here?"

My abruptness sobered him up a little. "What's happened?"

"Nothing. I'm fine. I just need to know."

"Well, me, obviously."

"Who else?"

"Anyone in the Office who knew you were coming, I suppose. We always put visiting operatives up in the cottage. What's this about?"

"Just making sure I'm covering all the angles. So, Quirk would have known, for example?"

"If he knew you were coming, then yes, of course. Are you sure you're okay? Things can get a little wild up there."

I assured him again that all was well. "Do you get many visitors?"

"One or two operatives from the mainland, that sort of thing."

"Have any of them ever reported anything unwelcome taking place in this house?"

"Nothing at all. Look, I'm coming up there. Something's happened."

"No need. I'm heading out soon. Tell me, though, who has a key to this place?"

He exhaled audibly. "Well, you know how it is. This is a small island, not a whole lot of crime, especially out of town. We hold keys, obviously, but, ah, there's also one under the little stone statue of the Three Legs of Mann around the side of the cottage."

"Anyone could have got inside?"

"I suppose. Why would they, though?"

"There's no alarm."

"There's never been any need."

"Is there any word from Quirk today?"

"Nothing. I did find out one thing, though, after our conversation."

"Go on."

"Morris Crossley did have blood taken from him. In the hospital, when they were trying to save him, for tests and blood typing, but also ... before that."

"What do you mean?"

"I went through my notes. Something he mentioned. I dismissed it as delusional at the time, but he claimed someone or something had come for him in the night, drawing blood from him. There was no way to prove or disprove his claim. Except…"

"Go on."

"I should have connected the two pieces of information. Later, when he was given a post-mortem, the histopathologist mentioned a small lesion in the skin on the inside of his elbow. Someone had drawn blood from him."

"You said the hospital took blood. It could have been from that."

"Wrong arm. Their incisions were very clear on his other elbow."

"Thanks. I'll be in touch."

I rang off. Interesting. I stared out of the window for a moment, letting that slot into place. Once I was properly caffeinated and had eaten a couple of the croissants they'd thoughtfully provided, I got dressed. Not unpacking my case had been the right thing to do. Once I was ready, I threw it into the boot of the hire car next to the bagged and frozen poppet, then left to take a quiet look around Thomas Quirk's house.

I'd assumed that Thomas Quirk's equivalent of the Crow's nest at the top of the Black Tower of Cardiff

Castle was going to be something equally impressive and forbidding, some ancient stone keep looming over one of the island's towns. I'd glanced at the visitor's leaflets that someone had thoughtfully left in the cottage and noted that the island had at least two fortresses that looked the part. One, Peel Castle, was even the focus for Moddey Dhoo hauntings, so presumably the location of another bridge to the otherworld. It sounded perfect for a Witchfinder General keen to keep an eye on things. It was even set upon a small islet of its own connected to the main island by a causeway – certainly the sort of place that the Lord High Witchfinder of the Isles might hang out. It was reassuringly ancient, too, stretching back to Viking days, a king with the unlikely name of Magnus Barefoot having built it a thousand years previously.

The ancient castle wasn't inhabited, though, none of its timeworn buildings even having roofs. It had to be a wild and windswept spot and, perhaps understandably, Quirk and his forebears had chosen to live in an altogether more comfortable and rather grand house in the west of the island.

The place looked deserted as I arrived. It was a grey stone mansion set back from the road, decorated with faux crenulations. It was very definitely a house, though; I assumed proper castles generally don't have nice big windows on the ground floor.

I parked the car up a little lane a good way down the road, then crept up the house's driveway on foot. The trees surrounding the building lashed and roared as if furious at my intrusion. There were no other vehicles to be seen, no sounds coming from within, no lit windows, no smoke coiling from the chimneys. There was no mention of the Office of the Witchfinder General anywhere, but the name of the house was provided on a brass plaque next to the grand arched front door. *Slieau Whallian*, it said: the name in Manx, according to my brief web search, of a hill where they'd once sent suspected witches rolling inside spiked barrels – spikes pointing *inwards* – to see if they survived.

My guess was that they didn't.

I used the elaborate iron door knocker to announce my presence. The sound boomed through the house. If Quirk was inside, I would maintain my pretence of being a visiting operative hoping to consult with him. If he were secretly the head of English Wizardry – or even the Warlock himself – then I was taking a considerable risk. I was relying on him also preferring to play his role of Office Keyholder for now, perhaps because he couldn't know who I had told about my visit.

Although, in hindsight, perhaps I should have informed *someone*.

No one came to the door. I rapped again, then put my ear to the wood, trying to detect anybody moving around inside. There was nothing. I walked around the perimeter of the building, peering into windows, knocking on any other doors I could see. Again, nothing. There was nobody around. Perhaps Quirk really was out of the country, and he lived alone, I knew. Just to be sure, I ran thaumometer checks round the property as I explored. Nothing registered a flicker.

The doors had good locks and there was a modern intruder alarm fitted. I dealt with both in the usual Office fashion, disabling them so I could slip inside without anyone knowing. No way of knowing if other, more arcane security systems were in play. If someone came, I could maybe still maintain my pretence as an honest Office operative, concerned for the well-being of my superior. Maybe they'd even believe that.

I stood in a dimly lit hallway, an elaborate mosaic floor beneath my feet. A wooden staircase led upwards, and there were three doors leading deeper into the house. There was a grandfather clock to one side – perhaps every Witchfinder was given one when they became a Keyholder – but this one wasn't ticking. No one had been around to wind it for several days at least.

My feet were loud on the hard floor and the wooden staircases groaned and creaked as I climbed. Like the library in Cardiff, the house was impossible to move around in quietly. The house barely looked lived in; it was grand, but there was no clutter, little in the way of decoration or softness. Quirk had lived here – there were supplies in the kitchen – but the impression I had was of a house used as an occasional shelter rather than somewhere comfortable to live. The air throughout was cold; colder than the outside. The sort of deep cold that houses accumulate after long periods of neglect. Perhaps Quirk, ascetic as he was, his mind on higher matters, didn't bother with anything so trivial as keeping his dwelling warm. Maybe he just threw on more old jumpers and continued.

And maybe, just maybe, he was a creature that didn't feel the cold.

I found one room on the first floor that clearly *had* seen considerable use. His study. There was a desk piled with books, and there were shelves into which many more volumes and rolls of paper had been crammed. It was all a long way from the sort of ordered tidiness favoured by Lady Coldwater – or Hardknott-Lewis. There were pads of scribbled notes upon the desk, next to an elaborate brass light with a built-in magnifying glass to allow the reader to pick out tiny details. That was at odds with my half-formed vampire theory: somehow, I doubted that powerful undead entities suffered from decaying eyesight as they grew old. It didn't mean that Quirk wasn't under the command or even enthralled to such a being, though.

A map had been unrolled on the desk, its curling edges held in place by a couple of books. It was old, with little depictions of sailing vessels upon the water and an elaborate compass rose providing orientation. A coastline filled most of the map. I peered in closely, trying to work out where this was in the modern world. Some of the place names were familiar, although the flowery script was difficult to read. I picked out Whitby, Newcastle, Berwick and, further north, Edinburgh. North-eastern England and south-eastern Scotland. What had he been looking at? Various books lay strewn upon the desk, several of them open and some with words and phrases underlined in pencil. Lady Coldwater would not have approved. I tried to read some of the sections Quirk had picked out but couldn't make much sense of them. There was also a piece of tracing paper by the side of the map, with a series of radiating lines and dots drawn upon it in pencil, like a depiction of a crooked star.

I skimmed a few of the titles on the bookcases. They were, perhaps, the sorts of volume you'd expect on the shelves of a Witchfinder: bestiaries and grimoires and the accounts of hauntings. Quite a few atlases, including a good selection of older, Victorian imprints. Several of the books I recognized: there was a copy of the *Malleus Maleficarum* there, and nearby, a copy of Samuel Bedfellowe's *The Old Ways*, that founding text in English Wizardry's mythology. The fact was odd in itself: the Crow had once told me that only twelve had ever been produced, and that the seven copies of it held by the Office were in London. Was this an unlicensed copy, or had Quirk simply borrowed it for his researches?

Was this the library of an English Wizardry fanatic? Or simply of a Keyholder in the Office of the Witchfinder General?

A lot of the books covered the legends and the magical fauna to be found upon the various islands under Quirk's control and there were also, I noted, quite a few on the subject of demons, revenants and the undead. Perhaps this was simply an area of special interest for him: Hardknott-Lewis had told me that he and Quirk had tackled the wight on the Isle of Wight. I took pictures of all the bookshelves and the desks, trying to capture the names upon the spines of the volumes, thinking to at least let Lady Coldwater know what I'd found. Then I moved on.

My thaumometer still hadn't registered a flicker. There was nothing there. I was about to slip outside again when my gaze picked out a low little doorway nestling beneath the rise of the staircase. A cupboard? Perhaps – but then I noticed the array of serious-looking locks. That was odd. I padded over and put my ear to the door. Once again, I heard nothing.

Repeating my usual trick to get through troublesome locked doors, I peered inside. It was not a cupboard. A flight of wide stone stairs led into the house's basement. The air down there was even icier than upstairs. There was the sound of something ticking or dripping. Using my phone, I looked around for a light switch and found a rusty metal box on the wall, connected to cables strung down into the darkness on a series of nails. The switch resisted briefly, but once I'd pulled it down, lights glowed from below. I had to duck my head to get through the low doorway – presumably Quirk, the tallest of the group of Keyholders as I recalled – would have found it even more awkward. Had he gone down there much? It seemed unlikely; the damp-smelling cellar was no place to store books.

I descended the stone steps. The stairs turned through ninety degrees to reveal a large, vaulted room. Bare light bulbs hung from the ceiling by their own wires, picking out every detail in a cold light. I'd been right to come down here: in the centre of the room, dominating it, was a large, oblong stone box.

A sarcophagus.

There could surely only be one reason for having a tomb like this in your basement. It wasn't a feature most people added to their homes. There are a lot of ridiculous untruths circulated about vampires, some of the myths encouraged by the Office to make the creatures seem more ridiculous. Garlic and holy symbols don't trouble them, and they don't start smoking and smouldering in direct sunlight, although they prefer to avoid it. Hardknott-Lewis had been correct; they can't turn into bats or wolves at will, but they can control such creatures – and any others, including most humans. They are fearsomely strong and impossible to kill.

Was it possible that the shadowy Warlock – ancient, powerful – was a vampire? It made sense in a lot of ways. It was also a deeply-troubling notion. On the few occasions that we in the Office had tackled them – so I'd read – the task had taken a large team of operatives, and even then, the outcome had usually been suboptimal. As Kerrigan had once put it, we generally finished in the silver medal position in such fights.

Was Quirk this vampire? Perhaps. Hardknott-Lewis had insisted that he trusted Quirk and that the two had tackled numerous undead and revenant entities over the years. Perhaps Quirk had been corrupted, transformed at some point. My doubts about the Crow surfaced again. It was he who'd sent me off alone into the wilds, insisting that the *head full of dark* matter was unrelated to the Warlock. But was it? It felt more and more like a trap I'd wandered into. Or, even if Hardknott-Lewis was to be trusted, perhaps Quirk had been creating a cover story, deflecting any suspicion that he was the Warlock.

Unlike the tomb in the Welsh graveyard I'd recently visited, this one was open, an ornate wooden lid heaved to one side, leaning against the tomb. From my vantage point, I could see that the sarcophagus was empty. That was good news; I was not going to come out on top in a fight with a vampire.

I hesitated briefly, drew my Office handgun, dialled up the anti-vampire round (which had a tendency not to destroy the creatures so much as to irritate them), then continued warily down the steps. Nothing leapt at me from the shadows. Nothing moved. The tapping sound was a drip of water in some distant corner. Thick dusty cobwebs hung from the high corners of the vault, adding nicely to the ambience.

I crossed the room to the heavy stone tomb. Carvings covered its sides. I studied them, moving my phone around to form shadows and pick out details. I thought I could discern ships and some sort of vast tentaclly sea-creature, but it was difficult to be sure. The marks were very worn and indistinct – a fact that was odd in itself. The sarcophagus had clearly been outside for a long time. Vampires do generally have their tombs that they return to in order to slumber and regenerate, and they do need some of the earth of their homeland within for the dark magic to work – but such tombs are never outside. Where had this one been, and why was it now here? I peered inside, lighting up every corner. A sprinkling of dried, grey earth coated the bottom. That was diagnostic; this was the lair of a vampire. Dread trickled through me; if Quirk returned now, I was trapped. No one knew where I was. I had little or no chance of surviving. And vampires, I knew well, could slaughter you easily without turning you into one of their own kind. That was an act – an *elevation* – that they saved only for the chosen few.

Another odd detail caught my eye: the lines of scrape marks across the stone floor, leading into the corner where the dripping sound was coming from. I crouched to study them. They looked recent, none of the dust that was elsewhere on the floor collecting in the grooves. It looked like the heavy stone sarcophagus had only recently been dragged into the centre of this vault. I followed the lines on the ground. In the shadows of the far end of the room, there was a slope leading upwards that ended in a set of large, horizontal doors. I must have missed them as I circumnavigated the house. Their existence made sense, though: there was no way this heavy stone tomb could have been brought in through the house. Most likely this was cellar access that had been added to allow garden machinery to be wheeled in and out, or perhaps, before that, for coal deliveries to be tipped into a bunker. I assumed the original designers of the house had not intended the chute to be used to lower in the sepulchre of a vampire. I crept up the slope and tried the outer door but it was securely locked.

I turned back to survey the room. What was going on here? If Thomas Quirk was, in fact, a vampire, perhaps even the Warlock himself, why had he moved his tomb and done so recently? Because he felt safer here than wherever he'd been? I thought back to the study upstairs; the maps and the books. Maybe they were part of his plans. Was that Quirk planning how he was going to move the sarcophagus, perhaps under the cover story of carrying out his Office duties?

Treading carefully, acutely conscious of the crawling

sensation trickling down my spine, I crossed back to the staircase and left the vault. The house remained quiet, but now I had the sensation it was watching me. That it was aware of me, crawling around within it. Maybe it would let me leave, and maybe it wouldn't.

I returned to the study. There had to be answers there. Now I picked out a little cup of grey-brown dirt next to the thuribles and flask. It looked like the same soil as that in the tomb. Had he been trying to find the right formula so he could manufacture more? Was that how it worked?

I picked up the square of tracing paper again. I'd suddenly worked out what they might be. The texts he had open mentioned various place names, but some were in Latin and some were incomplete. Each dot had to be a place on the map. He'd drawn lines based on directions or clues he'd found, then worked out where they intersected. I placed the tracing paper over the map and spent a few moments orientating it so that each dot lined up with an identifiable location. Once I found the correct alignment, I peeled back the paper to see what lay beneath the intersection point.

An island off the coast of North east England. Lindisfarne. I was vaguely aware of it; indeed, Hardknott-Lewis had mentioned it in passing five days previously. As he explained, it was tidal; cut off when the water was high, reachable on foot or by car at low tide. The question was, why had Quirk identified it? One obvious possibility was that the tomb in the cellar had come from there – but why? If he was a vampire and this was his tomb, surely he would know its location? Unless this was some sort of long-lost ancestral mausoleum that he'd been searching for? That was a possibility. Or it might be an alternative lair he was creating for himself. I knew that the actual stone of the tomb didn't matter so much as the sprinkling of home soil within – although vampires liked their traditions.

Another possibility, of course, was that he was innocent and researching potential supernatural threats. I needed to be sure either way.

I left the deserted house, deactivating the holdfast on the alarm and briefly reactivating the sesame so I could slip through the outer door. Nothing tried to stop me. I strode away, trying to ignore the troubling notion that the dark windows in the house's façade were eyes watching me.

But, Lindisfarne. The North-eastern tip of England. It was a fair way from the Highlands, but it was close enough to Scotland for my leads on Anders Kropotkin and Belinda Carraway to provide useful cover. It didn't seem like Quirk was on the Isle of Man; maybe I'd find him, or at least some clue to his whereabouts, on Lindisfarne.

14 – Moddey Dhoo

"A hound it was, an enormous coal-black hound, but not such a hound as mortal eyes have ever seen. Fire burst from its open mouth, its eyes glowed with a smouldering glare, its muzzle and hackles and dewlap were outlined in flickering flame. Never in the delirious dream of a disordered brain could anything more savage, more appalling, more hellish be conceived than that dark form and savage face which broke upon us out of the wall of fog."

– Sir Arthur Conan Doyle, *The Hound of the Baskervilles*, 1902

I was nearly back at my car when my phone buzzed with an incoming call. I expected it to be my Isle of Man contact checking in, or maybe Zubrasky – or perhaps even Sally – but instead, Lady Coldwater's voice rang out as I picked up. She had the tendency to talk VERY LOUDLY into telephones, as if the distance required you to shout or the technology was unreliable. I held my phone slightly away from my ear as we conversed.

"Danesh? Are you alive?"

"I am. Shouldn't I be?"

"Shut up and listen. I've been studying the doll images you sent me and comparing them with Jamie Tavish's poppet. This is more and more troubling."

"Why so?"

"The Crossley doll you found in the Museum confused me at first. I'm convinced it isn't local. Such artefacts are rare on the Isle of Man, and they generally have components from the sea and the mountain woven in. Mermaid's purses and herring bones; scraps of seaweed and sprays of heather. There was none of that.

No, this was not crafted by a local spellworker at all."

"You said you compared the dolls."

"I've studied the images closely, as best as I could without having the actual objects. I'm convinced that the knots and tangles were tied by the same hand."

"Then ... whoever made them had read the *Book of Shadows*."

"Or they were taught by someone who'd read the book."

I thought about that. "Which also means that these apparently random killings really are connected."

There was a brief pause on the other end. "What made you think they weren't? That's why you're looking into them."

I decided to trust her. I felt very alone on that windswept little island with Quirk's house nearby. "Honestly? I didn't really believe that they were. The truth is, we were using the case as cover for a completely differently investigation."

"*We* as in you and Hardknott-Lewis."

"Yes."

"I assume that what you're really doing is attempting to destroy English Wizardry?"

"That's the plan."

"I see. Nice of you to tell me that now, boy."

"I should have said. In any case, I'm beginning to think the two cases are intertwined."

"You see a connection between English Wizardry and the dolls? Tell me what you mean."

"Partly I'm still wondering about vampirism, given the bloodletting," I said. "Or the connection might be looser; maybe the operatives with the cursed dolls were getting too close to English Wizardry, and the Warlock sent one of his minions to stop them."

"Have you located Thomas Quirk?"

"No sign. Which may or may not be suspicious."

"Do you think he's responsible for these attacks? Can't you track his movements?"

"I don't know if he's to blame. Perhaps. He moves

around a lot, and not even his staff know where he's gone to half the time. It is strange that he's vanished at this precise moment."

The librarian let out a breath. "The more I look into these dolls, the nastier I find them. They're bloody malicious. The photographs of the third one you sent; where was that from?"

"That one was from my cottage. My bedroom."

That made her pause for a moment. A car whooshed past, rocking the car.

"You were attacked," she said.

"I believe so, unless it was another old doll. I mean, it looked fresh to me, but I am staying in an old Office safe house."

"From what I could see, the work on your doll was cruder," she said. "If I had to guess, I'd say it was assembled in a hurry."

"Yeah, that was my thinking."

"Did you touch it?"

"I did not."

"And it was in the room you sleep in."

"Yep."

"Did you experience vivid nightmares? Assaults that seemed very real."

"Oh yes."

"From what I've discovered, these dreams you've experienced; they may not be dreams at all."

"What does that mean?"

"There are many planes of existence and bubbles of reality. You know this. Most dreams are just that: dreams, inside our heads, but sometimes it's possible to be ... transported. Or external forces can intrude. We can find ourselves in shared, shadowy realms. It may feel like a dream because we're asleep, but it isn't."

"The dolls do this?"

"They may. You saw how incomplete the book is. The incantations are obscure. For this to work, the doll would have to be keyed to you, though. You had blood taken from you here in Cardiff, yes?"

"I *bled*; I don't know for sure if any was taken."

"Assume it was. Assume the blood was then used in the incantations woven into the doll planted in your house."

"By whom?"

"I don't know. From what I can see of the Tavish doll, there are dried blood stains inside its head, too. There's a pattern there. Were there similar marks inside the Crossley doll?"

I thought back to what I'd picked out by the light of my phone. "There were stains of some sort in there."

"Hmm. Have you destroyed your poppet?"

"It's deactivated for now. I want to bring it in for analysis. Have you get anywhere tracing the book's history?"

"I've made some progress. That's really why I'm ringing you. You'll recall I said that Alis Treacle started the Blood Sisters?"

"I do."

"The copy of the *Book of Shadows* we hold: I'm sure now that it was hers. This was her original spellbook containing the spells and curses she learned or discovered. The way they work are idiosyncratic, some not reproduced anywhere else in these exact forms. The handwriting, too, points to her. It changes, though, becoming harder and harder to read, as if she compiled the volume over a long period of time, perhaps as arthritis or some other affliction set into her fingers."

"That's no great surprise if this was her private notebook."

"No, but the history of the book is interesting. I uncovered a diary entry from her granddaughter saying that *she* had produced a copy of the book. This was fifty years after Alis's murder. The granddaughter knew the book was dangerous, knew it was being hunted, and she made her own copy before the family lost it."

"Who was she worried about? The witchfinders?"

"Partly. The book would have acquired a reputation; lots of people would have been trying to get their hands on it. I told you it was in a private collection in Suffolk until Oxford University recovered it. I know a little more now; it came into the possession of an antiquarian and self-styled Wizard called Samuel Deville. He was only distantly familiar with sanity, but he took his pursuits seriously. He kept the book very securely, let no one see it. That's why it's so decayed. It was turned in on itself for a long time. No doubt it affected him, too, deepened the poor man's madness."

"Did he have children?"

"He had no family. His researches consumed him, killed him in the end."

"Then Oxford University acquired the book, and then you did."

"The original book's timeline appears to be complete. It's hard to be sure, but the copy taken by Alis's granddaughter seems like the more likely source of the current attacks. We don't know what happened to that reproduction. Interestingly, there are also certain mistakes in all three poppets that I've studied. I mean, identical mistakes in each, knots in the tangle that differ from those described in the original book."

"As if the granddaughter mistranscribed the original."

"In all likelihood, whoever is making the modern dolls is working from that copy of the original."

I stared into the trees to one side of the road. Their high branches lashed in the wind. There were nests up there, black masses against the grey sky. "Do we know much about the Treacle family line?"

"The records are very incomplete. They would have tried to stay hidden. They would have been very protective of this book, certainly at first. It wasn't supposed to exist, making it dangerous in more ways than one. There has to be a good chance they wouldn't have let others make their own reproductions. It would have been passed down from generation to generation, a family secret, a dark heirloom."

"How many children did Alis have?"

"One daughter. She may have been pregnant with a second when they came for her. There was at least the one granddaughter, and then after that things get hazy. There are plenty of people around with the surname Treacle, but I haven't been able to place them into Alis's family tree."

"Will you keep trying to track down what you can?"

"Obviously. I've spoken to my contacts in the Pale Sisters, too, asked them to scour their libraries and archives for clues. We may find nothing; this enemy is very good at hiding in the shadows. The animosity between the Pale Sisters and the Blood Sisters obviously doesn't help. If this is some descendent of Alis, then we're largely in the dark. We also don't know what they're capable of."

"Is there anything in the book to do with mirrors?"

"Why do you ask that?"

"Just a theory."

"Someone like Alis wouldn't have had mirrors, or anything shiny or reflective. Their lives were muddy and drab, which I think emphasises how rare and precious her book must have been to her. As you saw, the text is degraded, but I saw no mention of mirrors."

"Okay. Thanks for all that. I appreciate it."

"Just promise me that if the attacks continue, if things get worse, you'll withdraw and get help, yes? We don't want you ending up like Jamie and the others. Or like your mother."

"You have my word," I said, and rang off.

I drove back into Douglas, deep in thought. Instead of returning to my cottage, I picked out one of the traditional hotels lining the promenade and checked in under a false name, giving them one of my small collection of alternative credit cards as payment.

The décor was shabby and faded, the carpets worn. There was a crack in the tall mirror on the wall by my door. Still, it would do; the place was quiet and no one knew I was there. Once the door was locked behind me, I used a different identity to book a flight to the mainland the following day using the hotel's reluctant WIFI. The plane was nearly fully-booked, it being a Monday morning, but there were a few single seats left. A couple of hops would take me to Edinburgh, from where I could head south for Lindisfarne.

I at least had a good view overlooking the sweep of Douglas Bay. The tide had fully withdrawn by now, revealing a wide stretch of sand and shingle and seaweed. People were running, walking their dogs, strolling by, their hair streaming behind them in the wind. In the bay, upon a little outcrop of rock, there was a small castle-like building for some reason. Odd. I made sure to stay back in the shadows, keep myself hidden behind the net curtains as I watched, just in case. I couldn't detect anyone surreptitiously studying my chosen hotel or waiting for me to emerge, but no point taking any risks.

I used the time to update MORIARTY, making no mention of the doll I'd found in my room or of my discoveries in Quirk's house. I did note my intention to head for Scotland the following day, carefully citing Anders Kropotkin, Belinda Carraway and Charles Raneleigh.

I ordered room service – somewhat dried-up sandwiches with shreds of lettuce that apparently constituted a salad – and then lay on the bed fully-clothed, trying to get some rest.

It was by the pricking of my thumbs that I knew something wicked this way was coming. Well, okay, my finger, not my thumbs. The one with the splinter began suddenly to throb sharply as I lay in the darkness. I really had to get it looked at; most of the time I didn't notice it, but it had been bad enough to intrude into my confused nightmare the previous night. Now it was hurting again. The room was dark apart from the glow of the promenade lights outside. I'd fallen asleep despite my intention to stay awake. I reached out to switch on the bedside light, see if I could see the splinter well enough to pluck it out with some tweezers, when a long, mournful howl echoed through the night. It was bestial, unearthly, falling through grating discords that made the hair on my neck bristle.

My phone said it was two o'clock in the morning. I rose and peered outside. The road and the promenade beyond were deserted. The colourful strings of lights strewn from lamppost to lamppost swung forlornly in the breeze. The sea beyond was a darkness, an emptiness, as if half of the world had been bitten away.

Then I saw that the road wasn't deserted. Stepping from the shadows between parked cars, a huge black dog padded into the middle of the road. It lifted its head to release another plaintive howl. The creature was huge; it looked more like a small horse than a dog. Its eyes were unmistakably red. The creature was casting around, nose in the air, sniffing something out. My thaumometer was on a table next to the window. It buzzed three times to alert me. I lifted it to study in the glow from outside. The device was flickering rapidly; high levels of thaumic activity were nearby. In truth, I didn't need the device to tell me that. I could feel the presence of magic in my gut.

Cŵn Annwn, Hardknott-Lewis had called the dog, but the correct name here, as I'd learned, was *Moddey Dhoo*. The name changed but the creature was the same: a huge, night-black spectral hound. Was it a portent of death, or did it appear for some other reason? Was it one individual or a type of entity? I didn't know. I also hadn't heard of it manifesting in such a public part of the Island's capital. Maybe people had seen it but had never mentioned it. People, in my experience, were good at ignoring anything troubling, anything that broke their safe, mundane world-view.

I stepped back into the shadows of my room to pick up my clothcutter knife from the bedside table. If the creature *was* summoned, there had to be a chance the blade would open up a tear in reality through which it could be sucked. Going outside to meet such a creature was not something to be done lightly, but I had my duty as an operative of the Office. More than that, I didn't want to see any poor innocent late-night reveller being ripped to shreds, especially not because I happened to be in the area. And, maybe I could learn something from the creature.

I picked up my handgun, too. I'd experimented with slipping it under my pillow like in the films, but the thing had made the bolster even more lumpy and uncomfortable than before, and I'd become a bit paranoid about triggering it as I tossed and turned. I dialled up the clothcutter round and returned to the window to see if the black hound had slunk any nearer.

The dog wasn't there; the road lay deserted. Nothing was moving. I peered down to the foot of the hotel, imagining the creature stalking me, sniffing at the hotel's door, creeping down a back alley.

The sound of a single, gentle footstep from behind me was accompanied by the swish of fabric. I turned in alarm. There was someone in my room. A person, not a hellhound. How? I'd obviously locked the door and checked there was no other way inside. I was aware of my thaumometer, ticking madly in my hand, registering high levels of magical energy. The smouldering ball of magical fury I carried within me blazed brighter.

I stepped back against the wall and flicked on the small pencil light I carried in my pocket. It picked out a woman. The cracked mirror by the door was behind her. Of course. The expression on her face was a snarl, and she was panting heavily as if she'd exerted herself in some great effort.

She threw herself towards me.

15 – Blood Sisters

Deep into that darkness peering, long I stood there
wondering, fearing,
Doubting, dreaming dreams no mortal ever dared to
dream before;

– Edgar Allan Poe, *The Raven*, 1845

I recognized her immediately. It was the purple-haired young woman on the aeroplane. The figure crouching by the grave in my dream vision. Damn; why had I been so stupid? I'd assumed my brain had randomly placed an unimportant stranger into my imagination, but that wasn't it at all. Too late, a few pieces of the puzzle slotted together. *This* was my attacker. This was the maker of the dolls. Despite all my efforts at secrecy, she'd followed me to the island, tracked me to this room. How? Too late again, I worked that out, too. The splinter. It wasn't throbbing randomly. The fragment of ensorcelled wood or bone or straw that I'd picked up from Jamie's doll was active. I'd carried it dutifully around with me, and by it she'd know exactly where I was at all times. And what was this? A direct attack because I was getting close? Because I'd invaded Quirk's inner sanctum? Whatever the truth of it, she'd clearly dispensed with the slow, subtle curse of her dolls to suck me into my own nightmares, and nor was she bothering to conjure up Night Hags to torment me.

She'd come herself to kill me.

"Who are you?" I asked. "Did the Warlock send you?"

Her voice was young. There was no mistaking the hostility in it. "You shouldn't have interfered, witchfinder. You should have let the dolls do their work like all the others. Killing you directly is satisfying, but it's too quick. Far, far too quick. You should have suffered long."

"Why are you doing this? Why did you kill Jamie Tavish and Morris Crossley?" I didn't mention Charles Raneleigh, as she couldn't have killed him; she wouldn't have been born at the time.

"I told you; this is a witch hunt. What did you think was going to happen?"

"I'm not hunting you. I'm trying to stop any more killings."

She looked amused at my words as we faced each other. "You misunderstand. The tables have been turned. This is not a hunt *of* a witch. This is a hunt *by* a witch. Oh, I wasn't sure about you; there's something in you that made me wonder. It's too late now. You know about my little dolls and you know about me. You have to die. Whatever you really are, wherever your heart really lies, you're still a witchfinder."

She lifted her hands and began to move them in rapid circles, describing complex patterns in the air. I'd seen that sort of thing before; this was a spellcaster preparing to throw an incantation at me. I could feel the power building in the room, like I was standing in a gathering electrical storm.

I tried to step forwards to incapacitate her, arrest her. I couldn't move. Some glamour she was working was preventing my legs from working. Instead, I tried throwing questions at her to distract her. Maybe I could even talk her down, find out who she was, discover something about the Warlock. Then again, maybe she *was* the Warlock. The possibility sent a chill of alarm up my spine.

"You stepped through the mirrors to get to me, didn't you?" I asked. "Just as you did the others. That was why Jamie had painted over the reflective surfaces in his house. Why are you doing this? How do you even find your way through the aether? It's too easy to get lost."

She ignored me. Her hands moved rapidly, the wince of exertion on her face. Whatever she was about to throw at me wasn't going to be good. I had my Stebsen's Ward reinforced belt on, but somehow, I didn't think that was going to save me, given that it never did.

"The hell hounds," I said. "Are they yours too? Are they some sort of backup plan to attack your victims if you fail?"

Again, she ignored me, her attention all on her spell. I could see the effort of it on her face. What had been her original intention? To send me mad by exposing me to the cursed doll, just as she had Jamie and Morris Crossley? Another apparent suicide of a troubled witchfinder? She was taking a risk attacking me in a public hotel rather than the seclusion of a remote house. She'd have to be sure of finishing me off, and she had to do her work quickly before escaping.

I tried one more time. "How did you get hold of the *Book of Shadows*?" I tried. "Alis Treacle's book?"

That was the wrong thing to say, judging by the look of fury that passed across her features. She knew the name, though. Alis meant something to her. Clearly, though, I wasn't going to get anywhere asking polite questions. I had to switch tactic. Dropping my torch, I lifted my gun, dialling up the holdfast round with my thumb on the knurled wheel, hoping to incapacitate her. Steadying my aim with my other hand, I fired.

The crack of the gunshot was piercingly loud in the enclosed space. There was no way I could miss – except that she swatted the bullet aside mid-air with a disdainful swish of her hand, barely breaking the rhythm of her movements. She scowled as if she really resented the inconvenience. The round thudded into the nearby wall. Would people come running? The hotel was quiet but a sound like a gunshot was surely unknown here. I prepared to fire again, the standard round this time, but another wave of her hand – the motion once again worked into the actions of the spell she was weaving – sent the gun clattering to the corner of the room. For a moment my hand was ice.

Her spell, meanwhile, was now a fizzing, spinning orb

197

of black energy between her hands, lighting up the room in its purple glow. There were glimpses of faces in it: the screaming, tormented features of people trapped in there, flashing in and out of visibility. This was foul sorcery. Okay. So, she knew I was an Office operative, but my hope was that she didn't know of my magical abilities. My own power was there inside me, coiling faster and faster. It was all I had. The dizzying rush of vertigo swam through my head. The power of it was alarming, threatening as before to consume me.

I had a moment. I gave her one last chance. She clearly had much greater control over her magical powers than I did; if I threw my magic at her, there was every chance I'd destroy both of us.

"You're about to commit a grave magus law crime," I shouted. "Stop this and we can talk. Please."

There was hatred on her face as she laughed at my words. With a dramatic movement, she threw her arms wide to hurl the hissing orb of darkness across the room at my head.

Acting instinctively, I held out my hands to ward off the attack. But I did more than that. Something within, some instinct, took control. The magical power flared within me, rising to meet her attack, rising to defend me. As before, it felt like I was exploding, or throwing myself off a high building. As before, the fury within expressed itself as red light and heat, flaring from my outstretched hands, just as it had when I'd slain Peter Warder and Thomson Fulger. This unknown woman was to be my next victim.

Except, this time it felt different, too. This wasn't an uncontrolled blaze of fire. Somewhere in that maelstrom, a part of me was in control – barely in control – tempering what I was doing. I threw my power at her, but also, I held some of it back. The spell I'd unleashed met hers, and there was a moment when the two streams of force met, clashed – and held. The spitting, fizzing sphere of malevolent energy hung in the air in front of my eyes, but it was caught. It came no closer.

Every corner of the room was lit by its purple and red fire. Through it, I could see my attacker's face. See the shock and confusion registered there. She'd had no idea I was capable of such magic – which was fair enough as I hadn't either. I moved my hand slightly, unleashing the tiniest amount of extra force, and it was enough to tip the balance. The seething ball of energy flashed towards my attacker. She screamed and was hurled against the door with a heavy thump. For a moment, she was consumed by the magical conflagration, then the fire died, and we were plunged into near darkness.

By the glow of the outside lights, I could see that she was moving. She was still alive. That was good – I hadn't magically slain another person – but also bad. I focussed on my magical power again, readying it for use to protect myself again. Attack her again if I had to.

She worked her way to her feet, an indistinct shape in the gloom. Her voice was hoarse, rough-edged as she spoke. "You'll pay for that, witchfinder. You'll regret the day you did that."

I found my torch on the floor near my feet, scrabbled it up in time to see her lurch towards the tall mirror on the wall near the door. She worked more magic with a rapid flick of her hand, a spell that I felt as much as saw. The oblong of the cracked mirror became limned in a blue glow. At the same time, I found I could now move my legs. I threw myself forward, hoping to tackle her, restrain her, but I wasn't close enough. She half-climbed, half-fell through the mirror into that shadow domain. I heard a cry, as if she'd met something unexpected through there, but it cut off immediately.

I shouted after her. "I'll find you, and I'll stop you. Tell the Warlock I'm coming. I'm coming to destroy you all!"

Whether she heard my words or not, I had no way of knowing. When I reached the mirror, it was cold glass, nothing more.

I didn't sleep any more that night. It took me half an hour of careful excavation into my own flesh with a needle and then a pair of tweezers to pull out the splinter. The wound stung sharply as I rummaged around in there. A red drop of blood welled from the spot as I finally held up the sliver of wood. It had been deeply embedded, almost like it had burrowed its way into my flesh. It didn't look like much: a tiny wedge of black. I threw it into the bin. If the thing was still active and trackable, my attacker could follow it to the landfill or the incinerator.

I lay back and listened to the sounds from outside. No more dogs wailed in the night. At four in the morning, a heavy mist rolled off the sea and a foghorn began to sound: a vast, low, mournful sound, baleful as the death-cries of some deep-sea behemoth. It was warning ships of the dangers of the island's rocks, but to me it sounded like the voice of Manannan as he threw his cloak over the island. I leaned on the sash window staring into the night, the icy cold air on my face. Was it heavy enough to stop planes flying? Was I going to be trapped here? The distant lighthouse across the bay blinked at me: six flashes, then a long pause, then six more. A lone car crept its way along the promenade, its headlights two cones of solid white in front of it.

When the first grey ghost light crept off the eastern horizon, I phoned my local contact. The raucous lamentation of the first gulls provided an accompaniment to our conversation. Kewin's voice was fuzzy, like I'd woken him up. Which, given the early hour, I probably had.

"Danesh, are you okay? Where are you?"

That was a bit of an odd question. Did he know I wasn't at the cottage? Had he come looking for me?

"Tell me," I said, "do you have the means to check the names of airplane passengers coming to the island?"

"What … yeah, we have an arrangement with the authorities. It's completely against GDPR regulations, but fortunately we're exempt from them. Which flight are you interested in?"

"Mine."

There was a pause while he thought about that. "Are you saying you were followed here?"

He sounded genuinely surprised. Maybe he was playing his part well, and maybe he genuinely had no idea about the attacks upon me. I decided to assume the latter. If he was going to write these books of his, depend on my cooperation, it was surely unlikely he was some sort of double agent or English Wizardry shill.

"It's possible. One of the people on the flight; I've seen them again."

"It's a small island."

"Not that small, trust me."

In the background, I could hear the faint clatter of computer keys.

"MORIARTY says you're leaving today," he said.

"Heading for Scotland, yes."

"You're finding your connections?"

"I think so. Still putting the case together. Do you also have sight of the passenger list for the Liverpool flight this morning?"

"Can't be sure who's going to check in, of course, but I can see who's booked. I assume you're looking for the same name on both?"

"I doubt they'll be on my plane going back," I said, "but it's worth checking. How long will it take? I need to dash to the airport soon."

"Give me half an hour."

"Thanks. But, ah, you won't see my name on today's manifest."

He didn't sound particularly surprised. "You switched to a fake ID."

"It seemed wise, given what's happened."

"What has happened?" he asked. Again, he appeared to be genuinely interested, genuinely concerned for me.

"I promise I'll fill you in on all the details if and when this situation resolves itself," I replied. "It might make for an interesting book if you ever wanted to write it."

"Okay, well, I appreciate that. And take care of yourself, okay? Come see us again some time. The island really is beautiful when you're not being pursued by vicious magical entities."

I was going to thank him and hang up. Instead, I said, "Oh and about Quirk. If he shows up or makes contact, will you let me know? Quietly, I mean. As in, unofficial channels."

"That sounds like you're suspicious of him."

Maybe I should have kept quiet. But if Quirk had sent my attacker in the night, it didn't make much difference now. "I can't be sure, but I do think you should be wary of him. I mean, we all need to be constantly wary, right? Once I know for sure, I'll obviously let you know. But … watch him, okay? And if things go badly for me, if I drop off the radar, say, and don't come back, go and look in his house. Take a team, and look in his cellar."

"You went inside. What the hell did you find?"

"Maybe it's nothing. I don't want to get you into any trouble, put you at any risk, but if I disappear, promise me you'll do that, okay?"

"Sure. And maybe I'll go take a look even if you don't disappear."

"Right. Quis custodiet ipsos custodes, right?"

"Exactly so, Danesh. Exactly so."

I showered and changed, then braved the hotel's restaurant for a cooked Full English breakfast and some depressingly weak coffee. I figured that three cups were the equivalent in caffeine terms of one normal one. The place was quiet; save for an older couple who weren't talking and a sales executive type in her crumpled blue suit sitting alone, there were no other guests. Nobody paid any attention to anyone else, and the waitress spoke only the bare few syllables necessary to find out what I needed. I wondered what they'd heard in the night, what they'd made of the attacks upon me. Nobody mentioned it. Perhaps they assumed someone in one of the rooms was watching a trashy movie.

I packed my bags, settled the bill and left. I wasn't going back to the cottage in the hills. My plan was to head directly to the airport, get off the island before anything else happened.

As I fired up the hire car, my phone buzzed to let me

know an email had arrived. My local Office contact had pulled out the passenger lists of my two flights, just as he'd promised. The names on the outbound list were all unknown to me, apart from that of my own fake ID. The inbound list, though, contained my real name – as well as one other that I knew.

My contact had done better that simply giving me a list of names, though. He'd also downloaded images from the airport's security cameras, pictures taken as we walked across the tarmac and into the airport's baggage hall, each tagged with the passenger's name via facial-recognition software.

There could be no mistake: the other name I recognized and the young woman with the purple hair who'd come for me in the night were one and the same. I wondered where she was now, whether she was still on the island. Most likely not; she clearly didn't need to resort to mundane public transport to get around.

That gave me pause for thought: why had she bothered to take a flight at all, when she could step between the worlds using mirrors? Perhaps the sorcery required to pull off the stunt was gruelling and dangerous, to be used only *in extremis*. Or perhaps she hadn't known where I was going to be sleeping and had pursued me in the real world so that she could hide the doll in my room in order to weaken me, tip me over the edge. Perhaps you needed to be familiar with both ends of your aether-walk before you attempted the journey. She'd tracked me after I'd visited Jamie's house, drawn blood from me in Cardiff, lashed up a doll, then come to plant it near me. In the image, she had a small rucksack thrown over her shoulder. Was the poppet in there? Had it been acting on me even as we flew across the Irish Sea?

But, if she didn't know where I was going to be sleeping, didn't know which particular mirror to step out of in the night, then that meant, so far as I could see, that she wasn't Office at all. She didn't have access to MORIARTY and wasn't, seemingly, under the orders of the Warlock. She hadn't been sent by anyone in the Office.

Or was this some elaborate bluff to throw me off the trail? I turned it over in my head, then gave up.

Mainly, I was wondering how it was that a woman called Alis Treacle, a witch horribly abused and murdered by my antecedents in the Office of the Witchfinder General in the seventeenth century, had managed to turn up on my flight to the Isle of Man here in the twenty-first century.

16 – The Winter Tree

One can only wonder why the Reverend Pates'
intricate and detailed cartographical designs were
accompanied by a text so wilfully difficult to
decipher. The usual assumption among antiquarians
is that he didn't wish his parishioners – or, more
likely, his ecclesiastical superiors – to fully
comprehend the pursuit to which he devoted so
many years of his life. One can only lament the loss
of his accompanying cipher book when one sees,
for instance, a map covering, if the title is to be
believed, "Parts of South Wales, Gloucestershire,
Herefordshire and the Shadow-woods of Western
Fairy Land." Similar sketches cover many areas of
the British Isles, for Pates was well-travelled.
Certainly the known geography of recognizable
areas is accurately rendered, and the Greenways
that connect to the fairy realm are clearly marked
and described. Alas, the annotations that describe
how to effect travel to the other realm are
indecipherable. One can only marvel at such
injunctions as "walk with eyes closed, the frozen
bell held aloft and rung with constancy." This
under a scribbled heading that suggests that, by
these means, the practitioner may achieve "The
Opening of the Way."

– A G Smiles, *Comments upon The New, Complete
Map of Fairyland*, 1879

I took the direct road back to the airport, the one we'd
driven along two days previously. At the Fairy Bridge,
feeling uncomfortable as though I was betraying
something, but not wanted to take any risks, I called out

to greet any of *themselves* that might be listening with a cheery 'Good morning!' You did not want to antagonize the little folk. There were a few other cars on the road, and I wondered if the passengers in them were also following the ritual.

There was no response to my greeting, but on the other hand nothing calamitous happened to the car as I drove. I figured that was good. I glanced in the rear-view mirror to be sure – and caught a glimpse of something. The road there is lined by tall trees, green fields beyond them, but in the shadows and the tangle of branches and twigs, I saw something move. At the same time, I felt the fizzing surge in my gut that told me something magical was occurring – just as it had when Alis Treacle had stepped from the mirror to attack me.

I thought about putting my foot down hard and getting away from there. Reach the airport, fly away from this island. But, the hell with it, I wasn't going to run. I was going to take the fight to them, whoever they were. Was this Alis coming for me again? Or was it common to feel the stirrings of something supernatural when you crossed the bridge?

I pulled into the verge, made sure I had all my usual Office equipment with me, then climbed out of the car to walk back down the road. Three or four cars roared by; I hoped they would think I was nothing more than an early morning tourist taking a look at the fairy bridge. I glimpsed the flicker of movement up ahead again. Branches were moving behind or in front of others, as if something was shaking them or pushing through them. There was, however, no wind that morning; the trees around me were still.

Was it some large animal like a deer perhaps? Except, I happened to know from my local guide that there were no deer on the island, just as there were no badgers, squirrels, foxes or snakes. Although, weirdly, there were wallabies.

This wasn't a wallaby.

I saw it again: dappled shadows moving against the darkness. There was something in the trees by the side of the road near the fairy bridge, something large. I walked nearer, and it receded, stepping deeper into the tangle of branches. Except, how was that possible? This was no large wood; there was only a thin line of trees between the road and the grass and brackeny scrub of a field. I stepped off the tarmac and between the boughs, hoping to catch a glimpse of whatever or whoever it was. As I crept forwards, conscious of the snapping and rustling of sticks and leaves beneath my feet, I drew my handgun. Hopefully no one whizzing by in a car would see the crazy armed guy creeping along the verge.

I stepped forwards … and forwards. Instead of thinning out, the trees grew denser about me, obscuring my view, making it harder to see where I was. How was that possible? I stopped mid-stride, listening, confused. I could still pick out the cars on the road, but they were distant, hushed. Far quieter than they should have been. These woods: there was something familiar about them, too. Hard to be sure, but they put me in mind of the forests I raced through in my nightmares, pursued by nameless horrors.

There was more movement up ahead: branches moving against the light. Or, no, not branches. Were they … antlers? They were splayed wide, high off the ground as if upon the head of some huge beast. I was immediately reminded of the Irish Elk skeleton I'd walked beneath in the museum. I'd read that such magnificent beasts had once walked these lands. Had one stepped from the ancient past to stalk these impossible woods? The early morning sunlight slanted in from the right, low and golden, and in that glow, I saw a huff of breath in the air, misting the primal scene.

I continued forwards, step by step. I was surrounded by trees, now, all sounds of the twenty-first century gone. I glanced at my phone to work out where the hell I was. No signal, no GPS lock. Wherever I was, I was off the maps. I could see no edge to the forest, nothing outside it. There were trees, trees everywhere. Once or twice, as I progressed, I thought I glimpsed the lines of buildings, the skyline of a town, between the shifting boughs, but they disappeared once I took another step. My breathing was loud inside my skull. Unfamiliar birds flittered and twittered in the skeletal branches high above my head. The ground was soft beneath my feet, a mulch of mud and decaying leaves. I breathed in the sweet smells of earth and greenery. The thaumometer was buzzing desperately, off the scale. I switched it off. Had I stepped into the realm of the horror that haunted my nights? Had I found a way into my own nightmares?

The light grew brighter as I wove between the boughs. Now I strode through a sea of spring-time bluebells, their scent buttery and sweet. Clumps of ferns unfurled their violin-neck curves. I turned and tried a different direction and it was suddenly summer, dappled golden light filtering through the green canopy above, illuminating the air around me. I walked through the wild woods, the warm air rich and drifting with seeds and buzzing insects. A few paces further on and it was autumn, lime-yellow leaves drifting from the sky like dying birds while I waded through scrunching leafmould. The chill crept into the air around me, and in a few more moments I was in winter. A patina of frost gilded the ground, while specks of snow drifted down through the still air. The air became a muffled silence. This was no visual illusion; I could feel the numbing cold creeping up my toes.

I stopped, lost, confused. Could I retrace my steps? I turned and tried stepping into my own footprints. Perhaps I could reach the road again, get away from here. What was this? Some trick of the little people? Some trap set by the Warlock? But the woods went on for ever, in all directions. Only the seasons changed as I crept forwards, blizzards giving way to bright hot sun and the windswept falls of dead leaves.

Then I glimpsed the antlered figure again, slipping between the trunks of two towering trees a short way ahead of me. I raced after it in pursuit, leaping over the knots of tree-roots, dancing through the boughs to find myself, panting, wide-eyed, under the eaves at the edge of a wide circular clearing. The trees were cliffs of darkness and green all around, but in the space between was a round plain of hummocky grass and, at its centre, a single oak tree, ancient judging by its size, wide and gnarled and grey, its bark lined like elephant hide. This part of the woods was warmed by hazy summer light, but the tree was winter-leafless, its boughs and branches black sticks save for a few last leaves clinging to its twigs and, in the highest branches, the black shapes of watching crows. There were round clumps of some other foliage up there, too: the tree was heavy with mistletoe. Woody strands of ivy wound their way from the ground and up the trunk, while the very lowest branches, heavy limb-like boughs, sagged almost to the ground under their own weight.

Strutting towards it was a naked human man. Except, not a man: his head was crowned with a set of pronged deer-antlers. They were no adornment or hat; they sprouted from his skull. As if grown strong from supporting their weight, his neck was thick, bull-strong. All his muscles were strong, but he flowed forwards with an easy grace, like a two-legged version of some woodland bull stag.

He glanced back at me once, disappeared behind the bough of the oak tree…

…then reappeared on the other side. Except, now he was altered, transformed. Now he was a man, still tall but with no antlers adorning his head. He wore a plain green suit of some thick wool, the style old-fashioned. His trousers ended at the knee and upon his ankles he wore thick woollen socks. He glanced around the glade warily, and despite his form there was something bestial lingering in his stance, in the dart of his head and the blank of his eyes. He was panting noticeably.

I could see the age upon his face, his beard grey, the pinch of some great effort lining his features, but I recognized him. I'd seen him in the picture Gilroy had shown me.

Arthur Stonewall stood there. *Myrddin*. The man English Wizardry called *Abaddon* and *The Destroyer*.

The man who, also, was very high on the Office's wanted list. If Hardknott-Lewis had been there he would surely have attempted to detain the man immediately.

Stonewall cradled something in his hands. He unfurled his grip to reveal the soft, lifeless form of some furry woodland creature. Sniffing, snuffling, he walked to the tip of one of the tree's outstretched branches and I saw, then, that what I'd thought were dead leaves or broken sticks hanging from the low branches were something else entirely. Other objects hung from the bare wood. They were animals and birds: a hare string up by its powerful rear limbs, robins and finches suspended by their stick-legs like Christmas baubles, blank eyes white. A squirrel, clawed feet splayed wide. Tiny mice and voles dangling by their tails. Woodland creatures and birds of all description. Stonewall reached up to the twiggy end of a bough and tied his latest addition to the collection.

As he did so, a shake ran through the great oak, as if a great gust of wind was whipping about the woods – although none of the other trees moved at all. A bright spark flowed from the dead creature Stonewall had attached. A knot of light. It moved up the branch to the trunk, then down to the ground. It lit up a diagonal scar slashing down the wide bough, as if the tree had been struck by lightning at some stage in its life. For a brief moment, the tree was limned in green, as if it were glowing from within. The silhouetted crows in the highest branches croaked in alarm, one or two taking fluttering flight before returning to their perches. The fulgent spot reached the ground at the base of the tree and blazed into a single, exposed root that crept a few inches out from the wood like a toe dipped tentatively into cold water. This glowed bright, bright, for a moment, and then the whole light show faded, and the tree was a black oak once more.

Stonewall knelt to the ground to examine the root. I saw that a small circle of earth had been excavated away to expose the great tree's root at that point. From the glow on Stonewall's face, I could see that the root shone with its own illumination.

Stonewall stood, as if satisfied at what he saw. A shuddering sigh went through him. He knew I was there, watching. This was all some show for my benefit. He turned to consider me, wiping his brow with a white handkerchief that he plucked from his breast pocket. It was a very human gesture. He was now, fully, a man, the gaze of intellect clear in his eyes. He passed his hand across the grey hairs on his head, as if checking to see if antlers still sprouted there. He glanced aside at the tree, something like regret or fear on his face, then stepped forwards to meet me. His skin was ashen, but his smile was wide. Now he walked slowly, as if each movement was pain.

Leaving the canopy, I walked into the clearing to meet him.

"Arthur Stonewall? I asked.

He stepped back from me, startled, and for a moment he looked at me with wide, panicky eyes once more, as if he were considering fleeing or charging. Then the human depths returned to his gaze.

"Arthur Stonewall. Yes, yes. And you: you must be Amoor's grandson. You're Danesh Shahzan. For a moment, forgive me, I thought it was Bi Bi standing there."

His voice was raw, a little cracked, as if he'd recently suffered from some illness, or his tissues hadn't yet worked out how to be fully human. Nevertheless, he looked delighted to see me, his smile wide. His skin was soft as I shook his offered hand. Despite his appearance, I could feel the iron power fizzing off him.

"I'm pleased to meet you, Mr Stonewall," I said.

"Please, just call me Arthur. And you must forgive me my initial appearance. Walking the forest paths … it is easier when one takes on *his* form and nature, but it is dangerous to do so for too long. Each time it becomes harder to revert, to recall the person you were. Each time he – it – takes you over a little more, but I needed to do so in order to reach you."

"You're talking about The Green Man?"

"Just so."

"You … became him?"

"I don't know about *became*. Borrowed perhaps? What is it you say these days? *Channelled*. He is always here, by definition, but the form is available if you know the right spells. It is like, ah, slipping into cold woodland waters. You don't *become* the water but the water engulfs you, soaks you, and they will drown you if you aren't careful. You must emerge to breathe before it is too late."

"Why did you come for me now?"

"The time seemed right. And the little patch of trees near the Fairy Bridge on the island where you were: it is easier to move between the realms at such places. The *Mooinjer veggey* granted me passage."

I looked around with some suspicion. "The little people are here?"

"That very much depends upon what you mean by *here*."

"Are you in contact with them?"

"Rarely, rarely. They only show themselves when there's no one around to see them."

I wondered how he knew. I tried again. "You came to find me because of Sally? She told you about me?"

He smiled at that. "Oh, she sends me frequent reports, has done ever since she first met you. Didn't she say? She is very careful, so very protective, and she has been through much, of course, but the communications always arrive, one way or another. Her latest missive was very clear on the point that you are Bi Bi's grandson. It is a fact that I obviously already knew, but I wasn't sure if you did, if you take my point." There was something ridiculously formal in his accent, like hearing a recording from the previous century. But then, of course, he was – what – 120 years old? 150?

"Why does she talk about me?"

Now there was a very definite twinkle in his eye. "Well, I'm sure you can work out the answer to that, my boy. Some things are very simple. I know how it is; even I was young once. The rush of love and the delights of lust; there's no denying it. Nor should you try. Quite the opposite, I should say, quite the opposite."

"Sally … said this about me?"

"Oh, she didn't need to spell it out. She's kept me informed about much that is going on in the world outside, but it is noticeable how very often you crop up in her accounts. She likes you, but she is wary of you, too."

"Are you wary of me?"

"A little. I wanted to meet you. You're Bi Bi's grandson, and he was a very, very good friend as perhaps you know. In truth I miss him still, every single day, even now. But then there is Witchfinder Danesh, the friend of Hardknott-Lewis, and I do not know for sure which is the real you. Perhaps you do not, either."

"You trusted me enough to bring me here, talk to me."

He nodded at that. "But there is much that I cannot tell you and much that I dare not, not yet. Still, you are in need of guidance and perhaps, with my assistance, we can discover where your heart really lies."

"You must know that I'm trying to destroy English Wizardry. And that they are trying to destroy me."

"English Wizardry, yes. That is a part of it. But there are great risks here, and long plans slowly being knotted. We cannot allow anything to endanger our design. We will only get once chance, in all likelihood, and it cannot be allowed to fail. You, my boy, are an unknown quantity to me, a variable in the equation. You are a shooting star, a drifting seed, and I do not know where you will land."

I gazed up at the tree with its hideous decorations. "And if you don't like what you see, am I trapped in these woods. Or do I end up as more fruit for your tree like all those other poor creatures? What if I don't like what I see in you, Arthur Stonewall?"

A moment of horror passed across his features at what I had suggested. "The tree? Of course not, no, no. That is unthinkable. It is true that if you are my enemy then it might be best if you were not allowed to leave these woods. But I mean you no harm, you have my word. I apologize if I have given you any other impression."

"Yet here we are, standing under a tree festooned with the decaying corpses of animals and birds that you have killed."

He looked up at its wide, spreading boughs. "This tree, yes. It is special; there is power here. Some texts refer to it as *darach dubh*, the black oak. The winter tree. But I did not kill any of the creatures you see here, I assure you. Or at least, one or two were on the point of their death already, but that is the way of it in the woods. The death of one brings life for others. It is true the spell might be woven quicker if I used the living, yes, but that would be to corrupt it, poison it. A fair end does not justify foul means."

"What spell? What is taking place here?"

He glanced to the ground, then back to me. "You will have many questions, I'm sure, and there is much to talk about. Amoor was the same, always trying to get at the truth. An admirable quality. I will tell you all that I can, I promise you. This that you see here, let us say simply that an incantation is being woven. A slow, deep incantation. May we leave it at that? The longer it is honed the more powerful it will be."

"A spell to destroy English Wizardry?"

"Ah, them. Yes ... and no. The roots go much deeper, of course. But I am weary after my journeying, and I am an old man. Shall we move to a different part of the woods and sit? Will you allow that?"

"I'm racing to catch a plane. We don't have long."

He waved that objection away with a swat of his hand. "No need to worry about that, at least. This little corner of the wood is ... cut off rather. The cycles of life and death, of summer and winter still take place here, but one is also removed from them. Time seems to ... get a little lost among these twisting pathways. We are ageing as normal as the outside world measures it, I'm afraid, but we can sit and talk for a time – for days and years if need be – and you will still be able to catch your aeroplane."

"If you allow me to leave."

He smiled in warm amusement at that, and dipped his head. "Yes. If I allow you to leave."

17 – Another Part of the Wood

Also called, simply, the Green Man or Herne the
Hunter, the Horned Man is a tall, powerful male
figure with deer antlers growing from his head. In
some accounts, he is able to transform at will into a
deer, allowing him to run with incredible speed.
Indeed, it is possible that he can become any
manner of woodland creature – possibly including
the trees themselves. The Horned Man is a sort of
guardian spirit or *expression* of woodland; a semi-
divine creature that guards and protects the trees
and the creatures that live amongst them.
  – Dr Miriam Seacastle, *Red Dragon, a Bestiary of
Modern Britain*, 1999

I walked behind Arthur Stonewall away from the lone
oak, following twisty, turning pathways that wound
beneath the reaching boughs. We stepped past both
broadleaf and pine trees. Once again, the seasons came at
us in a flurry: one moment we were crunching through a
layer of snow, then wading through ferny spring growth.
A few yards farther on, bright, hazy sun picked us out,
and then the leaves on the trees were sand and lime and
plum as autumn returned.

Woodland creatures fluttered and clattered in the
treetops and in the undergrowth. Then, in the distance, I
picked up the deeper roars of something much larger.
There was an edge of fury in the sounds. I glimpsed high
branches lashing and crashing across dips in the land, as
if some vast creature was over there, trying to force its
way through.

Stonewall glanced back at me as we walked. "Don't worry. They can't get in."

"What are they?"

He talked over his shoulder as we walked. Now I could see no path at all, but Stonewall appeared to know where he was going. "There are many creatures in the deep woods, but I imagine these are my enemies, desperately trying to reach me. I'm sure Sally told you that I'm being constantly harried."

"She was very protective of you. This is English Wizardry?" I asked.

"That's one name. It's them, or some malevolent entity they're controlling."

"What other names are there?"

Stonewall stopped for a moment, head on one side as he listened. "Well. Let's say the roots go deeper. You must know some of the history."

"Some," I said. "Will you tell me what you know?"

"Some," he said, "although I regret, I will have to keep certain facts to myself. Not because I don't trust you, in fact, but because it is dangerous knowledge. Dangerous for you, dangerous for me. Once you leave here and walk the world again, they might get to you and, if they do, they'll try to rip what you know from your mind."

I thought about the extraordinary lengths English Wizardry had gone to in order to reach Sally, following the trail of removed eyes the previous year.

"Especially if they know I've been talking to you," I said.

"Quite so. I've wanted to talk to you for a long time, but we were obviously wary. The Office is another threat to us – by definition, but also because you are right to believe that your organization has been infiltrated."

"You know about that? Do you know who the traitor is?"

"That fact is hidden from me, I am afraid. My attentions are rather on the bigger picture, the long term. But we decided it isn't you and almost certainly isn't Campbell Hardknott-Lewis, either."

"You and Sally."

"Yes."

I thought about that. I was pretty sure I agreed about the Crow, but it was good to have Stonewall confirming it.

"You called her Sally," I said.

"I did. Is that wrong??"

"I thought that was simply the name she chose to give me. I have no idea what her real name is."

He threw an amused grin aside at me. "I'm not sure what a *real name* is. It is the name I know her by, though, so it must count for something if you do, too."

The distant roaring raged again, but this time it came from a different direction.

"Are you absolutely sure they can't find their way in?" I asked.

"Well, they haven't so far. One of the advantages of hiding out in a Tanglewood."

"I don't know what that is."

"*This* is a Tanglewood. It's a part of the forest where the directions of travel, the usual arrangements of *forwards* and *backwards*, don't follow the normal rules. It's not separate; it's a part of the greater forest, and from here I can walk more or less anywhere, but it is also self-contained. It's not an island, but it is, conceptually, a peninsula. Try walking into it and you'll find yourself flipped around and heading out again."

We resumed walking. "How do you manage it, then?"

"Well, I discovered the answer to the puzzle. I found the map to this place long ago, the dance of steps to take. It is like drawing out a rune on the ground with your feet. The movements need to be very precise."

"Who discovered this secret?"

"The steps were scribbled on a piece of paper inside a copy of *The New Complete Map of Fairyland* by the Reverend Pates. Are you familiar with the work? I memorized the map he'd sketched and then destroyed it."

"Can't say I've heard of the book."

"Ah. Well. Probably for the best. Few copies now exist, and none, I hope, have Pates' own hand-drawn maps stuffed inside. I doubt even your Dorothy Coldwater has an original copy, although she may. Pates spent his days walking the greenways and forest paths searching for what he called *the shadow paths into the wild wood*, hoping to catch a glimpse of the faerie folk that he imagined were all around him. Which, of course, they were. One day, I must pass on what I know of this place to someone suitable. A safe retreat such as this is a treasure beyond value."

"When is the right time? And who will you tell?"

Stonewall didn't answer.

I tried a different approach.

"So, Sally also knows the way here? She's been to visit you? She was clear that if English Wizardry got their hands on her, extracted her eyes and recovered her visual memories, they could work out how to get to you."

"She has visited once or twice. She knows the paths to take – or at least, she knows the steps to take to reach the outer glades which I, in turn, can visit without exposing myself to the outside world. There are layers within layers. Mostly, Sally whispers her words into the green and they trickle their way through to me. Did you know that the trees talk to each other? Not just the trees, in truth, all of the green. One thing I learned early on in my researches, long before I encountered English Wizardry, is that there is only one forest. Did you know that?"

"I didn't. I don't see how that can be."

Stonewall stopped again, letting me catch up with him. We stood in a little clearing. He gazed up at the treetops around us, peering into the sky as if seeing something significant up there. Perhaps he was recalling the correct path to take, the right pair of trees to pass between.

"People like to parcel things up," he said, "dice and slice them, reduce them to their constituent parts. It gives us the wonders of science, of course, but perhaps it is also a failing, making us blind to the larger picture. Don't you think?"

"I hadn't thought about that."

"You've been busy, I know. Something to consider.

We love to map out the world, define little patches of greenery here and there, have you noticed? What is the modern word? Compartmentalize. But the wild wood remembers what it once was. There's only one sky and there's only one sea and there's only one forest. If you can follow the twisting paths you can step into any part of it."

"That can't be right. Lots of the world isn't forest."

He sounded delighted at my objection. I guessed he didn't have many people to engage with in philosophical debate. "Ah, but once it was. Some of it is underground, in the seeds and the roots, buried deep. Some of it exists only in the realm of memory, but it is there. It is always there."

We resumed walking. I thought about his words.

"You're saying that if you know the right paths to take you can walk from any patch of forest to any wood? In any other part of the world?"

He looked delighted as he looked back at me. "Just so, yes. If you prefer to put it like that. That was how I was able to find you this morning."

"In my dreams yesterday morning, I was running through the woods, pursued by something. It caught me ... and then a green light intervened. There was a figure, and it had horns or antlers, too. I assumed it was just something my brain had invented, but now ... was that you?"

"Forgive my intrusion. Yes. You were in need."

"How can dream worlds and real woods intersect?"

"Most dreams are nothing more than that: visions our brains conjure up. But sometimes our minds wander into other realms, especially if we are gifted magically. Your nightmares most likely started out as normal night time visions, but I imagine they've become something more over the years. Either it was you reaching out, or it was some external entity trying to get through to you."

I had so many questions: Sally, Alis, the Warlock, my grandfather. But, as I tried to form my next question, we emerged into another glade. This one lay in summer, the warm air glowing with floating seeds. In the middle, atop a slight rise, was a shack built from logs, with glass in its windows and the patchwork of a garden all around it.

"You have an actual cabin in the woods?" I asked.

"This is my home, yes," he said, looking confused, clearly not getting the cultural reference. "It's basic, but it provides shelter, gives me all I need. It is always late summer in this particular spot, which is pleasant. There is a brook for running water and I forage nearby for autumn berries and the like. Will you come inside so we can talk?"

A narrow pathway led around his vegetable beds and up some steps into the cabin. The interior was taken up by a large, single room. Bright sunlight beamed in through the windows, illuminating the million dust motes floating in the air. The place smelled of fresh wood and the dust of old books, overlaid with something floral. Bundles of dried flowers hung from the rafters here and there. There was a bed and a stove, and the walls were lined with books and papers, seemingly in a random jumble. A plain, square wooden table occupied the centre of the room. Upon it were more tomes and Stonewall's notebooks, along with a couple of candles in metal holders, thick wax dripping down them.

"Please, make yourself at home. I'm afraid I don't get many visitors. None, in fact, which is rather the point. I can offer you tea."

"I'm good, thanks," I said. "This is where you've lived all this time?"

He looked around, as if seeing the place for the first time. "Oh, for decades, now. I am able to pursue my researches in peace. It's all I need."

"Your researches into English Wizardry. I thought…"

I stopped. I'd walked over to his table to look at the books he had open there. One in particular caught my eye. I'd seen that work before – that and the drawing of the oak tree the book was open at. An oak tree surrounded by seven stars. For reasons I couldn't put my finger on, the thought that there were also seven

Keyholders in the Office crossed my mind. Was that relevant somehow? I thought about the oak tree in the glade with the dead woodland creatures hanging from it. What was going on here? A tiny thrill of alarm trickled through me. Hardknott-Lewis had once told me that only twelves copies of *The Old Ways* had been printed, with the Office holding seven of them. Here was one of the missing ones. Quirk had had one, too. Why did the book keep cropping up?

Stonewall saw what I was looking at. "Ah, Bedfellowes' work," he said. "You are familiar with it?"

"It's English Wizardry's bible. Their root text. Why are you studying it?"

A little smile passed across Stonewall's features. "I knew him, you know. Or at least, I met him."

"Bedfellowes? He died in the nineteenth century."

"He did. He was an old man at the time, one foot in the grave, and I was young, still a teenager, I believe."

I knew Stonewall had been involved with English Wizardry in the early days, before – I'd been told – turning against it around the turn of the twentieth century. Mormont, Stonewall: the extended lives of these people was easy to forget sometimes.

"This was in some sort of secret cabal meeting?"

"I was a fool, dazzled by the lure of arcane knowledge and secret powers. I soon saw my mistake, but I can't say the same for Bedfellowes. I found him dim-witted, to be honest, lost in his own delusions. He was gullible, flattered by the attention the group gave him, even though they laughed at him behind his back."

"Then, why study his words?"

"Well. Most of it is nonsense, fanciful at best, ugly and dangerous at its worst. But here and there you can find fragments and snatches of a deeper truth in his words. Reading between the lines can be inciteful. One or two of his statements have proved to be very accurate. Surprisingly so."

"Are you sure of that?"

He pulled a little three-legged stool out from beneath

the table for me, then sat in his plain wooden chair, giving a little involuntary grunt of discomfort as he did so. His old bones.

"There are a few passages in the book where he expresses very subtle and inciteful notions," Stonewall said. "In fact, it was your grandfather who first pointed them out to me. He was a very smart man. He had the ability to see things that were there in plain sight but which others had missed."

"Will you tell me about him?"

"Of course, of course."

I thought of the photograph Gilroy had shown me. "You knew him from the Mystical Council?"

"That was part of it, yes. Bi Bi was very active, but I was already consumed by my researches."

I returned my attention to *The Old Ways*. "What did my grandfather spot?"

"The writing style changes in certain passages," said Stonewall. "The sentences become longer and more grammatical, the thoughts more subtle, allusive. I'm convinced he was ghost-writing these sections, or perhaps that someone was implanting ideas into his mind. Bedfellowes insisted the words were all his, of course, but from what I knew of him, well, I doubt it very much. If you tried to engage him in debate, he would become rapidly flustered and confused."

"I presume you're talking about the Warlock."

Stonewall nodded with a frown on his features. "We can call him that, yes, although there are other names. English Wizardry are the immediate problem, of course, but in my time with them, I soon saw that there was and is a power behind them. A deeper, quieter threat. As I suspect you know, English Wizardry are a mask for the Warlock. I have devoted my time to discovering the identity and nature of our real enemy. Of unearthing that root."

"How close have you got?"

Stonewall made a little laughing sound. "A little closer than I was, but not as close as I'd like. He tried to recruit me in the early days, you know."

"You *met* him?"

"No, no. It was all carried out via intermediaries and interlocutors. The person or the entity we call the Warlock is very protective of his secrets. Obsessively so."

Evangelina Mormont had referred to the Warlock as *him*, too. I wondered if that was significant or if the two were simply displaying out-of-date prejudices.

"Did you meet Evangelina Mormont?"

"Oh yes. Now, she was a deeply scary individual. She made no attempt to remain hidden, quite the opposite. She loved the adoration of her peers. She was as bright as the midday sun but utterly unhinged. She enjoyed her cruelty. The Office should never have let her live, even hidden away in Oblivion. I was delighted when I learned that you had destroyed her, you and the estimable Dorothy Coldwater. What you achieved there was impressive."

I thought about Mormont's curious injunction to go to Oblivion. *See who else has been lying there all this time.* "Have you visited Oblivion?"

"Regrettably not. Some realms the green does not extend to."

"What about Annwn? The Welsh otherworld?"

"Oh yes, the wood very definitely extends there."

"From what you've learned, is the Warlock an operative of the Office of the Witchfinder General? One of the Keyholders perhaps?" I asked.

He gave that a few moments of careful consideration. "I talked about English Wizardry being a mask for the Warlock. It is my belief that the Office is, too, in part. Perhaps they always have been. I do know they've been deliberately weakened and undermined while being allowed to continue, to maintain at least an illusion of effectiveness."

"We've been infiltrated."

"I believe so, and, as I say, that was another reason Sally and I were wary of you. It is my belief that the Warlock is not an active member of the Office, but that someone high up is acting under the Warlock's influence."

"Who?"

Stonewall sat back in his chair to consider me. "Well, you tell me. That is what you've been investigating is it not?"

"Is it that obvious?"

"Given your recent experiences, it would be a dereliction if you weren't. You crossed into the green on the Isle of Man. Do you suspect Thomas Quirk?"

There seemed little point in denying this. "He may well be the traitor. He's a very good candidate."

"Who else? I presume your recent adventures with Evangelina Mormont gave you some useful clues?"

I studied his features for a moment: his kind, open smile, his blue eyes. Could I trust Stonewall? Sally had. She'd gone to enormous lengths to protect him, as had Auchter and Cornwallis and the others. People had died to protect this man. I doubted Sally had been deceived, and the truth was that I trusted her.

Then there was the fact that I needed Stonewall's help.

"Earl Grey is another possibility," I said.

Stonewall gave that some consideration. "My. That's quite a thought. The mighty and fearsome Earl Grey, Defender of the Realm."

"Do you think that's unlikely?"

Stonewall sighed. "Honestly, I don't know. It's always best to keep an open mind. Our enemy is very clever and very good at hiding in the shadows. I've never met Earl Grey, but I've watched him from afar. And your own Hardknott-Lewis? He's perhaps even more upright and unwavering than Earl Grey. Do you have concerns about the Welsh Witchfinder, too?"

"I try to keep an open mind. I trust him, but I also recognize now that this might be because I *want* to trust him."

Stonewall smiled at that. "That's just the sort of thing your grandfather might have said."

"What can you tell me about the Warlock?" I asked. "What have you learned?"

"You've been honest with me, Danesh. I'll do my best

to reciprocate. It is my belief that the Warlock is a very ancient and very powerful vampire. In human terms, he is utterly malevolent – although terms like *good* and *evil* are not ones he would understand. This entity does not think in such ways. It sees us as inferior, as *things*. We're fuel, we're cattle. He has no concern for what we think of him. He may not even consider that we are thinking, feeling people at all."

"A vampire as in, The Order of the British Vampire?"

"Once again, this is simply the current name, one of many. I'm convinced the group is real, yes, quietly pulling the strings. I believe that both English Wizardry and the Office are their tools, amongst many others. They've infiltrated the Office, controlling this traitor you seek, but I believe they were responsible for creating English Wizardry in the first place. That group is their puppet, its strings quietly pulled from the shadows."

"How big is English Wizardry?"

Stonewall looked amused again. How much did he know about me? "Well, their membership does seem to have been reducing somewhat of late. I suspect they are small, a few individuals willing to carry out their atrocities."

"And the Mystical Council?"

"They were too much of a threat to the Warlock. I'm sure he attempted to infiltrate them, too, weaken them, but I believe he failed. When he found that he couldn't control them, he did what he could to turn opinion against this sect of benign sorcerers at the heart of the British establishment."

"Do you know any more? Like, where this vampire lives? What his identity is?"

"Despite all my efforts, I do not. I can tell you I have been preparing to meet this enemy for many years. And then I heard about you and I became worried that you might … get there first. I know you have certain abilities, and that you're resourceful and intelligent, but I very much doubt such a confrontation would go well for you. Another reason we decided to contact you."

"Are you warning me off my pursuit?"

"Not at all. I'd like to offer what help and guidance I can. Perhaps even to work alongside you, if you're amenable."

"Any help you can give me."

"I will do what I can before you leave. A long road lies ahead of you, a dangerous road with no clear destination that I can see, but perhaps I can set you on the right path. I can only apologise for not intervening sooner. I would say this: even if the Office traitor is not the Warlock, don't underestimate the man you are pursuing. He is clearly dangerous and good at remaining hidden. And, if he has turned his back on the Office's tenets, he will have access to powerful confiscated magical artefacts, too, even setting aside what the Warlock may have given him."

"As well as the Office traitor, I'm pursuing a user I believe to be a witch," I said. "Alis Treacle. She's casting destructive curses on Office operatives and summoning demonic entities to torment them. Night Hags. She's subjecting her victims to serious cruelty. She's attacked me, more than once. I've come to believe she's another tool of the Warlock."

"Alis Treacle? That was who was in the woods when I came to your aid?"

That threw me. "Wait, you *saw* her? I get that you came to help me; that I was in some sort of exterior domain at that point, but I thought that the other presences were all in my head. Her and this malevolent, unnamed entity that's been haunting my nightmares for a long, long time."

Stonewall thought about that. "The borders between the subconscious and the shadow realms can be difficult to draw. I don't know who or what this entity you mention is; I wasn't aware of it when I came to you. But I was aware of a powerful folk magic user and the malice she bears towards you. You called her Alis Treacle, but I don't see how that's possible."

"Why?"

"I've never read her book," Stonewall said, "but I've read many accounts of it. She died, she very definitely died. She can't be pursuing you."

"I've been thinking about that. Perhaps the Warlock brought her back, set her on my trail. Perhaps she's some sort of vampire witch, with the powers of both."

Stonewall passed his hand through his greying hair. "I've never heard of such an entity, but if there's one thing I've learned over the years it's that I know basically nothing about what's possible. The realms are infinite. She – it – was tending some sort of grave, I saw. And there were dolls, dolls that looked like the paraphernalia in some incantation or curse. What did all that signify?"

"You *saw* all that?"

"As I say, what we call reality and illusion: the distinction can be vague. But that very definitely was not some invention of your subconscious. The details may have been twisted around, the landscape symbolic, but have no doubt, that was a forest clearing in the mundane world. You have encountered these dolls?"

"The curses woven into them send their victims mad, immerse people in their own nightmares."

"You mentioned Night Hags. As well as the hexes, the dolls probably provide a focus for those entities to manifest. The malign effects you describe are just the sort of thing the demons love to inflict on people."

"Can you tell me where the clearing is in the real world?"

"I know which individual wood it is in, as you would put it. I'm afraid I've become rather distanced from the outside world; I can't tell you how to walk there or drive there, but the paths and the groves and the trees you need to find within the woods – yes, I know those intimately. You would call that part of the green, Ashdown Forest in England. The High Weald of Sussex."

"Why there?"

"That I have no idea about. I assume it is or was significant in some way."

Sussex. It was useful I was returning to England that

morning. It was a long way from Scotland, certainly, but if I needed cover to pursue Quirk in the south, this could provide it. At some point I needed to check in with the Crow, too, see what he'd turned up in London. After this conversation with Stonewall, I was more inclined to trust him, now. Lincoln hadn't been in touch to tell me about any suspicions – which I assumed was a good thing.

"You have to consider the possibility that these visions are some sort of trap, though," Stonewall continued. "This Alis Treacle entity might have been showing you the place she wanted you to come. You have clearly survived her attacks on you so far, but she may be more powerful at this location for some reason."

"If it comes to it, I'll take the risk," I said.

Stonewall stood, his knees cracking audibly. He crossed the room to me then squatted to study me as if I were some interesting specimen.

"May I be allowed to touch your mind?" he asked. "I knew what Bi Bi was capable of and if you're anything like him, you have great powers, too. Yet, Sally tells me you are wary of your abilities. You are not properly in touch with your inner self; your powers flare up, out of control, in moments of stress, but otherwise they are dormant."

"I used to get, like, migraines or blackouts. I understand, now, that it was this part of me bubbling away, suppressed, then erupting at unexpected moments."

"This is better now?"

"A little. I still barely know what I'm doing."

"You are able to manifest your powers in the real world when you need to?"

I wondered what he knew about the killings I'd committed. Unleashing a sorcerous death ray probably counted as *manifest*.

"In moments of stress."

"Aha, I see. The body will do unexpected things to protect itself if it thinks it is threatened. Our innate magical abilities are at the mercy of the fight/flight mechanism just as everything else is. Your responses can be tempered and trained, though; you can learn to exercise control."

He looked pensive for a moment. "Then, of course, there's the fact that you're an operative in the Office of the Witchfinder General. That must be a significant conflict for you to bear, something your subconscious is desperately trying to reconcile."

"Yeah, you could say that."

"Well. Let us see what we can do to help. What I'm proposing won't hurt you."

"I'm not sure I like the ideas of you digging around in my head."

"I won't be able to hear your thoughts or anything of the sort if that is your concern. I should be able to see the ... topography of your mind. I wonder if something's been done to you. A deep curse or something similar."

I thought about my mother and everything she'd suffered since Az's death. My assumption had always been that I'd escaped any sort of magical attack or damage that day because I'd fled while Az and my mother were caught.

"Do it," I said. "I need to know."

He nodded and, saying nothing more, stood over me as if he were simply going to cut my hair. He laid his hands gently onto my head, in best Vulcan mind meld fashion. I felt nothing, other than the curious sensation of warm lights shining inside my mind – which was probably my imagination. Stonewall shifted his position a few times, moving his touch to the back of my neck (sending a shiver up me), to my temples, to the soft skin behind my ears.

When he was done, he stepped back, then returned to his chair.

"There is certainly great power in you. Great power. You do know you come from a long line of formidable practitioners, don't you? Bi Bi had so many stories of his former battles in India. Ah, it is such a shame that the Mystical Council is no more and that you are reduced to working for the damned Office. The landscape of your mind is ... complicated, though. There's something else going on within you. The blazing light is clear, but it's like it's buried beneath this jumbled mound of rocks. Perhaps this isn't any great revelation to you. These rocks, though: they look to me like they've been deliberately piled there, if that makes sense. In symbolic terms, they look like a deliberate blockage, a wall around part of your mind. That, or scar tissue covering some old trauma."

"Then it is a deep curse? I've been carrying it within me all along?"

"Honestly? It doesn't feel like that. Perhaps an act of malign magic is the splinter at its heart, but what I glimpsed, well, it looks more … psychological in nature."

"Psychological?"

"You must forgive me. I spent quite a bit of time with both Jung and Freud in the twentieth century. I haven't kept up, though, and I believe modern psychiatry has moved on. I may not be using the correct terms. What I saw in you, though: it felt like some unreconciled childhood trauma. It smelled to me like *guilt*. An internalised belief that you do not deserve to have these powers, or that you fear them or blame them for something. Does that make sense?"

Perhaps I had escaped a curse then. That – or I'd been spared for some reason. I wasn't sure which explanation was worse. "Yeah. Maybe."

"I can help you, if you would like," Stonewall said quietly.

"I am not going to let you delve around any more deeply in my mind."

"No, no, of course not. Nor would I wish to nor be qualified to, old boy. But I can provide you with some clarity, some perspective. Clear away the clouds and show you the whole landscape as it were. This accretion of scar tissue in your mind might not be magical in nature, but magic can still help shine a light. It will then be up to you to decide what you do with the knowledge."

"You mentioned a complicated picture. Did you detect something else too?"

"There is also this ... shadow there. It appears to be much more recent. Do you know what that might be?"

I told him about my close contact with the three cursed dolls and with Alis Treacle's *Book of Shadows*. I told him about the shadows that sometimes invaded my vision.

"Ah, that might well be it," Stonewall said. He looked concerned. "You are resilient; I suspect you have all of Bi Bi's powers of repair, but your ability to heal is not infinite, just as his wasn't. You are still recovering from your experiences. I presume you're using the mantras Bi Bi used to practice? The rituals?"

"I need to find out about them. Can you remove this newer shadow too?

"Again, I can offer you the clarity to see the harm for what it is. Gaining such knowledge is often the first step in healing, although it will take you time. Perhaps a long time."

"This help you're offering ... is it anything to do with the oak tree? The incantation you're weaving?"

"No, no. That is, or will be, a weapon to wield against the Warlock. The time for that is coming, but we are not there yet. We may only get one opportunity, and we need to be sure. No, I am offering you something different. As I say, a way to achieve clarity. It helped me, in the early days. It may help you."

"I need weapons, not clarity."

"For you, I suspect they are one and the same thing. What I'm offering: it is an ordeal, but not a very terrible one."

"An ordeal? Is it harmful?"

"It never harmed me, not in any significant way. Not in the long run."

That didn't sound particularly reassuring. Still, I considered for only a moment.

"Show me," I said.

18 – A Moment of Clarity

And to this spot Taliesin brought his master after his horse had won the race. And he caused Elphin to put workmen to dig a hole there; and when they had dug the ground deep enough, they found a large cauldron full of gold. And then said Taliesin, "Elphin, behold a payment and reward unto thee, for having taken me out of the weir, and for having reared me from that time until now." And on this spot stands a pool of water, which is to this time called Pwllbair.

– The Mabinogi

Stonewall led me between the smooth boughs of a clump of spring trees into another forest glade, a short distance from his cabin. There was no oak tree filling this clearing, but there was a dip in the ground, with rough steps winding down to the lip of a pool of water. Someone had delineated the edge of the spring with heavy stones. Weather-worn, moss-coated, they looked to have been there for a long time.

"A pool?" I asked. "What is this place?"

"Once again there are many names, although some call it the *Clear Spring*. It is part of the reason I built my house where I did."

"You didn't create this?"

"No, no. These waters have been here for a long time, I've no idea who dug the pool. Perhaps no one did and the waters well up here naturally."

I stepped to the edge of the pool. A set of steep stone steps descended into the water, but I couldn't discern how deep they went. A foot or two down, the still waters became inky black. One or two upturned leaves floated across their surface, like fairy galleons, but other than that I could only see the dark reflection of the overhanging trees and the clouds in the sky, along with my own face, peering in.

"Why is it called the *Clear Spring*? I can't see anything."

"Immersing yourself in it gives you the clarity I mentioned. It allows you to see. That's what it does."

"I thought you were going to tell me to drink from it or something."

"Alas, no. You must strip completely naked and descend by the steps you can see. The pool goes deep, but it has a floor. You will be completely submerged when you stand on the bottom but, still, you must go all the way. There is a ritual that takes a little longer whereby each week you go one step further down, but perhaps that is something you could return to in the future."

"The main thing I took away from that sentence was *naked*. Is that really a part of how the magic works?"

Stonewall looked amused at my objections. He'd clearly grown accustomed to running through the woods as a deer-man. Maybe I was lucky to have caught him with clothes on.

"Magic? Yes, we could call it that," he said. "I read an account – I'm not sure where now – of a miraculous cauldron being found in this pool at one time. It might even have been one of the cauldrons you'll be familiar with from the Mabinogi, perhaps even the one that brings the dead back to life. Certainly, these waters are restorative. As to being naked, that's entirely optional. I simply thought you'd want dry clothes to put on afterwards. I'll fetch towels and light a fire for you to warm up afterwards then leave you to it, shall I? When you're done, come find me in my hut."

"I just walk down the steps?"

"Simple as that. Remain fully submerged for as long as you can stand it. The waters are somewhat chilly."

I peered back through the trees. There was no sign of the cabin.

"How do I find your hut? If I get lost in these woods, I may never get out."

"I think you'll be fine. As I say, the waters give you clarity."

He cleared a space of leaves with his feet, then lit a small pyre of collected dried twigs and branches using – I was pleased to see – a box of matches. He crouched to blow on the flames, bring them to life. Once they were crackling away, giving off a strong heat, a line of grey smoke rising into the air, he nodded to me and, saying nothing more, left.

I paused for a moment. How had I ended up stripping naked in the middle of an enchanted wood in order to dunk myself in a magical pond? Strange how life turns out sometimes. Ignoring the nagging feeling that the whole thing was an elaborate jest by Sally, that she and Stonewall were watching from somewhere, I removed my clothes, folded them up for some reason, lay them on the ground, then gingerly dipped a single toe into the waters.

Jesus H – as my mother would say – *Christ*, it was cold. Shocking, brutally cold. I stepped in, the water over my ankles, and my feet screamed at me to find out what the hell I was doing. My flesh was already icy numb. A small, perverse part of me was tempted to literally take the plunge and throw myself into the middle of the pool, take the hit all at once, but Stonewall had talked about taking it one step at a time. If that was going to make the ordeal more effective, that was what I was going to do.

I took another step down, the water covering my calves, my thighs. With each movement, I heard myself emitting an involuntary gasp of shock. I was shaking uncontrollably, but I knew the next step was going to be much worse. I was right. The liquid ice grasped hold of my testicles, and I swore out loud through gritted teeth. The shock unleashed the magical fury that lay dormant somewhere inside. It raged up, the fight/flight response kicking in as Stonewall had explained. With an effort, I let it come, let it flow through me and away. I wouldn't use it – partly because I didn't want to fight whatever the pool was doing to me, partly because I feared superheating the water I was standing in and boiling myself alive.

I forced myself to step down, farther and farther, subjecting my soft belly, then my chest and neck to the freezing waters. The hell with taking it slowly; I needed to dunk myself and get the ordeal over with. My body was adjusting to the thermal shock; the worst of the cold was becoming distant. Either I was becoming acclimatised, or I was succumbing, becoming numbed.

Gulping a deep breath of air, I took the final plunge, swimming off the step beneath my feet into the glacial darkness of the pool. I plummeted, and panic shook through me. The pool was bottomless and my frozen limbs were too stiff and distant to swim me upwards. I flailed, trying to save myself, but the effort of it was enormous, and suddenly didn't seem worth the effort. I let myself sink.

Then, long moments later, my feet squelched into soft mud. I could hear only my own heart, labouring away in my chest, desperately pumping the same reserves of oxygen around my body. I could see nothing except for, high high above me, unexpected explosions of light. Whether they were real or only in my eyes, I couldn't tell.

I forced myself to stop moving, close my eyes, do nothing more than exist. Despite the bitter cold, my body was beginning to feel oddly warm. I'd stopped shivering. The cold crept through my brain and I had the odd sensation of old stones, weights I'd carried, freezing and shattering as the ice got into them. There was a light there, powerful and warm. I didn't need to be afraid of it, because it was me. I could use it, draw on it.

I floated for a time, letting the cold consume me.

When I was ready, with the simplest effort, I pushed towards the light. I seemed to swim – maybe fly – for a long, long time. The waters couldn't be this deep, could they? How far had I plunged? My oxygen-starved tissues sent alarms ringing through me. At the same time, a part of me remained calm, in control. I was going to be okay. I could do this.

I emerged gasping into the warm air of the little clearing. Nothing had changed out there. There was no audience; no trap had been sprung. I swam in little circles for a moment, then paddled my way to the stone steps. Finding them with my toes, I pulled myself out of the waters. The fire Stonewall had lit was glorious. My flesh was blue-purple as I towelled off the freezing waters.

None of it was a concern, though. I felt energized. Clear-headed. The magical power coiled away inside me, but it wasn't distant or suppressed. I could wield it as simply as I could move my own limbs. That was what it was; another limb. It was something like a snake, a king cobra maybe, deadly when it needed to be but otherwise placid. The potential in it was huge, I saw. There were colours to it that I didn't recognize, abilities and powers I would need to explore, learn to wield. But I knew that, in time, I would get there.

Once I was dry, and dressed, and warm, I sat for a moment by the crackling log fire and looked around me at the trees, playing with sending my mind's eye soaring upwards to the tree-tops, into the sky. The woods extended infinitely. Seen from above, they were a rolling green ocean stretching to all horizons. Nearby, a mere few steps away, was Stonewall's hut. The lines of the forest paths wound through the boughs beneath my gaze, like a map of nerves in some vast body. There, distantly, not so very far away, were the roaring, lashing monsters that were attempting to smash their way into this part of the woods. Compared to the wider landscape, they looked small. Somewhere further away were the real enemies. I was ready to face them now.

I returned to my body, stood, and walked the path to Stonewall's cabin. He sat at his desk, surrounded by his books and papers. He looked up at me as I entered.

"Ah, there you are. Was the experience helpful?"

"I think so."

He stood and came to look at me, not touching me this time but peering into my eyes.

"Yes, I can see it in you. A burden has been lifted. It is

still a sapling, pushing through the ground. Give it time and space to grow. Give it light. You are no longer fighting against yourself. Good, good."

"And the *Book of Shadows* hex? The effect of the dolls?"

"They're lifted too, I'd say. You're free of them. When you're ready, if we're both still around, by all means come back. I can teach you one or two other things, spells and incantations and the like, but the clarity the pool offers is the most valuable. Trust your own instincts. Lessons are better if you teach them to yourself."

I thanked him, ready to leave and face the world again.

"Do you need me to show you the way back to your vehicle?" he asked.

"Thank you. I can see the way."

He nodded with satisfaction, then picked up a small wooden box from the table. It looked hand-made.

"A parting gift for you, Danesh."

"Something my grandfather gave you?"

"I'm afraid not, no. It is a small thing, but it may be useful."

I hinged open the little box and within, resting on a bed of purple cloth, there lay a single acorn.

"It was dropped by *darach dubh* when it was last in autumn," Stonewall said.

"Is this what you've been working on? This is the spell?"

"No, no, not that. As I say, this is a small thing. Once we find the Warlock, that will be the time for the great spell. This acorn, though, is simply a way of calling me. When you need it most, perhaps if you find yourself facing the Warlock, crush it beneath your heel and I will hear. And then, together, we can face our enemy. Sally has one of these, and now you do too."

I thanked him again and left the peaceful, sunlit glade. The woods felt familiar to me, now; my feet could follow the path they needed to take without me having to think about it. It occurred to me that Stonewall had just done the thing he'd said he would do one day: pass on the knowledge of how to traverse the tanglewood, find this secret grove.

He'd chosen to give that knowledge to me.

Soon, I was emerging near the Fairy Bridge on the Isle of Man. The trees behind me were nothing more than a line of boughs by the side of the road once more. Two, three cars whooshed past me.

Despite Stonewall's reassurances about the speed at which time passed in his realm, I was suddenly running late. I'd lost a little time somewhere. Returning to my car, I raced to the airport and made the gate as they were paging the last, annoying passenger – i.e., me – to check in urgently. I had seconds to spare. The sign directing passengers to departures and arrivals showed a stick figure with two angled, stylized planes above its head. It reminded me oddly of the Horned Man. The woman on the desk – Shireen, according to her name tag – looked amused as I raced up to her, out of breath.

"I hope you enjoyed your stay on the island," she said, her smile wide.

"Thanks, yeah. It's been interesting."

"Do come back," she said.

The scary poster at security forbidding the carrying of weapons, explosives and dangerous chemicals made no mention of cursed folk dolls, so, just as Alis had two days previously, I figured I was safe to take mine on board the plane. I had my handgun, clothcutter blade and other Office equipment wrapped in a Veil: magically imbued cloth that fuzzes out X-rays and just about anything else. I was taking the risk that security wouldn't search my bag and find the weapons. If that happened, I'd have to start flashing my Office ID around and having some awkward conversations. Fortunately, the Veil did its job. Fifty minutes later, the little island was sinking back into the mist and the lead-grey sea, and we were heading back to the mainland.

As I walked down the steps from the plane at John Lennon Airport, my phone, once it had reregistered itself to a UK network, buzzed with a text. I still had the sender named as *Scary Librarian*. I thought I probably should change that.

Ring me when you can, it said. I phoned Lady Coldwater as I made my way across the tarmac to the terminal. I filled her in on everything I'd learned, without mentioning Stonewall and the changes I was experiencing.

"Sussex," she said, "interesting. That was Alis Treacle's home ground."

"Do we know any details of where she was buried?"

"Are you thinking that the grave you glimpsed was hers? The broken ground in the woods?"

"I think it might be."

"It's worth looking into, I agree," the Lady said. "The exact whereabouts of her burial place are unknown, until now at least. All we know is that she was thrown into an unmarked grave in unhallowed ground."

"Do you think it's likely Alis has returned?"

I could hear the librarian breathing as she considered. "It would require strong magic, and we've heard no whisper of it being worked. I'll talk to the Sisters again, see if we can discover anything. For now, best not to get too close to her I'd say."

"I'm going to tackle her before she comes for me again. I've had enough of being pursued."

"I understand, but you need to be ready. Pursue Quirk for now; that is what you're really supposed to be doing."

"For all we know, it's Quirk that has set Alis on my trail."

"That doesn't make it any safer to go after her."

I ignored her objections. "If Alis has been brought back, would she retain her powers?"

"Oh, if she's angry enough, yes, quite possibly. And I imagine she would cling onto a burning hatred of witchfinders, given what was done to her. Don't you think?"

"Yeah."

"That's why you need to be wary," the librarian said.

"Revenants can be … single-minded. Oh, there's also one thing I can tell you now. You asked me about mirrors in the book."

"You said there was no mention of them."

"There isn't. But I've looked again, and there are a couple of suggestions of using water to walk between the worlds. Lakes and the like, on quiet days when there are no ripples. Alis talks about weaving the incantations needed to turn water into *a doorway to another demesne*, to step across the distances. Then there's another account in the writings of Agneish Faygold that describes how Alis was cornered by her pursuers with her back to a lake, and then how she used the waters to escape."

"And you think she's repurposed those spells, learned to use mirrors and windows to reach places, bypass locks."

"As I say, her life would have been drab. Perhaps the modern world has opened up all sorts of possibilities to her, making her considerably more dangerous at the same time."

"When she came for me, planting the doll in my room in my cottage, she didn't use mirrors to reach me. She followed me and broke in."

"Walking the mirrors is dangerous. From the other side, the multiverse is a huge maze of reflective surfaces and portals and windows. They're not arranged to match the real world; you have to know where you're going. I assume she followed you to identify an access point – a window she could manifest through from the aether – and so gain access."

"What's involved in this magic?"

"It's mostly folk witchery; the spilling of a bit of blood, the uttering of the right syllables to put your mind into the right state. The book makes mention of runic circles too, though. I mean, it doesn't use those terms, but that's my interpretation."

I thought about that. "To make the openings permanent?"

"I think so. There's something else, though: the runes can *both grant passage and deny it*."

"Like a door that can be set to only open one way."

"I wondered about poor Jamie, you see. His mind was disordered, but surely he would have tried to return to his house when he found himself in that other realm, wouldn't he? Perhaps the magic prevented him from doing so. Perhaps there were runes drawn across the entrance that let him into that domain but not out."

"What would happen if such a barrier has been set up and you try to pass through?"

"From what I can tell, you'll be immediately turned around. You'll step back into the room, the world, you just stepped out of."

The inklings of a possible plan came to me. I had no idea if it would work. I set it aside to think about later.

"Can you make out the details of the runes required for this spell?"

"I can read them, given a little time. I'm not going to though; we've seen the malign uses such magic can be put to."

"And what if it's used for good?"

"Hard to see how trapping someone in another world could be a good thing."

"Please?" I asked. "I'm not going to use them for evil purposes. I thought you trusted me now?"

"As I say, this is powerful magic, with a high likelihood of it going badly wrong. You're not skilled enough to wield it."

"There's no risk then, is there?"

There was a long pause on the other end, enough for me to check my screen to see if I'd lost the connection.

Then she replied. "Very well, Danesh. I will attempt to recover them. Use them for harm and I'll come for you, though. With knives."

"I wouldn't have it any other way. Can you let me know if you learn anything from the Pale Sisters, too? Anything that might be relevant."

"I'll do my best to fit it in to my other duties. There is one more thing that might be of interest. This is also from Faygold, not the *Book of Shadows*. She names the troop of witchfinders who came for Alis, who were responsible for her capture, and then her torture and death."

"Can you give me the names?"

"I'll text them to you. Some of them are interesting."

"Interesting how?"

"You'll see."

She rang off. Her text arrived a moment later. It gave the names of the six seventeenth century witchfinders responsible for the persecution and death of Alis Treacle:

Murdo McTavish
Per Svenska
Fenton Crossley
Gregory Holston
Alfred Raneleigh
Piers Hamwell

I stood on the tarmac, a cold wind blowing off the Mersey as I studied the list. Fenton Crossley leapt out at me; I didn't know anything about him, but *Morris* Crossley had obviously been the name of the Manx victim I'd recently investigated. Then there was Murdo McTavish. Was it possible there was a family connection to Jamie Tavish there? Names changed over the years, especially when they weren't written down so much. It was surely easy for a *Mc* to be dropped over the decades.

And, Alfred Raneleigh too. The Crow's notes had mentioned a *Charles* Raneleigh, although he'd died – or been killed – three decades previously. Was there a link there? The other names meant nothing to me. So far as I could recall, I'd never heard of Per Svenska, Gregory Holston or Piers Hamwell. The names of Belinda Carraway and Anders Kropotkin had come up as possible victims, but I could see no connection between them and any of these names. Perhaps the whole thing was coincidence.

I replied to the librarian, thanking her for the names and asking, as politely as I could (using actual punctuation and complete words) if she would be able to look into the genealogical details of the names, see if there were any connections to the known victims in our day.

Her reply, when it came, was terse.

It said, Obviously.

I mulled the names over as I was shepherded into the terminal by an employee in a hi vis jacket. I couldn't just stand out there with jets revving their engines, it wasn't safe, was it mate? Inside, I emerged onto the airport's concourse. I had a little time before my internal flight to Edinburgh. I was checking out the possibilities for a decent cup of coffee while I waited when I glimpsed a familiar face in the small gathering of people greeting arrivals.

He was standing at the back, a grin on his crumbling baby-face. His stubble had grown into something of a straggly beard, now. It was rare to see him outside, in the real world. He'd been in the Office for years, and, so far as I could tell, had perfected the art of doing the least amount of work necessary in order to keep his position.

Digbeth had come to find me.

We stepped aside from the crowd so no one could overhear. "What's happened?" I asked. "Why are you here?"

"Hardknott-Lewis sent me. He's found things in London you need to know about."

"Why didn't he phone? Or use MORIARTY?"

There was a wary look in Digbeth's eye. "He couldn't be sure any such messages would be intercepted by the wrong people. You understand why, yes?"

"Sure."

"Let's find somewhere quiet and talk," he said. "There are things you need to know."

19 – Witch Hunt

Stars, hide your fires; Let not light see my black and deep desires.
– Shakespeare, *Macbeth*, Act 1, Scene 4, 1606

We bought coffee – Digbeth favoured something milky and weak – then ventured into the chill outside the airport to stop anyone overhearing us. We perched on two of the square blocks of concrete that had been set there in a higgledy-piggledy line as a defence against terrorist attacks – and which wouldn't be much help at all against any of the threats I worried about. People trundled past us pulling their rumbling luggage, but no one paid us any attention.

"Hardknott-Lewis returned from London yesterday," Digbeth began. "As I say, he sent me because there's a danger our comms are compromised. This has to be word of mouth only. He was very clear that we're not to communicate with him via phone or any other electronic means."

"He found something about Earl Grey?"

"Obviously, I don't know all the details of what you're up to, but the gaffer said to tell you that he has eliminated Earl Grey from his enquiries. Those were his words. DNA evidence has proven that Earl Grey is not the individual you're looking for. Does that make sense?"

"It does."

"I have to ask: what did you suspect Earl Grey of? I know we have to be wary of everyone, but Earl Grey? If he's gone to the dark side, we can all go home, right?"

"It's best you don't know the details."

"Of course, yes. I shouldn't have asked," Digbeth replied, he looked away. "Hardknott-Lewis gave me a few hints, enough for me to be prepared to meet you, and I've obviously read your MORIARTY logs. I assume there's more to what you're doing than this Alis Treacle investigation."

"To be honest, it's looking more and more like Alis is a part of the wider investigation after all. But I'd hoped to catch up with Thomas Quirk on the Isle of Man, and now I need to look elsewhere."

Digbeth's eyes narrowed slightly as he absorbed that. "Quirk is still a suspect, then. Do you think he's in hiding somewhere, preparing another attack? Or worse?"

"He's certainly a hard man to find right now. I urgently need to track him down and, well, *resolve* that situation before things get out of hand."

"We," said Digbeth.

"Huh?"

"*We* need to track him down. Another thing Hardknott-Lewis was very clear about. You know what the gaffer is like. *The danger has reached the point where the two operative rule is absolutely mandatory.* I'm to accompany you, watch your back, work with you."

That was going to be awkward, especially if I needed to wield my magical powers. At the same time, I was grateful for any help I could get.

"I'm boarding a flight for Edinburgh in two hours," I said. "See if you can get a seat."

"Why would Quirk be in Edinburgh? Or do you think Ian Majkowski's involved in this too?"

"Edinburgh because some leads in the Alis Treacle case lead me there. Quirk isn't in Scotland so far as I know, but I believe he's nearby."

"Let me go and see if there's room on the flight."

Digbeth shambled off, walking with an awkward limp. He hadn't done a great job of staying in shape, despite being only ten years older than me. I made a note of the fact. I'd never seen him involved in any sort of combat, but I doubted he was going to be much use if it came to it.

I watched him through the plate glass of the airport. He

was talking to someone on his phone while waiting in a queue at the information desk. He wasn't saying much, nodding his head. I knew little about his home life; I'd vaguely assumed he lived alone, but maybe there was a besotted partner somewhere.

He came back a few minutes later. "Booked a ticket on my phone in the end."

"It's the modern way."

"I've been thinking; something you said about Alis Treacle struck me. You talked about her in the present tense, like she's still involved. That can't be right; the woman obviously died hundreds of years ago."

"She didn't die," I said, "she was *killed*. Murdered. But, yeah, I'm beginning to think the truth might not be that simple."

Digbeth pondered that while staring into the distance.

"Interesting," he said.

"What is?"

"It may be nothing, but it's something else the gaffer said when he came back from London. Another thing he'd learned about and needed to look into urgently. It may be nothing, but I don't know, maybe not."

It was unusual for Digbeth to take much of an interest in anything. But if he'd come across something, I needed to hear it. He probably picked up all sorts of things sitting there at his desk all day.

"Tell me what he said."

"Your investigations into Jamie Tavish troubled the gaffer. He'd looked up the details of something in the Whitehall office's library; some detail of the magic that killed Jamie."

"Did he make any mention of runes?"

"Runes?"

"It's possible runic spells were used to trap Jamie through the mirrors. He could jump through but not return."

"Now that you mention it, I think the gaffer did go back to Jamie's house to study the scene in more detail after he read your notes. He also did say he'd been consulting the forbidden lexicons in London, and that he'd found out some of the spells used to kill Jamie were … archaic. *Strangely constructed* was the phrase he used."

"As if the person using them had learned them a long time ago?"

Digbeth nodded. "He also mentioned something else: a spell component that was *vampiric* in origin. I suppose he might have been referring to a sigil he found at Jamie's."

"Vampiric? He said one of the runes used to attack Jamie was vampiric in nature?"

"I'm reading between the lines here, but that's the impression I got. You know what he's like; need-to-know basis only."

"Yeah," I said. "Damn, though."

"What does it mean?"

"It means we'd be a damn-sight more effective if we communicated among ourselves properly. Like, say, if the librarian and Hardknott-Lewis compared notes. She could have helped him in his researches."

"How is the librarian involved in this?"

For one thing, she didn't appear to have received the memo about avoiding electronic communication with me. More likely, she *had* been told, and had chosen to ignore it. I really needed to get those runes off her.

"Never mind for now. A vampiric rune also confirms I was too slow to see what was right in front of me. Looks like the person or the thing that I've been pursuing – and that's been pursuing me – *is* tied up with the wider situation. The Warlock must be behind these attacks, too. He's been using Alis to kill Office operatives who are becoming a problem for him, and now he's doing the same to me. Why the hell didn't Hardknott-Lewis tell me this immediately?"

"He obviously thought it was safer to send me to tell you in person."

"Did he tell you anything else, give you any suggestion about what he thought I should do next?"

"I know that he was worried by the magic he'd uncovered. I mean, even more worried than his usual *very* level of worried. He was talking about the dangers of curses and other malign acts of witchcraft. He suspected Alis was in the thrall of the Warlock. For what it's worth, I think we should pursue her case, find this Alis Treacle, before confronting the traitor in the Office. We don't want her coming up behind us if we tackle Quirk. I mean, going straight for him might be exactly what English Wizardry and the Warlock wants us to do, right? If we strike where they don't expect it, pursue Alis first, it might throw them off guard."

I didn't like it; the Alis Treacle investigation had taken up too much time, and I needed to corner Quirk before English Wizardry cornered me. On the other hand, perhaps Digbeth had a point. And, Alis Treacle – whatever she was – *was* hideously dangerous. She needed to be stopped. Too many people had died at her hand. The extra time would be useful, too: I was still coming to terms with my newly unshackled magical powers. I clearly needed practice before they were fully under my control; from everything I'd read, these things can take *years*. Perhaps tackling Alis before the boss fight with Quirk made sense.

Digbeth was fidgety; he seemed impatient for us to be away. No doubt the prospect of physical danger alarmed him. "You said there were leads in Scotland? No surprise at all. Scotland's always been a nest of witchcraft."

"There are other victims there," I said. "It's possible they'll give us clues on how to tackle Alis."

"Right," said Digbeth. "Let's do it. We should check in for our flight."

We arrived at Edinburgh in the mid-afternoon, checking into separate hotels under yet more fake IDs. The night passed without any supernatural attacks taking place. The following morning, we were welcomed to the Scottish branch of the Office in a wing of Edinburgh castle by Herbert Wigwe, the acolyte I'd last seen in Downing Street that day. He'd grown up a highland Scot, his accent soft and musical. He greeted us warmly. He'd started sporting a beard that suited him, made him look wiser.

"Welcome to Scotland. I scanned through your recent log entries when I heard you were coming, Danesh. Had a few fun and games on the Isle of Man by the sound of it?"

"It was eventful."

"Ian Majkowski's not around at the moment, but he told me to be sure to extend all hospitalities to you. What happened to Mason Greentree – it affected us all, obviously, but Ian was a good friend of his. Bloody English Wizardry bastards, right?"

"Right."

He led us through several layers of security door to the Office's offices. The heraldic symbols of Scotland (unicorns, for some reason) were reproduced again and again throughout the building, on departmental signs and the like – although obviously not on our logo. I also had the very clear impression that steps were steeper in Scotland than those I was used to south of the border. I didn't mention it to Herbert as we climbed and climbed. I needed all my breath to keep up with him.

The offices, when we reached them, had fabulous views across the city. The craggy mound of Arthur's Seat lay to one side, odd so close to a city centre. Trams, buses and cars thronged Princes Street in front of us. Beyond, to the north, across the rooftops, bright sun picked out the waters of the Firth of Forth, including a red loop of the steel railway bridge. Beyond that, dusted with white, lay mountains that I didn't know the name of.

Herbert offered us an extremely respectable cup of coffee – I warmed to him immediately – then sat down with us to find out what we needed.

"Your notes mentioned Belinda as well as two other persons of interest," he said.

"Anders Kropotkin and Charles Raneleigh, yes," I said. "Is Belinda around at the moment?"

"She's on a shout at the moment, a bit of ghost activity in the Old Town. If she's not back soon we can go and find her. Do you think she's in some sort of danger?"

Her name had only come up because the Crow had mentioned her. And he'd only done so because she'd suffered a few psychological symptoms that might – might – be consistent with curses and Night Hag intrusions.

"It's a possibility, no more than that. You've also had a recent death here in Edinburgh, one Anders Kropotkin."

"Oh, aye. Sad case. We looked into it because a police officer in the know felt there was something a bit odd, *a bit off*, about it. But we didn't find anything. The guy had been suffering some personal issues, his girlfriend leaving him mainly, and it triggered a few childhood traumas as far as we could tell. He'd been prone to nightmares and sleep-walking as a boy."

"He sleep-walked right out of the windows of his third floor flat."

"Or he threw himself out, knew what he was doing."

"You obviously ran thaumometer checks and the like."

"There was a reading when we got there, right enough, but there is in many parts of Edinburgh. The *background hum* we call it. Something to do with the geology of the place. Or the history."

"I presume you've read about the cursed dolls I've been finding."

"Aye, the poppets, yes. Nasty wee bastards. We have our own versions of them up here, all heather and fishbones and malice."

"Anything like that at Kropotkin's flat?"

"We didn't *find* anything, but I guess we didn't turn the place over. If it was well-hidden, we might have missed it."

"Who's living there now?"

"Another private resident, not related in any way."

"It might be a good idea to keep an eye on them, check them for any troubles they might be experiencing," I said. "If there is a doll there, it will still be having an effect, especially on any children."

Herbert nodded and made a note of the task on his phone.

"And Kropotkin wasn't known to the Office in any way?" I asked. "As a user or an operative?"

"He was just a regular guy."

"He'd reported seeing huge black hounds in the back streets."

"We looked into that, of course. That was what caught our attention. We couldn't find anything."

"Tell me, do you have records of all your former operatives?"

"Down in the archives, we do. We don't have a library as extensive or famous as yours, but we keep our records assiduously. Can I ask what you're looking for?"

"I'd like to look into the death of Charles Raneleigh thirty years ago. Then I'd like to look for mention of some names I have from the seventeenth century."

"We can go now if you like."

"Sure you have time?"

"Oh, aye. There's a redcap outbreak I need to look into down on the border, but that can wait a while. Little buggers are always running round causing mischief."

The vault was deep underground, down many, many more steep flights of echoey stone stairs. Eventually we ran out of windows; we had to be underground, inside the rock of the volcanic plug upon which the castle had been built. Once again, heavy security doors barred our way while cameras watched us from the high corners. The vault was a modern, dry, well-lit room, the roof arched and the walls painted white. I could almost feel the weight of all that stone bearing down on us. Thankfully, there was no Scottish equivalent of Lady Coldwater to watch us suspiciously as we entered.

Herbert walked down the aisle of steel shelves, running a finger across the spines of the books.

"Here we are, case notes from 1992. Charles Raneleigh should be in here. We really need to get these old records digitized, but you know how it is."

He slipped on white cotton gloves and began to leaf through the book. It contained lined pages written in many hands, bound together to form the single volume.

The paper crackled as he turned.

"Here it is."

Herbert ran his fingers down the side of the page while I peered over his shoulder. Digbeth seemed uninterested, sitting on a chair by the door while we worked.

"Some mention of black hound sightings," Herbert said, more to himself than to me," the *Muckle Black Tyke*, fairly standard stuff. Ah, Ian Majkowski was involved; he was an Acolyte back then. Raneleigh was investigating possible witches' Sabbath associations in the Highlands. Then, a couple of weeks later, he pops up on Lewis and Harris."

"He appeared on two different islands?"

"Ah, no. Common mistake. Lewis and Harris is the name of a single island."

"Right. This is the Hebrides?"

"Aye."

"He was having a few psychological problems?"

Herbert nodded. "The black dog was coming for him in more ways than one, by the sound of it. Poor guy. The long winters in the north can be tough."

I made what sense I could of the handwritten log entries. Raneleigh's notes read more like diary entries, a series of private thoughts and observations. He'd been investigating what he referred to as *burnings*, mentioning the word again and again, as if they were a known thing.

"What are these burnings?" I asked Herbert. "Does that signify something?"

"Nothing in particular. I don't know of any folk practices or rituals or anything with that name, although obviously fire plays a part in many activities, especially in the winter."

"His disquiet comes through," I said. "See, he uses words like *hideous* and *unsettling*. I'd say he sounded pretty terrified by what he'd discovered."

"Here he talks about the nightmares he's been suffering, see," said Herbert. "In his dreams he found himself strapped to a tree while a fire was lit beneath him. These are some pretty vivid nightmares. He talks about his flesh burning, his skin and bone melting and dropping off him, the agonies waking him up screaming. Here, see, he says he had a strong fear of fire, something he puts down to his home burning down when he was a child. He was haunted by his nightmares. But that's common enough, right?"

"This follows the pattern I've seen, though," I said. "Here, too, he mentions in passing some blood being taken from him, wounds he couldn't explain one morning. But if this is related, why the gap of thirty years?"

"There's a name here," said Herbert. "A few pages back he talks about being contacted by a local woman who says she's seen a number of these burnings taking place and is terrified she's next. The locals are accusing her of witchcraft."

"It's all a bit *Wicker Man*," I said. "Have you ever witnessed anything like that in real life?"

Herbert shook his head. "Not in the least. This sounds more like an outsider's guess at the sort of dangers a witchfinder might face in the Isles. These are odd things for a local to say. The woman's name is here. Eta Carlisle. Does that mean anything?"

I shook my head. I'd never heard it. "There's no mention of cursed dolls or Night Hag attacks or anything of the sort. I can't be sure if this is related to my case or not."

Herbert closed the book and sat to think. "You said something in your notes about a possible link to seventeenth century witchfinders. Charles Raneleigh definitely had those connections. Like your Jamie Tavish, Charles came from a family of Office operatives. I looked into him."

"How far back did you go?"

"To the earliest days. I believe his family lived and worked in the south in the nineteenth century, but they started out in Scotland originally, and Charles came back as a young man. His forebear, the first witchfinder in the family, was Alfred Raneleigh. Would that be one of the names on your list by any chance?"

"It would. Can I see his entry?"

Herbert found another ledger, the red cover ink-stained, the pages dog-eared. Someone had gone to a lot of trouble to write down the names of all members of the Scottish Office of the Witchfinder General, including their years of their appointment, promotion and retirement – or, more commonly – their early death.

"Here," said Herbert. "Alfred Raneleigh."

"And he was definitely a forebear of Charles?"

"No doubt about it. It's not that common a name, and you know how it is: witchfinders are recruited from known and trusted families a lot of the time. The old boy and girl network, right?"

"Right."

I pointed to another entry. "There's a Murdo McTavish a few names away from Alfred Raneleigh."

"Aha. You're thinking he's a forebear of Jamie?"

"How could we find out?"

Herbert thought about that. "How long had Jamie's family been in Wales?"

"A generation or two. The notes at our end said he moved from the Borders, but whether that was on the English side or the Scottish, I don't know. We also don't know why he moved."

"For the tropical climate of sunny Wales perhaps?" said Herbert.

"Oh, yes, that'll definitely be it," I replied.

"Let's look through the records for Tavishes and McTavishes, see what that turns up."

Fifteen minutes of scanning found a series of McTavishes, generation after generation, all men. Then, in the nineteenth century, instead of a *deceased* or a *retired*, there was a note that one Alexander McTavish, an Adept, was moving to England – and his name, previously given as *McTavish* had now lost its *Mc*. Alexander Tavish was a name I did know: my researches into Jamie's past in Cardiff had found that name as a direct forebear. Alexander had kept on moving and had ended up in the valleys of South Wales. Assuming they were the same Alexander Tavishes, the connection was clear. Alexander had presumably altered his surname to fit in better south of the border.

"I don't get it," I said as I put these pieces together. "It looks like two of the six who killed Alis Treacle – Alfred Raneleigh and Murdo McTavish – were Scottish, but Alis lived in Sussex. A long way south."

Herbert nodded, as if that made sense to him. "You can probably thank King James for that. James VI, I mean, who became your James I."

"Why so?"

"Aye, well, Scotland went a bit crazy for witch trials in the late sixteenth century. The King was completely caught up in it, became a witchfinder himself. Did you know that? Not something the royal family like to publicize. James even wrote a book about it, *Daemonologie*, describing all the ways demons attacked men. Werewolves, vampires, they were all in there. Some say Shakespeare got his *weird sisters* from that book when he wrote Macbeth. There was an act of parliament, too, making witchcraft, or even the act of consorting with witches, punishable by death. Thousands of people were tried up here, and a lot were killed: strangled and then burned."

"When you say *people*, you mean women?"

"Mostly, aye. Not exclusively, though. The point is, we had a real surplus of witchfinders up here, and they became something of an export to England and Wales in the following years. Spreading the word sort of thing. Like … missionaries, almost."

I scanned the names one more time, but there was no sign of a Fenton Crossley, Per Svenska, Gregory Holston or Piers Hamwell. They, presumably, hadn't been Scottish, but local to Sussex at the time of Alis's murder. One of Crossley's offspring, I knew, had moved to the Isle of Man from England at some point. Svenska, Holston and Hamwell remained a mystery.

Six, though. I thought of my dreamland vision of Alis at the graves – or my actual meeting with her if Stonewall was correct. Perhaps it was a bit of both, given that the dolls I knew about were safely in the hands of the Office and not decorating a mysterious burial site. There'd been four dolls there, though, and she'd said it: *Four of the six.* One doll for each of her murderers, that had to be it. There were two still to add. Except, she'd also said, *One missing, one removed.* What did that mean? Who was missing and who'd been removed?

Then, of course, there was the fact of my own doll, hastily lashed together. What had she said? *There's room for you, too. Always room for you, witch finder.*

I sat back, trying to make sense of it all. Had she been set upon my trail by the Warlock? I was very definitely unrelated to the six named seventeenth century witchfinders. I knew for a fact that there'd been nothing like that on my mother's side, and my father's forebears had been thousands of miles away in India at the time. Apart from Anders Kropotkin, Belinda Carraway and myself, the people who'd been attacked had clear connections to the witchfinders responsible for Alis's death. Her killing spree seemed to be two things knotted together: a revenge plot and then the attacks on completely unrelated people. Perhaps the Warlock had allowed her to carry out her own vendetta as a side-hustle while she did his evil bidding.

Herbert returned the volume to its place on the shelves. "I hope that's helped in some way?"

"Could we talk to Belinda Carraway now?"

"Of course. If she's not back we can go and find her."

The grand edifices of Edinburgh's old town loomed around us. The stone was grey and grim, although finely decorated. The roads were black cobbles. A sheen of rain made every surface shine. Herbert slipped down a narrow alleyway, up yet more steps with an iron railing running up it. He stopped at a grand door, tall and wide enough to steer Highland cattle through. If you'd wanted to.

"She was investigating reports of a Code 11 here," Herbert confided in us. "She must still be inside."

"Don't you send two operatives on case like this?"

"When we can. This was considered low risk. And Belinda can be … unreceptive to offers of help. I think she sees them as a personal affront."

There was a brass plaque beside the door, the sort of thing a solicitor or a doctor might sport, but it had been polished so much that the letters were illegible, worn away to random runes. Herbert pushed open the door, shouting up to Belinda who he was. Answer came there none. I followed him inside, Digbeth a step or two behind me. Yet another flight of stairs led upwards. Once it would all have been grand – the ceilings stucco plasterwork, the floor detailed mosaics – but now everything was a bit shabby and cracked. There was a cold dampness in the air that suggested a building no longer used.

"What's the likely haunter?" I whispered.

Herbert shook his head. "Probably isn't one. It was a doctor's surgery once, though, so I suppose there's plenty of scope for trapped spirits. Would have been lots of operations carried out in a place like this, back in the day. You know, before anaesthetics and the like."

I glanced at my thaumometer. It was, indeed, flickering constantly around 1 – low-level – as if the whole city were built on top of something supernatural. Were there catacombs beneath Edinburgh like in Paris? I didn't know. Herbert saw me take the reading but didn't look concerned.

A scream came from upstairs, then, followed by a heavy clump as of some weight falling to the floor above us. Then another scream, and someone laughing, high-pitched enough to scrape up my spine. It became a shriek, shriller and shriller, until it passed beyond my hearing. My innate magical senses – previously dormant – opened one sleepy eye.

"I assume that wasn't Belinda's voice," I said.

"No," said Herbert. "It was not."

I drew my handgun. I clearly didn't want to use my new-found powers here, not with three – or two – other operatives to see.

Herbert was about to ascend, one hand on the wooden railing, when a flash of light came from above, blinding us all momentarily. As my eyes recovered, a ghostly form emerged out of the glow: a woman I thought, transparent, her hair lashing as if she were in a gale, her white robes trailing around her. Your classic *woman-in-white* ghost, once very fashionable. She descended through the air towards us, arms outstretched, her eyes alabaster and a hiss of purest hatred on her lips.

Leave here. You should not have come here!

As she spoke, her countenance changed. She went from being a young woman to something utterly demonic, features contorted in malice. I dialled up a clothcutter round on my gun, but I doubted it would be much use. My guess was this was an entity from our world, trapped here after its death, rather than an invader from another realm. A Touchstone might have worked – if I'd brought one, and if I'd had any idea what totem would appeal to his particular entity. Herbert, I noticed, drew his clothcutter blade. He glanced aside at me, the first flicker of nervousness on his features. He knew his knife wasn't going to achieve much either. We nodded to each other. We'd fight side-by-side. I stepped up to stand next to him.

The spectral form threw itself at us with an ear-blasting shriek – and then, even as I was raising my weapon to try a shot, a ragged hole appeared in her abdomen, like she was on fire and burning from the inside-out. And then, through her, I saw another form, another woman, this one reassuringly solid and definitely not floating through the air in contravention of the laws of gravity. She was about my age, short, her head shaved bald, and in her hand was the pointed steel weapon she'd used to skewer the ghost.

The blade acted like a lightning rod, earthing the woman in white, pulling her in. The creature writhed and wailed, but couldn't resist. Again, her shriek went higher and higher, the sound painful in my brain. The cacophony reached a crescendo … then cut out. The entity swirled into the steel weapon and was gone.

There was a moment of hush.

"Belinda," said Herbert, stepping forwards. "Good to see you safe and sound."

The woman seemed about as furious with us being there as she had been at the ghost. She scowled as she trotted down the remaining stairs.

"What the hell are you doing here, Herb? I told you I was fine. I can handle a wee bundle of spite and bile like that with my eyes shut."

"I never doubted it," Herbert replied. "Got a couple of visitors looking for you."

She glanced aside to me and, behind us, at Digbeth. Her gaze was piercing, very nearly as sharp as the makeshift weapon she'd used to skewer the spectre.

"You're Shahzan," she said, her tone making it sound like an accusation.

"Danesh," I said. "That was nicely done. What was she, a patient? A relative unable to handle the loss?"

"Neither of those. She was a doctor, Victorian times. Her name was Elsie Ingot."

I noticed then that the blade Belinda had used was, in fact, some long, fine surgeon's implement, the sort of grim item used to pierce soft parts of the body and extract tissue samples.

"Did she linger because she died from some disease? Or was she assaulted by a patient?"

"Neither of those things. She lingered because she was bloody furious at being overlooked, dismissed by the medical establishment her whole life. That's probably why she reacted so badly at seeing you lumbering in, invading her domain. I was in the middle of helping her when you came."

"Ah, sorry," said Herbert.

"It's my fault," I added. "I wanted to come and see you. We should put that implement you used with her body, help her find proper rest. If you know where her remains are."

My words seemed to placate Belinda a little. That had been the right thing to say.

"Oh, we will, don't you worry."

We scoured the property looking for any other supernatural incursions and then stepped outside into the light drizzle to return to the castle. I filled Belinda in on everything that had happened to me, my reasons for visiting – or, at least, the details I wanted people to know about.

"Can I ask you something?" I said.

"If you have to."

She walked with the same focussed fury with which she'd greeted us, and I was struggling to keep up. "Obviously tell me to fuck off if you want. But, I read you had some … difficulties a while back. They may be unrelated, but I wondered if any of my story was familiar?"

She'd listened attentively to what I'd told her, occasionally glancing aside at me as if seeing me with fresh eyes. "You said cursed dolls were planted?"

"To lower victims' defences, I believe, and to act as the focus for Night Hag attacks. Did you ever see anything like that?"

"I did not, but I didn't look, either."

"The episodes – the attacks – they stopped?"

"They did. Things reached a climax, like, and there was a bit of a showdown, and then I never suffered the attacks again. Can't tell you what a relief it was."

There'd been no mention of a crisis point in her case notes – a fact that I asked her about. Digbeth and Herbert were behind us, out of earshot.

"Aye, well, it didn't seem relevant. I assumed I was suffering a few frights in the night, my own stupid brain summoning up baddies, you know. But now…"

"Now you're not so sure?"

"That woman you described. The witchy lass with the spooky dolls. You should know that I saw her, too. I saw her every damn night. Couldn't escape her."

"Did she look like this?"

I showed her the picture from the Isle of Man Airport feed of the purple-haired Alis arriving on the Isle of Man.

Belinda's eyes showed me she recognized the woman. "How the hell do you have a picture of someone from my dreams?"

"Because she's real. I mean, she may well have popped up in your nightmares too, but she walks the Earth, no doubt about it."

"Why did she attack me then leave me alone?"

"That's what I'm wondering. Can you tell me what happened at this showdown?"

"Are you sure it'll help?"

"It might. I can't be sure. Obviously don't tell me if you'd prefer not to."

Belinda sighed. Recalling the events was clearly uncomfortable for her.

"You've been open with me. Very well, just between you and me, yes?"

"I'm very good at secrets."

Her eyes narrowed slightly at that but she otherwise ignored it. "So. In my nightmares, there was this clearing in a wood. There was a grave there, someone buried. Actually, two graves, I think. However much I tried to flee the place, I always ended up back there."

"The woman was there? What did she say?"

"She was *furious* about something. Look, I assumed this was *me*, some manifestation of my own mind, some buried anger. I don't … it didn't occur to me this was an attack."

"You aren't the first, trust me."

"She would shriek at me, laugh at me, say that she had to return there every night, and that now I would too. I would keep her company for the rest of time. She was going to dig a grave for me; a fresh grave beside the others. It was pretty grim if I'm honest. The thought of being buried alive – it's something I have a bit of a horror of. I mean, I'm sure most people do, but the thought really spooks me."

"For any particular reason?"

"Oh, just a daft childhood thing. A game that went wrong. I'll spare you the details."

I thought about Belinda's words. Alis had to return to the burial ground every day? That was interesting. I'd assumed she went occasionally, when she had some new victim perhaps. But always? Like a vampire forced to return to its lair, its mother earth?

Little lights came on in my brain. I'd wondered whether Alis Treacle was being controlled or possessed by the Warlock, but what if I'd had that wrong?

What if she *was* the Warlock? The attacks: they always came at night. I'd seen her walking in the daylight, sure, but the assaults were always when the sun was down. When a vampire – or something vampiric in nature – would be more powerful. Except, I'd fought her off. It had cost me, but I'd hurt her, sent her back through the mirror when she came for me on the Isle of Man. Surely the fearsome Warlock would be much tougher to fight?

"Danesh?"

"Sorry," I said. "The attacks stopped, though? She let you live?"

"And I don't know why. She seemed confused about me, like she wanted to destroy me but some voice was holding her back."

"You're a woman," I said.

"Thanks for noticing."

"No, I mean, you're the only female victim that I know about. I think that has to be relevant. There's revenge going on here for the actions of certain men, and the others who've been killed were all men, too. Facing a female witchfinder … it might have thrown her."

"Yeah, well. She wouldn't be the first there, believe me," said Belinda. "As I say, I assumed I'd imagined the whole thing. That was why I logged a few vague details but didn't pursue it. Now, I need to know more. I need to know a lot more."

"Can I ask," I said, "Do you come from a family of witchfinders?"

"Is that relevant?"

"It might be."

"My mother and her mother were in the Office. We go

a lot further back than that, though. All the way back. I had a forebear here in the very early days. They were obviously very different times."

"Do you know his name?"

"Ah, Holston. Gregory Holston."

She must have seen the look of recognition on my face. "You know about him."

"His name's come up."

"Something I should know about?"

"I think you should, yes. I'll send you all the details I have. It might not be easy reading, but it may help explain a few things. What it reveals ... I'm sorry. No blame attaches to you."

She nodded, but didn't reply. Perhaps she knew something about her forebear already. We walked together in silence after that, each absorbed in our own thoughts.

20 – Broken Ground

… but not everything passed so happily on our excursion into Ipswych. One of us known to all as Alis was taken by Hopkin's animals as we left the town by the postern gate. A number of Scottish were with them. We despatched three of their number through the veils to the realms of lamentation and thought we had made our escape clean but Alis as we discovered upon our return was left behind. It is to be hoped she met with some swift end but we fear it is not so. If the witch finders have her they will not spare to inflict all manner of torment upon her poor and broken body. Her daughter urges us to save her as we have saved many others and this is the end we must now pursue with all haste.

– Sister Agneish Faygold, *Accounts*, 1686

We drove from Edinburgh nearly to the south coast of England that afternoon and evening. It felt suddenly safer to be one more anonymous vehicle on the public roads. Once again, we used fake IDs to hire the car. So far as I could tell, no one was tracing us, but I wasn't taking any chances. I'd suffered no more nightmares, except for a brief rerun of the long-standing Az one. It was always distressing, but this time it felt almost like relief to be back in the familiar pattern, too. So far as I could tell, everything I experienced was safely inside my head.

South of the border, tanking down the A1, we passed signs for Lindisfarne. Digbeth caught me glancing to the side to pick out the buildings visible on the part-time island as I was driving.

"You're trying to see Lindisfarne?" he asked. There

was something in his voice that made me think the place meant something to him, although I hadn't mentioned it in my MORIARTY entries.

"The name came up," I said casually. "Hardknott-Lewis mentioned it, but I wasn't sure where it was."

"Aha. Tricky place to get to; you have to time the tides right or you get stranded. Or swept away."

"If I ever go there, I'll be careful."

After that, the conversation dried up as the hours ticked by. I tried to find out what he remembered about Jamie but it didn't appear to be much. I soon regretted not taking a flight to London. Digbeth, on the other hand, seemed content to stare out of the window at the passing landscape. Occasionally, he picked up his phone and answered texts.

Around Leeds, we swapped over and he drove. I'd had one message that I'd wanted to study. *Scary Librarian* had been in touch again. She'd tracked down one additional piece of biographical information: Per Svenska, one of the seventeenth century witchfinders on her list, had lived in Norfolk, although his family was originally Scandinavian. Three generations after Per, a daughter of the family had married one Piotr Kropotkin. Sure enough, Piotr had lived in Scotland and they'd moved up there. After that, there were no more Svenskas or Kropotkins in the Office records. The family had turned to more mundane trades than witchfinding. There had to be a good chance that Anders Kropotkin, the guy who'd died in Edinburgh, was a descendant. Which meant that, of the modern-day victims I knew about, only I had no connection to Alis's killers.

The other information the librarian sent was more useful: despite her clear reservations, she'd copied out the runes that Alis had used to trap Jamie in the mirrors. The list she'd sent was, as she put it, *almost complete*. She hadn't been able to transcribe everything from the *Book of Shadows* – either because they'd remained obscured, or because she was being exposed to too much destructive magical influence. What she'd sent would have to do. I thanked her profusely; I knew her well enough to know that she'd probably pushed herself, risked her health, to extract what she had.

I studied the runes on the screen, learning their lines, the flow of strokes needed to craft each. I could almost *see* them in a magical sense, see how they worked, how they flowed. It was like hearing someone speaking in a language you vaguely knew: the odd syllable here and there made sense, and the more you grew attuned, the more you understood. The well of magical potential roiling away inside me helped, too. As I practised the runes on the phone's screen, I could feel the flare of magical power as I got something right, drew the right lines, formed the right shapes. So much so that I had to be careful; I didn't want to work the actual runes into life and manifest something unwelcome inside the speeding car.

"You okay?" Digbeth asked. He'd seen me drawing away on my screen from the corner of his eye.

"Oh, sure," I said. "Trying to make use of my phone's gesture recognition stuff. I think I'll stick to typing."

He grunted but didn't reply. I spent the next few miles making sure I had the runes committed to memory then put my phone away.

We arrived in Sussex as dusk was falling, colour leeching from the world beneath a lowering sky. I wanted to put my plan into action in the early morning, ready for the approaching dawn. We found a country pub that did rooms – *The Lightning Tree* – and tried to find a few hours sleep. The full moon was peering through my window when my alarm buzzed at 4:00 AM. Who knew that there was a four o'clock in the morning as well as in the afternoon? I got myself together, made bad instant coffee with the room's kettle, then knocked gently on Digbeth's door. Ten minutes later, he emerged, nodding but not saying anything.

We pulled off the road a little north of a junction called Wych Cross to consult maps and agree plans. I had only a vague idea of the location of the burial site in the physical world, but I was also confident I could track the place down employing my new-found mystical (and highly illegal) abilities.

I didn't want Digbeth to know anything about that, though. Fortunately, he seemed perfectly happy to stay to *make sure no one else comes*. We parked out of sight of the road or any buildings, and I left him in the car. If I absolutely had to, I could phone him, but I doubted he was going to make much of a difference. As well as my powers, I had my Office weaponry and gizmos, and also, if it came to it, I had the acorn that I could use to summon Stonewall. Given that we were in the woods, I assumed he could come to my aid rapidly if I needed him.

When I was out of sight of the car, I took a moment to find my bearings. The tree trunks were dark shapes around me, vertical lines in the moonlight. The muddy ground was lost in darkness beneath my feet. I could hear the distant *whoosh* of vehicles on the road, but other than that I might have been gone from the modern world. Rotting leaves from the previous autumn gave the air a gentle tang. Unseen things rustled in the undergrowth. The map on my phone showed me a number of small lakes and ponds that might be the site of the little islet I was looking for, but there was no way to tell which was which. I put the modern technology away and closed my eyes, trying to reach that elevated state of mind I'd experienced after my dip in Stonewall's pool.

I soon saw it. It was like glimpsing a thread of spiderweb glistening in the moonlight. It wove between the trees, sometimes looping around and taking diversions as if a particular sequence of steps had to be taken to arrive at the protected grove. Walking as quietly as I could, my breathing loud in my ears, I followed the gossamer thread. I continued for maybe an hour. I soon lost track of where I was relative to the car and the road, but it didn't matter. Owls screeched raucously from the branches as I stepped by. There was still no sign of the glow of morning in the sky. I neither saw nor heard anyone else – although that didn't mean unseen things weren't watching me.

Eventually, I emerged into the clearing. I knew instinctively it was the right one. The gibbous moon had slid up the sky from behind the treetops, silvering the world in its flat light. The open space felt oddly like a spotlit stage. I'd been following the line of a chortling brook, its waters dark beside me, but now the stream spread to fill a pool of still water perhaps thirty feet across. In the middle was an island of earth, high rushes obscuring what lay at its centre. Perhaps in the summer, when the water was low, you could walk to it without getting your feet wet, but now I'd have to wade.

I closed my eyes again to listen properly, sift through the rustling and scurrying of the woodland to see if I could pick out footsteps or breathing. Nothing. Taking off my boots and socks, I rolled up my trousers and waded into the water. The waters were icy. Mud oozed between my toes as I felt my way forwards. I tried not to think of the pondlife that might be lurking there. I could see nothing beneath the surface. Occasionally, my feet found sharp stones that I had to work my way around. The owl screeched again in the distance. The water came up to my thighs, soaking my jeans. Then, thankfully, the ground began to rise and the waters shallow. My testicles weren't in danger this time. I pulled myself up onto the islet with the help of a clump of bullrushes, slipping and sliding onto dry – *ish* – land.

In the centre of the islet, I could discern very definite signs of magic use. A rough circle of branches had been set into the mud, animal skulls set atop them. I didn't know what all the creatures were: some were tiny – birds or rodents – while others were larger, rabbits or badgers. The largest of them had horns curling out of it – another sheep or goat skull like the one I'd found in the supposed grave of Owain Williams, back in the Welsh hills. It watched me from the depths of its hollow eye sockets with a clear look of malice. So I imagined. Scattered on the ground were scraps of twig and twine, a few straws of corn. This had to be where the dolls were lashed together and enchanted. Perhaps it was here, also, that the Night Hags had been summoned and set upon the trail of their victims.

There were also two little mounds of broken ground. I crept towards them, wary. The mounds were small for graves, although one was larger than the other. They both had stone slabs piled on top of them. Each was marked with a single, rough stone. As I drew nearer, I could also see the dolls. Four of them in a line, tatty bundles of twig placed there like sad children's toys. The real dolls – three of them anyway – were in the possession of the Office. These looked to be mere copies, placed there as markers. I could sense no malign magic coiling off them.

The arrangements of the graves, the trees and the water: the scene was definitely familiar to me from my dreams. This was the place. And the graves? The slabs on the mounds would be heavy to heave aside, but that would be no problem for a vampiric entity if that were what I was dealing with. Underneath, dug into that waterlogged ground, there would be a cavity, and a place where bones had been buried within the mother earth. Now, perhaps, they were something else entirely.

I set to work while I had time. I walked the perimeter of the islet, beating down the vegetation where I needed to expose the mud. The soil would be my canvas. Every few feet, I crouched to draw the runes the librarian had sent me. With each sigil, I added a small amount of my own magical strength, powering the runes, bringing them to life. It felt awkward at first, like balancing something wobbly upon the tip of a stick, but slowly my confidence grew. The shape of the symbols, the flow of the lines: I began to *know* they were right. I set them close enough together to make the circle complete, but far enough apart to give me time to go all the way round. I worked for the best part of another hour, glancing around again and again to see if anything had come, creeping up on me from behind.

When it was done, I walked the lip of the water once

more, checking for gaps and misdrawn lines. Once I was happy – it's a relative term – I withdrew to the centre to stand by the grave and wait for Alis Treacle – or the entity that had once been her – to return to her lair. The eastern horizon was very definitely thinking about starting a new day now, the first mauves and pinks shading the night sky. The air was completely still, no breath of wind, no rain. That was good. That was very good. A downpour might wash away the runes.

I crouched and waited, making no sound, my gun resting on my thigh, the silver anti-vampire round dialled up and ready.

I felt rather than saw the moment when my enemy arrived. Just as I'd suspected, she was using the waters of the lake as her gateway to and from the aether. I assumed the circle around the island allowed her to arrive from any angle – if that was how stepping from plane to plane worked. I felt the rush of magical force in my gut, and she emerged, seeming to spring out of the waters like a leaping salmon, yet without the water touching her. She stood for a moment, breathing heavily, wary of something but not sure what. She looked the same as she had on the plane and in my room when she attacked me: a young woman, purple-haired. She didn't appear to have noticed me. It didn't matter. I had her. There was no escape for her now.

Perhaps not for me, either.

I stood, letting the low rays of the rising sun pick me out. She saw me immediately, saw that she'd walked into some sort of ambush. She reacted immediately. I assumed she'd attack, fling vicious spells at me, but she turned and threw herself back into the water, into the mirror, the doorway to another demesne that would allow her to flee.

The runes did their work, flaring into life as she tried to pass back through her portal. She arrived not at her original starting point but on the opposite side of the islet. I turned to see her arrive, see the look of confusion and alarm on her face.

With a snarl, she ran across the island to throw herself

into the water at a different point. Once again, the sigil ring did its job, returning her to the island, trapping her just as she, once, had trapped Jamie. She was a blur of light trapped in a room of mirrors.

She knew what I'd done. She kicked at the ground with her boots, desperately trying to obliterate the runes, create a gap in the protective circle, but the wards I'd worked in repelled her with a *crack* of electricity. The look on her face was unexpected as she glanced up at me. I saw shock. Fear. She hurled herself again and again into the water, crying wordless screams of anger and frustration. She was a maddened wasp trying to escape a glasshouse. But, each time she vanished, she reappeared.

As I watched, a growing sense of disquiet crept through me. Why was she behaving in this way? I'd though to trap her so she couldn't leap away and return to surprise me as we struggled. I hadn't expected this desperate alarm, this need to flee.

These were not the actions of the Warlock, nor of any formidable magic user, vampiric or otherwise.

She tried one more time, fury twisting her features. She winked out of existence and then immediately back in across the islet. She landed in a huddle upon the mud, sagging in defeat.

After a second, she stood, panting heavily. When she'd attacked me in my hotel room on the Isle of Man, she'd been fearless. She'd made it clear she was hunting me. Then I'd struck her with the purple and red explosion of my own spell, throwing her backwards against the wall. The hunted-animal wariness in her eyes now was unmistakable.

"Let me out of here, you bastard."

"Answer my questions first."

"I'll take your fucking head off. Let me free!"

She raised her hand and threw a fizzing orb of magical fury at me, just as she had at the hotel. This time, more in control of my powers, I was able to parry it without too much difficulty. My timing was still a little off, sure, but I was getting better at it. With my palm open, I sent her

272

sphere of spitting, seething magic into the sky above us. I could have hurled it at her, but I chose not to. There were too many things I needed to know – things that did not make sense – and I couldn't be completely sure the spell wouldn't destroy her if it struck.

Her eyes were on the orb as I moved my fingers in the way I felt I needed to. Somewhat to my surprise, the magic obeyed me. The spell dissipated.

Her look was calculating as she considered me. "How did you do that? In the hotel, I thought it was some protection device, but this is *you*. How is that possible?"

"I'm not only a witch finder, just as you are not only a witch," I said. "What are you? Are you the Warlock? Are you that *thing*?"

"The Warlock?" She spoke the name as if it were unfamiliar to her.

"English Wizardry, the Office, the attacks on my family – are you the one behind it all? Tell me, or I'll destroy you."

Her response was a snarl of rage. "You don't know anything, do you? Let me free."

"I'll ask you again, are you the Warlock?"

"Obviously not, idiot."

"But you're under his sway? He controls you."

The look of bafflement on her face told its own story. "Why would you say that? I have nothing to do with that thing."

"Prove it to me."

"He – it, whatever – is nothing to do with me. That vile monster. Is that what you think?"

"If you're not a vampire, why are you compelled to return to your grave every morning?"

"*My* grave, witch finder? Do you really think that's what this is?"

I was having serious doubts on that score. I still had my hand raised, in case I needed to parry another blast of magical energy. Slowly, I lowered it.

"This *is* where the remains of Alis Treacle were buried, isn't it? Your remains."

The name reignited the fury in the woman's eyes. "What was left of her was placed here, yes. What does that have to do with vampires?"

"This is the place you have to return to as the sun rises. Every day or most days, depending upon how weakened you are."

"You're a fool. You know nothing. I'm not Alis."

"That's literally the name you used on the flight."

"Why do you care?"

"Tell me. Are you Alis?"

She seemed to sag. She knew I had her. "Of course I'm not, idiot. Yes, Everything I've done is for her benefit, an attempt to right the wrongs, but I'm not her."

This conversation wasn't going as I'd expected. My senses, my awareness of the magical had expanded alongside my control, and although the person standing before me was clearly dangerous, I sensed nothing *unnatural* about her; nothing vampiric or unliving. She was no ancient evil. The young woman with the purple hair: that was exactly who she was. Which meant that at least one person had told me lies. The question was, who?

"What are you, her descendant?"

"Why are you asking these questions? Destroy me if you can, before I destroy you, you evil bastard."

"Tell me," I said. "Please."

A look of defiance came into her features. "I was named after her. Alice with a *c*. I'm *Alice* Treacle."

"And you took her name, used the older spelling."

"It felt like the right thing to do."

"Why did you attack me? Why did you follow me to the Isle of Man and plant that cursed doll in my room?"

"Because you were getting too close! Because you're guilty, you're all guilty. I told you, one missing and one removed. I decided you would do nicely to take their place."

"How did you even know about me?"

"I was alerted when you tampered with the poppet in Tintern. The doll had been quiescent; I thought it had been removed and destroyed. Then, suddenly, it was awake again. I went to Tintern to watch, and there you were. The splinter you picked up was lucky for me. I tracked you, took your blood, created a poppet all for you."

"To bring my own nightmares to life and then to call a Night Hag to finish me off?"

"It's what you deserve, what you all deserve. Blind you, send you mad, tip you into drawn-out despair, make you suffer. I didn't want you to die quickly or easily."

"And the hell hounds? The black dogs?"

"Those creatures sniff around when doorways are opened. They aren't under my control."

"You told me there were six," I said. I gave her the names that Lady Coldwater had sent. "Are these the people you're talking about?"

Her fingers twitched as if she was planning more magic, but she didn't attack. "How can you know that?"

"You killed Jamie Tavish because he was Murdo McTavish's descendant. Morris Crossley's forebear was Fenton Crossley and Charles Raneleigh was descended from Alfred Raneleigh. Three witchfinders descended from those that brutalized and killed your forebear. Why Anders Kropotkin, though? His ancestor, Per Svenska, was a witchfinder, but Anders wasn't anything to do with us. He was completely innocent."

"Him? Oh, I watched him for a long time. He was no better, the way he treated people, his own girlfriend. The apple doesn't fall far from the tree."

"Piers Hamwell: he's the *one removed*?"

"His line died out long ago. There is no one left to pay the blood price."

"I don't understand about Alfred Raneleigh, though. You can't have killed him thirty years ago."

She looked like she wasn't going to reply, then clearly decided it didn't matter anymore.

"My mother. That's what started it all. She learned about our family history and set out to take revenge. She found this place, the little pit they threw Alis's remaining bones into."

More things slotted into place. "Then, the other grave?"

"It's hers, yes. I buried her next to her ancestor. As she requested."

"Who is Eta Carlisle?"

"Really? Are you that dim-witted? I'm insulted that *you* tracked me down. It's obviously an anagram. My mother's own way of acting in Alis's name."

"Wasn't that dangerous?"

"I told you; we need to keep her name alive."

"And the *one missing*," I said. "Belinda Carraway is a direct descendant of Gregory Holston, yet you let her live, didn't you? You couldn't bring yourself to finish her off."

Alice's head made little writhing movements as if she were grappling with difficult thoughts. She didn't reply.

"You let Belinda live because she's a woman," I said. "Six men murdered your forebear and you wanted six men to pay the price. Belinda threw your plan into confusion. What were you going to do, wait for her to have a son?"

"She shouldn't be part of your damned Office. You're all evil bastards."

"Yet you let Belinda live."

"I'm not a monster."

"You've personally killed three people, and not quickly or painlessly. You drove them into derangement, tried to make them finish themselves. You tried to do the same to me, too."

"Do you have any idea what happened to Alis?"

"Some."

"Let me tell you more, witch finder. She was blinded with red hot pokers because her captors were afraid of the *evil eye*. Over a period of months – long, long months – she was broken down, terrible agonies inflicted on her. *Exorcising the demons*. Your people did this to her. She also lost her wits and her mind. What I put those three through was nothing compared to Alis's suffering."

"I agree with you. That doesn't justify what you've done, though."

"No one else is going to right the wrong, are they? Not you, not anyone."

We faced each other on our little island in the woods. The sky was fully light now. Sooner or later, someone would come along and wonder what we were doing. The Warlock, the Office traitor: they were still out there. The question was, what *were* we doing? Which one of us was going to walk away from here?

Alice moved towards me. But she wasn't looking at me, she was studying the broken ground behind me.

"Out of the way, witch finder. It is happening."

I stepped back, wary of attack, although I'd sensed nothing. "What is happening?"

"You asked me why I came here every day. Now I'll show you."

She glanced up at the sky, judging how high the sun was.

"This is the right time. This is when she was killed. She succumbed to her injuries a little after nine o'clock that morning."

Ignoring me, Alice knelt on the ground beside the smaller clump of earth and stone. A hush fell across the little grove, a chill like a morning mist. I watched as a line of something like smoke rose from the ground to hover over the grave. I'd seen such manifestations before. This one was weak, indistinct. Unmistakably, though, there was a face in there. A woman's face.

This was Alis Treacle.

The look of sadness and hurt was clear in the thin, wavering twist of mist.

Alice, her descendant, spoke.

"I have righted the wrong, Alis. The offspring of those who tortured you have paid the price. You can rest now. Why are you not at rest?"

A voice came, a distant moan on the wind, but I couldn't pick out any words in it. By the way Alice drooped her head, I gathered she didn't either. This was a scene that had played out often. Alice didn't know what she had to do to give Alis release.

I knelt beside her. I could sense Alice tensing, wary of me or resenting my presence. I thought about her crimes: terrible unforgivable crimes. I thought about what had been done to Alis, too. Two wrongs didn't make a right – but then I thought about the people I'd killed: silently, magically slaughtered for my own ends, to save myself. Who was I to judge anyone? I thought about all the things the Office had done over the years – and would probably continue to do. And Alis … she'd been good, once, had cured people and helped people. Perhaps Alice could be that, too.

Here, beyond doubt, was another of our troublesome grey areas. Also – and this was little more than a hunch on my part – I wondered if there was a way to put all this straight without any more violence.

"Alice has paid your blood price," I said to the indistinct phantom. "Now I am paying hers. She won't suffer anymore. We won't pursue her. I won't pursue her. I promise you."

The line of smoke bobbed and sputtered. Whatever was left of Alis heard.

"Be at peace now," I said. "What was done to you, what we witchfinders did to you, it was unforgivable, a brutal act of hatred. I regret it. For what it's worth, I am sorry. We are sorry."

The mist bobbed once more. I thought nothing else was going to happen but then, with a sound like the exhalation of a long-held breath, it wavered in the still air. It thinned and dissipated, and the grave became nothing more than a mound of earth and a few old bones and stones.

Birds called from the treetops around us. Alice and I knelt in silence for a moment.

"She was worried … about me?" Alice asked.

"I think so. In the end, it was her concern for you that was keeping her tied to the physical realm. Not her rage or her pain, not the need for revenge, but her love for you."

"I didn't know."

"No."

"What you did … thank you, witch finder."

"It seemed like the right thing to do."

"You said you won't pursue me. What was that, the right words spoken to give Alis release?"

"I meant it," I said. "Do I have your word? No more revenge? Not for Piers Hamwell or for Gregory Holston or for anyone else?"

After a moment, she nodded her agreement. "Yes. It is over."

"Am I right in thinking you have a copy of Alis's notes?" I asked. "The *Book of Shadows*?"

"I do."

"I want you to hand it over to the Pale Sisters. Join them if you like, or not, but do that at least."

"The book, yes," she said. "Honestly, I'll be glad to see the back of it. The rest, I make no promises."

"No more Night Hags or poppets. No more waking nightmares and victims tipped into madness."

She nodded. "No more of that, yes. I'm free as well."

"And me?" I asked. "Will you leave me be?"

"You are not what I thought," she said. "Whatever is going on with you, I won't stop you. You *are* a witch finder, and yet you also are not."

"I managed to find *you*."

"And now you're letting me go free."

I stood and crossed to the edge of the islet. I set about unravelling the knots I'd spelled out in runes, tearing down the walls of the prison I'd trapped her in, unworking the runes with movements of my hands.

When I was done, she came up to stand beside me. "Where will you go?"

"North. I have urgent matters to attend to. You?"

She looked around, as if seeing the woods for the first time.

"Honestly? I don't know. Perhaps a holiday."

"Will you come back here?"

"Now and then, to visit her."

"Good," I said. "That's good."

I turned and walked away, wading into the cold waters to retrace my steps to the car.

21 – Quirk of Fate

Even by these three passiones that are within our selves: Curiositie in great ingines: thirst of revenge, for some tortes deeply apprehended: or greedie appetite of geare, caused through great poverty. As to the first of these, Curiosity, it is onelie the inticement of *Magiciens*, or *Necromanciers*: and the other two are the allureres of the *Sorcerers*, or *Witches*.

– James VI of Scotland, *Daemonologie*, 1597

There was an odd expression on Digbeth's face as I emerged from the woods. Surprise? Irritation? It was hard to be completely sure; the sunlight shining off the car windows made his features indistinct. He didn't move for a moment, the phone he'd been watching held frozen in his hands. Then he opened the door and strode the few yards to meet me.

"Danesh! You survived. You're okay! You've been gone hours; I was getting ready to come in after you."

"Have you alerted anyone?"

"Complete radio silence, as we agreed. I haven't seen anyone go into the woods after you. What the hell happened? Did you find the Alis Treacle entity?"

"I did."

"And?"

"That situation is now resolved.

"What does that mean?"

"She isn't anything to do with the Warlock."

"You were sure she was," said Digbeth.

"Yeah. I was wrong. I was seeing patterns where there were none."

Digbeth took a step towards the car, then returned to

where he'd been standing, as if he couldn't decide what he should do. "Then, it has to be Quirk, right? He's the Office traitor. He's the English Wizardry rat. The gaffer, before I left, said someone high up in the Office was controlling the Alis Treacle entity, using her as a weapon. It *has* to be Quirk. There's no one else it can be."

I turned Digbeth to look directly at me, confused by his words. It wasn't unusual for him to mix up details, get the wrong end of the stick. His case notes on MORIARTY were often a *mess*, poorly punctuated and contradictory. Digbeth being Digbeth.

"Hardknott-Lewis said that?" I asked.

"Yeah."

"You said that he said Alis was under the control of the Warlock."

Digbeth shrugged. "He had a number of theories. For all we know, the Office traitor is the Warlock, right?"

Digbeth's words made me think of something. A tiny detail that didn't fit into the wider picture. The runes that Alice had used and that I'd employed against her – the runes drawn from the *Book of Shadows* – the Crow had said that at least one was *vampiric* in nature. But neither Alice nor Alis had had anything to do with vampires so far as I could see. The suggestion seemed anomalous. Had those runes come from somewhere else? I needed to check with the librarian, see whether there was any truth to the statement. And, if there wasn't, the question was, why had Hardknott-Lewis said such a thing?

And why had he really sent me off on this trail in pursuit of Alice?

Out loud I said, "No, that's wrong. Alis Treacle was not under the control of the Warlock or anyone else. She was acting independently, pursuing her own ends."

My words seemed to baffle Digbeth for a moment. His mouth opened and closed a few times as he made sense of my words.

He took a pace back towards me and spoke in a conspiratorial whisper, even though there was no one nearby. His words, when they came, told me his thoughts had been running on similar lines to mine.

"Then, is it possible … is the gaffer leading us on a merry dance here? Telling us lies? It's almost like he wants us out of the picture. Like he's deliberately making us face these dangers to stop us asking awkward questions."

"You just said the traitor had to be Quirk," I said.

"Yeah, but … what if it's both of them? Think about it. They're old friends, right? Been on many little adventures together. What if it's both of them, working together to distract us, get us killed? What if it's been the two of them trying to destroy the Office all along?"

Was that possible? There was only one way to know for sure: if we could get to Quirk, we could pull the truth out of him.

"We need to move," I said. "Will you drive? It's been a long morning."

"Of course. Where are we going?"

"I lied to you," I said. "I wasn't only looking for Lindisfarne because Hardknott-Lewis mentioned the place in passing."

"You think that's where Quirk is hiding out?"

"I think there's a very good chance that's his lair, yes. I think he's moving his base from there to the Isle of Man but hasn't completed the process. If we hurry, perhaps we can get there in the light."

We sped off. It was a good seven– or eight-hours' drive, which meant night would be falling as we got there. I checked the causeway crossing times online. We were in luck: the tide was coming in, but the road would be passable, so long as we didn't hit any delays on the way up. We'd be stuck on the island until the early hours of the following morning, but that would have to do.

I texted the librarian, filling her in on Alice Treacle and telling her that the rogue copy of the *Book of Shadows* should be in her hands soon. I asked about the runes, too. While I waited for a reply, I watched the car mirrors, trying to spot someone following us. Again, there was no one I could detect. After a few hours, we swapped over and I drove while Digbeth returned to his phone.

The waters were lapping at the edges of the raised causeway that connected Lindisfarne to the larger island of Great Britain when we arrived. We were just in time. The light was fading behind us as we set off, the waters of the North Sea on both sides of us. Signs warned us of the dangers of stopping. Mud and seaweed were strewn across the road. Before long, it would be temporary seabed.

We reached the solid ground of the island without being swept away. Behind us, the first waves were exploring the tarmac we'd just used. The road led us through the small village on the island, past the ruins of the priory, its roofless arches and walls reminding me of the abbey in Tintern. Ahead of us, high on a rocky outcrop, was a small fortress, its high stone walls defying the storms that had to rage in off the North Sea.

"There?" Digbeth asked.

"Let's try."

It was old, I knew, dating back at least to the sixteenth century, although there were probably older, deeper foundations to the building. The island had seen a lot of conflict over the centuries, caught up in the squabbles between England and Scotland, as well as the assaults of Viking raiders.

We circled the old building, a chill wind blasting in off the sea. It was a lonely and inhospitable place. It felt like the edge of something. The waters were a muddy green-blue, but they crashed into flares of white spray as the wind drove them onto the rocks. My researches had told me that the building had been occupied off and on, which made it an unlikely location for a secret vampire's lair. There were doors, but they were locked shut.

"In here?" Digbeth asked.

Something told me we still hadn't gone far enough. The fortress looked the part, which made it too obvious. I looked around, eyes closed as I tried to sense where we needed to go. There was a murmur of … something. North of us, up the coast.

"This way," I said.

Minutes later, I saw the top of a stone ruin peeping over a rise in the ground. Tough-looking sheep chewed upon the thin, reluctant grass in the foreground. I knew the building was where we needed to go. We followed the curve of the coast line, leaving the village and the castle behind us. To our right, the sea merged into the sky in one mass of grey.

The ruins may have been a chapel, once, or some other religious mediaeval building. Its roof had long-since been blasted off by the gales. The walls merely hinted at the floor plan of the building it had once been. A doorway led into an interior chamber. This was more of a room, the buttressed walls tall, although it was still exposed to the elements – not only by the lack of a roof, but by glassless arched windows and, at one point, a great vertical crack in the seawards wall.

Stepping inside, the moan of the wind and the relentless crashing of the waves were muted. There was little to see, except for hummocky clumps of grass and some flat stones embedded in the soil. I slipped out my thaumometer to check. It was definitely registering something.

"There's nothing here," said Digbeth. "It must be somewhere else."

I couldn't tell him why I knew he was wrong. Once again, I didn't need him around to see what I was about to do.

"Watch the outer door," I said. "It's possible we've been followed. Keep an eye on the track from the village."

He nodded and slouched away.

I stepped around the room, looking for something but not sure what. I had my gun in my hand, anti-vampire round dialled up and ready. At the far end of the inner chamber was the tallest remaining structure. I'd assumed it was a chimney stack, but as I approached, I saw that it was the curve of a spiral staircase, the doorway off-centre to keep the wind out. I peered in. Cramped steps wound upwards a short way before ending in the open air where some upper floor had fallen off. They also wound downwards, into the darkness. Using my phone's light, I began to descend. The stairs were slick with slime, and there was nothing to hold onto. Half a turn, and I hit a brick wall. Literally. The way had been sealed off with cemented stones, floor to ceiling.

The stones were rough to my touch. Dry, though, without any of the algae coating the other surfaces. That was odd. The obstruction certainly looked old, though. It had been there for a long time. Except ... something felt strange about it. I put my hand to the stones once more and closed my eyes. There was something here I was missing.

Then I saw it. There was no wall there; it was an illusion. Some powerful and persistent spell had been worked into the old stones to keep people out. Pushing through was hard, a physical effort. I worked magic of my own, imagining a light that would show me the way. It guttered and sputtered for a moment, then stabilized as I got the hang of shaping it. I sent it into the wall to dissolve the warding magic.

The stones resisted, seeming to bend backwards as I pushed. I put more of myself into the effort, refusing to be denied. A few moments of struggle, and the wall gave. I thought the stones would tumble backwards in a thunder of rubble, but instead, they disappeared as if they had never been there.

Satisfied at this small victory, I carried on down. Cold, salt air blew up at me. I could hear the concussions of the crashing waves through the stones. Could I get trapped down there as the waters continued to rise? Had other sorcery been woven into these old walls to trap invaders within?

I reached the lower level. The chamber was dank, thick green algae colouring the walls. Unexpectedly, there was another doorway leading outwards to the sea. Flicks of water threw themselves over a small stone jetty out there. When a wave hit, the entire chamber boomed. I could taste salt on my lips. What had this been, some way of bringing goods ashore? Catches of fish?

In the far wall was another doorway, this one also bricked-up. Again, it looked like it had been sealed off for a long time, perhaps when some other part of the building had collapsed. I'd see if I could pull the same trick as I had for the first door.

Before that, something else demanded my attention. In the middle of the room, picked out by my light, stood an old stone tomb. The sides were worn, weathered. It had a lid of wood – which made little sense. Wood would soon rot in these damp conditions. I crouched to study the sepulchre, moving as silently as I could, senses tingling at the thought something might leap from within at any moment. Without touching the tomb, I moved my light around to exaggerate the shadows. The designs on the stones were unmistakably similar to the one I'd found in Quirk's mansion on the Isle of Man. They might have been a matching pair.

A few steps away, I noticed that deep ruts had been gouged in the ground. They headed from the centre of the room towards the jetty. I crossed to these, ran my fingers over them. Clearly, something very heavy had been hauled in – or out. There'd been two tombs here. Quirk had removed one, sliding it out onto a barge of some sort to take to the Isle of Man.

I stepped back to the remaining tomb. I paused, gun at the ready, blade at the ready, magic at the ready. The suspicion that this was a trap, that I'd been led there, nagged away at me. I had no choice but to open the tomb. Was it in there, the vampire warlock? Was this its long-forgotten lair? I steeled myself for a moment, crouching by the tomb. In a single action, I heaved the wooden lid aside and stepped backwards, gun held ready.

Nothing flew out screaming its visceral hatred. A moan came from the sarcophagus. A groan of distress.

I stepped warily back towards it to peer inside. A figure

lay there. He was old, thin, his bush of white hair matted and tatty. His features were drawn, sunken, but his eyes were open. They contained not malice, not fury, but fear. Perhaps, even, madness.

He did not arise to slaughter me. I recognized who he was immediately. Thomas Quirk lay in the tomb.

His voice was little more than a whisper. "No, no, leave me. No more of this, I beg. What do you want from me? Tell me what you want!"

He couldn't see who I was. I lifted my phone to show him my face. "It's me, Danesh Shahzan. What the hell happened to you? Why are you here?"

It took him more than a few seconds to understand who I was, his cracked lips moving all the time.

"Danesh? You're not … him?"

I set down my gun and offered him an arm, helped him out of the stone box he'd been entombed within. There was more magic here, some hex pinning him down. I tore it aside with some difficulty. When Quirk stood, he was more stooped than I remembered, as if he might snap at any moment. He was shaking noticeably.

"We have to get you out of here. I have a car."

"Yes, yes. I have to get out."

"Who was it?" I asked. "Who imprisoned you here?"

"I don't know. He wouldn't tell me. He wouldn't speak. He caught me in his magical bonds while cold, cold days slipped by, and there was nothing I could do."

This explained Quirk's disappearance, at any rate.

"Why?"

"He won't tell me! He comes through his portal each day to walk around me, look at me, but he never speaks. Never tells me what he wants."

"The stairs leading upwards?"

"No, no. The bricked-up doorway, there. That's how he comes through."

"Are you sure you don't know who he is?"

"I could never see his face. He wore robes, but there was more than that. His features were … blurred."

Blurred, right. *That* was something I'd come across

before. "He must have given you some idea why you were being held?"

"Nothing, nothing. He would simply ... study me."

"I don't think that was it. I think you were bait in a trap."

"Bait for what?"

"Quite possibly, for me," I said. "Was he a person or was he something else?"

"He wasn't the vampire I've been hunting I can tell you that."

"You've been hunting a vampire."

"Yes, yes. Long years I've been at it. I'm close, I'm sure."

We climbed the spiral stairs to the ground floor. I let Quirk go first in case he lost his balance. At the top, he sounded a little surer of himself, some of his strength returning.

"I have to thank you for finding me," Danesh. "I would have succumbed soon. Died."

There was no sign of Digbeth. Perhaps he'd gone back to the warmth of the car. I wished I'd brought water with me, something to give Quirk. Lindisfarne would be cut off, now, but we could take him to a hotel or something, get him warm.

Before that, though, I took the opportunity to ask him a few more questions.

"There's a tomb just like in your house on the Isle of Man," I said. "That was from here?"

"You visited my home?"

"I may have done, yes."

Quirk nodded, as if it were perfectly reasonable for me to break into the private house of a Lord High Witchfinder.

"There were three, once, according to my researches. Three rather old stone sarcophagi. The one down there, the one I removed to study and another."

"Where's the third?"

"That is a very good question indeed."

"Three vampires?"

"Yes. Three of them, yes. I've been hunting them for a long time."

"The Warlock."

"I think so, yes."

"In your house there was a copy of *The Old Ways*. Samuel Bedfellowes."

"That old book? Yes, yes. There are clues in it, vague suggestions."

"Is it your own private copy?"

It took him a few moments to work out what I was asking. "Hmm? No, no. Borrowed from London. All official. Well done for asking, though. Would you mind? I need to talk to my people; there was much taking place when I was taken and I need to catch up with them."

"Are you up to that?"

"It will only take a few minutes."

He was tough, no doubt about it. He walked away to talk to his people, heading outside into the darkness to get a signal.

While he did so, I took the opportunity to do something similar. Despite the purdah on electronic communications that he'd insisted on, I suddenly needed to talk to the Crow. He needed to know the truth about Quirk. And my discovery meant that there were some questions I urgently needed answers to. I went back downstairs and out onto the little jetty, picking my way along carefully so I didn't step into the waiting waters. I shivered as the sea lashed spray at me, but at least I wouldn't be overheard out there. The signal was weak, the phone crackly, but it connected.

"Danesh!" Hardknott-Lewis replied almost immediately. "How marvellous to hear from you at last. Where in all the kingdoms are you?"

"I'm on Lindisfarne. Where are you?"

"I am in Cardiff."

"Not London?"

"I was instructed to return to address some urgent local issues. Am I to assume you have made some progress in our case?" he asked.

"You need to know that Quirk is not the Office traitor."

"Are you certain of that?"

"I'm absolutely sure. It isn't him."

"Ah. I am very pleased to hear it. I found it hard to believe that Thomas might be our enemy."

He seemed to be taking the news of what I was telling him remarkably calmly.

"This doesn't leave many candidates, though, does it?" I said. "You told me yourself that our traitor definitely isn't Earl Grey. And we decided when I set out that Quirk and Earl Grey were our two likely culprits – except that, it was *you* who decided that, wasn't it? Just before you sent me off in pursuit of a very dangerous witch with a huge grudge against Office operatives."

"Danesh, I am not … wait, when did I say that Earl Grey is no longer a suspect? He was one of the reasons I was in Whitehall. I am still actively looking into him."

"Digbeth told me."

The Crow took a moment to respond. When he did, he sounded puzzled.

"Digbeth? When have you spoken to Digbeth?"

"He's obviously been with me since yesterday."

"I do not understand. What is he doing there? So far as I know, he is away on holiday, somewhere in the Mediterranean."

"I don't…" I started. But then, I stopped, because, suddenly, I did. I did understand. Digbeth. Damn. I'd looked into the name, checked so carefully, yet I'd missed it. There'd been a Digbeth active in English Wizardry back in the first half of the twentieth century. I'd made very sure that the two weren't related; that it was coincidence. Clearly, I'd been wrong. I'd missed a connection. Digbeth had been a snake all along, some distant relative of the Digbeth who'd been there next to Evangelina Mormont and the rest of the bastards in the good old inter-war days.

"Danesh?" the Crow said. "What is happening? What is Digbeth doing there?"

As if it were laughing at me, bastard that it is, the

universe chose that moment to confirm the very thing I'd just worked out. My phone buzzed with a text from Olwen. As I looked at it, Digbeth appeared at the sea door, his features eerily illuminated by the light of his own phone. His eyes were upon me. He nodded. He must have met Quirk.

Olwen, meanwhile, was relaying a message to me from Gilroy. She had no idea what it signified, but she echoed Gilroy's words. *Danesh will know what it means.*

Gilroy had been busy with his researches in his underground lair. I tried to keep my features fixed, give nothing away, as I studied the black and white photograph that had come through. This was no jolly parlour gathering; the wizards of the Mystical Council had clearly been on manoeuvres. I didn't recognize the setting, but it was a narrow street somewhere, the road cobbled, lit by what appeared to be ornate gas lamps. There was my grandfather in the foreground, along with two other figures I recognized from the first image Gilroy had shown me. There was no sign of Stonewall. They'd clearly been engaged in a fight: each of them was scarred or burned, clothing rent or slashed. There was none of the joviality I'd seen in the first image. Now they looked exhausted, their expressions grim as they paused to pose for the unknown photographer. On the floor, bound by heavy ropes were two individuals, the two they'd clearly struggled hard to subdue. One I didn't recognize, but the other, his face still in that moment and his features clear, was the spitting image of the Digbeth I knew.

The man standing a few yards from me.

Literally two seconds later, another text arrived, this one from the librarian. Damn, damn. Why hadn't either of these messages come an hour earlier?

Book of Shadows good, it said. And also, Vampiric runes? Don't be ridiculous. Don't you think I would have mentioned? Idiot.

"What's that, Danesh?" said Digbeth. "What are you looking at?"

He shouted over the rush and crash of the waves. Very

definitely, there was a sharper edge of threat to his voice. He'd seen Quirk walk free. He had to know that all his lies had been found out. What had his plan been? That Quirk would attack me in his shock and surprise? Or that someone else would be there to spring an ambush? It didn't matter. Digbeth had clearly decided to take matters into his own hands.

I tried to act unconcerned as I lifted the phone back to my ear.

"Can't talk now, sorry," I said to the Crow. "There's someone here I need to speak to."

"Danesh! What is happening?" I heard him say. "I have no idea why Digbeth is there. He is not acting upon my orders."

I killed the call and slipped my phone back into my pocket. The pocket where I'd secreted my handgun. Except, it wasn't there. I'd placed it beside the tomb to help Quirk out and hadn't picked it up again.

Damn.

Digbeth wasn't taken by my pretence for a moment. I watched as he raised his own weapon. He had a clear shot, even if I killed my light. I was too exposed there on the jetty. The waves were already grabbing at my ankles; all he really needed to do was wait. I wasn't going to survive for long in those cold, surging waters, dashed against the sharp rocks.

Digbeth seemed amused by the situation. "Looks like I'll have to kill you myself. It will be my pleasure. We should never have lowered ourselves by letting people like you into the Office. You don't belong. You can never belong, because however hard you try, you're not one of us, are you?"

"Digbeth, what the hell are you doing?" I asked. But, of course, I knew very well what he was doing. He was another English Wizardry foot soldier. He'd been acting under the orders of the Office traitor all along. He was a sleeper agent – almost literally so in his case.

I played for time, trying to pump him for information. It seemed to amuse him. I stepped forwards and he let me come, receding into the shadows, his gun always on me. I stopped in the doorway, the light from behind me faintly illuminating the scene. The room boomed to our voices and the thunder of the waves as they broke on the old stones. There was no sign of my weapon. Digbeth had taken it. He didn't know about my powers, though, did he? That was my only hope.

"Why did you persuade me to pursue Alice Treacle if you knew Quirk was here?" I asked.

He seemed delighted to explain how ingenious he'd been. "We read your careful logs and saw an opportunity. There was every possibility that Alice would do our work for us, destroy you without us having to lift a finger. Alas, that wasn't to be."

I thought back to my conversation with Digbeth at Liverpool Airport. He'd seemed to know about my investigations into Quirk but, in fact, he'd been clever. I'd let a few facts slip and he'd reacted as if he'd known them all along. He was smart; I'd been wrong to think him slow-witted. He'd made that phone call, too. Who had he been speaking to? It had to have been the Office traitor. They'd calculated that Alice might be powerful enough to finish me off, and then, when that failed, they'd tacked to a new plan, setting up an ambush on Lindisfarne.

"The doll in Jamie's house. You knew it was there."

"Obviously. I left it there deliberately, held by a hobble. When I read that you planned to visit, I slipped in first and removed it."

Damn, damn. They'd been running rings round me. No more.

I raised my hand, palm directly towards him.

"What are you doing?" he asked. The confusion on his face was sincere. He truly had no idea about me.

"I'm going to stop you now," I said.

"Do you really think you can defend yourself against a bullet with your hand?"

The coiling swirl of sorcery within me was winding away, but it was under my control now. Just about. I hoped. I let the cobra strike, blasting him with a spike of raging magic. I was wrong; I still didn't have the crafting right. The damn thing burned me as I sent it off, searing my hand with a spike of pain. It was a hell of a lot worse for Digbeth, though. When the flare hit him, he was thrown backwards. He fired his gun, but he was off-target, missing me by some way. He crashed into the far wall, a look of shock on his face. Which was fair enough, really. When he slumped to the ground, body awkwardly bent, he didn't move.

"Yes," I said to his lifeless form. "I think I can do that."

I walked across the room to stand over him, to make sure he was gone. There was no doubt about it. It was another death, another murder at my hands. I knew I shouldn't feel bad about this one because the bastard had deserved it. But then, so had all the others. I knew I should invent some alibi about how he'd died that didn't point the finger at me. But I was sick of lying, sick of the deception. If anyone asked, I would tell them the truth.

As it happened, though, the universe chose that moment to provide me with an excellent explanation. As I stood, I felt the tug of magical energy discharging, even as I picked up the flash of blue light on the wall to my right. The other portal was opening. Quirk's tormentor was on his way – the individual who'd created a trap to capture me. Perhaps he knew I was there and perhaps he didn't. It made little difference.

I stood in the shadows, preparing to face my enemy.

22 – English Wizardry

Then through the darkness I could see a sort of
patch of grey light ahead of us.
– Bram Stoker, *Dracula*, 1897

A figure stepped through the portal. He wasn't a tall man
and he wasn't wearing a long coat, but I recognized him.
His face was a blur, a scribble of crude lines, like I was
watching a video and his features had been pixelated – all
except his eyes, peering out at me.

*His face invisible … filled with fury, demon eyes, face
invisible.* Here he was, at last. The man who'd come for
Az and I on that distant day. The man who'd broken my
family and broken my mother's mind with the poison of
his curse.

He looked around, taking in the scene. Quirk was gone
and I had taken his place. He made a sighing noise that
might have been regret and might have been
disappointment.

He drew a gun – unmistakably an Office hand gun –
and pointed it at me. It didn't matter which round he'd
dialled up; any would kill me. Did he know the truth
about me? I'd killed Peter Warder and Thomson Fulger –
both of them his minions – and they'd learned about my
nature the hard way, but I couldn't see how word could
have reached their leader. Evangelina Mormont, also, had
discovered the truth at the end, also when it was too late.

He raised the gun to get a good aim. I wasn't going to let
that happen. I wasn't going to let either of us die before I'd
wrung some answers from him. I let the rearing magic
within me lash out before he could pull his trigger. This
time my control was good, the gun whipping from his hand
to skitter across the rough stone floor into a corner.

He didn't move for a moment. I couldn't read an expression on that fuzzed-out face, but the tilt of his head suggested confusion. He hadn't expected that. I hit him with more magic while he pondered. This was subtler, less flashy. It wasn't anything destructive: with a couple of attempts, I swept away the magical fog obscuring his features, bringing them into sharp relief.

The look of alarm that passed across his face was a joy to see.

"Earl Grey," I said.

"Danesh Shahzan," he said, venom in his voice. He stepped backwards towards the portal. I knew I could kill him before he got there.

"English Wizardry," I said. "It's you. You're the one who controlled Mormont. You're the one responsible for everything."

There'd been two people whose semen Evangelina Mormont's succubi hadn't collected: the Crow and Earl Grey. Mormont had let slip that only one of these remained to be harvested. I understood why, now. Hardknott-Lewis had resisted but Earl Grey had never even been a real target. One of the seven succubi had been a fake, a feint, deliberately weakened or instructed not to attack. One of those cauldrons was never going to be filled. Earl Grey had been included as a show to detract attention, to make him look like a victim.

When, all along, he was the perpetrator.

"You and Campbell Hardknott-Lewis," he sneered. "So upright, so honest. You make me sick. And yet, here you are, foreign worm, using your decadent magic. What will your esteemed mentor make of that? What will…"

He no longer had his gun, but he was still dangerous. In a blur of movement, half-way through his own sentence, his arm flashed out at me, hurling a throwing knife blade-first at my head. I could have swatted it away with a spell, but in the moment my instinct took over and I ducked, turned away to protect my face.

A second later, when I looked back, it was to see him disappearing through the portal. He would be closing it, sealing it from the other side. I wasn't going to let him do that. The stone archway hummed with unseen magical force, its connection to the complex tracery of spider-web lines through the aether. I had no way of knowing where it led, but I had to take the chance.

Not stopping to think, I threw myself after him into the magical gateway.

There was the briefest moment of terrible, life-devouring cold, then I found myself in an ornately-decorated, wood-panelled room. There was no sign of Earl Grey. Tall bookshelves lined the walls, filled with leather-bound tomes. A comfortable chair sat beside a table piled with more books. There were two doorways; he must have raced through one of them. In one wall, tall arched windows revealed a city skyline beneath a grey sky. The outline of the Shard and the BT Tower were unmistakable. I was back in London, some private mansion in the leafy north by the look of it.

Had he tricked me somehow, diverted me? From this side, the portal was a wooden doorway, tall and ornately carved, its wood weathered to silver as if it had once stood outside. It was an odd sight in the middle of the room: a door that went nowhere. And everywhere.

I turned around, deciding where to go, when there was a quiet *snick* sound, and then the sensation of magic being worked. Before I could move, something like snakes were flying around me. Snakes made of black smoke, winding faster and faster. I threw myself away from them, but succeeded only in stumbling. They were around my legs, too, and where they touched me, they solidified into ropes, utterly incapacitating me. I struggled against them, trying to work out how to unleash magical fire without burning my own skin. It was no good. I was soon trussed up like a fly in a spider's web.

Earl Grey stepped into the room through one of the doorways.

"Well, well," he said. "You continue to surprise me. I see that I should never have let you live. I should have done to you what I did to your vile, screaming brat of a brother. Instead, I'm going to kill you now. One more Shahzan removed from the board."

I tried again, using my magic in a different way. Rather than firing bolts of energy from my hand, I tried to *radiate* the power from my flesh. The bonds were strong, like the thick ropes used to moor ships, but I could sense them creaking under the onslaught of my attack. My skin felt hot, as if I were lying naked in the searing sun. Someone properly adept in the magical arts could no doubt exert the fine control necessary. I was not that person, not yet. I persevered through the pain. With a cry, ignoring the growing burning sensation across my skin, I put a few more drops of magical power into the spell.

My agonies mounted to a sharp point – and then when it was nearly too much, the bonds scattered off me, dissipating to threads of smoke, to air.

There was no mistaking the look of panic deep in Earl Grey's eyes. He hadn't thought I was capable of such an act. That told me many things: he was no user. He had access to powerful artefacts – stolen or given to him – but he had no powers himself. And that confirmed something else, too: he was not the Warlock. Earl Grey was in charge of the both the Office of the Witchfinder General and, secretly, of English Wizardry, setting the two off against each other to enhance his own power, pursue his own aims. But that was all he was. He was not the ancient evil that controlled so much.

"Do you have any other magic to throw at me?" I asked as I stood. "Or are you done? The Warlock isn't going to be very happy with you, is he?"

A sneer passed across Earl Grey's features at my words. "The Warlock?" I don't take orders from that *thing*. It's alien, degenerate. An invader. It's not one of us."

"But he put you in charge, didn't he? The head of the Office also running English Wizardry. You could demand more resources for the Office each time a magical outrage was committed. At the same time, you could ensure the Office wasn't too successful, too effective. Putting you there was a masterstroke."

"Putting me here was one of his many mistakes. He thought I would simply follow his commands."

"I saw you talking to him, didn't I? That day in Downing Street, the tall old man in the robes, hairless and very pale."

"Why should I tell you anything? These matters are well above you."

"Then I won't understand, will I?"

Earl Grey shrugged, as if it was of no importance. His gaze was darting around as he tried to come up with a plan. He was alone, I suspected. In his need for secrecy, he hadn't called any minions to his aid, because he didn't think he would need them. Perhaps there weren't many minions left.

"The Warlock tries to give me orders even now," he said. "I no longer listen. Abominations such as him corrupt the purity of true English magic. Just as you do."

"The scars on your back from the succubus attack. Hardknott-Lewis said they were deep."

Earl Grey shrugged. "A small sacrifice to make."

"Tell me why you let me go when I was a boy. Why did the Warlock tell you to take Az and not me?"

"Oh, but he didn't, did he? Take you both, those were his orders. Even then I was growing weary of his demands. Getting to your brother was easy enough, too easy, but you ran and hid and I let you live. How does that make you feel? I let you live because I wanted to annoy the Warlock, nothing more."

"Why did he want us dead?"

A weak smile crossed Earl Grey's features, a smile that didn't reach his eyes. "It's amusing, isn't it?"

"What?"

"How two enemies can end up on the same side when faced with a common threat. We're the same, you and I, both wanting to destroy the Warlock."

"We're not the same at all."

"The only reason you've been allowed to continue living is that I thought you might be a weapon I could wield. That's all you are. The Warlock is afraid of you, or some power your family wields. It was me that suggested to Hardknott-Lewis you be recruited. I tested you to see if you had real power, teased it out of you. Even if you kill me now, it doesn't change anything; I've still won. Sooner or later, you're going to fight the Warlock, and one of you will die. Hopefully, both of you, two with one stone. I can tell you anything, reveal all that I want, and it doesn't alter that fate. This is your destiny."

Maybe I could have hit him with some seething mass of magical death. Maybe I'd have immolated myself in the process. Instead of doing either, I ran at him and tackled him to the ground. There was something satisfying about physically hitting him. He was still strong, all wiry energy. We wrestled for a time, grunting in effort. Each time I felt my strength fading, I thought about English Wizardry and everything this man had done, and my rage came burning back.

I punched him hard on the face, then, before he could respond, pinned his arms to the floor while I squatted on top of his chest. He tried to rise, but he sagged back, spent.

I picked up his head with a balled fist and looked directly into his eyes.

"Tell me how to find him, what I need to do."

Earl Grey's response was a whisper. "Get your hands off me, mongrel scum."

I should have blasted him there and then, burned him to ashes. He'd done terrible things to my family, and to me, and to lots of other people too. He'd run English Wizardry, believed its lies, *lived* its lies. But I didn't want him to have a quick, easy end. The long-suppressed trauma in my mind, the old scar: it had centred around *him* and what he'd done.

So, instead, I thumped my fist into his face again. Once, twice, three times – each met with a crunching squelch. Blood dribbled from his ruined mouth. He groaned, and I held off as the pain of the blows throbbed through my singed hand. I was hurting myself almost as much as him.

HEAD FULL OF DARK

"I've killed you one by one," I said. "Killed the members of English Wizardry. Now it's your turn."

"Do it," he slurred. "You're an animal. It's only what I expect. Do it and he'll know. He'll come for you."

There are numerous inventive ways to kill someone using Office m/tech. A holdfast set to short range and placed upon a person's chest will place a neat stasis sphere around a victim's heart and stop their blood pumping for a few minutes. When the magical effect is halted, it leaves no physical trace. In that moment, though, I had no time for such subtleties. All I could think about was the voice of my mother, confused, asking me if I was Az as I spoke to her on the phone.

I slammed Earl Grey's head into his fine marble floor. He blacked out for a moment. When his eyes flickered open, he tried to speak. I bent closer to pick up his words. His last act was to smile again and whisper words into my ear.

"You think you've won. Go and see. Go and see."

He was pointing to one side. To the portal.

"Go where? What do you mean?"

He spoke one more word, more an exhalation of final breath than anything else.

Oblivion.

Earl Grey died. Another victim to add to my growing tally. More of Evangelina Mormont's final words also replayed in my head. *Mongrel scum. You know nothing. Go to Oblivion and see. See who else has been lying there all this time.* Words that had run through my head again and again, a video on a loop.

I stood. I was alone, and I had access to his private portal, his secret gateway to the aether. I crossed to it, the ornate doorway standing in the middle of the room, its carved frame glowing faintly blue. Rather than a runic circle drawn around it, this had sigils worked into the frame, some separate, some complex sequences knotted together. At its apex, there was a blank space where a seven-sided jewel or decoration had once been placed. By the look of it, Earl Grey's portal was an old and powerful artefact, granting its user the means to travel to many different realms. How much had he used it? Where had he travelled to over the years?

I couldn't know. I did know, my finger tracing the lines of the runes in the frame, which ones needed to be strung together to grant me access to the place I needed to go. I could read the language, now, or enough of it. There was a risk, certainly, but I needed answers. I could step inside without Hardknott-Lewis or anyone else knowing. I needed to see who, indeed, had been lying there all this time. A small voice in the depths of my mind whispered to me who it was, who it had to be, but I'd never wanted to hear it.

Enough lies. Enough deception. My fingers flicked over the runes, tracing *this* one and then *that* one, followed by a sequence of five. The frame glowed brighter and there was a deep humming sound that I felt in my chest rather then heard in my ears. The portal was connected to *somewhere*, but still the space filling the frame remained blank, devoid of any shimmering magical field. When I pushed my hand through it, nothing happened.

A key. There had to be a key. I returned to Earl Grey's body and searched his pockets. Eventually, I found it around his neck: a little gold star, seven-sided. I pulled it from him and touched it to the space at the portal's apex. Immediately, the air contained by the frame swirled and solidified.

Became a portal.

Had I connected it to the correct destination across the aether? Only one way to find out. Taking a breath, I stepped on through.

23 – Fade to Grey

I placed him in his resting-place for his long eternity and stood beside him for as long as I could bear it. Then I left him. There was nothing else I could do. The evil that has been done to him cannot be undone, and all that is left to me is to try and prevent such horrors from destroying anyone else. I shall take a day off from my duties – perhaps two – and then return to work more determined than ever to rid this world of the sorcerous and the unnatural.

– Campbell Hardknott-Lewis, Lord High Witchfinder of All Wales, *private journal*, 1991

Once again, I stood on a wide icy plain. Once again, I could feel the heat being sucked out of me with every passing second, my very bones turning to ice. I could breathe – weirdly, there was air in the Oblivion dimension – but once again I was being drained of my life-energy, my essence, on a more fundamental level. The science of that escaped me, and right then I didn't care. Maybe there was no science to it. I was already shivering, my jaw clenched painfully shut, my feet numb. Once again, my mood was turning dark, destructive. The whisper in my mind to lie down, give up, give in was clear, insidious because it sounded like my voice. It sounded like *me. It's all futile and you're worthless.*

I couldn't survive there for long, but I needed to know for sure.

In front of me, lines of detail on that infinite plain of greyness, I could see the iron spikes hammered into the ice. The markers of those buried in that most perma of frost. Others, I knew, perceived Oblivion differently. For Hardknott-Lewis it was an endless forest, some of the trees not trees but something like lignified people, self-crucified to the boughs they had become. I wasn't sure which version was worse.

Who else has been lying there all this time. I didn't have time to explore the entire forest of iron spikes, see whose names were written on the oval plaques welded onto each, looking for the needle in the haystack. I'd be dead before I got through four or five – dead or worse than dead: frozen into unending semi-conscious torpor. Winters in Cardiff could be bad, but they were never *that* bad.

Mormont had seen something, though – except, she'd been brought in under heavy magical sedation, bound with iron and unbreakable enchantments. They wouldn't have let her wander around at will – even if she'd been strong enough to do such a thing. Maybe she'd simply been told who was in there, or had been a part of the original operation under Earl Grey's orders. Maybe she'd been making the whole thing up to trouble me. I had to hope that the grave I was looking for was one of those near hers in the ice. Concepts of distance, of here and there, were less rigid in Oblivion than in the familiar world, but it was all I had.

The destroyed resting place she'd lain in, and that I'd visited last time, was still there: the hole hacked from the ice, the marker canted over at forty-five degrees. Moving as quickly as I could, slipping on the ice again and again, I worked my way towards it. I slid and slid, not getting any nearer the grave – and then suddenly, in the manner of moving in a dream, I was upon it. The deep hollow in the ice, where Mormont had lain until she'd been released, lay untouched. The name on the plaque hadn't been altered, either. *Evangelina Mormont*, it said, like it was just waiting for her to return. Either they didn't like to reuse the tombs, or no one else had been placed into Oblivion since she'd been released. Leaving the plaque there was maybe a risk, but the chances of anyone stumbling upon it were vanishingly tiny. Oblivion is, by all accounts, limitless in extent and only Office gateways are attuned to this particular needle in the infinite haystack.

I was shivering uncontrollably now, my body's reflexes kicking in to desperately preserve its dwindling heat. I cast around, skidding to the nearest graves, studying the names. One or two I recognized, the names of sorcerers and necromancers from the Office's back catalogue of bad guys. There were some fearsome names among them, but none I was surprised to see.

Then I found a plaque bearing a surname that was a shock, although the first name meant nothing to me. What did *that* mean? I filed the information away to think about later.

If there was a *later*. I was fading, now, my whole body so numb that I couldn't tell if I was still shivering. Ever been to a concert where the music is so loud you stop hearing it? It becomes, simply, how the universe is? That. That was the cold of Oblivion. I no longer felt it, but I knew it consumed me, and I also knew I was on the point of death. A long, long, infinitely drawn-out death, like slipping over the event horizon of a black hole and falling into it for ever. I'd brought Earl Grey's key with me, thinking I could use it to return, and it was clutched in my fingers, but my hand refused to respond when I told it to open. I put my hand to my mouth, thinking to breathe some warmth into my muscles, but I exhaled only cold mist, as if all my body heat was gone, radiated away.

Suddenly frustrated, I shook my hand … and promptly dropped the key to the ice. I had to pick it up, work the simple magic to return to our world. I knew this. It was the only thought left in my mind. I had to find the door I'd stepped through, slide the key into the ghost lock and work the relevant runes, and I could escape Oblivion. The door had to be somewhere near, although I'd lost sight of it. I reached for the key on the ice…

…and slipped again. This time, my numbed limbs couldn't adjust in time. For a moment, I didn't know where I was. Then wet, sharp cold bit into the side of my face, and I was lying on the ice. The key was there, right in front of me. And beyond it was another grave, no marker upon it, no name. Why was there no name? I could see from the dark mass entombed within the ice that someone was in there.

I slithered my way over to it, to peer into those frozen depths. The deep ice was like glass, and from directly overhead the features of the person entombed became completely clear.

It was Az.

My brother lay in Oblivion.

My thoughts were as frozen as my limbs. It took long, long moments for the words to penetrate. My twin was there. Az, killed when he and I were eight years old, the event that had kicked off a lifetime of loss and pain and guilt. Killed by an unidentified man. *Short man, long coat, his face invisible ... filled with fury, demon eyes, face invisible.* Killed by Earl Grey. Except, not killed. He was here. Why? Why had he been locked away in this private eternity?

And why had no one told me?

Az's eyes were open as he stared up at me from his cold depths. He was young; a child. The body doesn't age in Oblivion even if the mind, at some level, is conscious. His lips were blue; all his skin was blue, purple-blue, but I could see from his eyes that he was still in there. That was how Oblivion worked. Not a death sentence, because that was inhumane. A life sentence. An eternal life sentence. It was a terrible, terrible thing to do to anyone, especially one innocent of all crimes.

I couldn't move. The universe closed in on me, the darkness taking me. I was joining him, succumbing to the negative energy of Oblivion. I welcomed it, accepted it. All the life that I'd lived and that Az had been denied, lying here all that time, locked away, experiencing none of it. Experiencing nothing but cold, faint existence. This was the least I could do. I would lie beside him for the rest of eternity. At last, we'd be together again. At least he wouldn't be alone.

Again, as once before, a hand on my shoulder saved

me. A face, smearing into view above me – a blur, faint, as if glimpsed in tarnished mirrors. A familiar face. His lips moved although I couldn't hear words, but I knew he was speaking my name, shouting it. I pulled myself away, rejecting his touch, but I was too weak. He gripped my shoulder hard, the mouth moved again, calling out other words…

…and the universe and sound and warmth came rushing back in, throwing themselves at me in a flood. I was lying on a hard floor, familiar white walls around me. The offices in Cardiff. How was I back here?

Standing over me was the Crow, his black bird eyes intent upon me. His chest was rising and falling as he recovered from his exertions.

"Danesh? Can you hear me?"

I'd been in London and now I was here. Oblivion: it was connected to both places, and no doubt many others. There was no great mystery to it. It was a hell of a way to get around.

On balance, I still preferred to take the train.

My fingers and toes were numb. Pins and needles fizzed in my legs as sensation returned. I climbed to my elbows, my knees and, finally, my feet.

I faced Hardknott-Lewis, looking directly into his eyes. Funny, I'd always thought he was taller than I was.

"Az is in there," I said. "What the fuck is going on? Did you know?"

He was always so sure of himself, but now he opened and closed his mouth as she struggled to find the right words.

Eventually, he succeeded. "Can I make you a cup of tea? Or, excuse me, coffee? We can sit down and I will tell you everything, you have my word, everything that I know, at least. Can we do that? The corridor outside the broom cupboard is perhaps not the place for this conversation."

"You'll tell me everything."

"I promise. Would you like to lean on me? You suffered badly on your trip into Oblivion."

"I'm fine. I'll manage."

Neither of us speaking, we left the offices and crossed the main road for the grounds of Cardiff Castle and his private quarters in the Black Tower. The roaring traffic, the stone walls, it all seemed distant to me, abstract, as if some vital part of me hadn't escaped Oblivion. Climbing the stairs was an effort; my legs were filled with lead. The Crow slowed to let me catch up. His features were fixed, his expression grim.

We sat in his room, as we'd done so often, as if we were discussing the finer details of some operation. The portraits of the former Lord High Witchfinders watched us from the walls, the scowls of disapproval on their faces clear. They seemed to be leaning in as if to hear what was about to transpire.

"Did you know?" I repeated once we had our hot drinks, our little pretence at normality and civility.

The Crow sipped at his tea. His responses were muted, brief. "I did."

"For how long?"

"For ten years now. Well before your arrival, obviously."

"All this time, every day I've been here, you knew and you didn't say anything? How could you do that?"

He stirred his tea with his silver spoon, although he hadn't put any sugar in. Then he fixed me with a frank look.

"I wanted to say something. Truly, I wanted to, and often. But I could not see how your knowing would help. You seemed to me to be at peace with your loss, and I felt that knowing the truth would open up old wounds, cause you such pain. And, I knew that you would want to tell your mother, of course you would, but she could not be allowed to know the truth. How could we explain it to her? I knew – I know – that she has not been well since the loss of your brother, understandably so. Although, latterly, I believe, she is somewhat recovered."

"None of that was your decision to make. This is my brother, her son."

"I was wrong," he conceded. "It is perhaps worth mentioning that I was also under strict orders not to reveal the truth to you, although that should not have stopped me from telling you."

"Earl Grey."

"Just so. It was him all along, was it not?"

"Your research in London didn't tell you that?"

"They were pointing that way – until I was suddenly ordered back to Cardiff, presumably because I was getting too close. I assume he is dead now?"

"He is."

"Ah. Perhaps if I had seen him for what he was, not been blind to his failings, I might have wondered why he was so insistent on keeping the secret about your brother. I think he feared you, feared what you might become. A fear that proved prescient."

I had no time to think about Earl Grey. No time and no head space. The sins of the Crow were my concern now. The need for revenge.

"Were you involved in putting him in there? Were you there that day when he and I were playing together?"

"You have my word that I was not," said the Crow. "I had nothing to do with it. I swear this by everything that is dear to me."

"Swear it on Gregory's name."

That stopped him. He recoiled as if I'd struck him. I hadn't been sure, but there had to be *some* connection between the Crow and the other name I'd glimpsed in Oblivion.

Gregory Hardknott-Lewis.

"Ah," the Crow said, his voice even lower than before, barely a whisper. "You saw. I did wonder if you might."

"Who is he?"

"He's my boy. My son."

Some of Mormont's words came to me from our final showdown, her description of Hardknott-Lewis. She'd called me his little project, his would-be son. Was that what I was to him? Some sort of surrogate for a lost child?

"How? How did he end up in Oblivion?"

"It is, as they say, a long story."

"Did you put him in there?"

"I was ... involved. At the time, it seemed like the best available option. The only option. A curse was cast upon him, grim, destructive magic, and he was about to die, and so I..."

He stopped. He was crying. His eyes were liquid, but looked fully at me, refusing to look away, hide his tears. I had never seen him cry, or barely even reveal any emotion in all the time I'd known him.

"Did you love him?" I asked. "Your boy, did you love him?"

He recovered enough to reply. "Oh, more than life itself. More than everything. Far more than I love myself. You know, he would have been about your age if he'd stayed with us."

"Swear on his name you had nothing to do with Az being put into Oblivion."

The Crow pulled out his silk handkerchief, blew his nose, took a moment to regain his composure. "I kept the truth about your brother from you in order to protect you, and perhaps out of cowardice as well, but I swear, upon Gregory, that I had nothing to do with putting Az into Oblivion, and nothing to do with the attacks upon your family. I was not there when he was taken; I had no part in any of it. I was not supposed to even know, but I saw him just as you did, well after the fact, on one of my visits to see Gregory."

"Visits that you denied me for my brother."

"I know that I do not deserve your forgiveness, and I do not ask for it. But, for what it is worth, I am sorry. I wanted to show you, I truly wanted you to know. I thought that in time, once you were ready, perhaps if your mother was no longer, well, so vulnerable, then the moment might come. Several times I..."

I held up my hand to stop him. I wasn't interested in his protestations. "You must have suspected something about Earl Grey."

"Until recently I did not, you have my word. I made a mistake in assuring you he could not be responsible for any of the terrible things that have happened. I shall regret this to the end of my days. It is hard, sometimes, to think ill of those we look up to, and I should not have let doing so cloud my judgement. *Semper vigilans* I kept saying to you all, be wary of everyone. And then I utterly failed to apply that to myself."

"What did you find in London?"

"I rapidly dismissed all the other possibilities we discussed. Aside from Thomas Quirk, only Earl Grey was a candidate, but still I refused to believe it. Then a few days ago I found something."

"Tell me."

"As you know we in the Office have been rather slow to adopt modern policing practices. Thirty years ago, everything was on paper, and someone had gone to a great deal of trouble to redact those older archives. But I unearthed the originals, and I found Earl Grey's accounts of his actions as an Acolyte and an Adept, his ascension through the ranks to England and then to Witchfinder General."

"There was an account of the attack on Az and me?"

"No, no, nothing of the sort; I do not believe that was any sort of official action. But I did find some pictures of him from three decades ago, and the similarity to the sketch your mother produced, the one you carried out an image search on, well, it is striking."

"Show me."

He opened a drawer, fished out a folder and handed me a photograph. "This is Earl Grey on a field operation in the environs of Lancaster, tackling a nasty poltergeist haunting at a monastery."

I took the picture. For sure, it depicted a short man in a long coat, like someone from a *noir* film, but such an appearance was hardly evidential.

"How do you know this is even him? His face is blurred."

"It is, isn't it? And that is an odd fact, given that

nothing else in the picture is obscured. His hands, his coat, the buildings, the trees – everything is pin-sharp apart from his features. You can even see his eyes, but the rest of his features are ... hazy."

"How do you know this is Earl Grey?"

"The notes attached make that clear."

"He used some magic to obscure his features," I said.

"Whenever he needed to act with impunity, yes, I believe he did. Some glamour he was able to work at will, or perhaps the effect of an illegal magical artefact that he carried. Highly illegal under magus law, however it functioned. I believe he used it when he attacked Az and, by chance, he was photographed in Lancaster using it, too. There were several pictures missing from the archive; my assumption is that he removed any which betrayed this power he had. He must have missed this one."

I thought about Evangelina Mormont and Peter Warder on the day they'd tried to tackle Sally in her flat on Cathedral Road. Their faces had been blurred to my perceptions, too. My attention had repeatedly slipped off them. Had she worked the magic on Earl Grey, or had they both learned the trick from someone else? Or had the Warlock worked the glamour whenever it was decided it was needed? However it worked, the corruption had been going on for a long, long time.

"Why? Why did he go to all this trouble to eliminate Az?"

"He didn't, though, did he?" said the Crow. "He, well, if you will excuse me, took your brother off the board but kept him alive. Or, as alive as existence in Oblivion can be. That puzzled me, too. Forgive me, but he could so easily have killed your brother, destroyed his body in any one of a hundred ways that would have removed all evidence."

"So, what were they doing?"

"My best guess is that they kept him alive as a bargaining chip. Or perhaps as the seed for some sorcery that they thought might, one day, be needed. You know something of the magical history of your family now, do you not? It is possible that they feared you and took your brother as a ward against future threats. Forgive me, that is a grim thought, I am aware. You must be assured that no guilt attaches to you or your mother in this, none whatsoever."

"They could have simply wiped us out. Az, me, my mother."

"They could, but they also could not be sure that other Shahzans would not show up in the future. Your family is large on your father's side, is it not? You have numerous cousins and other relatives, scattered all over the world. The enemy we face is rather good at laying long plans, seeing life as a landscape rather than a portrait."

I thought about the few family weddings I'd been to over the years. The scale of them had always taken me by surprise. Cousins and cousins of cousins I made no attempt to keep track of.

"There are a lot of us," I conceded.

"That is a good thing. I believe the size and extent of your family is one thing that saved you and Az all those years ago."

"Saved me but condemned him to his life sentence in Oblivion."

"Yes."

I thought back to my showdown with Earl Grey. What had he said? *One more Shahzan removed.* Not *the last Shahzan* or anything so dramatic. *One more.* Maybe the Crow was right. We were a clan of users: vampire-hunters, demon-slayers, spellworkers, and there had to be others out there with such abilities. Perhaps the Warlock really was afraid of us, had gone to great lengths to control us, kill us. I thought about the risks I'd faced, the attacks and dangers thrown at me. The attack in St John's Churchyard Gardens, the possessed lion statue, the succubi: were they all, in some way, an attempt to quietly finish me off? Hardknott-Lewis, to be sure, had given me my orders, but Earl Grey and then the Warlock had given him *his* orders. And the Crow, at least, had warned me, warned me constantly, of the dangers I faced, the need to be careful.

"You said Gregory was on the point of death, suffering under the effects of a curse," I said. "Is that true of Az, too?"

The Crow looked troubled. "I wish we knew. That is the most likely situation, although there are certain death spells that have a reversal clause attached to them. If you know the right words, you can stop the curse actuating. If you do not, or if you use them incorrectly, however, then the subject is doomed, and there is nothing you can do about it."

I clutched at the faint hope he was offering. "So there's a chance he could be safely removed?"

"I am sorry, but we simply do not know. The risks are huge; removing him from Oblivion, even temporarily, could mean his immediate demise. He may be on the point of death because of some injury received or harm done to him. At least, now, he … lingers. This is another reason I chose not to tell you of his situation. I did not want you to have to face this dilemma."

"We must know something about his condition, the circumstances of his attack."

"Regrettably little. I have been unable to uncover any clues by studying him, and there are no mentions in the Office's archives about the attack upon you and your twin. Apart from missing that photograph from Lancaster, Earl Grey did an excellent job of covering his tracks. I dread to think what he has been up to all this time, the crimes he has committed, the horrors he allowed to continue."

"There must be a way to find out. Az deserves to live his life if that's in any way possible. Maybe, I don't know, Gregory can be helped, too."

The Crow sighed and stared out of his window for a moment. "Gregory is beyond help, I am afraid. The curse worked upon him was vile and cruel. The moment he is removed from Oblivion would inevitably be his last. But as for Az … as I say, I simply do not know. Even if it were possible to safely extract him, he is still a little boy. He is your twin, but he would be twenty years younger than you."

"Then I'll be his big brother. I'll be whatever he wants me to be, but we have to help him."

"What would we tell your mother?"

"The truth. She deserves to have that, surely."

The Crow nodded. "Revealing such information to a member of the public would require the approval of the Witchfinder General. But, of course, right now there is no such person, given that the previous one, ah, met his end."

"Then we can act. If Az can be brought back, then we have to do it. There's no question. In any case, when the dust settles, the next Witchfinder General is likely to be you, isn't it? You have to be the favourite, especially as someone from your department was responsible for exposing Earl Grey."

The Crow held up his hand as if to deflect the flow of words. "Perhaps, perhaps, assuming that the Office even survives this scandal. It may be that Earl Grey's betrayal of everything we stand for is the final nail in the coffin for us. It may well be that you have succeeded in destroying both English Wizardry and the Office of the Witchfinder General with the same blow. Given everything you've learned, and given the, ah, tension between your nature and your position, I would find it understandable if that was a happy thought for you."

In many ways, it was. Destroying the Office, undermining it, was exactly what I'd wanted. I'd never become a paid-up member of Sally's coterie, but I'd come to support what they were trying to do. But now? Now I cared about Az and my mother. And, sure, I cared about the Crow, too. And, more than anything, I wanted to see the Warlock ended. I wanted revenge.

"If anyone can pull the Office back from the brink, it's you," I said. "You could be another Emrys Robinson. You could be the second Welshman to be Witchfinder General."

"I doubt you would welcome such an outcome."

"Right now, I genuinely don't care that much."

The Crow nodded at my words. "Well. All in good time. You will not be surprised to learn that appointing a new Witchfinder General involves a whole series of extremely arcane and tedious processes and interviews, along with a considerable volume of forms to complete. But, yes, in principle, if I were in that position, then I would approve the request to return Az to us if we could be sure that it was safe to do so. Of course I would. We would have to tread carefully, and perhaps the Pale Sisters would be able, once again, to lend their invaluable help. But, yes."

"Then we need to find out about the attack on him. We need to know what harm was done to him and why."

"Yes."

"We have to track down the Warlock and wring the truth out of him," I said. "Earl Grey, evil bastard that he was, was just following orders a lot of the time. If what you say is true, and Az is being held captive to use as a bargaining chip or a weapon or whatever the hell it is, then it's the Warlock who will know."

Hardknott-Lewis nested his fingers together in his familiar gesture of deep thought.

"The Warlock is still out there, yes," he said. "It may be that, even now, you and I are dancing to his tune."

"What does that mean?"

"The Warlock made Earl Grey what he was, turned him, enthralled him, gave him English Wizardry, but then Earl Grey began to take his own stories, his own myths, too seriously. He started to believe all his *one true English magic* nonsense. It may even be that this is why the Warlock allowed Earl Grey to be killed. Or, at least, did not attempt to prevent you from doing so. Perhaps he was more than happy to see both English Wizardry and the Office struck such a blow."

I thought about that. "You're saying the Warlock isn't English. Earl Grey said something along those lines, too. And, you're not English."

Hardknott-Lewis smiled a sad little smile. "No. If it would help, I will swear upon Gregory for a second time that I am not the Warlock and that I do not know the Warlock's identity. If you ask me to."

"No," I said. "I believe you."

"And you, Danesh? Can you continue to set aside your doubts about me and whatever remains of the Office for a while longer so that we can pursue the Warlock?"

He looked at me, his hard eyes intent, and I could see the fear in him, the doubt. And, deep, deep down, something that I hadn't noticed before, the well of sadness and regret in him. It was clear he genuinely did not know how I was going to answer his question or what the future would hold. His implacable hatred of magic use – perhaps it made a little more sense now.

I thought about Sally and her accusation that I'd stay in the Office the moment Hardknott-Lewis asked me to. Then I thought about Stonewall and the Warlock and the fights to come. Somewhere in my mind, I was thinking about Owain Williams, too. The unspecified, unnamed threat he – or it – represented. Mainly, I thought about Az and how I was going to free him.

I needed to follow my own path, learn how to use my powers fully, face the enemies that needed facing. I'd brought down English Wizardry and I'd probably helped destroy the Office, too. But Hardknott-Lewis needed me, and maybe I needed him, too. Maybe Az needed him.

In his room, the only sound was the slow, slow ticking of the grandfather clock as the moments stretched out and his question to me went unanswered.

End

ACKNOWLEDGEMENTS

As ever, my thanks to my wonderful wife and our two daughters. All of this is for you. My eternal gratitude also to Elsewhen Press for believing in these books, for producing them with such care and attention, and for doing so despite all the threats of the Office of the Witchfinder General. I'm delighted to be a part of the Elsewhen family.

As with *The Eye Collectors* and *The Seven Succubi*, I'd like to extend a special thank you to "The Whisperer", my contact in the Welsh Division of the Office of the Witchfinder General, without whom details of the Office's inner workings couldn't have been brought to light. Events in this volume reveal who this individual is – but, naturally, names have been changed to protect the innocent. I can only hope that "Danesh" survives to continue whispering his stories to me.

Elsewhen Press
delivering outstanding new talents in speculative fiction

Visit the Elsewhen Press website at elsewhen.press for the latest information on all of our titles, authors and events; to read our blog; find out where to buy our books and ebooks; or to place an order.

Sign up for the Elsewhen Press InFlight Newsletter at elsewhen.press/newsletter

SIMON KEWIN'S WITCHFINDER SERIES
"Think *Dirk Gently* meets *Good Omens!*"

THE EYE COLLECTORS
A STORY OF
HER MAJESTY'S OFFICE OF THE WITCHFINDER GENERAL
PROTECTING THE PUBLIC FROM THE UNNATURAL SINCE 1645

When Danesh Shahzan gets called to a crime scene, it's usually because the police suspect not just foul play but unnatural forces at play.

Danesh is an Acolyte in Her Majesty's Office of the Witchfinder General, a shadowy arm of the British government fighting supernatural threats to the realm. This time, he's been called in by Detective Inspector Nikola Zubrasky to investigate a murder in Cardiff. The victim had been placed inside a runic circle and their eyes carefully removed from their head. Danesh soon confirms that magical forces are at work. Concerned that there may be more victims to come, he and DI Zubrasky establish a wary collaboration as they each pursue the investigation within the constraints of their respective organisations. Soon Danesh learns that there may be much wider implications to what is taking place and that somehow he has an unexpected connection. He also realises something about himself that he can never admit to the people with whom he works…

ISBN: 9781911409748 (epub, kindle) / 9781911409649 (288pp paperback)
Visit bit.ly/TheEyeCollectors

THE SEVEN SUCCUBI
THE SECOND STORY OF
HER MAJESTY'S OFFICE OF THE WITCHFINDER GENERAL

Of all the denizens of the circles of Hell, perhaps none is more feared among those of a high-minded sensibility than the succubi.

The Assizes of Suffolk in the eighteenth century granted the Office of the Witchfinder General the power to employ 'demonic powers' so long as their use is 'reasonable' and 'made only to defeat some yet greater supernatural threat'. No attempt was made in the wording of the assizes to measure or grade such threats, however – making the question of whether it is acceptable to fight fire with fire a troublingly subjective one.

Now, in the twenty-first century, Danesh Shahzan, Acolyte in Her Majesty's Office of the Witchfinder General, had been struggling with that very question ever since the events of The Eye Collectors. An unexpected evening visit from his boss, the Crow, was alarming enough – but when it turned out to be to discuss his thesis on succubi, Danesh was surprised yet intrigued. Clearly, another investigation beckoned.

ISBN: 9781915304117 (epub, kindle) / 9781915304018 (334pp paperback)
Visit bit.ly/TheSevenSuccubi

Red Dragon

A Bestiary of Modern Britain
Dr Miriam Seacastle
2022 FACSIMILE EDITION

Elsewhen Press are pleased to be able to produce this facsimile of the 1999 illustrated, limited edition privately published by the author but since unobtainable.

"Dr Seacastle's … Bestiary was the product of a great deal of solid research and investigation. It is a short volume … but there is much in the book that is precise. Not only that, she makes several rather inciteful remarks about actions taken by Her Majesty's Office of the Witchfinder General over the decades."
— **Simon Kewin**, author and OWG scholar

The original edition has all but disappeared, but we temporarily gained access to a copy from the library of the Cardiff Office of the Witchfinder General, from which we have been able to create this facsimile edition.

"A must-have for historians, students, and those interested in the OWG or indeed protecting modern Britain." – **Sally Spender**

An invaluable collector's item.
ISBN: 9781915304155 (epub, kindle) / 9781915304056 (72pp paperback)
Visit bit.ly/RedDragon-Seacastle

The Magic Fix series by Mark Montanaro

The Magic Fix

The Known World needs a fix or things could get very ugly (even uglier than an Ogre!)

"Did we win the battle?" asked King Wyndham.

"Well it depends how you define winning," answered Longfield, one of the King's royal commanders.

In fact, the Humans are fighting a losing battle with the Trolls. Meanwhile the Ogres are up to something, which probably isn't good. Could one flying unicorn bring about peace in the Known World? No, obviously not.

But maybe a group of rebels have the answer. Or perhaps the answer lies with a young Pixie with one remarkable gift. Does the Elvish Oracle have the answer? Who knows? And, even if she did, would anyone understand her cryptic answers (we all know what Oracles are like!)

The Known World is in danger of being rent in twain, and twain-rending is never good!

Did I mention the dragon? No? Ah… well… there's also a dragon.

ISBN: 9781911409731 (epub, kindle) / 9781911409632 (240pp paperback)
Visit bit.ly/TheMagicFix

The Enchanting Tricks

The Known World is still not fixed… and things <u>have</u> got ugly

In the Goblin realm, Queen Afflech was doing remarkably well considering the circumstances. She had seen her husband die, and both her sons killed within the space of a couple of weeks. That kind of thing does tend to bring you down a bit.

Losing three kings in a few days looked rather careless. But of more concern to the Goblin warlords was whether it looked weak to their enemies. They suspected the Humans were behind one death and the Ogres behind another. The Pixies were no threat, the Trolls would probably soon be killing one another again, and the Elves were irrelevant (or, to be precise, just annoying).

Meanwhile, King Wyndham wanted to show the Goblins that Humans were not to blame (apart from the two that might be to blame). Petra, the most famous Pixie in the Known World, knew exactly who was to blame and wanted to rescue them. Lord Protector Higarth was determined to help the Goblins with their predicament, whether they wanted Ogre-help or not.

But on the plus side, the dragon's gone; and there are still plenty of unicorns… maybe they can somehow solve everything?

ISBN: 9781915304193 (epub, kindle) / 9781915304094 (270pp paperback)
Visit bit.ly/TheEnchantingTricks

ABOUT SIMON KEWIN

Simon Kewin is a pseudonym used by an infinite number of monkeys who operate from a secret location deep in the English countryside. Every now and then they produce a manuscript that reads as a complete novel with a beginning, a middle and an end. Sometimes even in that order.

The Simon Kewin persona devised by the monkeys was born on the misty Isle of Man in the middle of the Irish Sea, at around the time The Beatles were twisting and shouting. He moved to the UK as a teenager, where he still resides. He is the author of over a hundred published short stories and poems, as well as a growing number of novels. In addition to fiction, he also writes computer software. The key thing, he finds, is not to get the two mixed up.

He has a first class honours degree in English Literature and an MA in Creative Writing (distinction). He's married and has two daughters.

Printed in Great Britain
by Amazon